WHEN
WE
WERE
ENEMIES

ALSO BY EMILY BLEEKER

WHEN WE WERE ENEMIES

A NOVEL

EMILY BLEEKER

LAKE UNION
PUBLISHING

Text copyright © 2023 by Emily Bleeker
All rights reserved.

Published by Lake Union Publishing, Seattle

www.apub.com

Amazon, the Amazon logo, and Lake Union Publishing are trademarks of Amazon.com, Inc., or its affiliates.

ISBN-13: 9781662509889 (paperback)
ISBN-13: 9781662509896 (digital)

Cover design by Shasti O'Leary Soudant

Cover image: © Andreas Kuehn / Getty; © Everett Collection / Shutterstock; © ebenart / Shutterstock; © Maria Heyens / ArcAngel

Printed in the United States of America

For my husband, Sam—
I wouldn't want to do any of this without you.
Tu sei quello. Tu sei l'unico.

CHAPTER 1

Elise

Present Day
Minskoff Theatre, New York City

It's funny how moments you've dreamed about for a lifetime can feel unexpected. As Hunter gets down on one knee and pulls out the dark blue velvet box from his pocket, I freeze in place, the wind whipping my dress around my knees outside of the Minskoff Theatre where we've just watched *The Lion King*.

"What is going on . . . ," I start to ask, knowing what a man on one knee means but also knowing this is not what we planned. We agreed the logical next step in our relationship was moving in together, not getting married. But then a singular voice rises from the crowd behind me, singing "Can You Feel the Love Tonight" in a rich baritone, and I turn to see we're surrounded by the cast of the show in full costume and singing in perfect harmony.

"Hunter?" I whisper as I take in the performers and the congregation of onlookers chattering to each other in excitement while they record the moment with their handheld devices.

The lights on the marquee reflect off the tears filling my boyfriend's eyes. For a moment, I wonder if he's been put under some magical spell—a love spell that's making him do something so romantic and unexpected and confusingly beautiful. A cameraman hovers nearby, shooting photographs. The clicking acts as a sort of percussion to the chorus swelling around us. The magic starts its work on me now. The cutting February wind, the stinging tap of icy snow on my cheeks, the burning tightness on the tips of my ears all fade away as I watch the man I've fallen in love with over the past six months mouth, "I love you, Elise."

And with that, he opens the ring box and says the words I know are coming. "Elise Toffee Branson, will you marry me?"

My grandmother's unmistakable three-carat princess-cut solitaire blinks back at me. My smile falters, and my knees go a bit weak. My mother must've given him the ring. Snuck into my apartment, maybe? Used her fame and charm to get my landlord to let her in. How does anyone say no to two-time Oscar winner, box-office blowout hit, second-generation Hollywood royalty, Gracelyn Branson?

The faces start to swirl and blur as the song comes to its harmonic conclusion. Everyone seems to hold their breath, waiting, just waiting endlessly for my answer. Truly, what could my response be at this point other than yes?

But, staring at the ring, I reluctantly recognize how unfair it all feels—being offered a ring I've worn before, asked a question I've been asked before, by a man I love less than the first, in front of all these people, all these cameras, all these witnesses? This isn't some movie where the girl can run off without saying anything while the confused boy with a diamond ring in his otherwise empty hands watches her disappear.

"Yes," I say as he slips the antique ring on my finger. The weight is familiar. If it weren't for all the lovely chaos going on around me, it might feel too familiar. I don't look at it, afraid of what it'll make me remember. I blink; a tear runs down my cheek. No one, including Hunter, needs to know the reason.

"Yes!" I repeat, this time with more feeling and loud enough to be heard over the street sounds. The crowd explodes in cheers and produces from . . . somewhere . . . long tubes with strings attached that explode glitter streamers and confetti into the air. The flurry of colors and sparkles swirls around us as Hunter stands to his full height and with his most brilliant smile, takes me in his arms, staring into my eyes, his warm breath coming out in clouds that surround me. He smells of Creed cologne, and before kissing me, he whispers, "You're my forever, Elise."

I nod, and he tips me into a dip and presses his lips against mine in a soft, tender kiss. I slip back in time to six years ago when Dean asked me to marry him and I said yes. When I took off the engagement ring after his funeral, I promised myself I'd never say yes to another man. And I thought I never would, but then I met *this* man.

Hunter lets me go, and I stand unsteadily, my head whirling from the kiss, the excitement, and the grief that colors it all. Though the proposal itself is perfect and thoughtful, and even though Hunter is generous and successful and gorgeous as all get-out, a part of me wishes I weren't in this moment. Because the only reason I'm here is because Dean isn't.

A limo pulls up, and the chauffeur opens the rear door. The decorations have settled into piles on the sidewalk, and Hunter rushes me toward the car with his arm around my waist.

"Shouldn't we help clean up?" I ask.

"No," he chuckles, "I've lined up someone to do that. So it's all taken care of."

"Good, because we'd be crucified on social media if we left all that litter," I say, sliding into the back seat, the throng having grown so deep, I'm almost afraid someone will get hurt as we drive away.

I settle into the leather seat as Hunter unbuttons his tux jacket and puts his arm around my shoulders. Threading his fingers through mine, he stares at my glittery hand like it's a new and fascinating creation. Champagne is cooling on ice, and what must be at least three dozen roses are on the opposite side of the car.

"Let's not worry about image for once, okay? We just got engaged, baby. You're gonna be my wife." He kisses the back of my hand, and the sincerity in his voice breaks down my defenses. His wife. I don't know if I'm ready for this.

"I'm not obsessed with image. But you and I know *some* people will pick this whole thing apart. It'll be a minority, but it'll be a loud one. I'm just running a risk assessment."

After fifteen years in public relations, I know all too well how some people will take any opportunity to criticize Hunter because he's one of the richest men in New York City. Add to that the fact that his new fiancée is Gracelyn Branson's daughter and Vivian Snow's granddaughter, and it's easier to just front-load every experience with apology tweets. The amount of love and hate that goes along with fame, especially inherited fame, is staggering. But as is often said about anyone in my situation, "Poor little rich girl has it so hard."

"Hey, Elise," he says, squeezing my hand and holding it to his chest, a slight edge to his voice. "Can't we be happy for a few minutes?" he asks cautiously but sincerely, putting my palm against his cheek.

That's all it takes. We started dating only six months ago, but there's one thing I know for sure—this man loves me. The smoothness of his freshly shaven jaw and the security of his arm around my body, holding me tight, shake me out of my negative spiral. Hunter Garrot just proposed to me in the most romantic display I've ever witnessed. And he didn't propose because of who my mom is or who my grandma was or how successful my business is, or anything like that. He proposed because he loves me, and I love him in return.

"Of course we can, handsome," I agree, stretching my neck to kiss him. When our lips meet, it's only Hunter and I—no flashbacks, no daydreams, no longing—just the man I love kissing me back. Like at the end of a romance novel, he leans down and pulls me in, and the perfection of his proposal is complete as we race through the streets of Manhattan.

If only I believed in happily ever afters.

～

"It's like a movie," my mother says with wonder as though she hasn't been in at least fifty films in her lifetime. She appears every bit the movie star she is, sprawled out on the dark blue velvet sofa that faces the full wall of glass windows looking out on Central Park. Her dressing gown cinches under her tactfully enhanced full bosoms, and her makeup-less face is shiny and red from a recent face peel. Very few people get to see Gracelyn Branson this way, and that's how she keeps up the façade of graceful aging.

"How's your skin?" I ask, gesturing to the residual redness on her cheeks and forehead.

"Oh, you know—same old, same old," she says, her lips slightly swollen from a recent injection of some kind. I try not to wince. "The press junket for *Over the Moonlight* is next week, and there's Oscar buzz already, so I need to look my best. I'll be up there next to all these young, gorgeous, polished babies. But I made sure Dr. Cook didn't go too overboard this time."

The "Can You Believe Gracelyn Branson Is in Her Seventies" articles and posts should come with a disclaimer listing all the things she does to keep her skin, teeth, hair, and figure looking effortlessly youthful. I try not to judge her for it. Being onscreen is her job—her passion. Aging under the hypercritical microscope of fame isn't easy. Just like a teacher needs to recertify, and an IT guy needs to stay up to date with all the new technology, my mom needs to make the investment in looking young.

"Fingers crossed for the nod. Jimmy has a chance this year too, right?" I ask, referencing my oldest brother. I'm the youngest and least famous of the family, and I'm glad I no longer have to take my turn accompanying my mother to the long and mostly boring awards shows. It used to be that each of the four of Mom's kids would take turns escorting her and Nonna during awards season if the actresses didn't have a boyfriend or husband to go with them.

That's how I met Dean—at one of the after-parties. I was standing in a corner, nursing a glass of flat champagne, and he was hiding from too many things to name: photographers, starlets, reporters, cougars wanting to attach their sinking star to his rising one. I didn't mind going to awards shows after that—because I went with Dean.

Then Dean got sick and died. And soon after, Nonna passed. Within a handful of years, it was back to me and Mom. But she stopped asking me to go after my meltdown at the Golden Globes five years ago.

I should have known better—it'd been a year of loss with Dean and then Nonna right after. I shouldn't have agreed to go with her. There were too many memories too easily accessible. I wasn't ready, and the general public got a close-up of my "private sorrow," or at least I think that's what the headline called it when I couldn't stop crying during a red-carpet interview and then went home before the opening monologue.

"It's better not to jinx it," she says, even though she was the one who brought up the whole topic of awards. "But I do have some news—I wanted to wait to tell you until after hearing about your big moment and all . . ." She sits up and raises her steaming coffee mug as though pausing to deepen the suspense in a scene. Half the time, I don't know if I'm talking to my mom or talking to my mom playing a mom-like character.

"Yes . . . go on." I nudge, knowing that showing I'm invested is the only way she'll get on with the story.

"Mmmm, yes, sorry." She puts down the mug as though she hasn't been using it as a prop. "I have a new beau."

Of course she does. Gracelyn Branson is rarely single for long. She's been married three times, and she cycled through relationships during the times she wasn't legally bound to one of her husbands, and even then, there was likely overlap I don't like to think about for too long.

"Who is it this time?" I ask, and it comes out more judgmental than I intended. Thankfully, my mother is too busy rearranging her dressing gown to notice.

"It's Mac Dorman," she says like she'd just said Brad Pitt's name. I raise my eyebrows, not knowing who the heck Mac Dorman is. The name sounds familiar but not familiar enough to bring up any memory of a face or recollection of a recent meeting.

"Who?" A warm whoosh of heated air pours from the overhead vents, rustling my hair and tickling my cheeks, reminding me how cold it is outside. I wrestle out of my wool peacoat as my mom sits up straighter, moving to the edge of her seat.

"Mac Dorman," she repeats slowly. "You know—the documentarian."

Oh yeah. Mac Dorman. I do remember him now. Shoulder-length graying hair, tortoiseshell glasses, and an air of superiority that follows him like a fancy cologne.

"The guy doing Nonna's documentary?" He'd called me at my office about six weeks ago and pitched something about telling the "true story of Vivian Snow." I'd seen him lurking about at various parties I'd attended with my mom but never actually talked to him. Mac Dorman is branded as the Ken Burns of celebrity biographical documentaries—but I think he makes them mostly because he's nosy. He's nominated for an Oscar or Emmy every year and has won a few, not that I'm keeping score.

"Yes! We started out exchanging emails, of all things, and then talking on the phone, and once we met in person a few weeks ago, the chemistry was unreal . . ."

"Too much information, Mom . . ." I wave away the image of my seventy-something mom with the snobby filmmaker.

"He's very talented, and I believe you'll like him more than you think. Has a lovely idea for the documentary about Mother." She pauses and glances at me out of the corner of her swollen eyelids. I wonder how much the skin peeling and spa treatments have to do with her new love interest and find it noteworthy how quickly our discussion has gone from my engagement to her romance.

"You know how I feel about that film. If he insists on making some sort of gossipy tell-all about Nonna, I prefer we're not involved. Otherwise, we give it legitimacy." I twist my grandmother's beautiful ring around on my left hand. I'm not used to it again. I wonder how long it took Nonna to get used to wearing it when she married for the first time. I wonder how long it took to get used to not wearing it when her husband died in the Battle of the Bulge a year and a half after their wedding.

"Nonna's story deserves legitimacy. It's a beautiful tribute, and he's not the only one who thinks so. Mac recently had a huge influx of funding so . . . we had a thought."

"We?" I try not to groan. Things are clearly getting serious with Mac. I can only assume my mother with her paycheck from her latest film is the "sudden influx." Like the skilled method actor she is, my mom takes on the interests and passions of any man she falls in love with. When she dated Kurt Harverson, the NASCAR driver, she decided "going fast" was a metaphor for life, so she invested in his NASCAR team. Likewise, when she fell in love with her yoga instructor, she helped build an ashram in Brazil that ended up being a front for a cult.

"Yes. He appreciates my input. I do have years of experience in the industry. And let's not forget the subject of this particular film is my own mother. Would you sit and listen?" She's getting defensive, and I'm forgetting it's not my job as a thirty-seven-year-old woman to make life choices for my grown-ass mother.

"Fine." Folding my coat over the back of the sofa, I drop my purse on the floor and sink into the cushions. I won't take off my shoes—I'm supposed to meet Hunter at Claro for lunch. If I stay here much longer, I'll be late.

My mother smiles, once again resetting her expression like she's ready for her next take. It's hard to stay upset with her for too long. To the outside world, her life seems easy, full of money, fame, beauty, and success, but in many ways, my mother's life has been a lonely, lost existence—the life of a fatherless little girl who flits between men like a hummingbird sipping what nectar she can find even as the flowers of her youth die off.

"Mac and I were thinking it might be lovely if you got married in Edinburgh."

"Scotland?" I ask, not understanding the significance of the random suggestion.

"No, dear. Indiana. Where your grandmother grew up."

"Indiana?" I gasp, my patience lasting not even halfway into one sentence.

"Yes," she says, raising her manicured hand, seemingly annoyed with my interruption. I wave for her to finish her cockamamie idea. It's better to say no after she's put it all on the line. "It would be a stunning modern peg for the film. The church in town where Mother and Father were married is lovely. We went there when you were little—when my grandmother passed. I have fond memories from my childhood as well. I tried to get your father to marry me there, but he insisted on Bali."

"It's a romantic idea, but I'm sure Hunter will want to be married close to home." *Or far away, or anywhere but Indiana,* I think but do not say. "And I'm not sure I want to be a part of this film. You know how I feel about being on camera." I'm barely used to the idea of getting married. I'm not about to have it recorded for all mankind to see.

"Well, you *have* to be in the film, dear. I already promised Mac you'd participate. And I think you're wrong about Hunter. When he asked for my help to get your grandmother's ring, I brought up the idea. He seemed very interested. Said that a small, off-the-beaten-path kind of a wedding would be perfect for the two of you."

My mouth hangs open as I try to process all the information downloading at a turtle's pace. Oh, my dear, sweet Hunter. He wanted to make everything easier in my life but often seemed to stray just enough away from my original vision that it became out of focus and unrecognizable. My watch buzzes, and I know from the staccato beat it's my boyfriend . . . no . . . my fiancé. He must be on his way to the restaurant already.

"I have to go." I tie my scarf, then slip on my coat and throw my purse over my shoulder. The dazzling late-morning sun reflects off the snow-covered landscape of Central Park and cascades through the windows.

I learned a long time ago that my mother, well-meaning as she is, will find any opportunity to make important moments in my life about her. Like how she insisted on singing "Dust in the Wind" at Dean's funeral and wore a black gown with a black veil to catch the attention of all the paparazzi clicking away with zoom lenses along the perimeter of the cemetery. Usually, I don't mind. But going over my head to make decisions about my wedding in order to impress a man is a bit much for me. I need to step back—to breathe. And I need to get the facts from Hunter.

"Yes, well—say hello to Hunter for me. Tell him 'Brava!' and that I can't wait to see the tapes. You'll make a beautiful bride."

"Will do," I say, waving and hustling toward the front door, more out of a desire to escape than the worry of being late. "Feel better soon, Mom!"

"Thank you, my love!" she yells out from her seat as I reach the front door. When I close it behind me, I'm fairly certain I hear her shout, "I'll have Mac call you."

The door clicks closed, and I wish I could close the conversation about Mac Dorman as easily. But I know it's not possible. Instead, one of three things will happen:

1. My mom and Mac will break up as quickly as they got together, and this whole documentary idea will evaporate along with their relationship.
2. I will have to wade through family drama by standing up to my mom, as well as likely standing up to all my siblings who will undoubtedly take her side.
3. Or the most likely outcome of all—I will get married in Edinburgh, Indiana.

CHAPTER 2

Vivian

Monday, April 26, 1943
Camp Atterbury

The sun sits low in the eastern sky. I fight off a shiver as the chilled morning air hits my bare calves. I wish I had one intact pair of nylons to make a good impression on my first day and to protect my feet from the inevitable blisters. As I walk down the dirt path toward the front gates of Camp Atterbury, a fine spattering of mud collects on the black leather of my new heels. Well, new to me. My friend Mary found them in the charity bin at the USO and put them aside for me. I should feel guilty about taking something meant for the poor, but with Mom still locked away and Dad's broken foot, we're closer to poor than we've ever been.

If I were singing in a real club in Chicago or even Indianapolis, I'd make more than a dollar a weekend. And then I'd have enough money to pay for Mom's doctors, and Dad could cut down on his hours at the factory, and Aria could have a normal childhood full of bobby socks and school dances.

Stop it, Vivian, I chastise myself. There's no room in my life for fantasy or big dreams. I'm nineteen, almost twenty, and I'm the only hope of keeping my family together. Mother lost herself in her sphere of dreams and fantasy, and look where that got her—locked away in Mount Mercy Sanitarium. So instead of voice lessons with experienced teachers and trips to the city for auditions, I got my secretarial training from Marian College and applied for a real job at Camp Atterbury.

After two interviews with the help of Mary who introduced me to Charlie, the handsome married officer I dance with at the USO most Friday nights, one typing test, and a few toothy smiles, I got the job working the switchboard at the front office for Camp Atterbury. I say front office, but I don't even know where the office is located, never having stepped foot on base.

The bus dropped me off on the side of the road in front of the buildings protected by not only a fence but the front gate I'm approaching, a guardhouse, and a sign with large lettering that says:

Main Entrance
Camp Atterbury
Internment Camp

I shiver, not only from the cold but from a sudden dread that runs through me at the sight of the gates, white posts with chain-link and barbed wire. This is a camp for prisoners of war captured in the European theater. And this is where I'm going to work.

Every part of my body tells me to turn around and leave. I suppose it's more necessity than courage that keeps me moving toward the front gate. Around the perimeter stand impressive lookout towers as tall as the bank in downtown Edinburgh. I can see uniformed men inside, milling about with big rifles slung over their arms. They're watching me watch them. I swallow and square my shoulders to look more professional.

My tweed suit coat and tailored skirt are a bit tattered but nice enough for a desk job; at least that's what Mary said. I smooth my hair, my fingers getting tangled and the wind and moisture in the air making it a mess.

Feeling eyes on me not only from above but also from the guardhouse, I walk up to the gate. The top half of the door swings open before I touch it. Inside stand two uniformed young men.

"Can I help you, miss?" the taller one asks. I'm pretty sure he's the more senior of the two.

"Yes. I . . . I'm here for the new secretarial position," I say, shoulders so straight I might throw out my back.

"You're the new secretary?" The young soldier, whom I'm certain I've seen at the dance hall at least once, looks me up and down. He gives me a little grin like he knows what I look like in my garter belt.

"Yes . . . yes. I am." My voice quivers slightly, making me feel weak, but the private seems to like my timidity. "I'm Vivian . . ."

"Vivian Santini?" He pronounces it Sane-tie-nye.

I nod. I've learned to accept any pronunciation that comes close to the correct San-tee-nee.

"Yes—you're on the list." A tall, smooth-faced soldier exits the guardhouse from a side door and waves to his partner. The white gate covered in barbed wire pulls back slowly, the opening barely wide enough for me to slip through. On the other side, I'm faced with another, loftier, set of gates.

The shorter of the two guards crosses to the locking mechanism and rolls back the second barrier. I search his waist for a gun. I don't like the idea of being surrounded by weapons. Papà has one gun. My little sister, Aria, found his old rabbit pistol under his pillow within a week of President Roosevelt's declaration of war. We tried to convince him it wasn't a safe place to store a loaded weapon, but papà insisted he needed it close at hand in case we're invaded by *I Tedeschi*—the Germans. I guess he forgot his own countrymen are also on the wrong side of the conflict. He refused to give the pistol up, even though living in central Indiana, we're pretty unlikely to see any fighting. But I understand the overwhelming desire to protect our family. He does it with a gun—I do it by providing an income.

I Tedeschi aside, the only other way I can imagine my father pulling a gun on a man is if he caught one trying to woo Aria or me, which keeps me from inviting any gentlemen callers into our home. Not that I've had time for a love life between work, papà, Aria, and school.

"That way." The taller guard gestures toward a long, white gravel drive, and the other man, Talbot I think his name is, ushers me in the right direction. The buildings on this side of the road are gray, unlike the white barracks across the street that house the American servicemen. I wonder if the different colors are symbolic. A large office building sits inside the barbed-wire barrier. Behind it is another fence topped with razor-sharp wire, the last defense against a potential prisoner revolt.

As I follow Talbot, the other soldier watches me walk away. I think I feel the men in the tower doing so as well. This attention from men—it's new to me. I'd always been a dowdy, quiet girl in high school and went to an all-girls college.

When I'm onstage, it's different. I feel bulletproof under those lights. But here, I feel the weight of their gazes.

I keep my heels out of the mud the best I can. It's been a wet spring, and the clouds rolling in signal another storm on the horizon. The deep rumble of thunder in the distance vibrates through my midsection, and I breathe in the prestorm scent. When I get home tonight, Aria will be a mess, covered head to toe in dirt from her garden; I'm sure of it.

Talbot walks ahead, opens the door to the building, and waits for me to step inside. It's warm, and the air is thick with a heavy, manly smell. A desk sits behind a window with a door immediately to the right and a sitting area with chairs to the left. A young woman works behind the glass, and Talbot gives her the same sickly grin he gave me at the gate.

"Hey, Judy. Is Gammell in?"

The girl has a plain face and a sweetly curled bob, and she responds with an innocence I find comforting. Her soft brown eyes are friendly and a welcome escape from Talbot's obvious glances.

"No—he's in the fields. Should be back shortly. Wanna wait?" She talks to him so casually; they must know each other. I have a shock of worry for the girl. Then a flash of gold on her left hand catches my attention.

She's married. Thank heavens. Talbot looks me over again and then back at Judy and shrugs.

"I don't mind staying, you know, for a little bit," Talbot says, and points to the chairs lining the walls by the front door. I take one of the seats but stay perched on the edge of the cushion, afraid of looking lazy if the lieutenant colonel walks in. I cross my legs, one over the other, at first. But when I notice Talbot watching, I quickly change my position, crossing at my ankles instead, tugging at the hem of my skirt.

Judy raises her eyebrow and seems to catch on to Talbot's interest. She sits up tall, as if her spine were a puzzle clicking into place.

"Sarah had fun last night," she says in a lowered voice but loud enough that I can hear. "We should do it again sometime. How about Friday? At the hall?"

"This girl sings down there on Fridays. I've seen her lots of times." Talbot looks at me and back at Judy, ignoring the question about poor Sarah.

"She does?" Judy squints through the glass and laughs. "Oh, by golly, yes! I remember you. Sorry, dear, what's your name?"

"Vivian," I say, a warm blush on my cheeks. I'm proud of my work onstage at the USO, but I wasn't planning to tell anyone at my new job about my stage persona.

"Yes! Vivian Snow." Judy says the name like she's reading it off a marquee outside a theater. Goose bumps break out on my legs and arms.

"Snow?" Talbot butts in. "I thought it was Santino . . . something or other."

"Snow is my stage name." Once again I'm little Viviana Santini, the shy daughter of immigrants who hid behind her mother's skirts on the first day of school and was too nervous to sing the solo in the first-grade Christmas concert.

"Ah. 'Cause your real name makes you sound like an immigrant," Talbot says matter-of-factly like he knows the ins and outs of such things. I switch my ankles to keep my outrage from being obvious. This is why I use a stage name. I've always been judged for being Italian. Both of my parents with accents. Wearing funny clothes. Living in a family with old-fashioned values. I have to hide so many things from my dad. My stage name is only one of them.

Judy seems to sense my uneasiness and leans across her desk to speak to me directly.

"Well, Vivian, that's no matter. I'm starstruck here. What brings you to Camp Atterbury? Are you doing a show for the boys?"

Before I can answer, Talbot intervenes. "Nah. She's just a secretary."

Judy gasps in exaggerated offense. "Gary! *Just* a secretary? Excuse me?"

"Well, you know what I mean . . ."

As Talbot and Judy debate, I sink back and stare at the door, wishing I could walk out. It's not that I don't want to work here. Judy seems fine, but Talbot . . . There's something about him that makes my skin crawl.

Just then, the door swings open like I'd willed it to happen. A uniformed soldier stomps in with mud on his boots that spills onto the tiled floor. Following behind him are three men in dark blue uniforms with the letters *PW* painted on their sleeves, pants, and worn leather boots.

The first two of the three men enter loudly, shouting and wrestling against their restraints. One is short, not much taller than me, but fills out his button-up shirt with muscle, not fat. The second man is taller, about Talbot's height, but slim, and he looks to be swimming in his oversized uniform. Both are covered in dirt. It's on their faces, clothing, and hair, and I smell sweat even though the morning has been crisp. The third man enters slowly, his whole countenance a stark contrast to the first two prisoners.

He's a touch above average height but not towering. He's slender but not gaunt, and he looks fit—as though he could run a few laps around a track without losing his breath. He has thick dark hair without a single silver strand giving any clues to his age. His eyes are dark, earnest, and friendly. And though he seems tidier than the other two men, he's just as muddy.

Agitation buzzes between the first two prisoners. But the third seems composed, collected, cooperative, resigned to the restraints around his wrists, focused on the conflict in front of him.

"È tutta colpa tua," the short man spits under his breath at the tall one. *This is all your fault.* The words come through in my mind as clear as if I'd heard them in English.

Italian. The only language spoken in my home for most of my life, at least until my mother went into the hospital.

"Quante volte te lo devo dire? Chiudi la bocca," the taller one grumbles back. *How many times do I have to tell you? Shut your mouth!* The strong language puts me on edge.

"Quante volte ti ho detto di smettere di toccare le mie cose?" the shorter man responds. *How many times have I told* you *to stop touching my things?*

The tension is building, both men clenching their fists like they long to punctuate their words with action. Talbot and the soldiers seem oblivious as they chat with Judy and stare at the door like they're waiting for someone else. I scooch even closer to the edge of my seat, wondering if I should alert them that the men look like they're about to fight.

"Adesso basta." *That's enough, now.* The quiet man still standing in the entrance mumbles in a calm but authoritarian way. Perhaps he's their commander?

"So che hai preso la foto. Restituiscila." *I know you took the picture. Give it back.* The shorter man continues without acknowledging the third man.

"Non ce l'ho! Hai una testa dura." *I don't have it! You're stubborn.*

Testa dura—literally meaning having a hard head. My father calls my sister that when he catches her wearing her gardening trousers to school or reading her books late into the night.

The calm man interjects again.

"Non ricominciare, Romano. Ti imploro. Te l'ho detto, troverai la tua foto." *Don't start this again, Romano. I implore you. I told you; we'll find your picture.*

The short man, Romano, takes a deep breath. He wipes his sweaty brow with his bound hands and finally gives in.

"Mi dispiace. Mi dispiace. Mi fido di te." *I'm sorry. I'm sorry. I trust you.* He sounds repentant at first but then adds with a touch of hotness, "Lui, non tanto. Ma tu, Trombello? Con la mia vita." *Him, not so much. But you, Trombello? With my life.*

As Romano makes a partial bow to the calm one, Trombello, the tall man fires back, "Nessuno vuole vedere la tua ragazza grassa, comunque." *Nobody wants to see your fat girlfriend, anyway.*

"Bononcini! Basta!" Trombello chastises when Romano leaps forward, his hand in a fist. In that half a second, Trombello jumps into action, grabbing hefty Romano by the front of his collared shirt, holding him back while also straight-arming Bononcini, who looks ready for the fight.

"Madonna mia!" I squeal, and jump to my feet, seeing the flow of the fight heading in my direction. At the sound of my shout, Trombello, with his hands already full—quite literally—whips his head over his shoulder. We lock eyes for a brief, almost imperceptible moment, and I can see the confusion in them.

I cover my mouth, surprised at my linguistic slip, but my moment of impropriety has its effect. In Trombello's hesitation, Romano's fist finds Trombello's jaw, and a crack that sounds like a dried-out branch breaking slices through the air, louder than the thunder. I recoil and close my eyes, expecting blood.

I hear a rush of loud, aggressive voices speaking in English and the frenzied shuffling of feet from the hall. In that bedlam, the door to the office squeaks open, and the bitter, damp wind touches my cheek.

"What the hell is going on here? Get these men under control and out of here. You've got to be shitting me. Whose idea was this?"

My eyes open at the sound of the authoritarian voice. The scene has changed drastically. Guards hold back Romano and Bononcini. Trombello lies facedown on the tiled floor, his mouth bloodied and Talbot's muddy boot on his back. A thick, middle-aged officer stands by the open front door, not seeming to notice the deluge of rain and cold air rushing in.

This must be Lieutenant Colonel Gammell. The boys I've danced with say he's strict, fastidious, and quick-tempered. I can see why. If he were a Looney Tunes cartoon character, he'd have steam coming from his ears.

His outraged masculine voice makes my chest tighten and my shoulders stiffen. My father's temper has the same effect on me. I try to be small and silent like I am when my father has an outburst. All the men in the room begin speaking at the same time, starting up the conflict again.

Hunched over, I glance around for an escape route, but all I can see are the outraged faces of angry men, and all I can hear are raised voices in two different languages, combining into a cacophony of confusion and commotion. There's no escape.

I close my eyes again and try to disappear, hide inside my mind while they fight in front of me. There's nothing I can do. Because, in this world of war, one nineteen-year-old girl is meaningless.

And just like inside my father's house and inside Edinburgh, Indiana—I'm stuck.

CHAPTER 3

Elise

Present Day
I-65 Indiana

The brownish-green grass of early spring flashes past my window at a blurry speed of sixty-five miles an hour. The sky is a bright, late-March blue, and it's warm enough to wear one layer on top of my long-sleeved T-shirt but still chilly enough that I'm not about to roll down my windows and take in the country air.

My flight was delayed by a few hours. Mac had sent me a first-class ticket, and I sat next to a silent businessman who thankfully spared us both from small talk or, God forbid, actual conversation.

When I checked my phone after we touched down, I'd expected the deluge of texts, social media notifications, calendar reminders, and one or two messages from Hunter. I had a few from my assistant and from Conrad, Mac's assistant, sending over my car rental and hotel reservations. But the one name that didn't show up was . . . my fiancé's. I checked at least three more times, wondering if his message had somehow been delayed by my lack of Wi-Fi. But eventually I accept that he hasn't texted me.

He's busy, I remind myself. *I get it.*

But Hunter was the one to greenlight this whole thing. I told my mom no at least ten times before Hunter got involved. Getting married in a small town in Indiana to appease my mom and appear in a Mac Dorman documentary is going to be torture. It's great PR for my mom and Mac, and this whole engagement has been a huge boost for Hunter's image—but all this press and attention are a living hell for me.

But that's when I feel self-centered.

How fair is it for me to push back? This is Hunter's first wedding. Yes, technically it's my first wedding, too, but I already planned my dream wedding six years ago. I wanted it all—five hundred guests, a tent in the backyard of my mom's Malibu house, catering from Tramonto Bistro, and Maroon 5 for our reception. We'd ordered a cake from Sylvia Weinstock and sent invites out to our friends and family. My dress, my perfect dress by Romona Keveza, an off-the-shoulder, fairy-tale-inspired gown with a crystal-encrusted belt was on order. I was scheduled to come in for the final fitting a few weeks before the wedding when Dean had his stroke.

Even before the stroke, I knew he wasn't cured. No one is "cured" of a glioblastoma, an aggressive and always fatal brain tumor, but I thought we had more time. I thought I'd marry him, take his name, be his wife for a few years. We'd even discussed having a kid, maybe two. That would be his legacy, our legacy.

Some people said it would be selfish to have children, but to me it seemed like the most selfless thing possible—his willingness to have a child he might never hold, who would only know him by pictures and through his movies. It made me love him more. But then he was gone. Boom.

And suddenly I was planning his funeral rather than our wedding. The sit-down dinner was changed to a funeral luncheon. And my dress—we forgot to cancel it, and another lucky bride got a huge discount on my dream.

I twist my grandmother's ring around on my left finger. It's starting to feel at home there again. But sometimes I wonder if I'm wearing it just for Hunter. Sometimes it feels like I'm wearing it to remember Dean and to keep alive the feeling that he's still mine in some way and I'm still his.

My phone buzzes.

Finally!

On my screen, Hunter's face grins back in a photo I took last August on a walk in Central Park, when I wasn't sure if he'd be a long-term commitment or another attempt at love that would fade into the background of my life. That was the day he told me he couldn't stand the nonexclusive nature of our "thing" anymore, and I took a risk and chose to lean into him rather than run away.

I answer on speaker.

"Hey, babe! There you are."

His deep chuckle makes my stomach bubble happily.

"Sorry! Lots of meetings this morning, but I'm glad you got in safe. How long till you get to the town? Edinburgh? Is that how you say it?" he asks with a slight Scottish accent.

He makes it sound like I'm visiting a mythical land like Narnia rather than an average small town in the Midwest. Though I guess to someone like Hunter, a simple, anonymous town like Edinburgh is a fantasy land, hard to understand for this man who's grown up in New York City with a philandering billionaire father and a distant, heart-broken mother—all under the media's microscope. Our childhoods were very different, my mother eccentric but involved, my father career driven but always there for me even after their divorce. But the media spotlight burned both of us at one time or another.

"It's apparently pronounced 'Edin-burgh' not 'Edin-burrow.' Made that mistake right off the plane. And it's not as remote as you'd think. Cornfields, for sure, but also towns and subdivisions. Middle America, I guess."

"The pictures Mac sent over make it look so quaint. But the church seems epic for a small town."

"Yeah. It's nice. I'm pretty sure I've been inside a few times, but I don't remember details."

"Is that where you did all your Catholic stuff?"

"Said like a true atheist there, Hunter." I laugh, not that I'm any more religious than he is. My mother claims to be "more spiritual than religious," but my grandmother had definitely claimed Catholicism as her religious affiliation.

My siblings and I were baptized at Nonna's request. And Nonna made sure I had my First Communion and even squeezed in Confirmation one summer when I stayed with her in LA. I was a true believer for a while. Even considered myself "very religious" for some time. But just like I grew out of my belief in fairy tales, eventually the realities and tragedies of life pulled me away from my religious beliefs as well.

"Well, I don't know what it's called," he says, laughing. "You gotta find out if a sinner like me can even be married by a priest and all that." It sounded like he put verbal quotes around "sinner."

"I think we're both sinners in the eyes of the church, babe."

"Okay, okay. Fine. You're a sinner—I'm a godless heathen."

"Who wants to date a saint?" I attempt a sexy rasp.

"Don't you mean *marry* a saint?" he corrects me, lingering on the word "marry." I don't know what it is about this guy, but he loves the idea of marriage almost as much as the idea makes me anxious.

"Ha—you know what I mean."

"I'm glad you don't mind my godless ways," he says, flirting. He's always been a flirt. I used to worry that meant he flirted with all women, like his father, but he insists he's worked hard to be the exact opposite of Kenneth Garrot when it comes to relationships.

"I love your godless ways."

"Even if they cause problems with the wedding?" He brings up the concern again and seems to be asking seriously this time around.

"We should be fine. You were baptized Catholic as a baby, so I think that's all they need. Possibly one or two other things. Gotta do that Pre-Cana class with the priest. If they ask about your views on God now . . . plead the Fifth if you're sold on this 'church wedding' idea . . .'"

My GPS interjects, directing me to take the next exit. I drift into the right lane without using my blinker.

"Our kids will get to watch the documentary." Hunter's voice returns, and I catch only part of what he's saying.

"Sorry, the GPS cut you off, babe," I say, dodging the question of kids with Hunter. I want them, obviously, but rushing into parenthood with a man I've loved for less than a year is different from rushing into a marriage. Children don't go away with divorce decrees. And I want to give my children a more stable life than I had. Thankfully, he drops the topic.

"Oh, that's fine. I have another meeting waiting. I was just saying I'm definitely still up for it. Can we FaceTime later? After your church inquisition? Is it dumb I miss you already?" The sweet vulnerability to his question doesn't match his public business persona. It's that tender part of this man that I love.

"Not dumb," I say, softening my voice to match his tone. "I miss you too."

The roads have narrowed, and I slow my speed. The GPS declares I've reached my destination.

"I'm glad I'm not the only one."

"Never," I say, settling into an empty spot on the one-way street lined with brick storefronts and old-timey streetlamps. Quaint. Just like Hunter said. And he's right—this'll look great on camera.

I pick up the phone and press it to my cheek. I like holding him close like that; it's more natural, intimate. "You're still planning to come out next week, right?"

He hesitates. In that quiet moment, I understand his plans have shifted already. This is what it'll be like as Hunter's partner, how it'll always be.

"I hope so, but the guys from Stockholm are talking about flying in next week, and if so, I gotta be here."

He's a romantic. He's loving. He's all in. But he's also only actually *here* half the time.

"I get that." Irritation bubbles up like it always does when I'm stuck in people-pleasing mode. I can be stern in my job, no problem. I can be kind but firm with my employees. But with people I love, it's harder. I give in, probably too much.

"I mean, I'll make it out there ASAP. I promise. You know how important this deal is."

I do know, but I also know how many important things I put on hold for this trip, how I shifted my schedule to work virtually. I moved much of my case load to Marla, my associate and VP, who is likely cursing my name right now—and who has made it no secret that she thinks this whole documentary thing is a terrible idea.

"You mad?" he asks coyly, as though he can read my mind.

"Not mad, really. Just . . ."

"Disappointed?" he asks, teasing, as though I'm a mom giving her child a guilt trip.

"Ha, no. More like . . ." I search for a gentle way to say that it feels like I'm making all the sacrifices in our relationship and he's making all the big decisions and that I feel overwhelmed and alone. But that's a lot, especially for a quick little "checking in" phone call.

Instead, I say, "I don't know. Nervous, I guess? You know how I feel about being on camera."

"You shine on camera, Lisey," he reassures me. "I've seen it before. It's in your genes."

It's always awkward when people remind me of the famous legacy I was born into.

"I guess . . . I guess what I'm really trying to say is . . ."

As I'm about to blurt it all out, a loud thump lands on the car window, and I scream like I'm in the middle of a carjacking.

"You okay?" I hear Hunter's voice distantly as I hold the phone away from my face to investigate the loud noise.

Outside the window stands Conrad, Mac's high-strung assistant who's been my main contact through the planning of this whole thing. I know him from the headshot he uses as a signature on his emails. He's holding the clipboard he used to assault my window and wearing a Dolce & Gabbana blazer and Colorblock sunglasses, looking about seven thousand dollars fancier than any Indiana native I've seen so far. He spins his finger in circles to get me to roll down the window.

I press the phone against my face and whisper, "It's Conrad. I gotta go."

"Conrad?" Hunter still sounds anxious from my scream.

"Mac's assistant," I say through pressed lips.

"Ohhhh, Mr. Text You Incessantly at Three in the Morning about Flight Options. Fun for you."

"Yeah, yeah, I wouldn't get on too high a horse there, mister. When you get out here eventually, I'll make sure he has your personal number."

"Wow. You *do* love me; don't you?"

Conrad attempts to get my attention again, a tap this time. I grab my computer bag and sling it over my shoulder.

"I think you'll have to check in with me tonight. This is going to be . . ."

"Fun? Exciting? Romantic? Entertaining? Memorable? Educational?"

"Don't you have a meeting to get to? Stop gaslighting me!" I say to Hunter, laughing as I slam the car door and pop the back hatch of the Explorer to retrieve my bags. Conrad watches, and I can predict the dialogue inside his head, "I'm an assistant, not a servant."

I say a quick goodbye to Hunter and hang up. But as soon as I take a deep breath of the cool spring country air, my real feelings return.

I'm here—where my grandmother grew up, met my grandfather, got married, had my mom. Where the only evidence my family once lived within this town's borders is the cluster of headstones in the local cemetery. I'm here to plan my own wedding, get interviewed on camera, be asked plenty of questions I'm sure I'm not prepared for. And at least for now—I'm doing it alone.

CHAPTER 4

Vivian

Monday, April 26, 1943
Camp Atterbury

"Is anyone going to answer me? What is the meaning of this?" the decorated officer bellows from the threshold, puddles gathering on the floor beneath him.

"I . . . I have the ringleader right here, sir," Talbot says. "I was waiting here for you to return, and these prisoners were brought in. This one started a fight with these other two and then lunged at the taller one. I got to him just in time." Talbot shoves his boot into Trombello's back. He flinches either from pain or, if he understands English, at Talbot's incorrect interpretation of the altercation.

Ringleader? Trombello was the peacemaker. He was the only one not involved in the conflict. Sure, he put himself between the two men, but it was to stop the confrontation from escalating, not the other way around. Someone must have seen that other than me.

"These three were fighting in the yard, sir," one of the guards adds.

"And why are they here in the offices and not in a cell?"

The guard points at Trombello on the floor. "That one asked for an interpreter, and the fight was by the gates, so we thought . . ."

"That you'd bring them into the administrative offices? Get them out of here, and put that one in solitary. They can request the use of an interpreter there. McNeil's a busy man. He can't be bothered translating these trivial disputes."

"Yes, sir." Talbot salutes and nudges Trombello with his foot. "Get up."

"All of you, out. Out! Have you all lost your minds?" The man I assume is Gammell pushes past the prisoners and guards and approaches Judy's wall of glass. I can barely keep track of what's happening as the guards usher the prisoners back outside.

I watch Trombello, in particular. He winces as Talbot forces him to his feet. He seems confused but passive despite the way Talbot treats him. Blood covers Trombello's chin, and there's a cut on his forehead from when he hit the ground.

"Mi dispiace," I mouth in his direction. *I'm sorry.* He must understand me, though he cocks his head to the side as if he doesn't.

The room empties, and Lieutenant Colonel John L. Gammell turns around as Judy points in my direction. I can't hear what she says, but the officer seems just as angry with me as he seemed with the prisoners.

"You're in the wrong building. You were supposed to sign in across the street. When Private Talbot gets back, he can take you." He's gruff and dismissive as he walks away.

Though I know he's wrong, my instinct is to sit still and acquiesce like I always do with my father. But then I think of Trombello laid out, bleeding. I think of the kind way he tried to navigate the dispute between the other two prisoners. I'm grateful such men do exist—ones who don't make me flinch.

"Wait!" I call out, but Gammell doesn't give my tiny voice any heed.

"Judy, get Major General Hobbs on my private line," he barks.

Judy lets out a compliant, "Yes, sir."

"Lieutenant Colonel. Please. Stop," I plead, louder this time.

Gammell's hand freezes over the doorknob, and he says something under his breath. He seems frustrated, angry, and more than a little damp, but I take his pause as my opening. I stand up and clutch my purse in my gloved hands, still wearing my hat and fully buttoned coat.

"That man—uh—the one on the ground—he . . . he didn't start the fight."

Gammell takes in a rumbling breath and lets it out before responding.

"Miss, I'm sorry, but I'm not in the habit of second-guessing my men." He turns to face me, his cheeks flushed. When he sees me, really sees me, his expression softens. When he speaks again, I feel like he's looking at me as a little girl with pigtails asking why the sky is blue. "Listen, sweetie. I'm sure you mean well, but we have it all covered . . ."

"I'm sure you do." I swallow and take a step in his direction. "But that prisoner wasn't fighting. He . . . he got caught in the middle." My hands tremble, but I hide it with a tight grip on my purse.

"I'm sorry, but . . ." He doesn't finish the sentence. He's losing his patience. "Have her report across the street, Judy. Call her a car. No need for her to wait." He looks back at me with a paternal expression of satisfaction on his face. "There you go, dear. We'll get you to the right place."

He's seeing me, finally, but not hearing me. Maybe hearing me even less *because* he can see me. He stands there, in his intimidating uniform with pins and patches I don't understand the meaning of, expecting something—what? A thank-you? I'm not ready for any bursts of gratitude yet.

"The other one, the big one, Bononcini, he took something, a picture of the shorter man's girlfriend, I think. And Trombello was trying to stop the fight. He was being a peacemaker. He was trying to stop it all."

Lieutenant Colonel Gammell tilts his head and squints his eyes. Now he's listening. A buzz of apprehension pounds in my ears as he searches me over with those sharp, probing eyes.

"Do you know these men?"

"No," I answer quickly.

"Have you spoken to them before?" He seems suspicious.

"No. Never."

"Have you been on this base before? What is your name again?" He looks toward Judy, who is about to answer when I speak up. I will be "onstage" Vivian. I will be confident. I will be warm. I will be clever if the circumstances allow.

"Vivian. Vivian Santini."

"Ah, so you're Italian? An immigrant?"

"Well, my parents are. They came to America after the war. I've lived here in Edinburgh my whole life." I speak clearly so he can hear that I don't have a hint of accent in my voice.

"But you speak Italian? Do you live with your parents?"

"My father and my younger sister. My mother is ill." I didn't expect to share so much on my first day, but I don't think Gammell will take well to any information being withheld.

"And you are totally fluent in the language?"

"What? Italian?" I pause. Could I lose my job if I admit to having the same heritage as the enemy housed here? But I've never lied about my family. So I tell him the truth. "Yes, sir."

"Yes, yes. Very interesting. And you're our new secretary. What will you be doing for us here at Camp Atterbury?"

"I . . . I was told to report here, to *this* office," I reiterate since he seems so determined to send me away. "I was told I'd be working the switchboard. Perhaps take a transcript here or there." I finish off with his formal title, "Sir."

"Hmm." His voice reverberates through his chest.

I tip my chin up, knowing he's trying to figure out whether he can trust me. To play it safe, to keep my job secure, I should've said nothing about the fight. I should've sat, half fainted, in my chair and then taken the offered car to a different job on the other side of the road.

"Well, that's unacceptable."

My stomach drops, but I don't allow him to see my alarm, turning up the corners of my mouth ever so slightly and hoping my lipstick is still nicely in place. I'll find another position. Perhaps not as well paid and perhaps not as close to home, but I can find something. Plenty of women have taken factory jobs with the boys away.

"I understand, sir." I bob my head and shift my feet. A bus will arrive on the hour. I wonder if I can wait in the guardhouse out of the rain. I'd rather endure Talbot's looks than the chill against my legs. I reach for the door.

"You aren't *leaving*, are you?" His full baritone makes me freeze in place.

"I thought . . ."

"Judy, set Miss Santini up in the office with you. The spare desk, there. We'll find another girl for the switchboard. We'll keep you here to give Judy a hand and help out when our interpreter, McNeil, is busy." I blink rapidly, dizzied by the changes happening right in front of my eyes. Then he turns to me, his face as stern as ever. "That is, if you're up for it."

"Absolutely. I would love to," I say, as though I'm accepting a date, not a job offer. I don't need to fake my gratitude. I should thank my lucky stars I got a promotion on my first day. Goodness, I should be grateful I even still have a job, but I have to be sure of one more thing.

"And Trombello?" I ask, holding on to my courage.

"I'll check into it" is all he says, but it's enough. Without any further discussion, he yanks open the door to a hallway that must lead to his office. Inside, several doors line a tiled hall. The first one looks to be the entrance to Judy's secretarial sanctuary, a room I'm sure I'll become well acquainted with. I expect the lieutenant colonel to stomp to his office, but instead, he holds the door open, takes a step back, and grumbles, "Welcome to Camp Atterbury, my dear."

"Thank you, sir," I say, rushing through into a new world, a new job, and potentially a new life for me and my family.

CHAPTER 5

Elise

Present Day
Edinburgh, Indiana

"There you are!" Mac calls out to me as he walks down the middle of East Main Cross Street like he's the king of the town. Mac looks just as flamboyant standing in front of me as he does on any news broadcast, TV show, awards ceremony, or after-party. His silvery-gray hair rests a touch above his shoulders, and a pair of dark-rimmed reading glasses acts like a makeshift headband, looking stylish and cool rather than utilitarian. He wears dark, crisp jeans that look like Conrad purchased them right before leaving New York, and his brown woolen blazer is tailored to his exact measurements. The whole getup is accented with a fuzzy tan-and-light-blue scarf tied in a messy but sophisticated knot around his neck.

I see why my mom is drawn to Mac. He has an air about him that makes it seem like he knows exactly what's happening now and has a good grasp on what will happen next. But every time I see handsome, older Hollywood men, I can't help but think of the unfair beauty standards in my mother's industry.

Though his teeth are capped and bleached, his face is lined, and he still looks like a well-kept version of his sixty-something self instead of the stretched, filled, and polished version of most women in the industry. While I don't agree with the double standard, I try not to push the idea of aging naturally on any of my clients, and I never shame them for their pursuit of eternal youth, impossible as it may be.

"Hey, Mac." I take his outstretched hand and meet his smile with one of my own.

"Great to meet you finally, Elise. You're as lovely as you look in your pictures, I must say."

I'm immune to false flattery, but I know how to take it as well as dole it out.

"You're even better in real life, Mac. My mother filled me in on all your best qualities. Can't wait to get to know you better." We continue to give compliments back and forth for a moment or two. I've witnessed this sort of feather fluffing my whole life and may have fallen victim to it if not for my father, who always kept me grounded. He left the realm of fame to live on his ranch in Montana after he and my mother divorced when I was a little girl. He's busy with his ranch and refuses to learn how to use the internet or a cell phone, and when I finally connected with him last week, his advice came too late.

"Don't do it, punkin," he said in his adopted western drawl. "Nothing grows well under those stage lights, especially new relationships. I should know."

That's the most I can get out of my dad about his relationship with my mother—a quip or two, maybe a sage musing while staring at the horizon. Being raised by actors gets existential sometimes.

He's the more stable parent, but I didn't spend nearly as much time as I would've liked with him on the ranch. During my teen years, when my mom was away at her ashram cult in Brazil, I learned what it was like to be a country girl, or at least my father's version. I think that's why I'm the only one of my siblings who didn't end up going to Julliard and using my mother's name to make it in Hollywood. I came to respect hard work and a touch of solitude.

I can't say that I never took advantage of my family's dynasty. I worked hard for my degrees, but when I started my PR firm, Toffee Co., I had an advantage as Vivian Snow's granddaughter and Gracelyn Branson's daughter. If I were a purist, I'd have kept my father's last name, McFadden, instead of using my mother's.

"I've got us a five-thirty appointment at Holy Trinity Church, right around the corner. You'll get a tour, and then you'll have your first sit-down with the priest, a 'get to know you' kind of thing. I'd love to get your first reactions to the building."

This is not a casual invite, though Mac makes it sound that way. It's on the shot list Conrad sent in his most recent email.

"Uh, I'm not really camera ready." I gesture to my rumpled traveling clothes and makeup-less face. "I'm all for being myself on camera, but this isn't a good look."

"No problem. I have Lisa here for hair and makeup. She can touch you up in the car. Do you have a top in a solid color, not black? Something more bridal like a pink or a purple? Oh. Or off-white, even. I don't think that would push the envelope too much, would it, Marty?"

Mac looks to the man standing behind him whose existence I had barely registered. He's short with a dark cap and carrying a camera case.

"Actually, the interior is pretty light, so I think a richer palette would give some contrast. No red or black."

"Sound good?" Mac asks, and I already hate my position in this project, more of a prop than a person.

"I have tops in all those colors, but I don't know that I'm ready for anything in front of the camera today," I say again, but he's not listening.

"You'll be great." He squeezes my upper arm in a slightly patronizing way, clearly unaware that I've spent years giving advice to clients about on-camera styling when needed.

Mac addresses me again, a low, dramatic tenor to his voice. "I'm beyond eager to start working together, Elise."

"Same," I say, matching his tone.

Nothing like jumping right in, I guess. And the only way to get myself into a pool of cold water is to dive in headfirst before I can think better of it.

~

After six minutes of sprint-dressing in the bathroom of the local diner, I exit through the glass door, satisfied with the deep plum-colored blouse I've tossed on with a tailored leather jacket, a pair of dark trousers, and heeled booties. No one can see my outfit under my puffy plum coat, but Conrad gave it a thumbs-up, and I'm guessing that means Mac approves too.

I climb into the back seat of the idling black Escalade to find a forty-something woman wearing all black with dyed red hair pinned up in a bun waiting for me.

"Hey there, hun. I'm Lisa. Just a quick little touch-up for you, okay?"

Mac jumps in, and we make the short drive to the church as Lisa applies my makeup and tidies my hair.

"The church is Holy Trinity Catholic Church, and we'll be meeting Father Ignatius. It's just an intro prior to the Pre-Cana class required for the wedding prep."

"They're all right starting without Hunter?"

"Yeah. It's just the basics, and we'll get you together for the next one, even if he's virtual."

Lisa has me open my eyes and applies mascara with a disposable wand. My nerves are starting to simmer under the surface. I can hold meetings with high-powered famous people. I can face PR disasters, Twitter gaffes, and celebrity feuds, but stepping in front of the camera to talk about myself and my family is suffocating. I feel like I did when Dean was filming in Maui and there was pineapple in my daiquiri, which I'm deathly allergic to. My throat closed up so fast I could feel the sides meeting in the middle, shutting off my airway.

Dean reacted immediately. Called for help. Gave me CPR. Obtained an epi pen from someone at one of the tables next to us. He saved my life. I wish Dean were here.

Lisa puts on a final coat of gloss, and I rub my lips together, chastising myself. Not Dean. Hunter. I wish Hunter were here.

Lisa produces a handheld mirror as the car slows. I barely look but say thank you, and when the car comes to a complete stop, Mac jumps out like he's escaping a kidnapper.

"By the way," Lisa adds once Mac is gone, "I'm a big Vivian Snow fan. I need to know: Was she really as sweet in real life as she seemed on camera?"

I'm usually uncomfortable when strangers ask about my famous family. But lately when I talk about my grandmother, it doesn't feel like an intrusion. Most tell me about how Vivian Snow made a difference in their life, and it's like she's resurrected for a moment.

"Absolutely," I say, and Lisa swoons. She's about to ask another question when the Escalade's door opens, and a sound engineer taps her out. He hands me a mic. I remove my outer coat, snake the mic through the back of my shirt, and clip it to my collar. After a few sound checks, he gives me a thumbs-up and dips out of the car, the same way he came in.

I hear a slate clap outside and Mac say action. The door swings open again, but this time Marty stands outside with a camera on his shoulder and Mac right next to him.

I straighten my jacket and blouse, rub my lips together one more time, and then work my way out of the elevated back seat, my feet landing on a cement curb. Ignoring the blank stare of Marty's camera and the smaller, handheld camera focused on Mac, I catch my first real glimpse of Holy Trinity.

I've been here before but never as an adult, and it looks almost as large as I remember. The church is built on a hill, the greenery sweeping up to the steepled tower and cement steps leading to the arched carved front doors.

"What do you think? First impressions?" Mac asks, his voice low and hypnotic like he doesn't want to wake me from some sort of trance.

"It's beautiful." I barely get the words out before my throat tightens again, not only from nerves but from a rush of feelings I can't turn off. As I take in the vision of the church through the barely budding trees, tears sting my eyes.

"Has it changed much since you were here last?"

I caress every sharp angle and delicate curve of the structure with my gaze. I've seen greater buildings. I've visited the Vatican. I've walked on the Great Wall of China. I've strolled through the halls of Versailles, stood in Palace Square in St. Petersburg, and gasped at the brilliant beacon that is the Taj Mahal.

But what this site has that none of the others did is a piece of my history, my origin; it feels like it's almost part of my DNA.

"It looks exactly the same as when I was a kid and . . ." I think back to the photo in the eight-by-ten frame my mother keeps by the side of her bed even to this day. "My mom has a picture of Nonna and Grandpa on their wedding day outside this place. Seeing those carved doors right now—it's like they could walk out any second."

"Really? It's that well preserved?"

"I think so. You should ask my mom for her parents' wedding picture. It's a little fuzzy, but you'll get the idea."

"What does it mean to you that you'll be married here in a few short weeks?" he asks in his interviewer voice.

I envision myself dressed in white with Hunter beside me in his tuxedo, the stair rails dripping with flowers and bells ringing in the background. Although I've been struggling to imagine our wedding day, in this moment, it seems so clear.

"I think it means . . . everything." My comment hangs in the air, a meaningful, pregnant pause after my heartfelt sharing moment.

"Let's cut there," Mac says to the crew. All the cameras lift or droop, no longer focused on me or the church. Mac places an encouraging hand on my shoulder, squinting through his lenses. "Wow. Elise, that was great. Exactly what we need. Honest, vulnerable emotion. Perfect. Keep doing *that*, and we'll be out of here in no time."

Every piece of encouragement from Mac rings hollow. I feel silly for falling under his hypnotic spell and spouting something so cheesy, so melodramatic. Now, that sentimental moment belongs to Mac and the documentary, impossible to take back. I need to be more cautious. Mac is either a skilled director or a master manipulator—either way, there's no doubt he's willing to do whatever it takes to get "the shot." And it looks like it's up to me to protect my family's dignity—as well as my own.

This could be an interesting few weeks, I think as I nod cooperatively at Mac's stage directions while Lisa touches up the liner slightly smudged from my tears.

"Perfect," she says, stepping back and smiling at me, although I'm sure she's smiling at the "granddaughter of Vivian Snow" more so than at "Elise Branson." But in this case, I'm not offended.

With the cameras rolling again, I walk up the long row of steps embedded in the hillside to the front of the church. I'd heard Mac talking about losing the daylight, so there's a sense of urgency in the air. And though I'm cold without my fluffy coat, and I have to make a concerted effort not to look directly at the cameras, I realize my hands have finally stopped shaking.

CHAPTER 6

Vivian

Friday, May 7, 1943
Edinburgh USO

The punch table is crowded, but I can't wait any longer for a pick-me-up. I've been dancing the jitterbug with Peter Thomas for the past half hour. I'm out of breath and covered in far more perspiration than is proper for a girl. I'm supposed to sing shortly, but I can't hop right off the dance floor and onto the stage without grabbing a cool drink.

The air is thick with the smell of cheap perfume, aftershave, and sweat. After performing here for six months, I know that as the night goes on, my senses will numb—the pinch of my shoes and the strange smells in the air will fade away, and all that will matter is the music. But I'm not there yet.

The next number starts, and I can see Peter scanning the room for me. He'd keep me on the dance floor all night if I let him. I duck behind a tall serviceman ladling two glasses of the red punch. It's actually one of the worst things I've ever tasted, barely any sugar in it due to rationing, and it leaves an off-flavor coating on my tongue. Occasionally, if we're lucky, there are chilled bottles of Coca-Cola waiting at the refreshment table, but not tonight.

I get to the front of the line and reach for the ladle when a serviceman snatches it out of my hand.

A voice in my head yells out, "Hey!" but another calms it immediately with a "You can wait." I'm convinced the first voice is that of Vivian Snow, singer, dancer, actress. But the second voice, the one that wins every time, the one that keeps me in line, is me, Vivian Santini.

"Let me get that for you." The man passes me a glass cup.

I take the cup, realizing he wasn't cutting in line after all. He just wanted to serve me a drink.

"Oh, thank you." I gulp the liquid quickly, trying not to taste it and wishing I were one of those girls who could quip back in the sassy way men seem to love.

"Saw you dancing out there. You're pretty light on your feet," he says, taking a mouthful of the punch, then grimacing. "Wow. This is really, really . . ."

"Terrible?" I say, laughing, placing my empty glass on the return tray.

"That's a nice way of saying it." He laughs and attempts another sip before putting his nearly full cup on the table. "It's truly awful. I'd rather drink old canteen water."

"We should really treat our soldier boys better, shouldn't we?" I joke, the sticky film already turning my mouth sour.

"We're going out there to get shot at. If we could only have something decent to drink before we go . . ."

"This feels like a travesty Washington *must* hear about. A new bill or something."

The soldier's eyebrow lifts, and he looks at me with a bit of a smirk when someone bumps me from behind, shoving me against my companion. He steadies me and calls out to the young private who hasn't noticed his misstep.

"Hey! Look where you're going. Aren't you going to apologize to the young lady?"

"Oh, hey, sorry," the distracted private says half-heartedly without turning around.

"Really, Private? That's how you apologize?" he says, reaching out to tap the kid's shoulder. I glance at his arm and notice a capital *T* under two bars. *He's a corporal,* I think. Which outranks the private.

I can't stand to see an altercation here, in the middle of what should be an escape from the war, over an accidental bump. I grab his wrist. His pulse is pounding. My heart's also racing.

"I'm all right, you know," I say softly. "It's no bother."

It takes a moment, but when the corporal finally recognizes my touch, it causes a shift in him. Instead of pursuing the unrepentant soldier any further, he switches his focus to me.

"You're a little darling, aren't you?" he asks like he's surprised by the revelation.

By following the movements of his eyes, I can tell he's taking in my curled and smoothly styled hair, then my dress, deep maroon with a white collar, cinched at the waist and falling below my knee. I have the new heels on, the ones from my first day of work, and a pair of lace-trimmed white socks, which look a touch childish but are necessary for dancing.

I usually don't like it when men give me this sort of once-over, thinking who knows what about my figure and features. But from this man, it bothers me less.

"I'm Tom. Tom Highward. I saw you dancing with Peter and thought I might squeeze a word in with you before he claimed you again."

"Well, hello, Tom. I'm Vivian." I smile like I was taught in the junior hostess training.

"Vivian, I feel like I owe you a real drink after that whole debacle. I can't complain, though. The prettiest girl in the room is standing here talking to me, so . . ."

"You're sweet," I say, blushing. The only way I know how to talk to these young men without stuttering is to pretend I'm a Hollywood vixen, like Rita Hayworth with Fred Astaire.

"You're sweeter than that punch, that's for sure," he says.

"There are plenty of things sweeter than that punch."

"Like, ice cream. Ice cream is a lot sweeter than that punch."

"I guess so," I say, clasping my hands in front of me as he shifts us farther away from the punch table. "Sometimes we have ice cream here. We even have hot fudge and peanuts when we're lucky."

What I don't say is that the USO dances are the only place I get those luxuries. I can't afford such things with the expense of my father's injury and my mother's condition. For me, even a little dish of ice cream is like heaven.

The quick swing song fades away, and a gentle intro from the band announces the first slow song of the night. Tom puts out his hand like Clark Gable and asks, "Would you do me the honor?"

I reach out to take his offer when the song intro fades and starts again.

The song finally registers—Vera Lynn's "You'll Never Know." The perfect song for a room full of soldiers all far from home. It's also *my* song—the one I'm supposed to be singing. Right now.

"Oh!" I jump back. "I've gotta go."

How could I have let myself get so distracted? I've danced with a hundred GIs in my time as a junior hostess. I've talked to countless more. But never, ever have I missed a cue.

I dash through the crowd of slow-dancing couples—GIs in their perfectly pressed uniforms, clasping girls in swaying skirts close and likely pretending they're the girls they left behind. When I get to the empty mic, the band is vamping the intro one more time, and Frank, the band director, a middle-aged farmer who takes his position very seriously, scowls at me.

"'Bout time, girly," he grumbles, and I mutter an apology, not even offended at his judgmental inflection. Pauly Jones, the thirtysomething piano player unable to enlist because he lost a leg in a combine accident when he was a kid, winks at me. It's the reassurance I need. I run a flat palm over my hair and turn to the microphone with a smile.

As the words flow out, gliding over my punch-coated throat and likely red-stained tongue, I feel her arrive—Miss Snow. My nerves calm; the sixty or so sets of eyes on me make me feel like being wrapped up in a warm blanket—the opposite of how I feel when I get attention offstage.

During slow songs like this, the hostesses allow the boys to hold them a little tighter than the manual suggests, and Carly Tawny, our senior hostess, resident mother figure, and my kinda-sorta voice teacher, turns a blind eye and goes into the kitchen.

As I croon to the slowly swaying crowd, I look for Tom. He's leaning against the back wall with his arms crossed, staring right at me, which sends an odd thrill through my body in a curiously enjoyable way.

As the song ends, the crowd applauds, and I step back from the microphone, looking toward Tom's towering figure. Seeing my interest, he peels his body away from the wall and takes a step toward the stage. He looks like he wants to say something, and I want to know what it is.

But I won't find out yet.

Because when the slow song comes to an end, I call out, "Lets pick it up a little, boys!" like I always do at this point in the night. "Shoo-Shoo Baby" starts to play. I sway to the beat, holding on to the microphone stand, and Tom settles back into his place on the wall. I can see him, and he can see me.

I'm onstage for an hour, and during that time, I sing the fifteen or so songs listed on my crib sheet. I dance and joke around with Tony as a part of a small bit we improvise from week to week. I banter with the soldiers in between numbers, ask where they're from, tell little jokes.

When I'm onstage, the time goes by in a flash. I close out with the sultry, heartfelt ballad "We'll Meet Again." If there were any wallflowers before, they're gone. And when voices from the swaying mass join in at the chorus, I blink back tears like I do every week, even though my father and sister are safe at home and no soldier has claimed my heart.

One thing both Vivian Snow and Vivian Santini agree on—war is terrifying, and many of these uniformed men won't return from it.

The music fades, and my tears recede. I give a slight bow and a wave.

"Thank you and good night."

The applause swells, and I gesture to the band so they get their share of the praise. The band will play a second set after a short break, and the men will trickle out and return to base in shifts. The girls have an obligation to stay until the end of the dance to guarantee enough dance partners and to add to their recorded service hours.

I can't leave either. Though I'm paid a small fee for my performance each Saturday, I spend the rest of my time here as a volunteer, so I follow the same rules of conduct. But Carly's given me permission to freshen up after my sets each week in a quiet spot in the kitchen where I can powder my nose and get a bite to eat and maybe a drink of water away from the heat and the crowd.

I skirt the always-congested refreshment table. A few servicemen tip their hats or give me a shy compliment, but most watch from a distance as I disappear through the set of swinging doors. I find Carly inside, arranging a platter of sandwiches and cookies in a pretty, geometric pattern.

"You were killer-diller out there, Viv. You've been practicing your runs; I can tell. And your breath control was banger. Everyone was on that dance floor. You know; I get asked every week how we ended up with a famous star here in Edinburgh."

I've been singing in the back room of Carly's apartment every Thursday night for a year. She was a music teacher at an elementary school before she got married, and though she's not a professional, she's helped me progress as a performer. I pay her back by babysitting a few nights a month. She's a young widow, and though there are more and more of those these days, she's been alone for longer than she was married. I look up to her for that—she's a strong and independent woman. And at thirty-two, she's more of a parental figure to me than my own mother.

"Ha, famous," I laugh, stealing a triangle-shaped egg-salad sandwich on white bread and a cookie.

"You don't know how many boys moon after you, Vivian. I gotta remind them over and over again that you're a hostess and can't date any of them. Otherwise, you'd have a line at your door."

"My father would chase them all off with his shotgun. Wouldn't that be a nice surprise? Fighting Italians in Europe *and* on the home front." I take a bite, grateful to have something in my stomach, even if it's void of flavor.

Carly laughs as she opens the door of one of the refrigerated units in the back of the kitchen. I hear the clank of the Coca-Cola bottle before I see it.

"Here. I hid this for you. Thought you might be thirsty after your performance."

"Oh, Carly! Thank you!" My mouth waters. She pops off the cap and passes the bottle my way. The carbonation sizzles and snaps; little sprays escape the top and tickle my fingers when I wrap them around the cold glass.

I take a long drink, almost too fast to even taste the syrupy cola. I know it's unladylike and that papà thinks that all sugary drinks are poison. He's always pushing watered-down wine on us instead of soft drinks. After smelling it on my mother's breath for so much of my childhood, I can hardly stand the taste of wine. He thought it would cure her mental ailments, but it only made them far worse. Now the only time I drink wine is at Communion.

The music starts up again, and even with a half-full stomach and a bottle of chilled heaven in front of me, the horns and strings are a siren's call. Carly pats my shoulder and heads toward the gymnasium with her tray in hand.

"Take your time, doll. Plenty of dances left for you tonight. No rush." She backs out through the double doors, and the sounds of the party tempt me as the doors swing closed.

I finish the last bite of my sandwich and have moved on to the cookie when I hear the doors burst open, ushering in the cacophony again.

"Empty your tray already?" I ask, spinning around on my heel with the top half of the cookie in my mouth. But it's not Carly standing in the doorway.

"Empty?" Tom asks, his hat clasped in front of him, his light blue eyes cold and warm at the same time.

"Oh goodness," I gasp, forcing down the partially chewed cookie. "You frightened me! I thought you were Carly. I mean, Mrs. Tawny."

"Sorry. I didn't mean to . . ."

"No, no. It's okay—Tom, right?" I ask, even though I for gosh-darn sure remember his name.

"Yes. And you're Vivian Snow."

I should correct him, explain it's a stage name, but I kind of like being Vivian Snow to this handsome young corporal.

"I . . . I am."

He moves to the opposite end of the kitchen island. I should mention the rules to him. We're not allowed to be alone with the men. I should ask him to leave the kitchen and dance with me where the chaperones can see us.

And I will.

But not yet.

"You were pretty fantastic out there." He places his hat on the counter and then picks it up again like he doesn't know what to do with his hands.

"Well, thanks." I put the cookie bits on a napkin next to the half-empty bottle of pop. "But I don't think I saw you dancing."

I *know* I didn't see him dancing; he was glued to that back wall, watching my every move, but I'm not about to let on that I was looking.

"I wasn't." He moves closer to me, and my breathing begins to grow shallow. My pulse thumps behind my eyes and in my ears.

"Well, why not? Plenty of girls out there would be happy to dance with such an interesting fella." He must've had plenty of offers.

"The girl I wanted to dance with was taken."

Must be Barbara. All the men moon after Barbara. Probably helps that she keeps her hem two inches shorter than regulation, and rumor has it she doesn't follow the rules about dating and drinking as closely as the rest of us.

Feeling the sting of rejection, I sweep the crumbs off the counter and into my hand and then take the last sip of my drink in one big gulp, forgetting my manners.

"You might be able to catch her now. The song's almost over, and if I remember the lineup, there should be a slow dance next." I point to the closed double doors and toss the crumpled paper and cookie crumbs into the garbage.

Tom takes his hat, folds it in half, and shoves it into his back pocket.

"I was talking about you. I wanted to dance with you," he says, placing one of his hot, rough hands over mine.

My body responds with a subtle but delicious tingle between my shoulder blades and down my spine.

"I . . . I'd love to." I've said these words hundreds of times to other GIs at the USO dances, but with this guy it feels different. I *want* to dance with him. His fingers close around mine, and he tugs ever so slightly.

"Let's get out there, then."

I'm blushing. Vivian Snow disappears, and once again I'm Viviana Santini, the shy daughter of immigrants. But he seems to like this shy girl as much as my stage persona.

"Excuse me; you can't be in here!" Carly calls out. I retrieve my hand and peek around Tom to see the petite brunette wrestling her way through the kitchen doors.

"Vivian! Is that you? You should know better, hun."

"No, it's not Vivian's fault, ma'am. I got lost looking for the latrine."

Carly raises an eyebrow and looks at me to make sure his story checks out. I shrug and nod like I both agree with the soldier and have no idea what's going on.

Carly stares up at Tom, resting her hands on her hips after putting down the empty tray.

"It's on the other side of the hall, dear." The tiny thirty-two-year-old says it like she's the mother of this grown man.

"Yes, ma'am," he says like a little boy caught shooting spitballs at the ceiling.

He walks toward the doors without another word but stops once he's past Carly. Over her head, he mouths, "I'll wait for you," and winks as he finishes his exit from the kitchen.

I want to wink back, but I don't want Carly to see, so instead I wipe the counter again. I'd like to claim I'm a terrible liar, but I'm shockingly proficient at the art of deceit. I have to be with a father at home who forbids his daughters to do anything or wear anything or go anywhere that might threaten his ideal of what it looks like to be a "good girl."

The truth is I learned early on how to tell harmless lies in order to fit into modern life. I've always wondered if that's why acting calls to me.

"Watch out for that one. I smell mischief." Carly points to her nose and then to the doors.

"You smell egg sandwiches."

"I smell mischief *and* egg sandwiches," she says, placing the tray in the sink.

"That sounds pretty unsettling."

"It is!" Carly laughs, loosening up.

The slow song ends, and my spirits drop, though I try not to let it show on my face. A jaunty swing number ramps up. It's not the same as a sweet slow dance, but I wonder if Tom knows how to jitterbug.

The golden wedding band she's never taken off glitters in the dim light as Carly places her tiny pale hand on my shoulder, abruptly very serious.

"Listen, hun; be careful, all right?" The faint wrinkles at the corners of her eyes remind me that she's seen more of life than I have. "We all know the rules, but I'm no fool—all the hometown boys are gone, and these polished-up young men in nice uniforms look like great husband material for you gals. But I see these boys when you all aren't around, and most of them have girls at home, some of them wives. You've got a good head on ya, so we've never had this chat before, but when a guy pursues a girl like he has a fire under his hat that he can't put out—usually that means he has his mind where it shouldn't be. The nice boys don't corner you in an empty kitchen. Remember that, okay?"

I've heard this warning before. I've even been the one to warn other girls when I've gotten intel about one guy or another. But Tom—I just met Tom. It's not like I want to do anything more than dance with him.

"Thank you, Carly," I say instead of all the other things I'm thinking. I fix a stray little curl that has fallen onto her forehead. "I'll be extra careful. I promise."

"You're a real doll; you know that, don't you?" she says. "Get back out there before the men storm the kitchen. At least four fellas asked me about ya after your set. You're gonna have to endure one more hour of adoration, you poor thing."

"I'll go out there whether you flatter me or not, so . . ."

"In that case . . ." She takes a deep breath like she's preparing for a long string of insults.

"I'm leaving! I'm leaving!" I call out.

As I spin through the doors into the hall, it feels like I'm already dancing. The cheerful timbre of the brass instruments urges my feet to move in time with the music. Emerging from the lights of the kitchen to the sparsely lit dance floor, I'm momentarily blinded.

"You sure know how to make a guy work for a dance, don't you?"

I don't need light to know who's waiting for me a few steps away. Without any further conversation, he leads me onto the dance floor where my feet answer the call of the rhythm. Despite his lanky, tall frame, Tom moves gracefully, like he's been dancing his whole life. He takes the lead, urging me into spins and twists and lifts with subtle flicks of his wrist. I immediately know that if I were smart, I'd heed Carly's warning, walk out of this dance, and stay away from Tom Highward forever.

Instead—I keep dancing.

CHAPTER 7

Elise

Present Day
Holy Trinity Catholic Church

The inside of the church is tidy and well maintained but less spectacular than I expected. The walls are yellowed eggshell, and the stained-glass windows hold none of the wonder and majesty of the grand cathedrals of Europe or St. Patrick's back in New York City.

"This will need some work before the wedding," the director of photography mutters to Conrad.

"The transformation will be impactful," Mac says with a broad sweep of his hand that shuts them up immediately. "Hey, darling. How are you doing?" he asks, taking my hands like I've witnessed the death of a much-loved pet. The cameras follow.

"It's . . . different from what I remember." The age of the structure would be hard to determine with carpet runners covering large portions of the oak flooring, but a notice on a bulletin board near the entrance narrows the founding date down to sometime in the 1850s. A giant wooden crucifix hangs above the altar, and I feel a pang of my remaining Catholic guilt that we're using this holy place as a setting for my mom and Mac's project.

"We're bringing in Terri Fitzgibbons, the wedding planner, and flying in flowers for the big day. Today, let's not focus on the aesthetics, okay? Let's focus instead on memories of your grandma and your first meeting with Father Ignatius."

"Sounds good," I say, and slip away from Mac. When the cameras are rolling, he's so welcoming, like we have a close friendship or like he's my actual stepfather instead of the man who's been sleeping with my mom for a couple of months. I think I prefer cold, snobby Mac. He seems more real.

I look up at the arched ceiling of the open, airy room and the choir loft. The beams are painted white, though I'm sure they were stained brown the last time I was here as a child. The cameras focus on my exploration, and it makes me nervous, so I block them out. Instead, I study the multicolored-glass windows made up of geometric shapes and lead lines. What would the off-white walls look like with the lights off and the sun shining through?

"What do you think?" a crew member asks. It's not Conrad or one of the cameramen. This man is only a few inches taller than me, with light brown hair combed over to one side. Younger than me, too, I think, but dressed in a light jacket that I swear my father wore in a film in 1989. He might be the location manager or a gaffer assessing the lighting. It's a little surprising being addressed by someone other than Mac with the cameras still rolling, but he must know something I don't.

I whisper, glad to have someone normal to talk to before Mac comes back.

"Cathedrals are breathtaking, but this"—I gesture to the glass windows and arched roof—"it's not showy or a waste of money or the result of some medieval pissing contest; it's just"—I search for the right description—"simple and beautiful and probably a labor of sacrifice and love when it was built."

He bobs his head, one finger over his mouth, taking in the multicolored glass.

"Hmm . . . poetic," he says with a touch of sarcasm that makes me think he's smirking. A quick check out of the corner of my eye confirms it.

"What?" I whisper, realizing why he's laughing. "You don't find a pissing contest to be an apt description?"

He takes his hand away from his mouth and clasps both behind his back. I can see his smile now. It's brilliant and gives me the sense he's been in far more mischief than his clean-cut look would suggest.

"Well, I guess I've never heard the term used in church or in reference to holy cathedrals."

"Oh shit," I say, covering the mic clipped under my collar. "You're right. Do you think my mic picked it up?"

He shrugs with a bemused expression on his face.

"You're no help."

"It's above my pay grade, I guess." He's still smiling.

"Mine too," I try to joke but end up biting my lip instead.

"Nervous?" he asks, still staring over my head.

"Yeah, pretty nervous."

"It doesn't run in the family, the 'on camera' thing?" His questions are casual and insightful. He must be part of the production team, likely taking mental notes or recording our conversation through my mic to share with Mac later.

"Nooo. No. Not at all."

"Why not? You don't seem shy."

"Ha. It's not that. I used to be quite the camera hog."

"What changed?" he asks.

I turn around and finally get a good look at my conversation partner as he continues to stare at the windows over my head. He's even more buttoned up than I first thought, but interesting enough to make me curious. I want to find out his name.

"My mom's acting coach said I didn't have 'the face' for it."

"The face for it?" he asks incredulously, refocusing his gaze on me.

"Yeah. He said my face doesn't work."

He gives me a quick once-over like he's searching for the supposed error in my features.

"I think he was wrong about that."

I blush. I shouldn't be surprised that I get along with the crew better than the primaries. It's been that way since I was little. They were the ones to sneak me a bagel from food services, or "crafty" as we always called it, or play a game of gin rummy during reshoots or carry me to my mom's trailer when I fell asleep during a late shoot.

Why I chose to run PR for sometimes self-centered, often out-of-touch movie stars, I'll never know.

"You'll see," I say. "I can't hide anything. My mom thought I was a prodigy or something at first 'cause when I was little, I never needed a tear stick, you know, the stuff they put on your lower lid to make you cry. But then she realized I wasn't crying on cue; I was crying for real because I didn't want to be in front of the cameras."

He chuckles, looking up at the windows again. As the sun starts to set, the stained glass on the eastward-facing side of the church swiftly loses most of its brilliance, and the windows on the west side change colors in the orange light, sending a blanket of golden hues through the nave.

The crew member grows contemplative, and a yellow triangle of light from the western stained glass falls on his cheek, making him seem warm, glowing.

"And what about now?" he asks seriously. "Do you want to be *here*? Now?"

I should answer, "Yes, I'm honored to be here," but I have a feeling this guy will know I'm lying.

"Actually—I don't know yet."

"That's . . . honest." He rubs his chin thoughtfully.

"Elise!" I hear my name called, and my head snaps in that direction. "Darling. This way."

Mac stands under the giant Jesus on a cross, waving at me like a member of the paparazzi trying to get my mom's attention. I wince. His whole attitude clashes with the reverence intended for this place.

An elderly-looking priest in a long black coat and a white collar, with graying hair and horn-rimmed glasses, stands next to Mac. He seems annoyed with Mac's volume and the hive of activity that's invaded his sanctuary. I want to apologize, smooth things over like a good PR agent would, but I don't work for Mac. God, I don't even work for my *mom*. If I do any smoothing, it will be for the sake of my conscience only.

"I better go do some damage control," I say, turning back to the production man and his tan coat, soft voice, and curious line of questioning. But—he's gone, likely called away by some voice in his earpiece while I was distracted by Mac. I glance around, not finding him anywhere, but I'm sure we'll see plenty of each other over the next few weeks.

I hurry down the main aisle to Mac, quick enough to show urgency without disrespecting the church. I can't help but think that in the near future, I'll be walking down this aisle very slowly with a veil over my face and flowers in my hands.

"This is Elise Branson, our bride." Mac gestures in my direction from the front of the sanctuary, his voice still loud enough to echo. "Elise, this is Father Ignatius."

"Hello, Father," I whisper solemnly, extending my hand.

"This way," he says, walking toward the back of the nave.

I slide my unshaken hand into my jacket pocket and follow the priest.

We enter a small office to the side of the church. Inside, a desk sits a few feet away from a rear wall that's covered in bookcases filled with books of all sizes. Some of the bindings look ancient and others like they came from the local thrift store. Two wooden chairs sit in front of the desk, and the windows to my right let in the dimming light of the evening.

Mac enters and takes a full turn around in the middle of the room like he belongs here. I stand in the corner as the camera and sound crew pack into the small space.

"Ben, the lighting in here needs some help," Mac snaps. A twenty-something with long hair in a ponytail starts rearranging the room.

So, the window guy isn't the gaffer.

Cameras go from handheld to stationary as everyone waits for proper lighting.

In the middle of the room, Conrad holds a pen and an open folder. He's explaining the Image Release form to Father Ignatius. The clergyman doesn't seem to like the idea of signing.

"What is this again?" the priest asks for the third time.

"It says that we can use your image on camera for the film. I sent your secretary a copy a few weeks ago but haven't heard back. We need it on file before we start filming."

Father Ignatius holds up the release form and reads it under his breath and then coughs and puts it back into the folder.

"I won't sign this."

"What . . . what do you mean? You approved everything already. I passed it by the archdiocese." Mac lets down his cool, composed mask for half a second, and I swear I see panic there. Father Ignatius closes the folder and leaves it with Conrad without a glance in my direction.

"I don't like the cameras," he says dismissively. "I told Bishop Lovedale this whole venture is fraught with pride and vanity. I can show you around the grounds and such, but Father Patrick will be on camera for the Pre-Cana and the ceremony."

"Father Patrick?"

"Yes, Father Patrick is here at Holy Trinity. I split my time between this church and three others in the area in more of a . . . supervisory role."

"So, this Father Patrick will be taking your place, then?" Mac asks, seeming calmed by the offer of a replacement.

"If you all insist on moving forward . . ." He pauses, as though Mac will suddenly see the wisdom of his old-fashioned values and cancel the whole film. But when Mac stares back at him, no change of heart evident, he continues. "Then, yes, he will be your partner in the proceedings. You can still reach out to me with any supervisory concerns or questions, and I can assist." He places the pen in Conrad's shirt pocket. "Off camera, of course."

"That's fine. As long as we can stay on schedule. Conrad, change the names on the release."

"Will do." The young assistant rushes through the cluster of crew members and out of the office while Mac leans against the desk, checking his watch.

"So, this Father Patrick—will he be available to shoot today? We had the first meeting on the schedule I sent over that you and your bishop approved."

"Yes, yes. He was out on a call, but I think I saw him come in. You have to understand—our first priority is our parishioners. I want that to be very clear." He holds up a warning finger, swollen and spotted with age.

"We completely respect that, and I promise to be careful with your time and Father Patrick's time." Mac nods, answering like he really understands, but I can see he's insincere. Once he realized Father Ignatius wouldn't appear on camera, he stopped really listening to him.

Mac glances at his watch again and calls me over and points to one of the chairs across from the desk. I wish they'd remove the empty chair where Hunter should be sitting.

"Sit on down, and we'll check lighting. Do me a favor and look over at Ben. Thanks, darling." He flips a chunk of my hair over my shoulder and then takes a look into the screens on the cameras to my left that will catch my profile.

"Ben, pull the desk this way a little." The desk is relocated with a screech.

Father Ignatius intervenes. "Wait a moment. Please don't move things. I didn't say anything could be changed in the room. I didn't give permission for that."

"Sorry, the lighting is better this way. We can put it all back after. I promise we won't disturb anything permanently," Ben explains in his slight New York accent.

"I . . . I . . . ," the elderly priest stutters, growing more overwhelmed. "I don't know about that . . ."

Mac straightens up, running fingers through his salt-and-pepper hair.

"Well, if *you* don't, then could we speak to Father Patrick? Perhaps you could locate him for me?" The tension in the room is growing by the second, and I wonder if we'll get out of here without a godly lightning bolt of retribution striking one or more of us dead.

"How can I help?" a voice from the back of the room chimes in. I don't have to turn around to know who's speaking. It's the man from before. The production assistant or whatever.

"Oh, thank the Lord," I hear Ben mutter as he adjusts a light behind me. I try to take a quick glance over my shoulder.

"In the camera, please," Mac corrects and then whispers over my shoulder to one of the crew. "The other priest is here. Get him miked and lit fast, and let's get moving."

After a momentary scuffle, I can hear the priest's footsteps crossing the floor. I sit up a little straighter. He crosses my line of vision, but I don't get a good look with everyone flocking around him.

"What do you think? Does he need any powder? Do I need to call Lisa?" a production assistant asks Mac.

I peek at the priest. I expected a slightly oily middle-aged clergyman. Instead, I lock eyes with the azure gaze I became acquainted with in the nave.

"Hey! It's you," I blurt out.

Production assistant Ben gives me a look that I translate as "Shut up; we're running behind." The friendly man sitting across from me, wearing a priest's collar, raises an eyebrow in my direction but doesn't say a word.

Damn it. He's the priest. I smile with tight lips. I told this priest I think cathedrals are pissing contests. And I swore. Right in front of him—I swore.

But I don't get far in my regret spiral before Mac settles into his chair. It's positioned off to the side with a fourth camera filming his reactions.

With the crew in place, Mac turns to me and with his camera voice makes the introduction official.

"Elise, this is Father Patrick Kelly. Father Patrick, Elise Branson. The bride."

"Nice to meet you," he says from behind the desk.

"You too," I say, pretending we've never met.

The assistant director steps forward with a black-and-white slate with digital numbers across the top and other information written on it in grease pencil. He holds it in front of Father Patrick's face, waiting for confirmation from the cameramen, and then calls out:

"*Vivian Snow: Bombshell*, Father Patrick, Take One."

And we begin.

CHAPTER 8

Vivian

Thursday, May 13, 1943
Santini Home

I have lip color, rouge, mascara, and eye pencil all tucked inside my purse, along with my mother's silver compact. Looking in the mirror, I add one more comb to my hair, hoping I've done enough to keep everything in place on the bus if Mary doesn't arrive in time to pick me up. In the mornings, I stand at my bus stop, fingers crossed I'll see her heading down the street with her red-nailed, long-fingered hand hanging out the window of her navy-blue Plymouth Special Deluxe.

Otherwise, I'm stuck on the bus. And with the days getting warmer, passengers let down the windows, so I can't trust I'll arrive at the base with my hair in presentable condition. Papà doesn't want his girls using anything "unnatural," which includes stiffeners in our hair, so I have to rely on a hairnet to keep my long strands in place and up to code. I'd like to cut it, but papà has a rule about that too.

At least makeup is easier to hide. Aria leaves me a wet washcloth in the mailbox at the end of the day when she gets the mail for papà. It's often cold as a snowdrift in January when I wipe my face at night, but I'll take the icy touch of the terry cloth over papà's fiery temper.

Before leaving the bedroom I share with Aria, I smooth the bedspread and check that the delicate perfume bottles are lined up in order on my dresser. That's the mamma I like to remember, the dark-haired beauty who collected lovely things from far-off places. I always knew my mother was beautiful. My father knew it too. She wore lipstick, and when I was young, I'd ask for an extra kiss on my lips before I went to school, hoping I'd get a little smudge of color on my mouth so I could be as pretty as her. She kept her nails painted red and her toenails, too, and when strands of silver began to show in her dark locks, she took to dying it.

But mamma had moods. When she got too wild, papà would calm her with a glass of wine. When she got too low, he'd pump her up with pills he got from a friend at the factory. I don't blame my papà; he didn't know what to do when she'd run off for days or even weeks, or when she'd stay in bed and talk about how much better off we'd all be without her. Papà thought he was helping. We all thought he was helping.

I sought refuge at school, and I found any way to stay late when I had the chance. Then when I was ten, my mother fell pregnant with baby Tony.

As her belly grew, something like a miracle happened. Her fits stopped, her wild, sleepless nights, the weeks of not knowing if my mother would ever return—gone. I'd crawl into her bed in the morning after papà went to work for the early shift, and I'd put my hand on her belly and feel the baby inside shift and wiggle, and I let myself believe a miracle had happened.

I knew other Catholic families whose houses were bursting with babies, and I often wondered why my family had so few. I had some idea it had to do with mamma's sickness, but once that baby started growing in her belly, I was convinced God decided to heal her.

We all thought she was better then, that she'd kicked the demons or whatever she called her fits and mood shifts that "followed her from the old country." And when Tony was born, my father seemed happy in a way I hadn't seen him before.

His anger was gone. And a peaceful softness took its place. At first, I was jealous of Tony, the baby who fixed everything, the baby who healed my mamma and calmed my papà.

But then I fell under his spell too. Baby Tony, with thick black hair and slate-gray eyes that might turn blue or brown at any minute. Before Tony, I'd said I didn't want children, even though it made Father Theodore cringe. Once he suggested I become a nun, and I considered it for a little while, thinking it a way to avoid having babies and staying home with an angry husband. I loved my baby sister, but I was required to care for her so often I felt like I'd already experienced parenthood. And I loved my imperfect father, but he made marriage and family seem like an immeasurable burden. Which I guess it was, but mamma's illness didn't only affect papà. I think that's what he forgot in all of this.

The day that mamma and Tony went missing, I was the one to walk Aria home from school to an empty house. I was the one who searched every room and called mamma's name out the open back door. I was the one to give Aria a snack of cheese slices and saltine crackers, and I was the one to find mamma lying in the creek with baby Tony still and blue in her arms. To this day, I won't wear blue, because it reminds me of the last time I saw my baby brother and the last day I considered mamma my mother.

The police and an ambulance came. Mamma was unconscious but not dead. Father Theodore says I need to repent for saying it, but sometimes I wish she'd died that day too. For the past ten years, we've had to scrimp and save and give up our hopes and dreams in order for mamma to stay in Mount Mercy Sanitarium. I had to work while going to school, and we pay more for her lodging and care every month than we do for the three of us.

Papà says she's sick and we need to understand. We take turns visiting her once a month, and I can tell every time he goes he hopes she'll be better, that he'll be bringing her home again. I used to secretly hope the same when I'd visit, that the doctors would find a miracle cure for whatever haunted my mother and she'd come home. I think I could forgive her if she'd sung to me when I had the measles or if she'd taught me how to put on lipstick or curl my hair or made even one single meal on the little white stove she'd begged papà for.

"Viviana! Your coffee is getting cold." Papà's voice shakes the house. Every time he shouts, I flinch. I don't like yelling of any kind. I'll do essentially anything to keep his irritation from boiling into fury.

Aria doesn't seem to mind as much, though she's naturally more adept at staying small when papà expands to fill a space with his loud voice or easily triggered displeasure.

"It's not like he beats us," she always says when I get agitated.

And she's right. He's not a monster.

Since we lost Tony, he's never once raised his hand or reached for his belt, and when he sees me recoil during his temper spells, he usually calms down and apologizes.

"Thank you, papà," I say, taking a long sip. The coffee is thick and bitter, and scalding hot.

"Sit down and drink. You're making me nervous. You're like one of those windup dolls that keeps moving and never stops. Moving. Moving. Moving. Then you run out of power, go to sleep, and get up and do it again the next day." We speak only Italian at home. I've tried to get papà to learn more English, but he claims he knows enough to work and to talk to the men at Amos Plastics, and that's all he needs.

"I have to catch the bus, papà. I can't be late."

"I don't like you on the bus, Viviana. It's not safe." He rubs the cast on his left leg. It's propped up on the kitchen chair, his cane leaning against the sink. I know it's hard on his ego to be immobilized, but what hurts more is the drop in income. It's the only reason he allowed me to get an office job.

Granted, he has no idea that the office is on the army base or that I'm working with Italian prisoners. If I'd asked him for permission, he would've given me a definitive no, but not for the reasons most would think. Papà isn't against his fellow countrymen being detained; he's ashamed of their part in the war. And he's afraid of the ramifications for innocent Italian immigrants like us trying to build a happy life in America.

"Papà, I've been riding the bus to Marian for school the past two years. Columbus is only a few miles farther, just the opposite direction."

"Stay away from army men. Don't talk to them. I see them on the bus; you know." Oh Lord, if he only knew how many military men I talk to every day at work and at the USO. But he doesn't know, and I'm not planning on telling him anytime soon.

"Even if they talk to me, papà, I don't talk to them."

"Good girl. Lonely men with no family nearby are not safe suitors for my daughter. Don't trust them. Never will."

"I'm not looking for suitors, papà. I'm just going to work. Besides, I could take the car if you gave me permission." I take another long sip of coffee.

"No." He slashes his hand in the air. "The engine is not reliable. If you break down, how am I going to find you?"

"I know how to work with the engine, papà. You taught me." I try to sweet-talk.

"And . . . and the gas is too expensive."

"But I'm making more money now. Besides, I could drive Aria to school and you to work when your leg is better." Aria is fifteen and does the mile walk to the high school with no complaint. But unlike my father, who thinks hardship will make his children more grateful and productive, I want Aria to experience some softness in life. I've been more like a mother to her than a sister. I changed her diapers when mamma forgot and combed out her tangled hair when mamma took to her bed or disappeared for days.

He ignores my reasoning and continues. "And . . . you'd put too many miles on it. Your mamma will cry when she comes home and sees her car with thousands and thousands of miles on it." He's waving his hands now. I know as soon as he brings up mamma, it's time to stop trying to convince him. At times, I think he's as delusional as she is.

"Yes, papà," I say, and kiss him on the head. He still has a headful of hair, and though it's more gray than brown, he looks at least ten years younger than his fifty-six years. He could easily find someone to marry if he were a free man. But divorce is a sin, and no one believes that as deeply as papà.

"The bus is safer for work."

I nod, not wanting to fight anymore and leave Aria to pick up the pieces before she walks to school. Why God gave us two broken parents, I'll never know. But with men fighting and dying overseas, I shouldn't wallow in my personal woes.

Aria comes in from the backyard, her cheeks red, hands covered in dirt and caked under her nails. With summer creeping in, my sister will spend more and more time outside tending to her garden. She got mamma's green thumb, seeming to pull life from the dirt. I think she finds as much escape in the tidy rows of beans and cabbages as I find singing into a microphone. Even though she's a junior in high school, she seems younger, preferring saddle shoes and cotton dresses or a pair of mamma's old coveralls.

"Bye, Viv," she calls out in English, wiping her hands on a towel by the sink. "Don't forget we have confession tonight."

"Ah, yeah, confession." I nod knowingly. I should be concerned with how easily Aria fibs around papà. We do go to confession at least once a week, but we also use it as an excuse to go into town. Aria usually sneaks into the cinema, and once a month I go to my singing lesson with Carly.

"Basta! In italiano!" Papà shouts. "Niente inglese in casa" is one of his rules, and like any other edict in the Santini house, we can only get away with breaking it for so long.

I quickly shift back into Italian.

"Confession tonight, papà."

"Yes. My good girls."

"You want to come too, papà?" Aria asks innocently, knowing he'll say no. Papà hasn't been to Holy Trinity since Tony's funeral. I've always thought that seeing the tiny box with his infant son lying inside made it impossible for him to go back. But he still wants us to go, insists upon it.

"No, no." He waves away the question like he always does. "But you can take the car this one time for church, Viviana, if you must drive," he says, as though the joy of driving the car were the only reason I'd want to take it out of the garage.

"Thank you, papà." I change the subject to food. "Chicken's in the icebox for dinner and tuna fish for a sandwich at lunch. I left two beers in there too. But no more than that. Remember what the doctor said. You can't take your pain pills with alcohol. So, either drink an hour before or an hour after, okay?"

"You say the same things every morning. I broke my foot, not my ears." He'd sound frustrated to anyone listening if they understood Italian, but I can tell by the softness in my papà's eyes that he appreciates my care.

"Love you, papà," I say, grabbing my light coat from the closet. I get it buttoned up, pin on my felt cloche hat, wriggle on my kid gloves, and sling my purse full of contraband makeup over my shoulder. He grumbles out a goodbye as I rush out the front door.

I can see why Aria's cheeks had such a lovely color to them. The air is brisk but warm when the sun drifts out from behind one of the generously sized, billowy clouds. The sky is a bright blue, the kind of blue that usually makes my stomach churn, but today I don't let the color take my thoughts back to that painful day. It's not that difficult because I have something far more interesting to think about. And that is—Tom Highward.

We danced the rest of the night, last Friday. He didn't leave my side. I rarely dance with the same man for more than two songs in a row, but I enjoyed the light pressure of his hand against my lower back, and each time a song ended, he placed it there again, making clear to the other servicemen I was taken.

I reach the bus stop a full ten minutes early. The cinched belt on my jacket reminds me of Tom's arms around my waist during the last slow number of the night. He hummed along, a deep melodic rumble enticing me to lean in with my whole frame, bits of our bodies grazing each other as we swayed.

After one particularly grandiose turn, he flicked his wrist, bringing me back into his gravitational pull so forcefully that we smacked into each other. He gripped my waist to keep me from falling, and I let him hold me so closely that we moved as one until I regained my senses and remembered the rules.

I'm so lost in my daydream when Mary honks her horn I nearly scream. The two women sitting on the bench and Mr. Thompson, standing on the opposite side of the bus stop reading a newspaper, all look up.

"Mary! Hush!" I reprimand with a gloved finger over my lips. "Sorry!" I address the others. Mary waves me over frantically, and I run around the front of the vehicle to hop into the front seat.

"Get in, already." She's tapping the steering wheel and looking around like we've just completed a heist and the police will soon come after us. Her flawlessly curled hair peeks out from under the folded silk scarf she always wears while driving. Her sunglasses give an added air of glamour and mystery, and the fresh coat of red lipstick makes her skin look like painted porcelain. Civilian employees at Camp Atterbury don't have to wear uniforms, but the dress code requires us to wear modest attire. Mary pushes the rules with her bright lipstick and a flash of color in each outfit.

"I'm in; I'm in," I say as I slide into the front seat and slam the door behind me. She stomps her foot on the gas, and the roar of the engine is drowned out by the rush of the wind through the windows, sending my hair into disarray.

"You're worse than the bus." I roll up the window on my side of the car before digging through my purse for mamma's silver compact and the contraband beauty supplies.

"Oh, hush; you know you can't possibly survive without me," Mary responds hotly, and I can't deny that she's right. Mary was my one link to modern life when I was a girl, and she saw me through all the problems girls usually turn to their mothers for.

Sure, Mary is boy crazy, can stomach hard liquor better than most men, and has been known to slip a thing or two into her pockets at Danner's General Store, but she's my best friend. She's also the reason I have my gig at the USO, my job at the camp, and the only reason I've held on to any dream of ever getting away from Edinburgh, as vague and seemingly impossible as that might be.

"I don't know if either of us will be alive at the end of this trip," I say after being thrown against the armrest as she takes a hard right turn onto Bryan Street.

"All right, all right, I'll slow down. You're beginning to sound like Carl. I swear he's more scared of me behind the wheel than any blitz."

As the car slows to a bearable, far more legal speed, I apply the last few touches of lipstick and then I notice she's watching me more than she's watching the road.

"What is it?" I ask, examining the color coverage in my mirror. I'm wearing pink rather than red because the lighter tint is far easier to remove at the end of the day.

"So . . . what did he say?"

"He?" I say, acting innocent, not sure if the "he" she's referring to is the same "he" I can't stop thinking about. She saw me dancing with Tom on Friday and asked me a few questions on the way home.

"About the roommate thing. What did your father say? If you can't put in a deposit this week, Dorothy says we have to put an ad in the paper."

"Oh, that." I close the compact with a loud click.

"Right after the wedding on Friday, Tammy will be on a train with Doug. It's a great deal, and if you move in, we can drive to work together every day. Plus, you'll be close enough to help out your dad and Aria, but you can actually live your own life, Viv. Get those headshots. Go on real auditions. Go on real dates with real men." She says the last bit with extra emphasis and wiggles her eyebrows. When she told me about the room-mate opening last Friday, I, in a moment of dance-induced delirium, said maybe. But now I realize how foolish the idea was.

"I can't. I'm sorry."

"Vivian!" Mary chastises me, and I can see her glare even through her tinted lenses.

"You know money is tight."

"I know, but I thought the job would help."

"It does," I say, knowing my father would be mortified I'm disclosing our financial difficulties, but if I can trust anyone, I can trust Mary. "But papà can't go back to work for another month at least, and with his medical bills and everything else . . . they need me at home."

"They always need you at home, Vivian. If you're not careful, you're gonna end up an old maid taking care of your dad instead of doing all the things you deserve to do."

"You don't get it. This isn't how it works in my family. I'm not supposed to move out until I get married, and even then, I'll always be expected to take care of my parents. It's just how it is," I say, knowing she's right. I hate to hear my greatest fears said out loud. It makes that version of the future seem too real.

Mary slows as she turns down the gravel drive leading to the main parking lot on the military base's side of the road. It's practically identical to the side of the camp where I work but without barbed wire and watchtowers with armed guards.

"Listen, sweetie. I get it." She puts the car into park and rolls up her window, removing her scarf and sunglasses to reveal a tidy and professional look. "My mamma and daddy didn't want me going away to school or working in an office, and I truly think the only reason they let me do any of it is because they don't have any boys, so it's their civic duty with the war and all, but dang it, Viv—I still did it. And guess what?"

"What?" I ask.

"No one died." She wrestles the rearview mirror toward her and touches up her lipstick again, pressing her lips together with a final smack. "I have Sunday dinner with my parents every week after church, and though my mamma might never forgive me if I don't settle down in the next few years, I swear she's a little jealous. Told me just the other week she's taking driving lessons so she can get her own license."

Hearing about Mary's nosy but normal mother makes that scar inside my soul start to itch. To distract myself, I turn the rearview mirror toward my side of the car and check my lighter shade of lipstick.

"I can't, Mary. I'm sorry. With papà sick and mamma . . . gone . . ." I stop there, unable to say much else. I want to tell her how sick mamma is, that we have to pay for her medicine and her treatments and her room and board and that most of the time when I visit her, she barely remembers my name. But I can't. Even Mary doesn't know that mamma is in an institution. Papà told everyone she went to live with her sister after the "accident" because she couldn't bear to live by the stream where Tony drowned. He taught Aria and me to lie.

"Do you think she'll come home to help take care of your father?" Mary asks, and I hear real sympathy in her voice.

"Uh, no, she's not . . . ready to move home yet." I smooth my hair one more time and check my teeth for any rogue color and try to look casual as I bluff. As far as my friends and neighbors know, mamma comes to visit twice a year, and we go out to see her once a month at least. I confess my lies when I do actually go to confession, but Father Theodore rarely makes me say penance. I try not to take it as an endorsement of my deceit but rather an acknowledgment that in some way God understands.

"You're a good girl, Vivian Santini." Mary tucks a stray hair into my hairnet and rubs in the blush on my cheek. "But you can be good and also be yourself; you know that, right?"

I lean away from her nurturing touch and open the car door. There are so many things I can't explain.

"Well, thanks for the ride." I exit the vehicle quickly, the crunch of the gravel under my heels taking me by surprise. Mary follows, slamming her door and leaning against the car hood as she adjusts the buckle on her shoe.

"You're welcome," she says, dropping the whole roommate discussion, which is a relief. She squints in my direction. "See you after work?"

I'm already walking toward the road crossing, the towers and fences looking more friendly every day that I spend inside their confines.

"I have to work a little late and then voice lessons with Carly. I'll catch the bus," I call back to Mary with a wave and rush across the road without another look back.

Even with its foreboding fences, towers, guns, and barbed wire, I'm not scared of the camp anymore. In some ways, it feels even safer than the offices where Mary works. She tells stories of all sorts of fellas on base talking her up, but on my side of the road, the men are prisoners. Sometimes I find the uniforms and regulations and the overall otherworldliness of the Italian soldiers comforting.

That simplicity is strangely similar to what I feel onstage—I do my job; I do it well, and I don't have to worry about much else until I step out of the spotlight or cross through the locked gates at the end of the day.

CHAPTER 9

Elise

"Uh, will your fiancé be joining us?" Father Patrick asks when Ben claps the slate and steps out of frame. Mac's in his position to the left of the desk, listening closely and watching both camera angles through a monitor.

"Eventually. But Hunter's stuck in New York working on a big deal. So he won't be here until he ties up some loose ends . . ." I swallow, my throat dry and my brain tired from the long day of travel, my eyes aching from the lights.

"Oh, that's right. Mr. Garrot's in finance or banking," Father Patrick confirms. Hunter Garrot is a household name. I'm sure Father Patrick's heard of him, but I also appreciate that he doesn't act like he *knows* him just because he knows *of* him.

"Yes. CFO. He should be here next week," I say, bluffing. I'm not sure if Hunter will visit next week or anytime in the next month. But, image-wise during filming, it's important I make it sound like he's interested in the wedding plans and appears to be a reliable partner.

"I look forward to meeting him officially," he says, rearranging some papers on his desk. "So, we'll start your Pre-Cana classes when I have both of you here, but for now—can you tell me a bit about yourself?"

"What do you need to know?" I ask, body language open, straight back.

He chuckles and crosses his arms on the desk. The dark vestments he wears don't match the warmth of his personality.

"Okay, I'll start, then. How long have you known your fiancé?" He picks up his pen like he's ready to take notes.

"We had our first date last summer."

"Oh, wow." He writes something down. "Pretty recent, then. Love at first sight?" he asks as though he's a hopeless romantic teen referencing a 1990s romcom. His conversational way of speaking puts me at ease.

"No. Not really. Hunter hired my PR firm, and we hit it off in our first meeting." I quickly add, "I switched him to a different supervisor when he asked me on a date, to keep things aboveboard. But it clicked from there."

"When did you get engaged?"

"February. It was very cold . . ." I pause, thinking back to the big performance on Forty-Fifth Street, the confetti in the air, and the crowd cheering. I'm sure Mac will want the footage from the photographer that night. "And romantic. Very romantic."

"I'm sure." He's listening to every detail intently.

He's easy to talk to, and our conversation is natural despite my embarrassment about the inappropriate comments I made in the nave. But it's hard to ignore the black-and-white collar. The girl who used to believe so deeply can't help but wonder if he's silently judging her with each question.

"There were singers and people dancing and confetti—so much confetti," I say, and he chuckles.

"It sounds like a fairy tale."

"Yeah, it kind of was." I try to sound wistful, grateful for the ethereal proposal, rather than diving into my honest feelings about fairy tales.

"A whirlwind romance?" he asks. That's what the tabloids called it: "Elise and Hunter's Whirlwind Romance—A Second Chance at Love." In the entertainment business, there are three topics that steal headlines: engagements, babies, and scandal. It won't be long before I'll have to be careful about what dress I wear to keep pregnancy rumors at bay.

"Yeah, I guess, but . . . this isn't our first time around," I clarify, a touch defensive after being questioned one too many times by friends, colleagues, and reporters about the advanced pace of my relationship with Hunter. "We're old enough to know what we want."

"Oh, I didn't realize that." Glancing at Mac and then me, he inhales, shuffling through the papers again. "One of you was married before?"

"No, no. I was engaged. Not married. Is that a problem?"

"Ah. No. Engaged is not an issue." He closes his folder again after making a note. "There are rules about marriages and divorces or annulments that would make the process more"—he searches for the right word—"more complicated."

"Ah, yeah. I'm Catholic enough to remember your stance on divorce." I narrowly avoid rolling my eyes.

"Ah. But are you Catholic enough to agree with it?"

I open my mouth to make a safe statement about divorce and religious beliefs, but then I think of my grandmother and how much she suffered for her faith.

"I can't say I agree," I answer honestly. I'm about to explain my reasons when Father Ignatius chimes in from the darkness behind the lights.

"It's an important principle in the church, though not popular in the world."

"I know," I say directly to Father Patrick to discourage more interruptions from Father Ignatius. "My mom told me stories from when my grandma, Vivian, was married to director Martin Twilson. He all but ruined her career. Broke her cheekbone one night because she kissed her costar in a scene. She had to back out of the film. And the way he was to my mom . . ." It's not my story to tell, but I've reviewed enough versions of her never-before-seen one-woman show to know about the late-night visits, creaking floorboards, threats if secrets weren't kept. "Anyway, Nonna stayed with that man for far too long because she was taught divorce was a sin."

"That's heartbreaking," Father Patrick says with what seems like empathy. It doesn't make me feel better, strangely.

"It was. It's hard enough for someone to get out of an abusive relationship. But then to have their church guilt them into staying? It's not right. And my mom taught me that no one should stay in a situation that's hurting them."

"Well then, you're more Catholic than you think," he says, a gentle smile emerging slowly. "No one's expected to stay in an abusive marriage. Acting to end abuse doesn't violate the marriage covenant."

I'm almost taken in by his soft response, but I remember sitting in those pews and seeing my sweet grandmother's face fall as we listened to the homilies denouncing divorce.

"I appreciate that sentiment, but you've gotta know that's not how it feels to faithful parishioners."

I expect continued pushback or another canned line that clearly comes from some religious document, but his response surprises me.

"I know."

"You know?" I echo, unsure if I should believe him. The collar and the cross above his desk make me ask one more question. "How? Because running a marriage retreat in Angola doesn't count."

Father Patrick shifts in his seat, checking the positions of the cameras and the crew behind them and possibly Father Ignatius, who has remained mute since his first outburst. Then he looks back at me and exhales.

"Uh, my sister. She . . . she got married when I was a teenager. She was only eighteen but pregnant, so she thought it was, you know, the right thing to do." He swallows and clears his throat. "They had two girls—Ruth and Liza. Her husband, Jim, was an unhappy man; okay—he was a mean man. An abusive man." He pauses again like he's gathering the energy to finish the story. The residual trauma I read in his face makes me wish I hadn't forced him to open up—not just to me or this room full of people, but potentially to a worldwide audience.

"You don't have to tell me. I believe you know." I stop him with an outstretched hand. I've put him in an impossible position.

"Let him finish," Mac mumbles, and even with the cameras focused on me, I roll my eyes, annoyed.

"You're under no obligation to tell me anything, Father. I signed on for this, not you. I'm used to it. The tabloids had a picture of me before my grandmother died. One time, a pap dressed up like a nurse to get pictures of my grandma in the hospital." And then I remember the worst incident. "Goddamn ZMT flew a drone over Dean's funeral."

"Ahem," Father Ignatius clears his throat at my curse, reminding me I'm in a church.

"Sorry. Sorry," I say to the general darkness and then back to Father Patrick. "I think you shouldn't have to do this whole 'share everything' bit unless you really want to."

He takes a microscopic glance at the cameras and then speaks.

"Well, thank you, Miss Branson. That's very thoughtful of you," he says, nodding his head casually, but I can tell he means it.

I'm relieved that he's not going to share the rest of his story. Not because I don't want to hear the end but because it's nice to see someone say no to all this Hollywood shit.

"Call me Elise. Miss Branson is my mother. Er, or Ms. Branson. Madame Branson?" I try to turn it all into a joke, mostly because all this fame stuff *is* a joke but also to take the focus off Father Patrick.

"Back to your question. I haven't been married before. Neither has Hunter." I restate my earlier answer so I can get us back on track with the interview. Later I can ask Mac to exclude that whole abuse conversation. "We're marriage virgins"—I hesitate—"but not actual virgins."

I clarify, in case it's important. "Just our first marriages. Shit. Do we have to be virgins?"

Father Self-Righteous coughs again as I stumble through my answer. No one would guess I'm the head of a multimillion-dollar, internationally acclaimed PR firm. It's been a long day. I need a good meal and a solid night's sleep before getting in front of the camera again.

"Uh, ha. Um, well, I won't write anything in your file, and we'll have a nice long chat about what's required before your wedding day when your fiancé is here."

"Sounds delightful," I say, heavy on the sarcasm.

"It's not as terrible as it sounds. I promise. But while I have you alone. Do you . . ." He lowers his voice and leans forward as though the microphones can't pick up even the shifting of his hair. "Do you mind if I ask you one more personal question? Then we can get into the wedding particulars."

"Maybe?" I say, reserving the right to say no if it turns out to be too personal.

"I thought it might be more appropriate to ask you before your fiancé arrives to avoid any awkwardness."

My eyes widen, but I don't stop him.

"What happened to your first engagement?"

It takes a moment for the question to make sense.

"You don't know?"

"Oh, I'm sorry. Is there a summary here somewhere?" He opens the file folder again.

"No, uh, no. It was a pretty public thing, so I always assume most people have heard . . ."

"I really don't keep up with the Hollywood rumor mill." It's the closest to pompous he's sounded in our back-and-forth, and I snip back sharply.

"Brain cancer isn't exactly hot gossip."

"Brain cancer?" he asks. His brows turn in, and the humor drains from his voice.

"Yeah. Six years ago, my first fiancé, Dean Graham, died from a brain tumor. Two weeks before our wedding," I say frankly, not because I don't care anymore, but because I don't want to be vulnerable in front of this stranger and potentially millions of strangers once the documentary is released.

"Dean," Father Patrick repeats. Hearing his name in a priest's mouth again after all these years gives me chills. "Yes. You said there was a drone flyover at his funeral, right?"

"Yup."

"That's terrible. I'm truly sorry."

I nod, wanting to move on.

"So," Father Patrick finally speaks again, "how does it feel to be planning your marriage to Hunter?"

I answer quickly with a pat line and a stiff smile.

"Great. It's been a long time since my first engagement. I'm ready for a new chapter." I shift in my seat, and after a few more moments, I dart a glance toward Mac, checking in. He seems fine with the turn of topics, which means I'm on my own.

"Sure. I can see that," he replies, raising his eyebrows like he knows I'm hiding my true feelings. He doesn't follow up immediately with another question. Instead, he sits in the stillness like it's a refuge, studying me, perhaps waiting for additional details or a trace of emotion. I brace for a deluge of questions about the worst time in my life when Father Patrick takes out a blank piece of paper and abruptly changes the subject.

"Have you considered wedding dates?"

A weight the size of a boulder lifts from my chest, and I can breathe normally again. He's letting me off the hook like I did for him. We've got each other's backs.

We move on to more basic details of the wedding and my Catholic upbringing but nothing particularly controversial. Autopilot clicks on, and I play the part of bride, daughter of celebrities, and granddaughter of a legend.

As we speak, the sun finishes setting, and the windows go from yellow to orange to black.

"It was nice to meet you, Father," I say, holding out my hand as we close out our conversation, cameras still running.

Despite his formal uniform, it feels strange to call this handsome stranger a paternal name. I liked him before, when I assumed he was part of the crew, when I hoped he could be a friend during this whole fiasco. But his chosen career and what it stands for—though commendable—places a barrier between us and removes the option of close friendship. Because Father Patrick has given himself and his life over to God, and though I can't admit it openly and still get married in his church, I've come to believe that the God we used to share might not exist.

"You, too, Miss Branson." He takes my offered hand casually in a firm but gentle grip. When my fingers slide across his palm, over the desk with neatly stacked documents, gilded pens, and religious relics, I feel something I haven't in a long time. An electric charge powered by an unseen battery. I yank my hand away, wondering if he felt it, too, but he shows no sign of the lightning bolt in his expression or manner as he returns to his seat and rests his hand genially on the desk. My hand burns like it's been scorched.

"I told you to call me Elise," I say, and Mac calls cut.

And as Ben removes my mic, I wonder if there's a loose wire somewhere that generated the electric charge or if it could've been a giant dose of static electricity? Or maybe I just imagined it. I'm not sure. Sitting here in a room filled with crosses and Bibles and priests, it's easy to wonder if God might have something to do with it. But I spent a good part of my life believing in God and never experienced anything like what I felt tonight when I touched Father Patrick's hand.

CHAPTER 10

Vivian

Tuesday, May 18, 1943
Camp Atterbury

I cover my mouth with the back of my hand as I yawn, trying to look professional and poised. Next to me sits Lieutenant Colonel Gammell and his NCO assistant, Command Sergeant Major George Simpson. When Gammell said we'd have a late night, I didn't expect to stay past dinnertime. I called Aria at five o'clock and told her where to find all the ingredients for the meal I'd planned.

I haven't had a moment to consider the consequences of staying late. I can barely keep my mind focused on switching back and forth between Italian and English, which I do over and over again until I can hardly tell the difference between the two languages.

Across the room are five empty chairs for elected officials from each of the five one-thousand-man compounds. Each group has one spokesman to present projects to the lieutenant colonel.

Combined, the five compounds make up the entirety of the prison. I've learned they're all self-managed and run with a military structure that leans heavily on preexisting rank. It's a system of rules and regulations I know little about but find fascinating. I've heard the phrase "Geneva Conventions" more in the past two weeks than in my entire schooling.

As I've become accustomed to my position, I've taken on more responsibilities, but I don't find them a burden. Of course, I have routine duties of filing and typing and answering calls and putting them through to this building or that office. I haven't had any official training as a translator or interpreter, and McNeil, the military translator/interpreter, seems to take offense at my role, though we rarely cross paths. He manages the disputes in the brig, like the fight I witnessed on my first day, and I manage the translation issues in the office with the lieutenant colonel.

Though I'm kept far away from the rough-and-tumble bits of prison life, that incident in the front office keeps replaying in my mind like a reel of film at the Pixy Theater. I keep looking around each room I walk into for Trombello's face. I rarely venture deep enough into the camp to see many prisoners. Civilian staff is welcome in the mess hall, and I've heard some good things about the food, but Judy eats with her husband across the street most days, and I don't have any other friends around here other than Mary, so I usually end up eating a sandwich at my desk when she's not around.

"Thank the Lord, only one more," Lieutenant Colonel Gammell grumbles under his breath as I pass him the file for the fifth and final set of compound representatives. He's not as grouchy as he seemed when I first met him. He's softened more than I'd expected.

"More letters home. Different food rations. Warmer winter wear. More rec time. These men act like this is summer camp and not war," Gammell's NCO, Simpson, blurts out.

I've heard this same sentiment about the US POW camps from my family and neighbors. I don't know where my opinions stand on the matter, but I do know I'm glad to have a job. So I stay busy and mind my own business.

"We follow the rules, Sergeant. That's all we can do," Gammell says dispassionately, still reading the file.

Simpson doesn't take Gammell's hint and continues with his rant.

"They get fatter every day. Have you noticed that? Is that the strategy? We fill their ranks so full of overweight, out-of-shape baby-men that if they were to escape, they'd be out of breath trying to wrestle into their gear before battle."

Gammell doesn't acknowledge Simpson, and I remove myself to the other side of the room where a full pitcher of water sits. I take it to the lieutenant colonel first and fill his glass and then to Sergeant Major Simpson.

"You can't tell me our boys are being treated the same in prison camps overseas. You just can't," Simpson says as he drags the cup across the wooden desk and then takes a long drink. I'm relieved by the silence and hope that'll be the end of the conversation.

But when he slams his glass on the table, gesturing for another refill, I know he's about to go into round two. I stand in front of him in my tweed dress suit, teetering on aching feet wedged into heels that were not meant to be worn for ten-hour days, and his eyes narrow.

"What do you think about all this, huh?"

My mouth goes dry.

"Me?" I ask, my voice timid like it is when I placate papà or comfort mamma during one of my visits. I'm well versed at staying calm in the storm. I think that's the only way I keep from being swept up in the tornado.

"Yeah, you." His voice lowers. He places his elbows on the table, leaning forward. "You heard all the requests and complaints today. What do you think?"

"Oh, well, I . . . I agree with what Lieutenant Colonel Gammell says. The Geneva Conventions are important." I glance at Gammell, hoping he'll jump into the conversation, or blurt out a command or something, but he doesn't look up from the file.

"You're a modern working girl. You've got your own mind. What do *you* think?" There's a smugness to the question. I have no choice but to answer.

"My father's against it. He doesn't think we should shelter people who tried to kill our men."

"I didn't ask what your father thinks," he says in a condescending rebuke.

I try to slow my breathing, collecting my thoughts again.

"I know a lot of the local farmers think the investment is worth the money since most of the prisoners will replace the workers who are drafted and at only a fraction of the cost."

"Are you a farmer?"

"Well, no."

"Then try again, dear."

"Well, I guess I think . . ." I pause, flipping through my opinions like I'm searching through the phone book. "I can see it both ways."

He glares in a way that might seem playful, but there's nothing friendly behind his eyes. I wrestle through the muck of years of doing as I'm told and listening agreeably when a man speaks. I dig into the place inside of me I know is brave and smart and unwavering, like I'm onstage with the spotlight turned my way for a solo.

"I guess I believe in the Golden Rule and that we've gotta follow through on our promises if we expect the other side to." Simpson's eyes narrow, and another opinion rises in me. Instead of pushing it away or swallowing it, I let it float out like there's an audience waiting on the edge of their seats to hear my soliloquy. "And, anyway, don't you think that once these fellas see what America is really like, what they're fighting against, that they might change their perspectives a little? Can't believe a lie when you're staring at the truth."

"Should've known you'd say that," he says as he shoves his glass away like it's poison. "Heard if you eat enough garlic, you can smell it through the pores on your skin. Your pretty perfume can't cover that up forever."

Gammell takes off his glasses, irritation legible in the carved lines of his face and his raised, overgrown eyebrows.

"Sergeant Simpson. That's enough." He slaps the manila folder closed with a crashing thud. I jump. If my heart weren't already in my throat, it'd be there now. "We follow the Geneva Conventions and pray our enemies have the same integrity. And, Miss Santini." He wiggles a finger in my direction. I'm worried he'll reprimand me for speaking out of turn, but I'm grateful to have a reason to turn away from Simpson. "I hear the men in the hall. Please let them in if you would."

"Yes, sir," I say, replacing the pitcher of water on the cart and heading to the door that leads to the hall. I know my cheeks must be flushed. I can't change that, but I can straighten my shoulders, shake my hair back, and blink the tears away while the officers aren't looking.

Through the thin wall, I hear the men approaching and find homey comfort in the rise and fall of male voices speaking a language that, until now, I've only heard in my most intimate circles.

I set my smile as though I'm about to film my close-up and swing the door open. Red-faced, ruddy-haired Talbot stands there. It takes all my effort to hold on to my warm expression. He's the last man I want to be friendly to after witnessing his role in the altercation on my first day. Not to mention enduring his inappropriate comments when I check in at the gate each morning and leering stares when I leave each night.

I can tell he's just as surprised to see me as I am to see him.

"Oh," he says, standing up straighter, and he stutters for a moment like he's missed his big cue.

"Lieutenant Colonel Gammell is ready to see you now." I step back to make room for Talbot as he calls out to the prisoners behind him.

"Line up. Single file," he says in English. It's questionable if the dark-haired men understand him, but they fall into line despite the language barrier.

"Vi ha chiesto di disporvi su una sola fila, per favore," I translate automatically. *He asked you to line up in single file, please.*

"What did you say to them?" he asks as the men shuffle into a line.

"I told them to line up, like you did."

"I didn't tell you to do that."

"I know, but . . ."

"Let's go," he says before I can explain. The men follow without my assistance. Talbot walks past, shooting me a look that leaves me on edge.

I hold the door open as the prisoners enter dressed in their Royal Italian Army uniforms with a PW band around their upper arms. It's unsettling seeing the men dressed in enemy regalia rather than their blue prison uniforms. They smell of musty wool, warm sweat, tobacco smoke, and I swear, the faint remnants of spent gunpowder. They stare straight ahead as though they've been coached on proper behavior. I wonder if they're having rebellious fantasies. Might they be imagining a time where we all are *their* prisoners? When their army occupies our country?

As images of Italian soldiers with guns advancing on our small town run through my head, the last prisoner enters. Unlike the rest of the men, this soldier breaks protocol ever so slightly, letting his gaze stray to meet mine. His dark, warm brown eyes glow with a kindness that doesn't match the warlike pictures I've created in my mind or the heartless enemy soldiers I see on the news film strips at the movies. And then I realize—I know those eyes. It's the prisoner I saw my very first day on the base, the one whose gentle command of the situation spurred me to speak up in his defense. Trombello.

Our connection is brief but mutual. He knows me and I know him, and I can see the questions in his eyes. Who is this woman? Why does she speak Italian?

I have my own questions. How did a man who seems invested in peace come to be a prisoner of war? What part of Italy is he from? Is it close to where my parents were born? Does he have a hidden temper like my father? Does he know what it's like to lose someone close to him? Does he have a family back home worrying about him? And most importantly—why does this stranger seem so familiar to me in some unspeakable way?

The prisoners take their seats, and Talbot stands by the back wall. I return to my small desk. My nerves have me rushing, but I try not to show it as I settle into position. Graceful. Self-assured. The leading lady.

As soon as I pick up my pencil to take notes, Lieutenant Colonel Gammell clears his throat and starts the proceedings.

The lead delegate is named Tessaro. He's a corporal in the Royal Italian Army and speaks with a thick Tuscan accent aspirating his *c*'s heavily. He's a small man with coal-black eyes, and his blazer has four red *v*'s on the left arm. The second man wears a tattered and unkempt uniform, likely not laundered since his feet landed on American soil. His hat tilts to one side, and his lighter complexion and striking blue eyes make him stand out from the other Italian soldiers. His name is Ferragni, and he speaks in broken English that I can tell Lieutenant Colonel Gammell and Sergeant Simpson can barely understand.

"Tell him not to bother," Lieutenant Colonel Gammell says to me quietly.

"Chiedo scusa, signore. Io posso tradurre. Parla liberamente, per favore," I say with a respectful and almost formal attitude. *I'm sorry, sir. I can translate. Speak freely, please.*

Lieutenant Colonel Gammell needs to trust my translations, so I speak to the prisoners with precision. They have more on the line. It's a heavy responsibility that I can't believe rests on my shoulders.

Gammell continues, and I translate seamlessly. Trombello sits silently. His uniform has no fancy bars or pins or badges. He looks to be a lowly foot soldier. I wonder how he ended up elected as a representative, a position usually given to those farther up in rank.

"You men have been elected by your peers and superiors to represent your compound in matters of importance." Gammell reviews their responsibilities as he has with every other group.

Tessaro covers the major business points, adjusts his uniform jacket, checks the sewn-in flags and awards on his breast, and then hands the floor to Ferragni.

"Something must be done about the food," Ferragni says in English, pronouncing each word with particular care, as if he practiced.

"The food?" Lieutenant Colonel Gammell asks. I repeat in Italian.

"Yes. The food is . . . how do I say?" He turns his eyes upward, looking as if he were running through a list in his head.

"You men eat better than our boys in the field," Sergeant Simpson interjects.

"We eat, but there's not . . . uh . . . beauty in it."

"Beauty?" Simpson scoffs, turning to Lieutenant Colonel Gammell. "For God's sake, they're prisoners." Talbot seems to agree, nodding at the outburst. I don't translate.

"Could you be more specific in your objections? What is the problem with your rations?" Lieutenant Colonel Gammell ignores Simpson and speaks directly to Ferragni.

"What is this Jell-O? It moves like a woman but tastes like colors. And the meat is like brick in mouth," he says with disgust, his hands moving as rapidly as his lips.

I hold back a laugh, wishing that Ferragni would let me translate his words directly rather than stumble through in broken English. Although I doubt that anyone who didn't grow up with warm focaccia and fresh basil in a red sauce over homemade al dente pasta would understand.

"What do they expect? Veal parmigiana?" Simpson says, butchering the pronunciation in a low aside only meant for Gammell and perhaps me.

"Parte terza. Capitolo due. Articolo undici," Trombello says, looking right at me.

Lieutenant Colonel Gammell also has his eyes on me, waiting for a translation. And though I don't understand his comment, I translate it exactly.

"Part three. Chapter two. Article eleven."

"What is that supposed to mean?" Simpson asks.

"I'm not sure what you're referring to," Gammell responds.

I translate for Trombello.

He explains directly to me, not to the lieutenant colonel.

"Le Convenzioni di Ginevra. Capitolo due. Articolo undici. Si terrà conto anche della dieta abituale dei detenuti. Ai detenuti saranno inoltre concessi i mezzi per prepararsi da soli gli alimenti aggiuntivi che potrebbero possedere."

And I understand immediately.

"The Geneva Conventions. Chapter Two. Article Eleven. The habitual diet of prisoners will also be taken into account. Prisoners shall also be afforded the means of preparing for themselves such additional articles of food as they may possess," I state plainly, and Lieutenant Colonel Gammell nods without comment. He flips through the pages of the dogeared booklet with the Red Cross symbol on the front, and though he doesn't show it, I can tell he's impressed.

The booklet is our holy document. Here at Camp Atterbury, it's our religious scripture. And Lieutenant Colonel Gammell might as well be a cardinal. He closes the booklet and looks at each man in the eye as he gives his response.

"All right. I'll consider your requests with this article in mind. If you'll give Miss Santini a list of specific changes you'd like to petition, we can reconvene in a week to discuss my assessment."

I translate into Italian without looking up as I write the date so I can make sure it gets into his diary.

"Any further items?" he asks Ferragni.

"Solo uno, signore. Soldato Trombello?"

"Just one, sir," I translate.

Trombello stands in front of his chair, adjusts his cap and his coat, and then settles into a stance with his hands clasped behind his back and his feet spread wide apart. His voice is calm and assured. This time he speaks, not to me, but directly to Lieutenant Colonel Gammell and Sergeant Simpson.

"Nella sezione due, capitolo quattordici, articolo sedici della Convenzione di Ginevra del 1929 si afferma che . . ."

In section two, chapter fourteen, article sixteen of the 1929 Geneva Convention, it is stated that . . .

He's quoting the Geneva Conventions again. Simpson and Talbot stiffen at its repeated mention. I focus on Trombello's impassioned speech, keeping my translation as close as possible to his planned-out narration.

"In section two, chapter fourteen, article sixteen of the 1929 Geneva Convention, it states that 'Prisoners of war shall be permitted complete freedom in the performance of their religious duties, including attendance at the services of their faith.' We've come to propose the construction of a Catholic chapel here, on the grounds of Camp Atterbury."

"A chapel?" Lieutenant Colonel Gammell asks, looking as though Trombello has requested a purple peacock to wander the grounds of the camp.

"Yes," Trombello responds, his dark eyes glistening with intensity. "Canon law requires the eucharistic celebration to be carried out in a sacred place."

"I thought fascists were godless," Simpson interjects with an edge of pious fervor.

Before I can translate Simpson's comment, Trombello says, "Dio non è un politico," with intensity, showing he understands more than the basics of English.

His statement translates to *God is not a politician* or more like *God has no place in politics*. Which isn't the case according to what my father says of Mussolini.

"God is not political," I translate, somewhat loosely, to which Trombello raises his eyebrow. *If he understands what I'm saying, why doesn't he speak for himself?*

Gammell consults the manual again and seems to find it matches Trombello's reference.

"Go ahead," he says, sounding reluctant but resigned. "Tell me what you have in mind."

"Of course." Trombello speaks in Italian, while I translate, his hands moving in front of him as he gets more comfortable in front of the officers. "It will be small. I have plans." Trombello holds up a roll of papers, and Lieutenant Colonel Gammell gestures for Ferragni to bring them to the table. "We can use the leftover construction materials that currently sit out to rot in the back lots. Very little money will be spent. We have craftsmen of all trades who've already pledged their skills. All we will need is access to tools and permission to spend recreation times on the erection of the building."

"Hmm," Lieutenant Colonel Gammell says as he listens to my translation and reads the pages in front of him. "This looks manageable. Twelve feet by seven. Not exactly a Notre Dame, now, eh? You'll have to get the other compounds to sign off."

"I already have signatures, sir," he says in Italian as I continue to translate. Ferragni places the document in front of both officers. I can see from where I'm sitting hundreds upon hundreds of handwritten names. He looks through them, and then Simpson does the same.

"Well, I'll have to review your proposal. But as long as the cost is negligible and the timeline presented is held to, I don't see why not. I'd like to pair you with one of our engineers to check these plans and keep things on the up-and-up." He writes a few notes as I translate his decision. Trombello takes his seat with a smile at the corners of his mouth and a tremble in his hands I hadn't noticed before. "Any further matters?"

There are none, and after a few formalities, the men are dismissed. Talbot stands at the doorway, scrutinizing each prisoner as they walk past as though they could've acquired a weapon during their time in the security checkpoint. As Trombello crosses the threshold, he glances back over his shoulder and meets my curious gaze. There it is again, the bouncing energy that makes me want to sing and hide at the same time. I won't smile at this prisoner. I can't let myself.

"Hold up there. Your plans," Lieutenant Colonel Gammell calls out, holding out the rolled pages Trombello had presented to the panel.

"Hey, Padre. You forgot something," Talbot says roughly, calling him *Father* sarcastically.

As the young Italian soldier crosses the tiled floor, I can see that Trombello's legs are long and muscular, his hands browned by working in the sun. He's a peacemaker but also an able-bodied man who could fight if he needed to. Which makes me even more curious.

"The Lord be with you," he says in accented English to Gammell and Simpson.

Lieutenant Colonel Gammell nods back and grumbles something I can't hear as Trombello exits with his arms full of papers.

"I'll need you to take minutes and act as an interpreter for those meetings, Miss Santini," Gammell says.

"I'm sorry. Which meetings?" I ask, flustered. I was actively taking notes but not paying close enough attention to understand his meaning.

"The chapel construction committee. With the prisoner who presented today. The one who knows the Geneva Conventions as well as his Bible."

"Oh. Yes, sir," I say, matter-of-factly, trying not to reveal the terrible thrill of danger that takes me by surprise.

I'll be working with him—the prisoner with kind eyes. I'll get to know his voice and he mine.

But there can be no more hidden looks, and I can't indulge any level of intimacy.

This isn't like the innocent flirting when I dance with soldiers at the USO or the winks and giggles I give to the men in the audience when I'm performing. This man is a prisoner of war, an Italian prisoner of war. He may seem safe and kind and religious, but I don't know who he is on a battlefield. Besides, even if he's untouched by fascist fanaticism, it's dangerous for a daughter of Italian immigrants to appear to have any special interest in these enemies of America. Especially when many in my country already think I should be numbered among them.

CHAPTER 11

Elise

Present Day
Camp Atterbury

A week into the shoot and I'm already tired of so many things.

The lights have been giving me a headache. And though we've been outside most of the day, I can't seem to kick it.

It's cold but unpredictably so. Some parts of the day feel like spring is about to burst through. Then as soon as a cloud crosses the sun, we're tossed into the depths of winter. So far today, it's warm enough to wear my leather coat and the mustard-yellow scarf Lisa added to insert a splash of color into the not-yet-green landscape of browns and grays. But who knows how long this temperature will last.

I'm also tired of Mac's dual personality, friendly in front of the lens, terse and narcissistic in the rest of his interactions. He wants authenticity on camera but also micromanages every step of the process, which makes authenticity on my part a near impossibility.

This morning, his booming voice echoes through the open fields of Camp Atterbury, disturbing the peaceful surroundings. He told me twenty minutes ago to take a five-minute break so he could address a technical issue. I'm starting to think it's not going to be resolved any-time soon.

I'm seated on a folding chair one hundred yards away from the crew. They're surrounding a small white chapel in the middle of a long, mowed field. This little building is the crowning achievement of the Italian prisoners—the hand-constructed POW chapel—the Chapel of Our Lady in the Meadow. The building doesn't have any doors on the front, just a glass façade protecting the altar and intricately decorated interior. The red-painted steps have crosses embedded in their cement, and a small cross is carved into the side wall. Apparently, my grand-mother walked here when she was an unknown secretary with a dif-ferent last name. She hadn't told me about this part of her life, and for the first time in this endeavor, I'm taking in her story like an outsider.

An adorable elderly woman named Dottie took us through the camp museum earlier this morning. I like to imagine she's always lived here, knew my grandma when she was a young woman, before Nonna's fame and before her stage name removed the Italian roots from her movie-star persona.

But that dream is an impossibility. Dottie didn't move to Nineveh until after the war and didn't start working here until her husband retired. His name is Stan, and he's out working with the maintenance crew in a supervisory capacity.

Dottie sits in the row behind me in her own chair, waiting to finish our tour. She's wrapped up in an ankle-length dusty purple Lands' End jacket that looks so warm, I'm tempted to buy one tonight at the outlet mall. As Mac shouts again and gestures wildly to the gaffer, Dottie sighs and retrieves a tattered paperback novel from one of the giant pockets on the front of her coat. It's been years since I've let myself get lost in a book, and there's something about the swishing of the pages and her unwavering focus that makes me want to sit next to her and peek into the fictional lives she's devouring.

My phone dings, and I look at that instead of the book.

It's Hunter.

We had a call this morning, and I shot him a text with the basics of my new knowledge when I first sat down for the break. A fifteen-minute turnaround is pretty fast for the busy CFO, and his name still brings up butterflies in my midsection when it flashes on my screen.

HUNTER: Hey babe! You still on break?

ME: Yeah. Might be a while. Mac is yelling—a lot.

HUNTER: Ha.

ME: Yeah. He's a blast.

HUNTER: Sounds like you're learning some interesting stuff at least.

ME: Totally. It's kinda surreal.

HUNTER: I'm sure. But nothing too scandalous, right? You said it's a camp? Like—like the racist ones from WWII?

ME: Uh, you mean internment camps? For Japanese citizens?

HUNTER: Yeah. Is it shit like that? 'Cause, I know I'm not the PR specialist but that seems like it could be a nightmare if Vivian Snow worked at one of those.

The comment makes me pause for a moment and not the business side of me, more so the fiancée side of me. Is he worried about the nature of the camp because he wants to protect my family from scandal . . . or because he doesn't want to be wrapped up in a scandal?

ME: From what Dottie said, it was different. POWs. Italians first and then Germans.

HUNTER: Dottie? Prisoners of war?

ME: Dottie's our tour guide. And they were prisoners of war. Mac seems to think it's a great detail, so we're going with it. I didn't know these camps existed.

HUNTER: Me either. Seems risky to bring it up. Maybe do some low-key opinion testing. Can't they just stick with the wedding angle?

There it is—that paranoid warning bell inside my head. I'd be fine getting married in my mother's living room or eloping to Paris—or spending a year or two engaged instead of this mad rush to the altar. But maybe when a philandering father like Hunter's is also a blowhard who is often on the extreme side of most social, environmental, and political issues, the son's image as a "good guy" becomes more important than his image as a successful businessperson. And that's why I'm here, freezing cold in the middle of small-town Indiana and making a film that supports that narrative.

ME: Friendly reminder from your fiancée—none of this was my idea.

I hit send and watch for bouncing bubbles indicating his response, the warning bell growing softer the longer I stare at the screen. Still nothing.

I'm being ridiculous. The distance and solitude are getting to me. Hunter and I spend plenty of time apart because of our careers, but this is different. I'd planned to work on this project with my fiancé, not alone.

I'm just lonely. Hunter is a good guy. Hunter loves me. He wants to be my husband and the father of my children. My warning system is more sensitive than most because of the way I grew up and because my mom falls for users and scammers far too easily.

I stare at my phone, thumb hovering over the pop-up keyboard as I consider the addendum of an emoji, when I hear Conrad calling my name.

"Mac said to take an early lunch, but food won't be here till noon, so you can sit in the car if you want."

"In the car?"

"'Cause it's cold," he says, like an automaton reciting lines.

I glance over at the cluster of dark vehicles parked in the distance. The sun is bright and the air warm enough to keep my extremities from freezing, but I'm not sure how long that'll last without the down jacket I stupidly left behind at the hotel. But I also don't like the idea of sitting in a running motor vehicle for who knows how long.

"Could I wait in the museum?" I address the question to Dottie and Conrad. The POW museum is a five-minute car ride to the main entrance of the camp. The first walk-through of the facility was fascinating but also rushed, highly monitored and controlled by Mac's editorial eye. I could easily spend another hour soaking in all the newspaper articles, photographs, and artifacts from a time when my grandmother's life was on the cusp of so many changes.

"I would, dear, but we close for lunch in fifteen minutes or so." She looks at the delicate watch with a dime-sized pearl face and thin silver band curled around her arthritic wrist. "I'm meeting Stan at the cafeteria for a bite. If you'd like to see more of the camp, I can take you back to the museum afterward."

I ask Conrad for permission with a raised eyebrow.

"I guess I could have Marty pick you up after he grabs the catering. As long as you keep your phone volume up."

I turn my ringer on in an exaggerated movement so he can clearly see it.

"Then it shouldn't be a problem. Take the first car."

"Let's go, Dottie. We're free!" I say, waving to my elderly accomplice as Conrad talks into a walkie-talkie. Moments later, one of the hired cars pulls up. I help Dottie into the front seat and then climb into the back. She guides the driver through the twisty, wooded lane before hitting the main road.

The base was quiet when we arrived at the Chapel in the Meadow this morning, but now it's full of life.

We're waved through an open gate that closes behind us. Following the asphalt road through rows of barracks, I notice fewer uniforms and more people dressed in civilian clothing. Men, women, and children walk together in what seem like family groupings dressed in bright, colorful, flowing garments, heads covered and many faces as well. The children are bright eyed with dark hair. One woman, heavily pregnant, walks slowly with three little curly-haired kids behind her.

"Who are they?" I ask, interrupting Dottie's detailing camp division of labor and payment methods during the POW era of Atterbury.

"Oh yes! You noticed. This has been an exciting time at the camp." Dottie turns around as much as she can, explaining breathlessly, "We've been asked to take in guests from Afghanistan as a part of Operation Allies Welcome. Since September of last year, we've provided a temporary home to over five thousand refugees who come through our base before finding homes and jobs or settling with family here or elsewhere in the world."

I stare out the window at the bustling community of Afghans, its members gathering in small clusters but clearly all headed in a similar direction.

"I didn't know."

"I didn't either, not till lately. I thought some of us Midwesterners never would've opened up, but now so many people are on board. We're having fundraising nights and fabric drives."

As Dottie's smooth narration continues, I try to imagine these families fleeing their homes and the trust they had to put into the hands of an army that lined their streets in a controversial conflict for decades. Now, they are starting over in a whole new country and culture—their bravery brings tears to my eyes. I've seen hard things in my life; I've lost great loves, and I've made frightening decisions, but I've never been brave—not this kind of brave.

I'm lost in my thoughts as the car comes to a stop.

"We're here." Dottie starts to unbuckle, but I rush to get out so she doesn't have to climb down from her elevated seat all by herself.

The building is almost identical to all the others on the base—off-white metal sheeting, green roofing, and steel utility doors with push handles. The Afghan refugees enter through a side door, bundled up against the chill. I wonder what seasons are like in their hometowns.

"The cafeteria has adapted the menu for our visitors. It took a little bit for Stan and me to come around, but I'm starting to like Afghan dishes. And Naghma, our head chef, passed on a few recipes for us to make at home. Care to grab a bite? You won't regret it."

The cafeteria is bustling and filled with the rich, tantalizing aroma of spices of Central Asia. The scents of turmeric, coriander, and cumin fill the air, along with the melodic spikes and dips of conversation in their native languages. It sounds musical, and I wish I could understand their conversations.

Although I wasn't intending to join Dottie and Stan for lunch in the cafeteria, the aromas are so tempting that I decide to sample a few items.

"I'd love to give it a try. Thank you," I say, eager to participate in the hubbub.

Dottie waves to an elderly man who is sitting at one of the long cafeteria tables across the room. He is wearing a workman's uniform and has a full head of white hair. He sees her and grins broadly in a way I can imagine on the face of a much younger man.

"I should warn you—he's a sweetheart but half-deaf, so if I yell, it's for his own good."

I smile. My parents never stayed with someone long enough to whisper about their idiosyncrasies with strangers. I hope to reach that stage in my relationship one day.

"I won't judge," I promise as Stan makes his way to our spot in line. Two small kids in front of us keep looking back at me with curious, playful eyes. The third time I catch their interested glances, I give them a wave with the tips of my fingers. The girl smiles and hides behind her mother's arm, but the boy giggles and boldly waves back.

"Well, hello, beautiful!" Stan says in full volume to his wife when he reaches us, kissing Dottie's cheek and placing his hand on her waist.

"Hello, stranger." She returns his playful cadence, though at a volume I would never have guessed could come from the tiny woman. She leans into his embrace.

"You brought a friend." He gestures in my direction. My nerves flutter. I wait for Dottie to mention Vivian Snow or Gracelyn Branson, one of my brothers' names, or even my father, Clark McFadden. Or, God forbid, Dean.

"Yes, this is Elise. She's on a tour of the base today for a movie."

"A movie? Are you a reporter or a movie star?" he asks with a wink that I can't resist. I never knew my grandfather; he died before my mom was born, but I love to imagine he would've been like this charming octogenarian.

"Nope, nothing as interesting as that. But your wife is going to be famous in no time. She's a natural in front of the camera," I joke.

"Dottie—I thought you gave up your days as a pinup girl when we got married." He looks at her with mock horror. She blushes so brightly that I wonder if there's some truth to his jest.

"Stan." She smacks his arm.

"Don't get me wrong; you're beautiful, but I wouldn't want some handsome heartthrob to steal you away."

"I'd be worried, too, if I were you," I say, playing along with the bit.

We reach a stack of plates and silverware. I follow the kids' lead on the protocol. The little girl goes slowly, like she knows she's teaching me a new skill. The servers fill my tray with rice and sauces, and then I grab some naan and a lightly fried dessert of pastry dough at the end of the line.

The kids sit at one of the cafeteria tables, and I pass them wistfully as I follow Stan and Dottie to their seats. I'd love to talk to the kids and their mom. I'd love to hear what life was like for them before, during, and after their flight from their home. Then again, bringing up those painful memories to satisfy my own curiosity could be cruel.

"You're brave," Dottie says. She has a brown paper bag perched on the edge of her full tray with a small bottle of white milk. "I always take a cold lunch in case things don't settle well."

"This looks amazing." I dig in hungrily. My mouth's full as I watch all the tables populate with staff and refugee families. The seat next to me creaks as someone takes the empty space. I glance over my shoulder, flavors and heat exploding on my taste buds.

"Miss Branson." Father Patrick greets me. He's dressed in a casual-looking but still priestly uniform with dark slacks and a black blazer, holding a tray full of food very similar to mine.

"Whoa," I blurt out through a full mouth of food and then swallow quickly. "What are you doing here?"

"Thanks for the warm welcome," he says, laughing at my shock.

"Father—they have *Gosh-e fil* today. It looks delectable," Dottie says.

"Which dish is that?" I ask, scanning the selection.

"These." He points to the sugary fried dough on my tray.

Dottie speaks louder this time. "They taste like elephant ears from the fair from when I was a girl."

"Careful, Dot. The kids are gonna think we ate actual elephants." Stan winks, and I wonder if they could possibly adopt me.

"Does someone write your lines? Are you wearing earpieces linked to a comedian somewhere? You guys are too hilarious."

"Hey, don't encourage them," Father Patrick interjects.

"I can't help it. They're too darn charming."

"No argument here," Stan says, his hands up, grains of rice hanging off the tines of his fork.

"And bonus—Dottie knows everything about the history of this place. Which I'm finding completely fascinating." I take another bite as Dottie brushes off my compliment.

Father Patrick dusts the rice off the table into a napkin.

"Before Operation Allies Welcome, I knew there was a base here, and we celebrate a mass at the POW chapel every fall but nothing else."

Dottie's whole body bounces on the bench. "Yes, Father is a history buff. We've become good friends."

She winks at the priest.

"You're gonna make Stan jealous," Father Patrick says in a very loud mock whisper.

"Too late," Stan says with a grin, standing up slowly from his bench seat. "On that note, I need to steal this lady for a few minutes if you two don't mind. Father, could you keep an eye on the young one till my wife gets back?"

"Of course," Father Patrick agrees.

Dottie taps my arm to get my attention.

"If they call you back to the set, you can leave. I'll have Stan drive me back in his cart."

"Sure thing."

"Thanks, dear," she says sweetly as though I'm one of her grand-daughters. As they walk off together, Stan takes his wife's tray, returns it, and then claims her hand for himself.

"Are they really like that?" I ask, enthralled.

"Like what?" Father Patrick asks, not as interested in their timeless love story as I am.

"In love. Are they really that in love?"

He shrugs, also watching them leave, and turns back to me. "I have no reason to doubt it. Do you?"

"Nah, not really. I just . . . I guess I haven't seen any relationship close-up without noticing all the flaws."

"Well, there are always going to be flaws. No marriage is perfect, just like no painting is without its brushstrokes if you get close enough."

"Okay . . . ," I say, not sure I understand what he means.

"I see it this way. I remember going to the Louvre and seeing *The Raft of the Medusa* by Théodore Géricault, something I'd always believed was a perfect masterpiece. But up close, only a few feet away from the canvas, if I put my toes right up against the line on the floor that kept the public from touching it, I could see the final brushstrokes on the surface of the painting, which I'd never seen from far away, or in a book, or through a screen. But you know what those strokes helped me understand?"

"Maybe?" I think I know where he's going with the analogy, but I want to hear him say it. The way he talks is so steady, and the way he thinks, so much more reflective than what I'm used to.

"That Géricault was a man, just like me. His hand wasn't a gilded creation free of the constraints of human frailty. His brush wasn't a magical instrument endowed with mythical powers. Everything I do as a man is covered in textures, and seeing that in Géricault's work reminded me it's okay to be imperfect."

"So, a 'we're all flawed, so God needs to fix us' kind of a thing?" I push back, catching on to his undercover sermon in the nick of time.

Father Patrick tilts his head and assesses me for a moment, which I'm learning is a habit of his. I stare back at him without flinching.

"Not everything I think about has to do with God." He returns my unbroken stare.

"So that wasn't a replay of one of your sermons?" I raise my eyebrow in a blatant challenge.

"Not a replay. But . . ."

"But . . . ? Remember, you can't lie." I take a bite of my cold food, knowing I've found a chink in his armor.

"It's an idea I've been playing around with for a long time." He's not looking at me now. He's focused on a spot in the air above my head, or something behind me.

"How long?" I ask, and take another bite.

"A while, I guess."

"No lying . . . ," I remind him, pointing at him with my fork.

"That's not how it works," he says, laughing.

"I guess you've never heard of the Ten Commandments." I shovel another bite into my mouth, knowing I'm being ridiculous. But he's playing along. And I like that.

"Nope. Never." He's back from whatever far-off place I'd lost him to momentarily. "I went to the Louvre my senior year of college."

"Before all this, then?" I gesture at his collar.

"Yes, before I was ordained."

"Hmm." It's my turn to evaluate him. "So, a million years ago, then?"

"It's been a while, but the moment stuck with me."

"Did you finish? Your degree?"

"I did, actually." He nods without providing any further information.

"What did you major in?" I pop one of the fried pieces of dough into my mouth and crunch through the crispy edge, crumpling with pleasure when its airy sweetness hits me.

"I have a master's in divinity."

"And—" I don't let him off the hook, tossing another treat into my mouth.

"Fine. My BA was art history, and I had a minor in secondary education."

"You went from art to religion? That's an unexpected jump."

"It was *very* unexpected."

"Oh yeah? Not part of your five-year plan after your undergrad?"

He shakes his head and looks into the space beyond again.

"No. Not at all. Things changed pretty soon after that trip." I don't know why, but I'm relieved when he looks at me again.

"And that made you change your trajectory?" I match his generalities.

"It did."

"Must've been monumental."

"Completely." I can see the emotional fences around him. I want to break through. His title and his vestments must work well to keep the world out, but I'm longing to sound a trumpet and make his walls come crashing down.

"There are no cameras here, Father. No silent partners or mics or lights." I fold my arms on the table and close the space between us so no one else can hear our conversation. His breath brushes against my cheek, and my elbow grazes his as he matches my position. The walls wobble ever so slightly.

"It's hard for me to talk about—it's easier to . . ." He cuts his sentence off like he's struggling against invisible restraints.

"Talk about everyone else's problems?"

"I was going to say, 'get lost in service,' but yes, when it comes down to it, I'd rather focus outward."

"But . . . honest question." I touch his sleeve. "How do you ever learn how to help others resolve their trauma if you're still caught up in your own?"

He's going to say God, I think, knowing how easy it is to look to a supernatural power to self-medicate the pain.

"Well . . ." I hang on the edge of his silence, ready for the story to pour out, when a tap on my shoulder sucks me back to reality.

It's Conrad, live and in person. Swear words flash through my mind, but I smile instead of saying them, though I wouldn't be surprised if it looks more like I'm gritting my teeth.

"There you are. Food's ready on set." He gives a side glance to my empty tray but doesn't call me out. "And Mac is ready, so I need to get you back in hair and makeup."

"Thanks. I'll be out in a few minutes," I say, hoping he'll wait for me in the car. He checks his watch and doesn't move.

"It's a little more urgent than that," he replies, pushing.

I catch Dottie out of the corner of my eye. She's leaving with another assistant, and I understand I won't be finishing this conversation with Father Patrick today. I pat his forearm in closing.

"To be continued?" I ask, arranging my used utensils and garbage on the tray.

"Absolutely," he says, and then, "Let me get that for you."

I waver, not wanting to look entitled or like I'm treating him as a servant. But that's my work mind talking. Hunter is right—I don't know how to let go and enjoy a moment.

"Well, thank you." I offer the tray up, and he takes it from my hands.

"Yeah, thanks," Conrad says from behind me, and his kindness, in contrast to Father Patrick's, sounds forced and formal.

"No problem," Father Patrick says as he walks toward the gray bins.

I don't wait for him to return, mostly because I think Conrad might murder me if I don't get out the door. As we walk to the car, he fills me in on the complications with the cameras and his personal frustrations as an assistant. I listen patiently and climb into the back seat, Dottie already loaded in the front. She turns around and shows me her dentures in a sweet smile. We're friends now, and that makes me feel a little less lonely.

"It's such a shame," she says with a little sigh.

"Yes! I want to know so much more about this part of the camp. If there's a gap in our filming schedule, could I volunteer?"

"Oh, I'm sure we could make that work. We always need volunteers, but that's not what I was talking about."

"Oh, no?" I drop my phone into my lap as we pull up to the Chapel in the Meadow. Conrad starts unloading the bags of food from the back hatch. I meet Dottie at her side of the car. She takes my hand as she descends from the elevated front seat.

"I was talking about Father Patrick," she says once she's found her equilibrium. "Isn't it a shame he's unavailable? You two sure seem to have hit it off."

I don't know what to say, but with the blush spreading across my cheeks, it must be easy for Dottie to see how I feel.

"I think you're reading far too many romance novels. Besides, he's a priest and I'm engaged." I wiggle the finger holding my grandmother's ring.

She waves her gloved hands like she's washing away the statement.

"I'm sure my imagination is running away with me because of the stories, you know, about your grandma and that priest." She says it like this is a well-known fact. If I'd been drinking water, I'd have given a spit take.

"I'm sorry, what?" She starts walking toward the chairs we'd abandoned close to an hour ago. I rush after her.

"Your grandma and the priest who helped build this chapel." She points at the handmade structure. "The rumors about their love affair used to be whispered all around the camp. You never heard?"

"No!" I insist defensively. "She'd *never* even think about doing something like that. She was far too faithful . . ."

"Sorry, dear. I'm sure it was just silly gossip," Dottie says, seeing my reaction. I probably freaked her out with my explosive response.

"It's okay. Gossip is a part of the job," I say without digging further. A gust of chilled wind hits us, sending a shiver up the back of my arms and neck. Dottie tugs her zipper up to her chin.

We both let the topic go.

I've heard so many salacious and totally untrue tabloid stories over the years. How Vivian Snow was engaged to Ronald Reagan until Nancy put a hit out on her. Or that Vivian Snow was bald, and she kept young children on her payroll to grow hair for her wigs. Or that she'd been abducted by aliens and secretly replaced by a reptilian creature who wore her skin suit.

A priestly love story from her prefame years has never been one of them. I should dismiss it as quickly as I do the other rumors, but Dottie's little aside sticks with me.

I pick at my salad, my stomach already full. I don't know if I linger on the idea because I'm in Nonna's hometown, learning about the chapter of her life I know the least about.

Or is it because of a fleeting but very real moment I'm trying to ignore. One that Dottie, an eighty-year-old stranger, picked up on. That moment at the cafeteria table when I temporarily forgot about the ring on my finger, and the enigmatic Father Patrick became a captivatingly insightful man with a smile who made me want to talk for hours—instead of a man of God.

CHAPTER 12

Vivian

Tuesday June 1, 1943
Camp Atterbury

"We'll start clearing the meadow next week and then break ground as soon as it's dedicated. The foundation can be poured and set by the end of the month." I take notes in English shorthand as a group of prisoners talk in Italian around a table that's draped with structural drawings on butcher paper.

The six Italian prisoners and I are the only inhabitants in the small boardroom other than a guard standing in the corner. This is our first official committee meeting.

I attended two weeks of preplanning with Trombello and Ferragni where they handpicked the rest of the men at the table and worked through preliminary details for the chapel. I took notes and translated communiqués between the main office and the Italian representatives.

It meant extra pay, which we desperately need, but it also meant increased familiarity with the prisoners. Which isn't an issue when it comes to gruff, middle-aged Ferragni, but Trombello—he's different. There's an inexplicable and intense curiosity that spikes inside me whenever we cross paths. I can't indulge it. So, I've made a concerted effort to keep my distance from Antonio Trombello because I can't risk doing *anything* that would put my job in jeopardy.

Papà's leg has become infected, and without my income, we'd sink further into debt. I paid mamma's hospital bill last month before paying anything else, knowing she was on the verge of expulsion. But it gobbled up my whole paycheck, and if I lose my job here, it won't be long before we're not only worrying about where mamma lives but where we'll live too.

The gig at the USO brings in very little. I heard about an open call in Chicago for the Midwest Talent Agency, and I know, I know if I could get in there, I could start making more money. But I need a headshot for the open call, and those cost money. And I'd need more money for bus fare to the city. Let alone finding a way to get there without papà knowing.

Tom thinks I could be a model; he tells me all the time when we dance at the USO. Every time I see him, he begs me for a date. He's figured out my work schedule, and most days he walks me to and from the bus stop outside Atterbury or Mary's car on the days my schedule aligns with hers.

I don't know how he finagles the free time, but he's in the Eighty-Third Infantry Division, which is signified by the yellow-and-black symbol on his sleeve. They're called the Thunderbolts, and according to Tom, they're a step above the average soldier in basic training. He's hoping to move on to Ranger training by the end of the summer, and I like to cheer him on toward his dreams like he does for me.

Carly is wary of Tom but understanding since he'll be moving on sooner rather than later. Mrs. Portia, a gray-haired former schoolmistress and the only paid member of staff at the USO, has already put me on warning with Tom—I'll have my card pulled if it looks like I'm encouraging his advances. But it's not easy to dodge his determined advances. Not to mention that he's handsome, charming, and has a brilliant smile.

"Signorina Santini." Hearing Trombello say my name in his sweet, steady baritone brings me back to the present moment.

"Yes?" I respond in Italian, finding it easier than forcing the prisoners to stumble through their limited English vocabulary.

"Is that possible? The timeline?"

I glance at the notes I've taken and shrug.

"Lieutenant Colonel Gammell will have to look it over and give his approval."

"Sure. Sure. But what do you think? Possible?"

"Oh," I say with a slight gasp. "You want my opinion? But . . . I don't know much about building things."

Having an opinion often means running up against someone with the opposite ideals, which is why I usually keep my thoughts to myself. Trombello beckons me to the table, not accepting my nonanswer. I glance at the guard, Mike Craig, one of Tom's buddies. He stares off into space, apparently lost in his own daydreams.

"Would you like to see?" Trombello asks. I do want to see the plans. I'm intrigued.

I slide out from behind the small desk in the corner and put down the notepad and pencil. I smooth my skirt and walk across the room. I expect Trombello to watch, as most men do, especially soldiers, but he doesn't. He turns to the rough sketches at the table and the rudimentary architectural plans drawn out in pencil on oversized pieces of butcher paper.

"It's not very big, but God can fit into even the smallest places; don't you think?" he asks as I take in the pencil outline of a small, rectangular box, topped with a modest cross. When I first heard Trombello propose the construction of a "chapel," I'd imagined a fairly substantial structure—not one of the grand churches in Indianapolis, but a moderately sized, solidly built, and attractively appointed house of worship that would welcome the faithful. But this is a small building, open to the elements, with no pews or stairs and barely big enough for two or three men to stand side by side.

"I believe God can be in all of us if we welcome him," I say, quoting Father Theodore.

"Yes, exactly," Trombello says, like we understand one another perfectly.

He introduces me to the new committee members. The names are familiar, and I remember bits of information about each man.

First, Simon Gondi. He's a short but strong-looking man who comes from a long line of masons in Florence. "My ancestors built the Cathedral of Santa Maria del Fiore, and we've never turned away from a challenge. This will be like playing with sticks and stones," he says, full of a bravado I've grown used to in Italian men.

Next, I meet Cresci, so tall and thin that I worry for his health. He's from Spello, Umbria, and did road work before being conscripted. When he speaks, I see he has more teeth missing than intact.

Gravano, from Savona, wears thick glasses and likes to wink at me when no one is looking. Trombello explains this winking soldier studied architecture before the war. He bows and says in broken English, "Beautiful girl. To meet you is to be delight."

"Thank you."

The fourth man sits quietly with his hands folded in his lap. He's the youngest of the crew and seems unused to the rough culture of the military and masculine competition. My little brother, Tony, might look much like him if he'd lived to be a man.

"This is Libero Puccini. He's a master craftsman with the chisel and hammer. There's a grand rock by the front gates of the camp that he's been tasked with carving, and he'll be doing a similar carving for outside our Chapel in the Meadow in time for its dedication."

"Nice to meet you all," I say, tipping my head in a semibow.

"So, you're Italian, I assume," Cresci asks, his voice whistling through the holes of his missing teeth when he speaks.

"Yes, well, my parents are. They're from Salerno. I was born in America, though."

"Your blood is Italian. You just live in America," Cresci states with a finality that reminds me of my father's declarations. "If they'd stayed only twenty years more in Salerno, your father and brothers would be sitting here with us."

"I . . . I don't know about that . . ."

"Don't let Cresci disturb you, Miss Santini. We're only glad to speak with a beautiful woman who reminds us of home; am I right?" Gravano interrupts, speaking to Trombello.

"Don't ask *him*." Gondi tags into the conversation. "I'll spare you and say yes for all of us." Then he turns to me with a paternal tone in his voice. "You seem like a good girl. I'm sure you make your papà proud."

"Yes. Thank you." I don't explain that my father would be furious if he knew I work with Italian POWs. I'm not exactly a "good girl" unless good girls lie to their fathers.

A whistle sounds outside, and Puccini, who sat silently for the whole meeting, jumps up. Cresci drops his feet from their perch on the table's edge with a thump. I've been around long enough to know this means it's dinnertime in the camp. Most nights I've left before the whistle blows, but I can smell the culinary creations each day as I walk through the gates. Although the food smells irresistible, for lunch I usually eat at my desk or occasionally walk across the street to the base mess hall and eat the plain ham sandwiches and multicolored Jell-O on the days Mary and I are on the same schedule, abandoning the tempting call of garlic, fresh baked bread, and simmering tomatoes.

"È ora di cena!" Cresci shouts out, announcing dinner as though he's declaring the end of the entire war. The men at the table collect their plans and belongings and make their way to the door without another moment of discussion. Each man says a formal farewell,

Gravano winking as he says his goodbye. Everyone's lined up by the door within a minute, all except Trombello. He's from Salerno and the only one in the group with true manners.

"Thank you for your assistance, Signorina Santini," Trombello says in his accented English, his first attempt of the evening.

"You're welcome, Signor Trombello," I respond, copying his formal address. I fall back into Italian. "I'm glad to help, but I don't know that I've done much."

"You have and you will. Without your language skills, we might not be as far along as we are."

"I know nothing about building a chapel. I only know about going inside one." I blush. He's giving me far too much credit. I'm not taking down their meeting notes out of the goodness of my heart, but because I've been ordered to by my boss. Ultimately, I'm a bit of a spy.

"Well, that's a blessing too." The men keep looking back at Trombello with impatience.

"Hurry. All the bread will be gone," Ferragni calls out.

"Trombello, line it up or you'll all go hungry," Mike, the guard, says sternly. Trombello gives a slight bow.

"I must go or there'll be a mutiny."

"I understand. It smells delectable."

"It's lasagna tonight. And a Monday, so that means Vigo has been baking bread all day."

My stomach grumbles and knees tremble at the idea of a home-cooked meal I didn't have to make myself.

"I haven't had a real lasagna since my mamma . . ." I stop. How can I finish that sentence without sharing more than I'm willing to? I refocus my comments. "I'll bring your plans to Lieutenant Colonel Gammell. You should have a response soon."

Loudly enough for the other men to hear, he says, "Join us! Plenty of the officers come to the mess hall or get bread or pastries from the bakery door. A few ladies too."

"Yes, yes. Come, signorina," the men chant in Italian.

"Come," Trombello says, this time in English.

"Come with us or stay here. Doesn't matter to me, but we have to go," Mike says.

"Really? You think it's okay?" I ask Mike. He shrugs.

"Can't say for sure, but Lieutenant Colonel Gammell is in there all the time. I sneak in sometimes. It's better than anything on base or even in town."

It's a tempting offer, and my stomach growls at the hope of warm ciabatta. I already told papà I'd be working late tonight, and as long as I make it to the seven-thirty bus, I'll be home around the same time I've been slinking in on nights I'm required to sit in on these meetings. It's one more lie, but a small one, wrapped up inside the original lie. So, does it even count?

"I need to take some things by the front office. Can I have a quick moment?"

"Sure. If you can move fast."

"Lickety-split. I swear."

Mike grunts and adds, "Fine. Meet us in front."

"Thank you!" As the prisoners file out, I collect my papers and the plans and walk swiftly back to the office. Judy has already packed up for the night. I drop the load from my arms onto my desk in a neat pile, unlock the bottom drawer where I keep my purse, put on a quick coat of lipstick and powder, and then sling the bag back over my shoulder.

It's already well past my normal quitting time, so I punch out my timecard and then rush out the front door into the warm evening air.

The men wait on the lawn, six Italians wearing POW uniforms and one uniformed US soldier with a gun in his holster and a frown on his face. I fall to the back of the line, and we follow Mike like ducklings waddling behind their mother.

"Your mother, she's passed?" Trombello asks me in English as we walk. I'm surprised by his question, forgetting that Italians are more direct.

"Uh, no. No. But she doesn't live with us anymore. She grew very ill after my brother died and has never . . . uh . . . recovered."

"She's *in ospedale*? Um . . . in the hospital?"

I nod, finding it simpler to let him create whatever picture he's developing in his mind than divulge the truth.

"And your *padre*? He's close?"

My father is a little easier to talk about, especially around these young men who remind me so much of him. We follow the gravel path toward the homey scent of dinner, and Trombello falls back to walk beside me.

"Yes. I live with my father and sister in town. He works at the plastics factory but was injured after Christmas and hasn't been able to return to work."

"So, you are the mother and the father, eh? You work here and take care of your family?" His accent is heavy but easy to understand. It'd be easier to speak in Italian, but I like the privacy English provides us from the rest of the crew.

"I do my best," I respond, blushing again from his praise. Unlike most men, his words seem sincere and not meant to soften me up or seduce me. He's never looked me up and down or complimented my eyes or lips or hair. He is looking at *me*—who I am as a person, and that's refreshing—and rare.

"And your life—what do you want for it?" he asks as we join the line that must lead to the food. Gondi and Cresci are complaining about being late. The guard drops the line at the back of the queue and then walks to where I stand with Trombello.

"You don't have to wait. You can go to the front," he says, his voice as sleepy as his eyes.

"Thanks, Mike!" I wave as he walks away but stay in place next to Trombello.

"You want to stay with us criminals?" Trombello asks.

"As long as you promise to reform your ways," I joke back.

"On God," he says, touching the points of the cross and looking up to the sky.

"You promise . . . uh . . . Trombello." I use his last name since I'm not sure how to refer to these men. Do I use their rank or formal address?

"Antonio," he corrects. "And I promise."

"Ah, redemption," I say with some grandiosity, and our voices mingle in laughter that is the same in any language. A few heads turn and take note of our interaction. "Antonio."

I say his name a little quieter, remembering my vow not to get too familiar with the committee members—just in case.

"So, your life. After war. After your padre is healed. You do this?" He points to the green-roofed bunkers that surround us.

"Stay in the military?" I ask, making sure I'm reading his gestures right.

He nods.

"No, no, not at all." I wave my hands, canceling out the very idea that I might do this forever. "But if I could do anything?"

"Yes. Anything."

"Acting," I say sheepishly. "Singing, maybe."

"Hollywood!" he bursts out like he's found the answer to a million questions in that moment. I pat the air and lower my voice.

"Shhhh. Yes . . . yes . . . that's the dream, you know? But for now—Chicago?"

He steps back and looks at me with wise eyes, his hand cupping his chin.

"No. Hollywood. That's where you go. I see now." My face flushes, and I know it's not from the balmy air blowing in from the south or the scented heat pouring out of the kitchen.

"Well, thank you." I give him a tiny but overly proper curtsy, my cheeks aching from smiling. Halfway through my bob, there's a tap on my shoulder and the rumble of a familiar voice. Surprised, I stumble a bit, but a strong hand around my waist keeps me from falling.

"Tom!" I know his touch. His hand at my waist has become familiar from dancing at the USO, and his voice follows me home at night in my memories.

"Hey, doll." He stands close to a foot taller than me and shoots down a brilliant smile from his lofty perch, leaving his hand on my waist.

"What are you doing here?" I ask, stepping back until his hand slips away. I notice something stiff and off about him. He's not even looking at me; he's staring at Trombello.

"I waited for ya by the bus stop. Thought you might be working late when Private Craig told me he left you over here waiting for dinner."

"Oh, I'm sorry! We had the chapel committee meeting today, so I'm taking the later bus, and Signor Trombello invited me to try the lasagna. Mike said it was no big deal, so I thought I'd give it a go . . ."

"Private Craig shouldn't have left you here alone." Tom stresses Mike's full, official name, and I realize I've fallen into using his name casually.

"Oh, I'm fine. This is the chapel committee right here, and this is Antonio Trombello. He's from my parents' hometown in Salerno." I pronounce the Italian names and town with an accent that sounds out of place sandwiched between my midwestern vocabulary. "You should see the plans they've drawn up—it's amazing. And Signor Puccini, he's the one carving that big rock out on the east side of the base."

I make proper introductions.

"This is my friend Corporal Tom Highward. Oh, sorry. Il mio amico Corporal Tom Highward."

Tom barely takes note of the introductions.

"You wanna eat here?" he asks. I can see his angle now. This is kind of a work around to the "no dates" caveat at the USO, and he knows it. "You know—as *friends*." The word sounds like sticky poison in his mouth, and my heart rate climbs as I sense tension in the normally charming guy.

"Um, sure. Sure. That's fine," I say slowly, processing through the possible fallout. It's not a date. It's not against the rules of my position here at the base either, as far as I know. Judy eats with her husband almost every day.

"Ci vediamo la prossima settimana," I say, telling the committee members I'll see them soon. Then I turn to Trombello. "If I hear anything sooner about the schedule, I'll make sure you know."

"Grazie, signorina. See you next week . . . if Hollywood doesn't take you first," Trombello says with a tip of his head, hands behind his back looking very official in my opinion.

"Hollywood doesn't even know I exist yet," I say timidly.

Then as we start to move past the waiting prisoners to the front of the line, Trombello acknowledges Tom with a quick, "Ufficiale."

"What's that supposed to mean?" Tom asks, lunging forward. I grab his tensed bicep and pull backward with no effect.

"Officer. He just called you an officer, that's all."

Trombello doesn't respond to Tom's aggressive move. He remains firmly in place, and I can imagine him as a soldier. His chest rises and falls rapidly, his pulse pounding at his jugular at double speed.

"Tutto bene, Padre?" *Are you all right, Father?* Ferragni asks in a low mumble.

"Padre? You think I don't know what that means?" Tom says, his body a brick wall, heaving like it's undergoing an earthquake.

"Father. It just means father," I explain, pulling back on Tom so hard that I'm certain I'll leave a mark on his arm.

"I'm not stupid, Viv. I know what it means. But do *you* know what it means? That's what I'm wondering 'cause I've been hearing some things about this guy. I think this one could use a reminder." He points a finger into Trombello's firm, broad chest.

"It's a joke," I say, thinking back to when I heard Talbot first use the phrase right after Trombello's proposal to Gammell. "Because he's in charge of the chapel committee. Right, Signor Trombello?" I ask, hating the trill in my voice I get when I'm nervous or frightened.

"You wanna tell her or should I, Padre?" Tom asks, his aggression swelling and exploding with a fingertip shove into Trombello's chest. "Or should I say—Father Antonio?"

"Father Antonio?" I ask, cocking my head, my eyes connecting directly with Trombello's.

He nods with a seeming internal peace I wish I had. And at once I understand a lot of things.

"You're a priest," I gasp.

Trombello bobs his head again, his eyes locked with mine.

"Lo sono." *I am.*

"I didn't know priests could join the army," I say, feeling stupid for not understanding his role in his community sooner.

"Padre, tocca a noi," Ferragni says, beckoning the priest to move away from the conflict with a tug on his sleeve.

The committee members have gathered around, and I can see why—Trombello's not only their friend and compound leader; he's also their religious guide.

"We should get inside," Tom says, backing away from the clogged line and the crowd forming around us. He yanks at his uniform, straightening and smoothing the fabric until all that remains wrinkled is his forehead.

He offers his arm and I take it, waving goodbye to the committee members.

"Buon appetito, Padre," I say to Trombello as we head up the steps toward the dining hall, trying out his official title and wondering at how curious it feels in my mouth.

"Buon appetito, figlia mia," Trombello says to my back, his words meaning *Enjoy your meal, my child.* It's a paternalistic greeting I've heard from the priest at Holy Trinity every Sunday since I was christened. It makes me feel more like a confused child than I have in a long, long, long time.

CHAPTER 13

Elise

Present Day
Rest Haven Cemetery

I haven't been to a cemetery since visiting Dean's headstone at Westwood Village Memorial Park when I was in LA. It's hard to avoid the memories as we walk through the grounds of Edinburgh's Rest Haven Cemetery, where my grandmother and grandfather are buried. It's nothing like sunny Westwood with its grand mausoleums and graves of celebrities with benches and meticulously maintained gardens surrounding them. But here, seeing the headstones—two dates carved into them and only a dash between to represent the life that person once lived—reminds me of how short it all is, how fragile.

My sadness will translate well on camera since it's perfectly okay to fight back tears about my grandparents. No one needs to know that some of those tears are for my long-dead fiancé.

The map I hold has a highlighted line that should lead us to my grandparents' headstones. The cemetery sexton, a short, balding man wearing a white collared shirt under a khaki windbreaker, leads the way through the tidy but dreary paths. The temperature has dropped after a few days of warmth, and everyone makes jokes about Mother Nature's mood swings. Conrad even approved a winter coat for the shoot today, but not the purple one I came with. He purchased a more flattering jacket from the local outlet mall last night and styled it with a bright green scarf that Lisa says goes perfectly with my eyes and skin tone. Right now, I'm glad the cashmere adds an additional layer of warmth.

"Almost there," the sexton, Mr. Christianson, says as we enter a part of the cemetery where the headstones have a worn look, their carved markings dulled from years of standing as sentinels above the long departed six feet under the ground.

We approach a simple pair of headstones: one with my grand-father's name and the dates of his birth and death and one that's a brighter gray granite, clearly more modern, with my grandmother's married name and the dates of her birth and death.

"Here they are. Our town's little secret—Mr. and Mrs. Vivian Snow. Well, a secret till now at least." He gestures to Mac and the camera crew following our trek through the graveyard.

"Yeah, Nonna wanted to be buried here with Grandpa and her parents, but she knew it'd be a hassle, so she had half her ashes buried in Hollywood and the other half here. We had the big funeral as a family, but my mom was the only one present for this one."

Actually, it was my mom and her boyfriend, but I don't add that. I'd like to think it's to spare Mac's feelings, but really it's to protect my mother from looking like the mess she is.

"We worked under total confidentiality. I didn't even tell my wife," the sexton says, like the covert operation had the importance of a state secret.

"I can't tell you how much that was appreciated," I answer, playing the PR game perfectly, though at the time, I was so wrapped up in my grief over losing Dean that I had little room for the intricacies of the double burial. I still hold some guilt for that to this day.

"Of course." He turns to the cameras and speaks to them directly, breaking the fourth wall, which must make Mac cringe. "I've never shown anyone this grave. Though Miss Snow's husband's headstone has been here since before my time and has received a visitor or two."

He points at the stone with the name **TOM HIGHWARD** carved in it. Born June 9, 1921, and died December 23, 1944. I take a second glance at the dates.

"Are you sure this is the right spot?" I look at the map again and spin around, checking the surrounding headstones.

"Yes, no doubt at all. I maintain Miss Snow's plot myself."

Mac steps forward, concern obvious in his furrowed brow. "Is there a problem?"

I look back at the headstones and consider saying nothing, but it's hard not to wonder if someone messed up royally after my grandmother passed away. I step closer to Mr. Christianson.

"You're sure this is my grandfather's headstone?" I ask in a whisper. "Because these dates—they aren't right."

"This is the only Tom Highward in the cemetery. Maybe it's a mistake on the headstone? But if so, I'm not aware of it," Mr. Christianson says, huffing like I've offended him. "His sister used to visit once a year till her passing in 1996, lovely lady. You'd think she'd have said something."

"His sister?" I ask. I've never met a great-aunt on my grandpa's side. All I've ever heard was that Nonna and Grandpa got married. Nonna got pregnant. Grandpa was transferred. Nonna hid her pregnancy while she sang with the USO Camp Shows. She took a few months off for an unexplained illness (to have my mom) and then moved to Hollywood after Grandpa was killed overseas.

"Yes, his sister. But never his parents. Rumor is they disowned him when he married your grandma. This is Vivian Snow's husband—Tom Highward—no doubt in my mind."

"I'd like to hear more of what Elise has to say," Mac says, his rich voice calming Mr. Christianson. "Elise, continue." I want to roll my eyes at his over-the-top officiousness but stay camera ready instead.

"So, I didn't know any of what he just said—about Grandpa's family disowning him. I'd be shocked if he was a wealthy man. But besides that, this says Tom Highward died in December 1944. But Nonna said he died in battle months *before* my mom was born. And she was born in March 1944. Maybe this is supposed to read 1943?"

"In battle? He was in the military?"

"Yeah, they met at Camp Atterbury. He died in the Battle of the Bulge, I think. I'm sure Mac has the timeline. Right, Mac?" I ask, but Mac doesn't respond. Instead, he crosses his arms and leans back into his heels, observing the conversation, like he's waiting for something to happen.

"The Battle of the Bulge started in December 1944 and ended in January 1945. The headstone date seems right if he died at that battle. I'm a bit of a history buff so I know these things," Christianson says to Mac, seeming proud of himself. "I know for a fact the dates are correct on the battle," he reiterates. "If you don't believe me, it's easy to look up."

I'd never fully researched my grandmother's story; it never seemed to matter. It all made sense the way she told it. But these headstones shift my perspective until it's like I'm looking at the picture from a new angle.

"No, I believe you. I hate to doubt Nonna's recollection, but she must've gotten the name of the battle wrong, I guess. So, he died when my mom was six months old?"

"Well, not so fast. There definitely *is* something fishy here," Mr. Christianson says, stopping my rationalization.

"Yes?" Mac asks eagerly, urging pensive Mr. Christianson on.

He points to Tom Highward's headstone.

"Well, normally if someone dies in action, he gets a headstone provided by the VA. You can see one there." He points at a tall white headstone with a cross at the top and small black lettering. "And over there." He points to a flat metal plate on the ground a few steps to the left with a Star of David, the rank of sergeant in the US Army, WWII, and the dates of the person's birth and death. He then points back at my grandfather's headstone. "This is a civilian headstone. It's possible that your grandmother didn't know how to apply for a VA headstone, but if your grandfather's body was repatriated after the war, it's unlikely."

"See; I think someone made a mistake. Either the dates are wrong or . . . this can't be his headstone," I say to both Mac and Mr. Christianson.

"There's not another Tom Highward here," Mr. Christianson says, looking up from something on his phone. "I have access to the cemetery plot map, and there's not another Highward other than your grandma buried here."

"Well, shit." My head is swimming. My grandmother is buried here, well, at least half of her remains are. I know that for sure. There's relief in that knowledge. But I never knew my grandpa. His headstone, right or wrong, and the story of his heroic death have been enough for all of us till now. "Does it really matter after all these years? We can cut this bit and move on."

I stare at Mac, my arms crossed at the mess we've stumbled into, but he's still distant, watching. I make eye contact with Conrad off camera and Marty, but no one budges. Someone should say cut. We can't keep sorting through this confusion on camera.

Mr. Christianson pipes up again, still scrolling through his phone.

"I still may be able to help. You said they met at Camp Atterbury? Do you know when?"

I wait for Mac to speak up with the "Gracelyn Branson approved" timeline, but he remains fully in observation mode, like a scientist watching his little lab mice run around the maze he's placed them in and then recording their progress.

"Uh, I can estimate from what I've been told," I respond when Mac fails to. I do the calculations from when my mom was born and the marriage dates and the tale of their romance. "Sometime in early '43 I think."

"Okay, that means he was in the Eighty-Third Infantry." He's back to his phone. "They trained at Atterbury and fought at the Bulge, which works with this being the 'real' date. It's only more circumstantial evidence, but I can look him up on the AAD if that'd help."

"The AAD?" I ask, unable to guess the meaning of the acronym.

"The National Archives has an AAD. Uh, Access to Archival Databases—I can look him up. An image of his headstone might even be linked. That would solve the mystery right there."

Mr. Christianson scrolls through his phone, and I study the headstones.

"Um, Mr. Dorman, I think we have a problem." Mr. Christianson holds up his device and looks past the cameras to where Mac stands with his hands behind his back. He walks toward the sexton with one raised eyebrow, obviously in his "in front of the camera" persona.

"How so?" he asks, nonchalantly, the frozen ground crunching under his shoes with each step.

"Uh, we should talk about this—you know—in private." The middle-aged man darts his gaze between the cameras and then me before he returns his eyes to Mac.

"Whatever you have to say can be said in front of Elise, right?" Mac asks me directly. I can sense Mr. Christianson's nervous energy in his tight grip on his phone and the slight tremble in his thick fingers. I do want to hear it, whatever it is. Especially since I have a sneaking suspicion that Mac already knows exactly what Mr. Christianson has to say.

"Of course," I say, forcing my frozen knees to unlock so I can join the men looking at the phone.

"Well, if you insist." He uses his neatly trimmed nail to point at a name on a website he's pulled up on the phone. "He didn't die in the Battle of the Bulge. If this is him—if this is in fact your grandfather—Thomas Highward of Philadelphia, Pennsylvania. Then, yes. There's no military record of him dying in France or . . . anywhere else during the war for that matter. He was in the Eighty-Third Infantry, but he's not listed among their casualties." He tosses up his hands and gives me an apologetic look.

I glare at Mac as Mr. Christianson's information sinks in, suspicion rising inside me.

"Did you know this?" I ask Mac, who doesn't seem surprised in the slightest. In some effort to sensationalize this story, did he hold back important information? Some family secret that should've stayed in the family?

"Who, me?" he asks, his graying hair blowing across his face. "I'm as surprised as you are." Then, without letting me rebut his only half-convincing denial, he turns to Mr. Christianson. "Is he even buried here, then?"

"That's what I want to know," I add, heat building up under my coat. I'll have to tell my mom—something. As I wonder what I can possibly say to her, Mr. Christianson and Mac continue their conversation.

"I . . . I can look at the plot maps. But"—he holds up his antiquated phone—"you can request a copy of his military records. Might take a few weeks, but it would shed some light. Not all service records are available to the public. But for family, that's a different story."

"Yes. That's perfect. Let's do it." Mac runs his manicured fingers through his hair and holds the unruly strands away from his face. "And what about the cemetery records? Can we take a look at the ones from 1944?"

"I have them in the office." Mr. Christianson turns and weaves his way through the headstones without even a moment of hesitation.

I follow with more caution. Mac signals to the camera crew, and they hustle with all their equipment behind us. I'm not sure if they're still rolling or not, but I don't hold back when Mac catches up with me.

"What do you know that I don't know?" I ask in a low voice, hoping that if Marty is recording our conversation, it won't get picked up.

"Nothing. I swear. You can trust me, Elise," he says, matching my pitch.

I don't believe his denial. There's no way Mac Dorman waltzed into this town without doing his research. He wanted this to happen. He set us up. I don't know what the truth is, but I do know that Mac has found something salacious, and he wants the cameras focused on my face when I figure it out. I hope I'm wrong, that I've grown too skeptical in my years of PR and in the shadows of my family's fame. But I doubt it.

We make our way to a small white building with a green roof and shutters. Mr. Christianson stops outside the door and rubs his feet on a black mat. The door jangles when he opens it, and the inner darkness swallows him up.

"I guess we're about to find out," I say as I clean off my own shoes and follow Mr. Christianson inside.

It's warm in here, and the wood-paneled walls are as comforting as they are tacky. Mac follows close behind, holding the door for a cameraman and a boom mic operator who settle into strategic positions in the room. Mr. Christianson closes a file drawer and plops down a green book with red binding on his desk.

"Here it is." He flips to a yellowed page and reads it under his breath before landing on one spot that he taps his finger on repeatedly. "That's odd."

"Is it a mix-up with the plots?" I ask, skirting around the edge of the desk and planting myself by his side. It's a half-typed and half-handwritten form with scrawling, elegant handwriting filling in the gaps.

"No. It's your grandparents' plot. That's for sure."

"Then, what is it?" Mac asks, sliding up on the other side, sandwiching Mr. Christianson between us.

"Your grandmother purchased her plot in 1949 and paid for the perpetual maintenance plan."

"And Tom Highward?" I ask. "What about his plot?"

"That's the thing. It was purchased in 1947." He hands me the ledger and points out the handwritten record.

"Nineteen forty-seven?" The date screams at me, and I pass the book to Mac.

"That's three years after the date on Tom Highward's headstone," Mac states the obvious.

"Nineteen forty-nine makes sense for Nonna's payment. That's the year *Summer in Salerno* came out. Her breakout hit with MGM. She'd have had the money for it at least." I know the date like it's a national holiday. My mom pushed my grandma to tell the story over again every time she wanted to impress someone.

Though it was Nonna's talent that carried her career and her beauty that launched it, it was her story of being a war widow that truly captured the hearts of her fans. I check the cameras again—still running. My stomach clenches, and tension grips my shoulders.

This could be really bad.

"Nineteen forty-seven is late but accurate enough for Tom Highward with repatriation; uh, that's when the bodies of our soldiers were brought back from Europe and the Pacific. *If* he'd been in the Battle of the Bulge, but—"

"As far as we can tell, he didn't die in that battle," I say, the series of terrible realizations pouring in so fast, I feel like I'm drowning.

"Exactly," Mr. Christianson says like Sherlock Holmes.

"So, who paid for the headstone?" I ask, noting that he'd mentioned my grandmother paid for her plot in 1949.

"Antonio Trombello?" Mr. Christianson reads off the ledger. The name rings no bells. Likely a distant Italian relative stepping in to help his bereaved niece or cousin.

"Is there any way for us to know for sure who, if anyone, is in that grave?" Mac asks theatrically.

"'*Who if anyone*'? Seriously?" I scowl at Mac. "Don't you think there's an easier explanation. The dates are wrong, or the headstone is in the wrong place. You're jumping to some majorly outrageous conclusions. Right, Mr. Christianson?"

The sexton is quiet. He shrugs and looks back and forth between me and Mac and once or twice at the camera.

"There's no way to know for certain without an exhumation."

The word "exhumation" hangs in the air. I feel nauseated, and I start shaking my head, but Mac looks right at the sexton without taking note of my reaction.

"What would that take?" Mac asks, grasping his chin contemplatively.

"Cut. Okay? That's too much," I say, running my hand across my throat in a slicing motion. I can't play along anymore. Mac continues to ignore me completely and readdresses Mr. Christianson, who's situated both literally and figuratively between us.

"Well, uh"—he swallows loudly, sweat beading on his brow—"it starts with the family giving the go-ahead. There are some forms and such."

The family. He's not referring to me and my brothers. No. My mother is the closest next of kin, and if Mac is the one asking—I can't predict what her response might be. I'm done with this ambush. I start to remove my mic.

"Where are you going?" Mac asks as I yank wires out from under my clothing.

"I told you—I'm done for today. I'm not signing any papers, and I really don't want my mom dragged into this mess. I'm here to film a documentary about my grandmother's early life. I'm giving up time at work and letting you film my goddamn wedding. But digging up my grandfather? That's just gross, Mac."

"Hey, no one said we're doing anything of the sort. I just want to know the procedure . . ." I can hear the BS in his claims of innocence.

"Thanks for the tour, Mr. Christianson." I drop the portable mic on the table and then rezip my coat, preparing for the cool breeze outside, ready to walk if Mac refuses to provide transportation.

"Elise," Mac calls after me, but I don't stop. Let him have his little chat about digging up my family and any secrets my grandmother may have had. Clearly, he wants to use us to bolster his career and make money.

I pull out my cell phone to call my mom but pull up Hunter's number first. He's a "take no prisoners" kind of businessperson, and I could use an enthusiastic cheerleader right now. I wish he were here. We'd be an unstoppable team, plus it'd feel good to have his arm around me while I had a good cry into his shoulder. But I'll settle for a call—for now.

Conrad hovers with a clipboard, asking me where I'm going.

"I'm going for a walk," I say as I finish dialing and the phone starts ringing. I put on my gloves, yank my zipper up as high as it can go, and pull on the stocking cap from my pocket. I'm so warmed by my anger that I barely feel the cold wind swirling through the frozen cemetery. Phone to my ear, I walk toward the brick entrance, waiting to hear Hunter's voice, with absolutely no idea where I'm going other than— away. Away from all these complicated questions about Nonna and my family. I'm not sure that I want to know "the truth" if it's anything other than the beautiful story I've wrapped myself in for my entire life.

CHAPTER 14

Vivian

Friday, June 4, 1943
Holy Trinity Catholic Church

"This is all I can remember. I am sorry for this and all my sins." I say the ceremonial words through the gridded partition, waiting for Father Theodore's response. I confessed the small lies to papà and the big lies about mamma. I confessed my growing feelings for Tom and how I'm finding it difficult to resist the temptation to go on a date with him. I confessed my occasional rebellion against papà and my prideful nature and my struggle against vanity. I also told Father Theodore about the incident with Tom and Trombello at the mess hall and how it makes me feel lost and confused.

What I don't share, what I can't force myself to say in this little box and in front of God, is how often I think about the young Italian POW whom everyone calls Father.

"No improvement from your mother, then, dear?"

"No, Father. I . . . I don't think she'll ever get better," I say calmly, even though I want to drop my head onto the armrest and cry. I've come to understand this fact more and more lately, but it's still hard to say it out loud without feeling like I'm dooming my mother to a life of imprisonment in a sanatorium. I used to imagine we'd find some magic cure, a pill or treatment or elixir, but I fear that hope is dying.

"And your father—do you think you might tell him soon about your position at the camp?"

I shake my head, though I'm not sure he can see it through the grate.

"Forgive me but—no. I can't. He'd make me quit. I know he would."

"I see," Father Theodore says with a familiar sigh that's a mixture of empathy and judgment. I don't begrudge him the judgment, and I'm grateful for the empathy. "With that in mind, then it's important to remember that if you allow this new young man to court you, it should not be entered into on a foundation of deceit. Proverbs, chapter twelve: verse twenty-two. *Lying lips are an abomination to the Lord, but those who act faithfully are his delight.*"

A delight. I've always thought I was deeply trustworthy, and I desire being "a delight" in the eyes of God, but when Father Theodore asks me to be honest about Tom, a dam builds inside me. Being honest is good; I know. But being honest is also hard—really hard.

"Yes, Father," I say in submission, but that "yes" is yet another lie. What "yes" really means is I'll try to do better, and I'll look for ways to tell the truth more often. But that's all I can commit to. Somehow, I feel that, although Father Theodore doesn't understand, God does.

Father Theodore finishes our session with words of guidance and then prescribes penance. Penance is actually my favorite part of the sacrament of confession because no matter how I feel walking into the church, stepping out, I feel clean and refreshed.

When I exit through the grand doors and into the humid night air, I'm lighter than when I walked in, and my mind is clear. I rush down the stairs to the street like I'm flying, ready for new opportunities.

Check-in for the dance is in ten minutes, and the dance hall is several blocks away. I let my renewed energy carry me down Main Cross Street, as close to running as propriety and my shoes allow.

I'm eager to make it to my gig because we need the money, yes, but also because Tom is likely to be there. I haven't seen him since that tense lasagna dinner at the POW mess hall. After the confrontation, we moved to the front of the line and were served immediately. We then joined a group of US guards and officers in the mess hall. Tom sat beside me, his back straight as a rod, a different man from the one I'd been getting to know at dances and on walks to and from the bus.

I watched Tom engage in small talk with the surrounding men and officers and nibbled at the meal I'd been so looking forward to without tasting it.

I wasn't brave enough to turn around and look for Trombello and the rest of the committee, but every bite I took reminded me that there were other eyes watching the whole dinner play out. And when I took my tray to the dish return, I found the young priest doing the same by my side.

"Did you enjoy your meal?" he whispered in Italian, the clinking of our plates acting as a perfect cover.

"Yes," I said, my smile plastered on. "Buono."

"I know Marco will be pleased. He was a chef before the war." He hitched a thumb over his shoulder. "Everyone's waiting to hear your review."

"Me?" I asked loudly, dropping my fork with a noisy clank. I lowered my voice to a whisper again. "Me? Why?"

He shrugged, a little smirk crinkling his sun-bronzed cheek. "You remind them of home—sisters, girlfriends, mothers, and wives."

My anxiety swelled like a sponge taking in water. I had that feeling again, of being watched when I'm not onstage. And as flattering as that comment was, I also knew it wasn't safe for me to be the object of affection for men who are our enemies.

I checked my watch without responding to his compliment, aware of the line behind us and knowing Tom was somewhere in the room watching too.

"I've gotta go," I said, in English this time, my heart pounding. Trombello searched my face, his eyes taking in what I couldn't say out loud. I'm not sure if it was the whisperings of God inside the man or if it was the man inside the Godly vessel, but when he stepped aside so I could pass by, I could tell he understood.

"Sì," he said and then, "Buona serata," or *good evening*.

And with that, I snatched my purse and rushed out the door, ignoring the hundreds of eyes watching my exit. Tom didn't follow me. He also didn't show up at my bus stop that night, nor has he shown up any night since then.

I've found no way to excuse his anger in line that day, or his behavior during our dinner. Yet I find his sudden absence painful. His mute punishment hurts far more than the raging fury of my father's explosions. I'd choose papà's brazen fire over Tom's silent frozen wasteland.

I'm just as confused about Trombello. But I don't let myself think about him. I keep my feelings locked away like a box in a dark closet.

But Tom doesn't fit in a box. He's unruly. He pulls me too close on the dance floor; he begs me for dates he knows I can't accept; he meets me at my bus stop and finds me in line at the internment camp instead of staying safely on base. He's made himself impossible to ignore—and then he disappeared without warning. No wooden crate or steel strongbox could keep him; I'm sure of it. And that only makes me think of him more.

If he shows up at the dance tonight, I'll perform in front of him as though he's no more special than the other uniformed men staring up at me. Perhaps he'll remember why I first caught his eye and thaw out of his deep freeze. Or, if I'm very lucky, when I see him, I won't get that flip in my stomach that makes me desperate for the warmth of his attention.

As I approach the burgundy door in the brick-lined alley next to the dance hall, I hold my arms away from my sides to keep the perspiration from soaking into the cotton of my summer dress. I'm one minute late. When I knock, Pauly, the piano player, opens the squealing door, and relief comes over his face.

"There you are, girlie. Frank was 'bout to panic. He sent me to drive out to your place to hunt you down. Where have you been?"

"Church," I say, wiggling past his belly as he holds the door open for me. The sign-in is gone along with the senior hostess. I feel like a trapdoor has unlatched beneath me.

"Church?" he says, sounding puzzled, with a bit of outrage.

"Pauly, where's Carly? You know, Mrs. Tawny? I need to check in."

"Mrs. Tawny? I don't have any clue. Only thing I've got a clue about is warm-ups. A whole new shipment of young'uns came into Atterbury this week, and the place is 'bout to get a whole bus full, so we need to get warmed up and playin'."

"I don't have my card checked yet." I hold up my hostess card. The only way a girl is allowed to dance in this hall is with a signed card.

"I'm not so worried 'bout you dancing as I am you singing," he says, basically chasing me into the familiar hall. Fans do little to cool the already oven-like heat of the room. Girls with perfectly curled hair and pressed dresses set up chairs and arrange plates of sandwiches and cookies on the refreshment table. The windows are open, and there's a slight breeze that'll mean nothing in a few hours when the room is a mass of humanity.

"There you are," Carly says, lifting a giant punch bowl to allow a newer girl to straighten the tablecloth underneath.

"Am I too late?" I ask, holding up my card. Carly wipes her hands on her apron and sighs.

"Too late?" she asks, one eyebrow raised. "I don't know what you mean. Got you on my list already."

"You got me on your list?" I repeat slowly.

"Yup, right here." She holds up the sign-in sheet, pointing to the last name on the list that looks a lot like, but definitely is not, my handwriting. She's giving me a pass, and all I have to do is play along, and she'll sign my card later on the sly.

"Oh goodness, I'm so forgetful," I say fairly convincingly, and return the card to my purse. Carly slips her arm through mine to guide me to the coatroom where I can stash my belongings.

"Yes, you are," she says, loud enough for the room to hear, and then more quietly asks, "Now, where were you really?"

"Church."

"Church?" she asks with the same doubting incredulity as Pauly.

"Yes!" I hang up my things, powder my nose, and reapply my brightest red lipstick that matches the tiny red roses on my white dress. "What do all of you think I am? A heathen?"

"No. But it's Friday night. Who goes to church on a Friday night?" She smooths my hair in a maternal gesture that reminds me of my absent mother. Frank shoves his head through the door, yelling.

"Vivian Snow, get your ass on the stage." He's joking but also not, and Carly's hands go to her hips.

"Frank Broward! You watch your language," she shouts back, and follows me out to the main hall, still talking.

"Is Tom coming tonight?"

"Get onstage, V.," Frank orders. I'm walking quickly, but I refuse to run. The girl running from confession to the USO was Vivian Santini. Now that I'm checked in, my lips coated in Montezuma Red lipstick, and ready to step onstage, I'm Vivian Snow, and no one rushes Vivian Snow.

And Vivian Snow doesn't get distracted by silly little problems with men.

"I don't rightly know," I say, trying to sound like Bette Davis in *The Little Foxes* as I climb up onstage and tap the mic while the band warms up behind me.

We do this every week, and I'm used to the simple sound system and the echo off the empty floors and barren walls. During our lessons, Carly always says, "A full room lies to you while an empty room tells the truth." And she's right.

I feel like a star when I sing to the cheers of GIs who might ship out at any moment. But when I sing to an empty room, I can't help imagining what I'd sound like on a record or on the radio, and that's when doubt tugs at my hem.

After sound check, I switch back to hostess duty. It's easy to tell which soldiers are new. They take in everything like a child on their first day of school. Each batch looks younger and younger to me.

"Hello, soldier. What's your name and where are you from?" I ask a young, wide-eyed GI with trembling hands who hasn't stepped away from the back wall since he checked his hat. The other men are talking and laughing with each other and the hostesses, but this one seems out of place in the big room full of soldiers and pretty girls.

"I . . . I'm from Mississippi. Clinton, Mississippi," he says with a heavy southern accent.

"Well, isn't that nice," I say, my usual opening response. "And your name?"

"Thelwin Patterson. Though . . . though . . ." He stutters a little, and I see why he's less social than the other men with their tongues of velvet. "My family calls me Winnie."

I can imagine a sweet little house with a large porch and white rocking chairs as this young man walks down the dusty drive, still in uniform, a pack slung over his shoulder at the end of the war. "Winnie!" they call out, and all run to embrace him.

"Mind if I call you Winnie too, then?" I fight the instinct to adopt his accent like we're in a scene together.

"You . . . you can call me . . . anything . . . you . . . you want," he says.

"Don't you want to know my name?" I say, knowing I'm flirting but seeing it as a necessary part of my job.

"S-sure do." He's nice, this Winnie. Young but nice and too sweet to face a line of gunfire.

Don't think about it, I say, scolding myself.

"I'm Vivian." I put out my hand and shake his daintily. His palm is drenched with sweat.

"Hello, V-v-v-v-vivian."

Frank starts his announcements in the background. They're boring and slow, and it's nothing like the city clubs where the bandleader is as much of the entertainment as the musicians. But even with his monotone and literal reading of the rule book, the crowd listens attentively.

It's a hot room tonight, and I can't wait to get in front of it. For now, I'll settle for a quick dance or two with Winnie before my performance. It'll help to keep my mind off the stacked-up boxes in my rhetorical closet. I look up at Winnie and bat my eyelashes, hoping he'll seize this opportunity to heroically ask for a dance instead of waiting for me to drag him onto the dance floor.

Just as he pushes his glasses up and opens his mouth—Private Gary Talbot from the front gate at Camp Atterbury taps me on the shoulder.

"Look who we've got here—the famous Vivian Snow." Gary smells faintly of alcohol, and though he's not drunk, it's clear he's on his way there. He's not the first soldier to sneak in a beverage, and it's usually tolerated as long as they keep their hands to themselves and don't get too sloppy.

"Talbot," I say coolly.

"You charming this young soldier? That's not really fair. He's brand-new here, and you still owe some of us old-timers a dance before you move on to new prey."

"I think Private Patterson was charming me. Isn't that right?" I wink. Winnie starts to say something, but his stutter slows him down.

"I'm sure if he's such a gentleman, he wouldn't mind if I stepped in for a dance."

Talbot takes my hand without asking. I want to yank it away, but it's frowned upon to turn down a soldier unless he's getting too friendly. And since Winnie hasn't gotten up the gumption to ask me yet, I have no other choice than to dance with Gary Talbot.

I'm not clear if Winnie says yes or no to the interruption. It doesn't matter because Talbot guides me onto the dance floor and puts his hand on my waist. My stomach rolls, and I wish I could shake it off.

As the music swells, he spins me out and then back in. I try to let my body follow his lead but find his movements jerky and harsh; it's as if he were barking orders and I were saying, "Yes, sir!" with every twist and turn. He flicks me inward so his arms come around me from behind. His hot breath is on my neck, heavy with whiskey and tobacco.

"You're more fun than I thought you'd be," he says, and twirls me out again like he's playing with a spinning top.

"Well, you're exactly what I thought you'd be," I say when he finds a way to bring me close again.

The dance ends quickly, and I break away, leaving Talbot standing in the middle of the dance floor, alone and out of breath.

I escape to the women's bathroom and hide for another song, patting my face with water and wishing I'd remembered to slide my compact into my pocket when I checked my purse. I walk out with Brenda and Tracy, seeking safety in numbers. Both girls chirp on and on about the new men. I scan the room.

Talbot is dancing with another girl; Lucy, I think her name is. I feel for her, but I'm glad that I got away when I did. Winnie isn't leaning against the back wall, and I don't see him out on the dance floor or by the refreshments.

I wonder where he went . . .

Then, out of the corner of my eye, I see someone far more familiar. It feels like a rock drops into my abdomen. Leaning against one of the painted metal posts, sipping a cup of punch, and talking to little Pearl Benson is—Tom Highward. He's smiling at her the same way he smiles at me—broad and bright like he's seen only sunshine his whole life. Pearl giggles and twists her artificially lightened hair. She drives in from Columbus with her roommates. Pearl's not shy about her quest for a husband, though she denies it whenever Carly and Mrs. Portia confront her.

"Is that Pearl Benson over there with Tom?" Carly asks, coming up beside me. The next song starts, and a refreshed set of dance partners takes the floor. But not Tom and Pearl. They stand talking like they're the only two in the room.

"I hadn't noticed," I lie, which has apparently become second nature.

One thing I can't lie about—it hurts to see Tom stooped over Pearl Benson like he can't take his eyes off her, like he wants to kiss her.

"You hadn't noticed, my eye. Don't be fibbing at me. You just went to church." Carly puts her hands on her hips like she does whenever she's scolding one of us. Usually, her high-pitched voice and spirited attitude have a way of getting me to laugh, but not tonight.

"I went to church and asked God if I should say yes to Tom's date," I blurt, wishing Carly were really my mom and could comfort me. She gasps.

"He asked you out?"

"A million times," I say.

"Doesn't he know you can't say yes?"

"I told him. A million and one times. It's why he's mad at me." Her mouth twists up in a sour expression.

"That's not fair. You don't make the rules, Viv. He's cruel to blame you."

"It's not cruel to want someone so badly you'd risk everything. People do it all the time," I say, thinking of *Love Affair* with Irene Dunne and Charles Boyer who fall in love and then promise to meet in

New York, but Irene gets hit by a taxi on the way to the Empire State Building. Love. I think about my father caring for my mother after she took away his only son and lost her mind. Love.

Carly shakes her head and tsks.

"I know what you mean. When I was your age, I'd have given up my job here in a heartbeat if it meant I could have one more night with my Larry. But look where that would've left me—husbandless *and* jobless." She puts her hand on my shoulder and squeezes it empathetically as she watches Tom flirt with Pearl across the room. "It doesn't seem like Tom is your guy anyway, so I guess it's better you said no all those millions of times."

"My thoughts exactly," I say as the song comes to a close. I tear my eyes away from Tom and Pearl and face Carly. "Time for my first set. Everything look okay?"

She looks me over, smooths my hair again, and pinches my cheeks lightly.

"Everything is perfect, as always." And though it's Carly saying it, and Carly isn't more than fifteen years older than me, I pretend she's my mom and give her hand a squeeze.

As I take the stage, introduced as Vivian Snow, I greet the room and get a round of exploding applause and whistles. And as my voice fills the room, now distilled by the swaying bodies dampening the echoes of the space, I pretend Tom never existed, that my mom is watching in the wings, and my true love is out there somewhere waiting for me, possibly even on top of the Empire State Building.

CHAPTER 15

Elise

Present Day
Streets of Edinburgh

"Tell her to call me immediately," I grumble through the phone at the third of my mom's assistants to give me some lame excuse about why she can't come to the phone. I hate being aggressive with her employees, but I can't stand the possibility of Mac getting to her first. Someone needs to look out for our family's best interest, and it's becoming clearer every day that that someone is not Mac Dorman.

I called my oldest brother, Jimmy, and started to fill him in, but he's on set in Iceland and had to go almost immediately. "We don't need more scandal" was the last thing he said before rushing off to makeup. I considered calling my other brothers, but Chris hasn't talked to Mom in six years since she orchestrated a failed intervention for him in Fiji, and Lawrence is on a cleansing retreat for who knows how long, which really means he's getting face work done and going on some fad diet at a modern-day fat farm. My dad mumbled something about warning me not to get involved and then sent his love, which didn't exactly translate through the phone.

It sucks to feel alone.

I dial Hunter's number again. I left a message earlier when my first call went to voice mail, and I'm disappointed I haven't heard from him. I need someone sane and on my side to talk me down from my panic. And if I need to pull the plug on this small-town-wedding thing, he should be the first to know.

The phone rings. And rings. And goes to voice mail.

I leave a message.

"Hey, babe. I know we're supposed to talk tonight, but—like I said, I need you to call me right away. Um . . . I love you. Bye."

I hang up and sigh, and my warm breath turns to a moisture cloud in the below-freezing air. It's started to snow, and though my new winter coat keeps my top half warm, my thin jeans are close to soaked through, and my heeled booties are not only pinching my toes but doing a shit job at keeping out the slush on the side of the road.

When I left the cemetery, I had no idea where to go. Part of me felt like running, sure that one of the black production SUVs would be on my tail immediately. But after I took several evasive turns and called every one of my mom's phone numbers and assistants without luck, the spire of Holy Trinity pierced the skyline above the houses surrounding me. So I'm heading there.

I text and walk, sending a message to Farrah, my assistant, asking her to keep working on connecting with someone from my mom's team.

When I find myself at the bottom of the hill where the church perches, my fingers are throbbing from the cold, and my feet are so numb that I can't imagine what kind of aches and pains I'll have as they thaw.

I climb the snow-dusted steps; the white layer is thin where they've been shoveled very recently. I leave my footprints behind to be filled in by the peaceful but rapid descent of the late winter storm.

Reaching the door, I test the handle and find it unlocked. I'll slip inside and wait for my mom's call and hopefully avoid catching the attention of either priest.

The door swings open with a squeal. It echoes through the shadowy, empty entry. The only light comes from the stained-glass windows. The rope connected to the belfry is tied up to the right of the entry, undisturbed. I wonder what it sounds like, though I'm not tempted to take a pull and find out. When the door closes, the bowels of the church turn eerie. My footsteps echo as I walk down the carpeted aisle, sidestepping the antique vent in the middle of my path.

In the dark like this, I can almost believe I've stepped into a holy place. The giant cross above the altar appears to float, and I stop at a row of pews in the middle of the hall, intimidated by its tremendous presence. The stillness and dimness create a feeling of anonymity, and despite my frozen hands and damp hair, I settle into a pew and lean back with my eyes closed.

As I take deep, calming breaths, I think of all the people from this small town who've sat here, prayed, worshipped, wed, mourned. They're part of my history, my past. If my grandmother hadn't taken that job with the USO while she was pregnant with my mom, if she hadn't followed her dreams and gone to Hollywood, this church on the hill could be mine, and that graveyard could be my future.

A door squeaks open from somewhere inside the church, and I jump. A sliver of light shines out from behind the altar. If I let my imagination have its way, it could look like a portal bringing a supernatural being into the church to give me words of wisdom. But in the dim light, my fantastic thought dissolves as a man dressed in priestly attire comes into focus.

"You can turn on the light when you come to visit," Father Patrick says in an official priest voice, making me wonder if he realizes who I am.

"I . . . I'm sorry I broke in." I sniff and shove my wet gloves into my pocket, positive I look like a drowned rat.

"Miss Branson?" he asks. I think I hear an extra lilt to his question that almost sounds like amusement.

"I hope I didn't frighten you. I just needed a minute out of the storm," I say, and sniff again, melting snow dripping down the sides of my cheeks, back of my neck, and into the top of my shirt.

Father Patrick makes his way to me. I wish the lights were on so I could read his expression. Then again—the brightness would expose my embarrassingly disastrous state.

"That's why the door is always open. There are lots of storms out there," he says, sitting in the row in front of me but turning around enough that I can see his eyes and the easy, welcoming expression on his face.

"I know you're being all deep and figurative, but there's a literal storm out there."

"Sure. But there are lots of places to find shelter from that kind of storm. You chose the church. I think there's usually a reason for that, even if the one in need of respite doesn't know it."

"Damn, you're deep today," I say, making a joke, the parable he's spinning hitting a touch too close to home. "You don't lock the doors—ever?"

He shakes his head. "They did for a long time, probably twenty, thirty years. Especially after the mall was built and we got more occasional tourist traffic. But what good is God's love when it's limited or conditional? And since when does sorrow follow a nine-to-five schedule? We decided to keep the doors open to all who need to find rest and comfort here."

"You're not worried about vandals or theft?"

"I mean, the cameras and motion detector by the front door help." He holds up an older version of an iPhone with a list of alerts on it, and I laugh loud enough for it to echo around the room.

"Here I thought you were gonna give me some speech about God protecting you, but it's a doorbell camera like the rest of us have."

"God's busy. It's a bit much to ask him to take care of something when I could solve the problem with two-day delivery of a door cam."

I laugh again and shake my head.

"Look at you, a funny priest. I bet you and Father Ignatius have a classic 'butting of heads.' I feel a movie plot in this somewhere."

"We have our differences of opinion; that's for sure," he says, putting the phone away and then getting serious again. "You're dripping."

"Oh, I know. I'm making a mess. These must be antique." I wipe away a trail of melted snow, and a pool of cold water soaks into my already-damp pant leg. "I can call a car in a few minutes. I'm waiting for a phone call. Or I could walk to the library and wait there. It's not that far . . ."

"No, no. Stay as long as you need. I don't want you to get cold. One moment," he says, returning to his office. I take off my coat and keep it turned in on itself to trap all the moisture. He comes back carrying a terry cloth towel, flipping on a row of can lights on the way.

"Here." He passes me the towel, and I use it to dry the bench and then my face and hair. "Do you need coffee, tea?"

"Coffee sounds like heaven, but please don't make a new pot for me."

"Mrs. Thompson, our volunteer secretary, bought us a Keurig last year, so one cup of coffee is almost too easy."

"Cameras and coffee machines—I'm impressed. But I don't want to be a hassle. I plan to get out of your hair soon."

"You're no hassle, Miss Branson."

"I'm sure you have better things to do than bring me towels and hot drinks—things like feeding and clothing literal refugees. That's pretty amazing work you do, by the way."

"I could tell it affected you when I saw you on base." He pauses and searches my expression like he's trying to figure out an interesting word problem or brainteaser. I wait for some pointed or deeply religious question, but instead he says simply, "Working with the families on base is humbling."

"I told Mac he should talk to the people at Atterbury and possibly do a segment in the film about your efforts."

"Well, I don't know about that."

"When do you go again?" I ask, finally warm and nearly dry, and blissfully distracted from the crisis I'll have to address as soon as my phone rings.

"I teach a class there on Thursday."

"A class? Like, a religious class? I guess I assumed most of the refugees were Muslim."

"Oh, it's not religious. I teach art therapy," he says in a rush. Then I remember his background before joining the priesthood, and a new burst of respect ignites in me.

"That's right. Your art degree."

He shrugs like he's uncomfortable with acknowledging his accomplishments. After making a career out of the egos of Hollywood stars and millionaire businesspeople, I find his modesty fascinating.

"You've got lots of layers there, Father."

"One or two, I guess."

My phone buzzes in my coat pocket, and I jump.

"Oh shit!" I say, digging through the rumpled pile of fluff.

"Your call?" he asks, not even flinching at my second swear word of the conversation.

"Oh God, I hope so." I retrieve the buzzing device out of the coat's zippered pocket. But it's not my mom or her assistant or even Farrah. It's Hunter. I want to talk to him, I really do, but a small part of me wants to hit the cancel button and call him back later, fill him in without Father Patrick listening in the background. That way I can keep talking to the unusual clergyman who still hasn't told me his, I assume, tragic backstory that I want to know. No—that I crave to know.

"Your fiancé?" Father Patrick asks, seeming to catch on to my hesitancy.

I nod.

"You should get it."

He's right. Plus, how would it look to not pick up my fiancé's call? Father Patrick is supposed to take us through the rest of our Pre-Cana. Marry us. Send us on our way into marital bliss. I wouldn't blame him for judging me if I dodged Hunter so cavalierly.

I hit the green button and put the phone up to my ear. Father Patrick takes my towel and coat and excuses himself as I answer.

"Hey, babe. Got your message. Everything okay?" I can hear traffic sounds in the background. I'm guessing he's in the back of a car in transit between meetings.

"Not really." I try to whisper.

"What's wrong? Are you safe?" There's an immediate edge to his voice.

"I'm fine. It's just more drama with this documentary."

"Oh, thank God. You scared me." Hunter's tone softens. If he were here, he'd be running his fingers through my hair to comfort me. "What's up? More delays? More Mac stuff?"

"A lot more Mac stuff. He wants to dig up my effing grandpa." Saying it out loud makes me chuckle at the audacity of the man.

"What?"

"Yeah. Some really crazy stuff has come up. There's a possibility my grandpa, my mom's dad, didn't die a war hero or whatever shit I've been told my whole life."

"Oh my God, really? Like, some big scandal?"

"Yeah, like maybe my grandpa ran off or Nonna lied or some other crazy theory."

Hunter is silent for a second, and all I can hear is the whisper of someone in the background. The driver?

"So they want to run the DNA?" he says a moment later.

"I don't know what the hell they want to do, but I'm trying to put the kibosh on it. You gotta try to talk to my mom and have her say no. She's sweet on you. Plus, you two were the first to buy in on this project.

But this storyline isn't good for any of us. Even just a rumor could do a lot of damage. Jimmy's freaking out."

"Well, maybe he'll finally help out, then." A double bump in the background and the sudden absence of traffic noise lead me to believe he's entered a parking garage.

"No, you know how he is. His career is the only love of his life."

"I know. I know."

"This whole thing is getting out of control," I say, feeling so alone, helpless.

The sounds of car doors closing and murmurs of people chatting fill the quiet on the other side of the phone.

"Hey, babe. I've gotta go to my next meeting." He's distracted. "But know I've got your back no matter what, okay?"

"Even if it means no wedding in May?" I wait through another long pause before he responds.

"Really? It's that extreme?"

Father Patrick emerges from his office with a steaming cup in his hands. He puts it on the pew next to me, mouthing the words, "For you." I give a wordless thank-you but have to turn my back as he walks away because his kindness brings tears to my eyes that I don't want him to see.

"Well, yeah, Hunter. What if the story about my grandpa's all been a lie?"

"That's what you're worried about?" he says.

"It would be huge. Huge. And with that kind of a bombshell—this documentary won't be some quiet release on a random streaming service."

He's silent. Clears his throat and then asks, "And that's a problem?"

A stab of betrayal pierces my chest like a heated dagger.

"You were worried about the whole POW thing, but this is no big deal? My whole understanding of my family, my mother's origin, are in question. And it'll be on a screen for the viewing public to see, and people like Mac and his anonymous partners are going to profit from it. Get awards. Get richer off ruining my family's name."

"'Ruining' is a bit strong, Lisey. And to be clear—I was worried about your grandma being connected with internment camps until you explained the POW thing. That's different from a family scandal. DNA is a bitch, and plenty of people are now finding out these kinds of secrets. It's a relatable theme, actually."

Now I can't stop the tears. Out slips a small sob that I'm sure Hunter can't hear, but I'm afraid Father Patrick can. A frustration that goes beyond Hunter and beyond our conversation boils inside of me.

"But they get to do it at home, in private. They get to choose who knows their secrets. Why don't I get that choice? I'm not consenting to living in the public eye because my grandmother was famous. Or my mother, or father or brothers, or, God, even my fiancé."

"Elise, do you really think you're any different from the rest of us?" Hunter's tone is no longer soft. He has that hard, cutting tone I sometimes hear him use at work.

"What?" I ask, my voice low and now obviously filled with emotion.

"You run a PR business dealing with the kind of publicity you seem to despise, and you benefit from your clients' scandals continually."

"I want to help them—shelter them from melodrama like this 'cause I know what it's like."

"You're giving yourself too much credit," he says in a biting way I've never, ever heard him wield with me. "You also help them profit off publicity—good *and* bad. If it were anyone but you—you'd agree with me. This is an opportunity. All of it. The documentary, the wedding, even the freaky DNA shit."

"I . . ." I feel like I'm having a conversation with a stranger. "I should let you go."

He exhales into the receiver.

"Sorry, babe," he says. I recognize this voice. "You caught me at a bad time. I'll back you up on whatever you decide, but think on it—okay? There's a reason sex tapes are good for careers—people like seeing their heroes naked. It's possible your grandma wasn't a saint. Maybe she did lie about your grandfather, but maybe there was a good reason for it. You're doing that PR thing again and jumping to the worst conclusions. I bet it's not as terrible as you think."

"Uh-huh," I say, irritated at his lack of concern. I'm out of new words, so I pull out some old ones. "Have a good meeting."

"Talk tonight?" he asks, and I don't know if I'm lying when I say yes.

"Love you," he says.

"You too," I respond out of reflex, and we both hang up.

I sit, stunned, and take a sip from the warm mug Father Patrick delivered during the call. The coffee warms me and stings in a familiar way at the back of my throat. I feel more lost than when I was wandering in the snow.

"Everything okay?" Father Patrick asks, back in his spot in front of me.

I shrug, confusing thoughts going through my mind. *Is everything okay? No. Will it be okay? I don't know yet.*

"Can I sit here for a little longer?" I ask as the wind slams against the windows. I shiver at the idea of going outside.

"You can sit here as long as you need. I have confession at seven; otherwise, I'd offer you a ride."

"It's all right. I'll get someone to pick me up in a bit," I say, taking another sip.

"I'll be in the sacristy if you need me," he says as he walks away.

When he reaches the altar, I call out irreverently, "Can you turn off the lights again?"

He flicks them off without saying a word.

"Thank you."

I sit in the dark, listening to the snowstorm as it surrounds my sanctuary, asking questions, searching for answers.

What if I can't stop Mac? And what if my grandmother was a liar? What if she made up a nice story about my grandfather to cover up something even more embarrassing or scandalous or horrifying? What if I quit the documentary—will Mac go on without me? Will Hunter leave me? And what if he's right—about the documentary, about my career, about me?

What if my whole life is about to change? Again.

CHAPTER 16

Vivian

Friday, June 4, 1943
Edinburgh USO

"Uh, Miss Snow. Can I have that dance now?" Winnie is waiting for me at the bottom of the stage stairs. His cheeks are red, and sweat drips from his hairline. I've seen him on the dance floor off and on throughout the night, and every time he caught my eye, I made sure to send a wink his way.

"Absolutely, soldier," I say, needing a break from searching the room for Tom and Pearl. It was bad enough to see them flirting right in front of me, and when they took to the dance floor, it was worse. Now they're nowhere to be found—their absence is devastating. My mind fills in every minute with excruciating detail.

Winnie is the perfect distraction. He swings me onto the floor with the fluidity of Fred Astaire. Excitement surges with each twirl. As the music swells, Winnie puts his hands on my waist and raises an eyebrow, and I know what he's about to do. I give a tiny nod as he picks me up and tosses me from side to side and then pulls me through his legs, and I twist, close to airborne.

The other dancers make space, and a circle of spectators gathers to watch. His wide grin makes him look childlike, not like a scared little boy but like a boisterous kid running up and down a football field or cheering at a baseball game. The song ends, and the onlookers applaud as both of us breathe heavily. A new song starts up immediately. The tempo is slow and luxurious, and though I'm parched and exhausted, I follow Winnie's lead and let his thin but strong arms keep me upright.

"Where'd you learn to dance like that?" I ask, still catching my breath.

"My mamma owns a dance studio in Clinton. When someone in the class was short a partner, she bribed me with Red Hots to get me to fill in."

"I think I'm gonna need to send your mamma a thank-you note because—now don't go back and tell your bunkmates this . . ." I push my pointer finger into his shoulder. "You're the best dancer I've met in a long time."

Winnie stumbles, and I catch him with a light touch.

"I don't know what you're getting on about—I've got two left feet right now," he says with a slight stutter, the redness fading from all parts of his face but his cheeks.

"You're not gonna fool me on this one, buddy."

I'm laughing at his humility and youthful innocence, intoxicated by the bubbly buoyancy of his practiced footfalls, each like a sip of champagne. I'm still giggling as he flicks me out for a gentle, graceful spin. I close my eyes, enjoying the pace of the waltz, knowing I can give myself over to his lead.

But as I extend my right arm halfway through my turn, a strong hand roughly grasps my wrist. My eyes fly open. I'm pulled between the gentle touch of baby-faced Winnie on one end of my wingspan and the tough grip of a stone-faced Tom Highward on the other.

"May I cut in?" he asks me rather than Winnie. The glossy glower in his eyes makes it more of a demand than a politely worded request.

I have little say in the tug-of-war. I'm furious at Tom and sympathetic to Winnie, but the rulebook specifies that my preference means little—the negotiations remain between the two men. Like most of the choices in my life, I'm strung between the hold of men making decisions on my behalf.

Winnie looks at Tom and then back to me, shrugging and releasing my hand. I don't blame him for not wanting to fight.

"Thanks for the dance," he says as he's swallowed up by the crowd of overheated, lonely soldiers and tired, lonely volunteers. He crashes into a couple. The soldier glares at Winnie, who apologizes to the dancing pair and to me as well.

Tom yanks me toward him, and I follow his lead, though it's tight and possessive in a way that frightens and thrills me.

"That's too close." I wriggle against his firm chest where I'm pinned. I can smell him—a tang of sweat and the heady hint of whiskey but also a warm, spicy scent underneath it that for the briefest second makes me want to nuzzle in even closer instead of breaking away.

"Didn't seem to be a problem when that kid had his hands all over you."

I ignore the accusation and push away enough to put some room between us, hoping none of the senior hostesses saw. They're lenient but not blind.

"I'm not sure what Pearl lets you get away with, but I'd like to keep my job."

He sneers wryly.

Fury boils at my temples. He knows he's upsetting me, and what's worse—he *likes* it. If only I were feisty like Scarlett O'Hara—I'd slap him right across the face and run away, tears streaming down my cheeks.

But I'm not a romantic heroine, so I stay, pulled in by an invisible magnetism that refuses to let go. We sway back and forth with little rhythm other than the steady rise and fall of his chest and the faint beating of his heart. I wonder if he can hear mine, too, or feel it through my thin cotton dress.

"Don't you care?" he whispers, the words and his hot breath tangling in my hair. His voice is thick with emotion.

"Care?" I ask defensively, tilting my head back so I can see his expression. I expect him to be looking off into the distance, but he's not. He holds my eyes hostage. A tingling electricity rushes across my skin and swells through my whole body. It's hard to breathe, and I have an odd urge to cry.

"What you do to me. Don't you care?"

His fingertips press into the pliable flesh at my waist, and though he maintains regulation distance, I feel closer to him than ever. It's like a part of me and a part of him extend past the mortal barrier of flesh and meet in the space between.

"I . . . I . . ." Even if I knew what I wanted to say, there's no way I'd get the words out when he's touching me this way.

The music stops for an announcement. I can't hear it. Tom holds me and shifts from foot to foot like a band's playing in his imagination.

"You don't even know how perfect you are; do you?" He touches my hair and shakes his head like he's remembering something sad.

"Nobody's perfect."

"You are. I swear to God, you are."

The floor starts to clear, and reality returns with the flip of a switch. This is my least favorite moment—when the lights come on and all the dreams of the night evaporate. The strong-jawed hero who held you close transforms into a farm boy from Kansas with a dead front tooth and semicircles of sweat under his arms. And the girls who walked in with perfect pin curls and matte lipstick now have flat hair, wobbly legs, and faded lines on the back of their calves where they'd drawn nylon seams.

I already know what Tom looks like without the spell of music, but it still happens—the undoing. Though he stares down at me, transfixed,

I can see his eyes are blurry from the drink I smell on his breath. And behind him, arms filled with her belongings and holding a uniform hat in her small, manicured hands, stands Pearl—watching us.

He finally loosens his embrace enough for me to break away. I step back, leaving him staring for half a heartbeat at a ghost. I don't wait for his reaction or say a polite farewell. I rush off the dance floor and dive into the coatroom, his voice calling after me and my wrist still stinging from when he'd grabbed it earlier. I grapple past the girls giggling by the door and find my hat and clutch in my cubby, tears streaming down my face. I hold my breath and lean my forehead against the wall. I've gotta get myself under control and fast. The bus will be here soon and will be packed.

Mary's not here tonight, so if I miss the 10:12, I'll have to wait another half hour for the last bus of the night, and there's no easy way to explain coming home that late from what papà thinks is a church function.

I dry my face and powder my nose to try to cover some of the obvious evidence of my heartbreak.

"Bye, Viv," one of the girls says as she walks past.

"Yeah, bye," another adds, and then another, giving me privacy for a moment longer. With a deep breath and another swipe of lipstick, I pin on my hat and slip on my tattered gloves that have been sewn back together too many times over the years.

"Hey, Viv. There's a man out there wanting to talk to you," Carly says, popping her head into the coatroom. She's all dressed for her walk home.

"I don't want to talk to Tom."

"It's not Tom, hun. I haven't seen this guy before. He's not military, but someone let him in, so he's gotta have clearance of some kind. Seemed official."

"I need one more minute." I check my face, dress, hair, hat, and wish briefly I'd brought some cotton to pad the blister on my heel.

Hopefully Tom and Pearl are gone. They're probably on their way to whatever lookout spot girls like Pearl go to with willing men.

"Thanks, doll," Carly croons as I walk past. I look around for the mystery man. "I swear he was here. But if a fella can't wait more than a minute to talk to you, might not be worth your time."

Frank and the guys have already packed up and are ready for their drink at Nip and Sip across the street before heading home.

"See ya Thursday," Carly says, squeezing my hand as we enter the alley together. "Call me if you need to talk before then, okay?" she whispers as we part ways.

My time is running out. I rush to the end of the alleyway. I get no farther than the sidewalk when a tall figure stops me.

"Miss Snow?" The mystery man steps out in a brown tweed suit and dark tie with a matching fedora. I let out a small yelp and then cover my mouth, embarrassed.

"Sorry to frighten you." His lined face makes me certain he's seen more in life than what Edinburgh, Indiana, has to offer. "I tried to find you inside but got shooed out by a stern, matronly woman." I immediately know he's speaking of Mrs. Portia.

"Yes," I laugh into the back of my hand, no bus in sight yet. "Mrs. Portia runs a tight ship."

"She'd be a right-fit yeoman; that's for certain." He has a city-like clip to his speech.

"You a sailor?" I ask, eyebrow raised.

"Eh, in my youth. Too old for that now." He waves like he's shoving those memories into the past where they belong.

"I was gonna say, we don't get many sailors here." I take a step toward the crowded bus stop, and he follows.

"I wouldn't think so."

The bus turns onto East Main Cross Street, and I pick up my pace.

"I'm sorry; this is my bus. I must go . . ."

"Hold up one moment, Miss Snow, if you would. I've got something important to talk to you about." He's out of breath and struggles to match my pace.

"I can't miss it. I'm sorry." I'm starting to panic as the crowd on the street fills the bus to the brim.

"Forget about the bus. We'll get you a cab. Give me a minute of your time." He's stopped now and searching through his coat pocket. He retrieves a business card and holds it out. "I work for MCA. We're booking talent for USO Camp Shows, and I've been looking for some fresh faces like yours. I saw your moves on the dance floor, and that was a nice set onstage. There's a casting call next month in Indianapolis. I want you there."

I stare at the card, the bus doors creaking closed behind me. This is the open call I've dreamed of attending, the agency that could potentially transform my career.

"MCA? As in Jules Stein? Or . . . uh . . . Benny Goodman and . . ."

"The Dorsey brothers, Guy Lombardo, Kay Kyser. Yes. All of them."

I take his card with trembling fingers, admiring the raised letters printed on stiff off-white paper. The bus engine revs as it drives away.

ARCHIE LOMBARDO
MUSIC CORPORATION OF AMERICA
TALENT SCOUT

"Mr. Lombardo . . ."

"Archie. Call me Archie."

"I'm just the singer. You'd need to talk to Frank Broward, our bandleader. I'm sure he'd be very interested."

Archie tilts his head and takes out a cigarette, no longer out of breath but looking overheated. He lights it and then takes a deep inhale before letting out a cloud of smoke that catches in the streetlight like fog, and then he spits a stray piece of tobacco into the street.

"The band ain't invited, doll. That's for you." He points at the card. "I put the times on the back for the call. Wear your prettiest dress and bring a nice photo. Anything will do if it's wholesome, but you seem to got that act down already."

"Act?" I ask, turning the card over, wondering if someone's setting me up for a big joke.

"That little 'pure as the driven snow' thing. It's a compliment. I promise."

It's not exactly the praise he claims it is, but I'm too busy taking in all the numbers and words on the card to care. I already know the audition is a little less than a month away. It's at an address in an unfamiliar part of Indianapolis. I'd have to get the car and the day off. I'd need to save up gas money and fix up one of my dresses to look professional enough for the call. I'd need a photograph and an excuse to give papà. I'd need . . . a miracle to happen.

My hopes deflate, and I slide the card into my purse without another word.

"I can count on you being there, then? Right?"

"I'll try," I say, and it's the closest I can get to the truth without lying. "I'll try, but I probably won't make it" is what I should say.

"Listen, missy. You've got it. You know what I mean by 'it,' right? You're cute and got nice legs, and you could model, sure, but you've also got something on that stage, and not many girls your age have it." He points to the dance hall with his cigarette. "You have all those boys dreaming about you tonight and all those gals wishing they could do what you do. That's one room of people in one little town. One day it could be the whole country or the whole world; you know that, right?"

It's like all my fantasies have come to life, but I know this isn't a dream because in a dream I would say yes unequivocally. I wouldn't have problems with mothers or fathers or expectations or money. Instead, I watch the smoke from his cigarette twist into the sky, drifting away like a dream upon waking.

"I . . . I better go. Thank you for this." I hold up the card, the most priceless item I've ever had in my possession and possibly the most useless.

"Wait. I promised you a taxi." He points to the taxi stand across from the bus stop. The idea of riding in a cab anywhere sounds so cosmopolitan, but I don't know how I'd explain it to my father.

"Oh, no thank you. But it was nice meeting you, Mr. Lombardo," I say, shaking his hand lightly.

"Archie. And it was my pleasure, Miss Snow," he says, placing his hand over his heart with a short bow. "See you on the first?"

I don't say anything in return. With a quick curtsy, I walk away, down the street and toward home. If I walk quickly, I can make it there before the next bus even shows up. I'm only a little over a mile from my house. Plus, I need some space to think, away from Mr. Lombardo, away from his charming words and his eyes that see far more in me than I ever have.

CHAPTER 17

Elise

Present Day
Camp Atterbury

"This is for you," Mehrvash, or Ash as she suggested we call her, says as a little girl in a long-sleeved blue T-shirt and patterned cotton pants holds up a coloring book page. She's neatly filled in a dog character with markers and added little hand-drawn stick figures smiling and waving.

"Thank you!" I say, smiling at her as I inspect the drawing. "It's beautiful."

Ash is the interpreter assigned to the shoot for the day, and she relays my message in Farsi. I attempted to say a few phrases when Father Patrick introduced me to the class, but they giggled so much at my errors, Patrick suggested I let Ash step in.

Father Patrick and Ash have been invaluable today. With their help and the strict guidance of Atterbury's PR rep, we've spent the day touring the facility and exploring the refugee program up close. Last week when Mac finally caught up with me after our fight in the sexton's office and begged me to continue with the project, this was my bargaining chip.

I told Mac that if he'd include a segment on the refugees in the documentary and references for the charitable organizations that assist in this work domestically and internationally *and* pledge a percentage of the profits to the cause, I'd continue with the documentary.

After some discussion with attorneys and the officials at Camp Atterbury, Mac signed off on the deal. And so, we're here, and it's been a full day of filming. Mac is in and out, hardly engaging with the subjects, but it doesn't matter to me how much of a selfish jerk he is because I finally, finally feel like this project has some meaning.

I've spent two of the past five days volunteering at the camp under the guidance of Father Patrick and his team. At first, I organized donations and helped in the kitchen, but at the end of the first day, Patrick invited me to his art therapy class.

I can't speak the language, and I don't have training in mental health or public service, but something about the camp calls to me and makes me want to do more. I spend so much of my life helping the privileged create and maintain a beautiful image that's sold to the public to keep them wealthy or famous, and I've enjoyed being behind the scenes in the society I was brought up in, but volunteering here hits differently. It isn't about making people look a certain way but about making actual change.

"I think that's you and that's Esin," Father Patrick explains, pointing to the figures. Ash relays the analysis, and eight-year-old Esin nods her head.

"You are such an artist," I say to the girl, who giggles when Ash tells her what I said. "It's my turn. I'll draw one for you," I say, taking out a blank piece of paper and some crayons. I draw a little girl with dark hair and a tall woman in a long purple dress shaped like a triangle who is supposed to represent me. I write *Esin* in English under her figure and *Elise* under mine. Ash takes a moment to write both in Farsi beneath my crayon letters and then passes the final drawing to Esin. She hugs it and says, "Thank you," in English and walks back to her seat. Mac gives a thumbs-up, and I hold on to my happy face, even though I'm still not in a good place with Mac.

"I should at least learn how to say thank you," I say to Father Patrick and Ash, embarrassed that as an adult I can't even learn one phrase in Farsi, while Esin is working to master an entire second language.

"We can work on it next time," Ash says. The day is almost over, and there likely won't be a "next time," at least not with Mac involved. He reported at the beginning of the art class that he's gotten everything he needs for this segment.

I had lunch with Esin's family members, and they've signed a release to have their story told through the documentary. Mac says he'll find a way to parallel the Italians' and Afghans' respective experiences in the camp. And I can see the similarities in their storylines.

More than 88 percent of the POWs left Camp Atterbury and the other 174 branch camps in the fall of 1943 when Italy left the Axis powers and joined the Italian Service Unit of the US Army. They spent the rest of the war in temporary housing in places with labor shortages until it was safe to be repatriated. Some stayed and made their homes here.

He'll never admit it, but I can tell he knows this timely storyline will add more weight to his production. We still haven't found common ground on the whole "grandpa grave" issue, but my mother's flight lands tomorrow morning at eight o'clock, and I for one will be relieved to have her here. The wall of assistants and agents she's built around herself over the years is virtually impenetrable when she wants it to be.

Father Patrick is preparing for the end of the day, and as soon as the kids file out, Mac will head back to the hotel. We have a dinner planned at Cracker Barrel, but I'm tired of the overly starchy menu, and other than talking with Lisa, I have little to look forward to, conversation-wise. In my free time these past few weeks, I sneak away to the small diner on East Main Cross Street in downtown Edinburgh. Their coffee is rich and as strong as their free Wi-Fi, and when I need to get some work done, Big Red's Place has become my makeshift office.

As he says goodbye in what sounds like flawless Farsi, I watch Father Patrick interact with the class. The dark-haired and bright-eyed refugee children are eager to please. Father Patrick explained how the art projects provide an escape from the trauma of having to flee from their homes without warning and landing in a new and foreign country. Joy is useful, especially when it's in short supply.

The children leave with friendly waves, and Mac barks some orders to his crew. Lights quickly disappear and are packed away in hardbacked boxes. Ash walks up to me with her hand extended.

"It was lovely to meet you," she says, a slight accent turning up the last syllable in every sentence she speaks.

"You too. I mean it. Here . . . take my card. I'd love if we could keep in touch." I rustle through my bag and retrieve one of my business cards. She hands one back to me with yellow-and-blue coloring on the top and the name of her organization: *Language Over Borders*.

"Yes—thank you. This means so much," Ash says.

"I'm not kidding. I want to learn more. Not only about language but about everything you do." Father Patrick watches discreetly as he collects the papers from the desks.

"Well, thank you. I'll pass it on to my superior. Any exposure helps." She smiles and places the business card in her blazer pocket.

"Yeah!" I say with an awkward level of exuberance. We stand in this uncomfortable space until she speaks again.

"Well, I better head out. See you next week, Father," she says, waving at Father Patrick. I wave a goodbye, too, wondering what exactly I want from her. Gratitude? No—I don't want her to look at me as some celebrity savior. I want her to look at me as an equal—a colleague.

"Oh, by the way . . ." Ash pauses, stepping out the door. "I hope you don't mind my saying so, but I'm such a big Gracelyn Branson fan. *Toy Department* was on every night after school, and my mom let me watch it while she made dinner. I always say your mom was my first English teacher."

And there it is. I'm not a coworker or a friend. Not even a top PR professional. I am Gracelyn Branson's daughter.

"I . . . I'll pass it on," I say. She waves again and then leaves. Mac and his crew are right behind her, Conrad the last in line.

"You coming?" He's given up on his pretend politeness since my little standoff with Mac and now treats me with just enough disdain to keep things real, which I actually appreciate.

"I'll be out in a few. I promised Stan and Dottie I'd say goodbye."

Conrad checks his watch. "Mac's blood sugar is crashing, and we ran out of protein bars, so we don't really have time for a social visit."

"It'd be rude if I didn't . . ."

"Can you do it in ten minutes or less?"

I start to push back, but Father Patrick chimes in with "Ten minutes. No problem."

"Thank you, Father Patrick," Conrad says in an overly chipper voice, such a contrast to the irritated tone he takes with me. Everyone likes Patrick. He's smart and empathetic, and most of all, he's easy to work with, which will take a person far in show business. Also, he's not hard to look at either. If I were going to cast a heartthrob priest on a TV show about forbidden desires, he'd be perfect for the role.

I like all these things about Patrick—the kindness and the intelligence and yes, even his frustratingly distracting good looks. But what I like most is his friendship. He doesn't care who my parents, grandparents, or fiancé are, and working by his side has created a casualness that lends itself to conversations on art and travel, even politics, and deeply intellectual discussions on religion. The only thing we don't talk about is his mysterious past. Well, that and my relationship with Hunter. Which is odd because that's the one conversation Father Patrick is supposed to have with me and, at some point, my fiancé.

"Yes, thank you, Father Patrick," I echo after Conrad leaves, mimicking the assistant's kiss-up tone.

"It sounds meaner when you say it that way," Patrick says, laughing and dropping art supplies into the bin.

"Well, that's because I'm not *being* nice," I explain.

"Ahhh, yes. That makes sense, then."

"Right?" I say with some sarcasm but then soften. "But in all seriousness—thank you."

"No problem. I'd like to see Stan and Dottie again anyway. Plus, I do have an ulterior motive."

"Ooooo, am I taking confession now?" What could Father Patrick have to confess to me?

He stores a clear bin in a closet, and I dump a dustpan of paper scraps into the recycling bin.

"I wouldn't go that far," he says, flicking off the lights. I retrieve my belongings from behind the desk.

"Now I'm dying to know." I join him by the door. We haven't been alone since my snowy-evening visit to the church. The darkness and tranquility of the empty room remind me of the peaceful feeling I took with me when I left the church that night.

"It's nothing outrageous aside from the fact that gossiping is a sin, and I'm positive this is gossip."

"Ahhh, now I see." I understand immediately what he's leading up to.

"Have you heard anything? Official?" he asks, leaning against the doorframe with his arms crossed. Last week he owned up to hearing most of my conversation with Hunter.

"I did a bit of my own research." I hold up a finger and lean in for suspense. "Tom Highward came from a wealthy family, and when I say wealthy, I mean Bill Gates wealthy but, like the 1940s version."

"You didn't know this?"

"Not at all. Tom Highward was this totally nebulous hero figure to all the grandkids. I don't think my mom even knew he was rich. Which is surprising because I found plenty of articles on Newspapers.com about Tom's life as a socialite and gossip columns about his joining the army, and even rumors of his marrying secretly and having a love child. But my grandmother was never mentioned until"—I point my finger into his shoulder as I add each detail—"she signed with MGM and was referenced as a war widow. But as far as I could tell, the Highward family had nothing to do with my mother before or after she was born. The younger sister who used to visit Tom's grave passed away in '96. I saw pictures of her, but I know for sure we've never met. She has a daughter who lives in Manhattan, though."

"Wow—you found out a lot. Are you going to reach out to the cousin?"

"You read my mind." I poke again, which must've been one poke too many because Patrick grabs my finger before it hits his shoulder again. "Sorry, I'm getting carried away." I smooth the fabric and pat the area like he's been hurt. "But to your question—yes. I'm not positive she'll know anything, but as soon as I get my mother's permission, I'm calling this cousin. She's flying in tomorrow morning. My mom—not the cousin."

"Ah, the fabled Gracelyn Branson."

"Yes, yes. Academy Award–winning Gracelyn Branson." I emphasize her preferred title.

"That will be . . ."

"Interesting," I say, completing his sentence.

"I think I was going to say fascinating, but interesting works too."

"You know what, you go ahead and laugh, but when she starts trying to use her womanly wiles on you, we'll see who's laughing," I say, grabbing the door handle. I don't open it because he's leaning against the door and would fall if I did. In this position, however, my hand accidentally rests against his bicep. He doesn't move at first, as though he recognizes something important in the moment we're experiencing—like it's a pocket of existence where his collar doesn't matter, and my last name doesn't either.

"Me. I'll be laughing," he clarifies, but the steadiness in his answer sounds like it has very little to do with laughter.

"We shall see," I say, brushing past him as I turn the handle and walk out to the hallway. He stumbles but doesn't fall.

"Hey, you almost killed me," he accuses, catching up to me halfway down the hall.

"You promised Conrad we'd be ten minutes. I'm helping you be a man of your word."

"Then we better go this way," he says, guiding me through the mazelike corridors to the mess hall to find Stan and Dottie.

"Hey, you two," Dottie calls from her seat at the cafeteria table. She's sitting alone with a novel open in front of her as she eats. The air is fragrant with spices, and I wish I could eat here rather than force down the fried chicken and waffles waiting for me.

"Hi, Dottie. No Stan tonight?"

"He had a call on the walkie, but I have my book to keep me company," she says, holding up her romance novel and taking off her reading glasses. "But I'd take you both over Francesco and Maria any day."

"I can't stay, but I didn't want to miss saying goodbye."

"Oh, that's a shame. I was hoping we could have dinner, but I'm glad you stopped by. I have something for your show." She takes out her oversized purse and retrieves a legal-sized manila envelope from inside. "I found some pictures in our archives you might be interested in. I don't think anyone realized we had the real live Vivian Snow working here years ago."

"Pictures of my grandma?"

"A few. Also, the chapel."

"That's great. Thank you!" I take the offered envelope.

"Will you be back on base anytime soon?" I don't think I'll be back. Hunter will be here soon, and after filming a few segments together, we'll wrap for a few months until the wedding.

"I want to—I really do, but it depends on the filming schedule." I dig in my bag and retrieve one of my business cards for Dottie.

"This is fancy," she says, squinting and holding up her glasses to get a clearer look. "CEO? Well, look at you."

She tucks the card into the back of her novel like a bookmark, and my cheeks feel warm. It's not often someone finds me impressive. It's impossible to see the North Star when it's high noon.

"Call me, okay? Even if I can't make it back before we wrap, I want to see you," I say, and add, "And Stan."

"Of course. I was just telling Father Patrick we need to have you both over for Sunday dinner, wasn't I, Father?"

"She may have mentioned it," he said, mouthing, "Like ten times."

"I saw that!" Dottie said, batting at him with her bent, arthritic hands.

"I love the idea. Thank you, Dottie." I check my watch. I've already stayed too long. "Well, I better get going. There's a van full of hungry crewmates waiting for me."

"Sounds good. Bye, dear." She puts her glasses back on and opens her book as Father Patrick follows me to the exit.

"Want me to walk you out?" Father Patrick asks, and I shake my head.

"Nah, I got it. But I'll see you on Thursday for filming."

"See you then," he says, and we part ways at the cafeteria door. He heads toward his car, and I jog across the parking lot to the large SUV in the corner. Marty, Ben, and Lisa are waiting for me inside.

"Sorry to make you guys wait," I say, climbing into the empty spot in the back. "Wait. Conrad and Mac left already?" I ask, looking around.

"They just left. No worries. We barely finished packing up," Marty says as he pulls out of the lot and follows the grid-like streets off the base. I apologize again and then stop because everyone in the car is in wind-down mode, looking at phones and returning texts. I'm about to take out my own device when I remember the envelope of pictures in my lap.

I slowly unwind the red string from the top flap. A cluster of black-and-white photographs pours out when I tip the envelope to the side. I arrange them in a neat stack, small ones up front, bigger ones in the back. The first few are blurry pictures of the Chapel in the Meadow during different phases of construction, each with a date on the back. The next few are of men working shirtless or in their PW uniforms with rolled-up sleeves, tools in hand, and big smiles.

When I reach the slightly larger prints, they change from action shots to group photos. The first shows a gathering of POWs in a field facing a man in religious vestments. Next to him stand a woman and a man performing in some way. I look closer, wishing I had a magnifying glass, but after a second of self-doubt, I know I'm right. It's my nonna. I flip the card over.

On the back is written *June 7, 1943—Dedication of the Ground for the Chapel in the Meadow by the Most Reverend Amleto Cicognani.* No mention of any other individuals pictured. But it's her. I'm sure of it. Positive.

The next photo, same size, is of a smaller group of men. On the back I read—*chapel construction committee.* The next photo shows my grandmother smiling next to the same man she'd stood beside in the picture of the dedication. It's a version of my grandmother I'm unfamiliar with.

As a child, I knew her as a glamorous woman with rich brown hair, long eyelashes, and perfectly colored lips that always had a compliment for me. She doted on me, her only granddaughter. She would wrap my hair in rags to give me long ringlets, and we'd stay up to watch the late-night shows, and she'd point out her friends or my mom's friends and tell me stories, and I'd fall asleep in her bed. As she aged, she grew frail but graceful in her frailty. She let her hair go white and her wrinkles set in. I respect that.

Sure, I know the glamour shots of her early career and her days as a pinup girl. But the fresh-faced innocence and unrestrained joy on her face in this photo—these I've never seen.

I flip to the next picture. This one is of my grandmother sitting at an outdoor desk, men in a field behind her working, a soft, close-to-seductive smile on her face. The next one is similar, with less of a smile, the background fading away, and I can see the future superstar rippling under the surface.

I turn the pictures over. Both are blank, though I have no doubt they must be from the same time as the other images—1943.

The next photograph is of a young Italian POW in a tidy prison uniform with the letters *PW* shouting out from his sleeve. He, too, is smiling, like my grandmother, but looking away like he's embarrassed by the attention, laughing. He's handsome with thick dark hair and a strong jaw, clean-shaven. And though the other picture is fuzzy, this man could be the same one pictured next to my grandmother at the dedication of the chapel grounds.

I turn this photo over, assuming it, too, will be blank, but it's not. Written in the same loopy handwriting that I'm starting to think belongs to my grandmother, are a name and a date.

Father Antonio Trombello—1943.

Antonio Trombello. That name—it's the one I've been looking for. Such a common name, and with few other details, my cursory research has found a plethora of Antonio Trombellos. But here he is—the man who purchased my grandfather's grave and headstone. He was an Italian POW.

Marty pulls into the covered drive outside the Haymark Garden Inn, and everyone piles out. I shuffle the photographs back into a stack and slide them carefully into the envelope again, not sure what to do. I could give them to Mac; that's what Dottie intended. And I see why—the photos provide a visual timeline to the construction of the Chapel in the Meadow and proof my grandmother was an integral part of that process.

But what about Antonio Trombello—this man who took pictures of my grandmother and made her smile more radiantly than I've ever seen? No. Not Antonio Trombello. *Father* Antonio Trombello, the *priest* who paid for my grandfather's grave.

I haven't forgotten Dottie's comment about Vivian Snow's rumored love affair with an Italian priest at the camp. And now it's clear why that rumor started. The question is, Do I want to spread an unsubstantiated story about my own flesh and blood?

"You getting out?" Marty asks. Back in the driver's seat after unloading the equipment into the lobby, he's ready to park the SUV for the night.

"Oh yeah. Sorry." I slide the envelope into my bag and climb out of the car. My mom will be here in the morning, and then I can get at least some answers. Until then, my grandmother and Father Antonio Trombello, whoever he may be, will have to wait in the darkness of their envelope.

CHAPTER 18

Vivian

Friday, June 4, 1943
Streets of Edinburgh

I walk away from Archie with my head held high, hoping I look like
Katharine Hepburn in *The Philadelphia Story*. When I step off Main
Cross Street, just past the last streetlight, onto our pitch-black road, a
chill runs up my spine.

If papà finds out I walked home alone, he may never allow me to
leave the house again. But the greatest danger in this darkness isn't my
father's fury—there are real threats out here, too—the kind that *make*
fathers overprotective.

I hug my torso. It's hard to navigate in the darkness, and I'm not
surprised when a rock catches my heel. My ankle turns, and the strap
on my shoe snaps. I stumble onto the road, my shoe half-off. I rub the
sore spot on my foot and try to inspect the damage to my only pair of
presentable show shoes.

"Dang it."

Headlights rushing down the road blind me. A horn blares. I
slap my hands over my ears and jump off the pavement with a squeal,

leaving my damaged shoe behind. A Chrysler runs over my abandoned footwear, shredding it into a mangled bit of leather and cork.

"You okay?" a young man's voice calls from the inside of the dark car, sounding as frightened as I feel.

"Keep driving, Ernie. She's probably drunk," a woman's voice, high and judgmental, orders.

"You don't know that," he scolds. "Hey, you. You all right?" he asks again. I clear my throat, not sure if I can find my voice.

"I . . . I'm fine," I say, my cheeks burning, more embarrassed than traumatized by the near miss.

"What in heaven's name were you doing in the road?" the woman asks as though I've committed a crime equivalent to murder. A rush of giggles trickles out of the lowered windows. Likely, they're just girls leaving the dance and heading home to Columbus with a brother or friend playing chauffeur and bodyguard.

"My strap broke on my shoe . . . ," I try to explain.

"Vivian?" From the back of the car, a deep and familiar voice interrupts my explanation.

"Tom?" I squint through the darkness, mortified.

The car—I recognize it finally. It belongs to Pearl's brother. He drives her and a gaggle of other girls to the dances every other Friday. Too young to join the army and with no reason to be at the USO, Ernie plays cards in the alley behind the Nip and Sip till the dance ends.

So, I've been practically run down by Pearl and her gangly little brother with Tom Highward in the back seat. Fantastic.

Tom gets out of the car, slamming the door hard and making it creak on its frame. He staggers a bit, still intoxicated.

"What the hell are you doing out there alone?" he slurs.

"I'm walking home," I say, chin up, defiant.

"You can't walk home. It's not safe."

"You sound like my father," I say hotly. "I'll be fine." I heft my purse up under my arm and take a wobbly step with only one shoe on.

"You almost got run over." He grabs my elbow. "You're not walking."

I try to yank it out of his grip, but the alcohol seems to give him extra strength. He holds tight.

"Hey!" Embarrassed and angry, I gasp, wanting to run away as fast as my bare left foot will allow me.

"Get in the car, Vivian," he orders like the military man he is.

"I'll walk, thank you very much." No way I'm taking a ride from Pearl and all the out-of-town girls who'll talk behind my back because I dance with more soldiers than they do, calling me a tramp for singing with the band.

"You get in that car or I'll put you there," he says, a fiery twinkle in his eye that makes me wonder if he's serious.

"No." I tug at my arm again. He uses his strength to yank me back and flip me over his shoulder like a sack of potatoes, my legs dangling in the air.

"Stop!" I squeal, outraged and confused.

"Get that door open." It screeches open, and with very little effort, Tom tosses me into the back.

I land on top of two shrieking girls. I was right—it's Adelia and Samantha from Columbus. In the front seat with Pearl's brother sits my least favorite uniformed man—Talbot. He watches the entanglement with amusement.

"What do you think you're doing?" Pearl yells as Tom wedges himself back into the packed car, helping sit me up, half on the seat and half on the leg of the girl next to me. My upper body presses against his side, my head touching the roof of the car.

"We're taking her home."

"We're doing no such thing."

"Your idiot brother about flattened her. It's the least you can do," he says bitterly, like he suddenly can't stand Pearl or her brother or anyone in this car.

"Hey now." Talbot tries to calm the escalating conflict.

"I can walk," I say.

"Tell Ernie your address," Tom insists.

Everyone in the car seems to understand Tom isn't about to change his mind. I give Ernie directions to my street.

As we drive, a warm wind cuts through the stuffy, overheated interior, but it remains unbearably hot and sticky. The others make small talk and shift in their seats to try to access the brief nibbles of a breeze. But Tom doesn't seem to be aware of much more than me.

Even with my aching elbow and bruised ego, I'm glad he kept me from running away. The only heat that matters is where his hand touches my bare knee and my body presses against his. This heat feels good, and it spreads as I watch him look over every inch of my face and linger on my lips, like he wishes he knew what they taste like. I've seen this look from men before. It usually frightens me, or disgusts me, but for some reason it feels different from Tom. His touch and his look make me want to get closer, and I don't know why.

The mile to my street goes by quickly, and when we pull over, Tom helps me out of the car like a gentleman this time.

"This your house?" he asks, pointing at the Browns' A-frame at the end of North Holland Street.

"Oh, this one? No. I live that way." I point in the general direction of my house. He glances over my shoulder and then back at me.

"You don't want me to know where you live?" His brow furrows. "Do I scare you?" He sounds hurt.

"No . . . not at all," I say, though it's partially a lie. Sometimes he scares me. But that's not why I don't tell him where I live. "My father's old-fashioned. He thinks the only place a young woman belongs is at home or at church. He wouldn't like to know I was at the USO."

"He doesn't approve of your band?" he asks, walking me to the end of the street. Pearl hangs halfway out the car window, watching closely.

"He doesn't know about it. Any of it."

"Not even Atterbury?"

"Nope. None of it. Thinks I work at Cummins engine company."

"What? Is he antigovernment?" He recoils, offended and a bit suspicious.

"No, no. Not at all." I rush to fix the misunderstanding. "He's against the POWs being here—at Camp Atterbury. Wouldn't want me working there."

"I don't blame him. How do you think it makes us enlisted men feel when you all fawn over those greaseballs?"

"Greaseballs?" I echo. Tom seems oblivious to the offensive nature of his comment.

"Yeah. The Italians. We're fighting those bastards, and they're being fattened up and playing summer camp on Uncle Sam's dime. Then they flirt with our girls behind our backs, stealing them away while we're out fighting their brothers and cousins. You can't blame a guy for getting jealous." He pauses his rant to take a swig out of the flask he keeps in his breast pocket. I take the opportunity to cut in.

"It's not like that," I try to explain defensively. "It's the rules. There's a book where it's all written down . . ."

"But maybe you like that," he interrupts, his breath scented with whiskey. "Is that why you danced with that kid tonight? To make me jealous?"

"No," I respond immediately. "It's my job. We're all just doing our jobs." I'm angry but getting more frightened by the minute of facing my father's wrath. "I have to go. My father will be worried."

"Running away again?" he shouts, reaching for my sore elbow. This time I evade his grasp before he can clamp down or toss me back in the car. Talbot and Ernie coax Tom into the car as I glance around, watching for lights inside the neighboring houses.

"Everything all right?" Talbot asks very officially, like he's on duty.

I nod, relieved to see Tom settle in the back of the car. He presses his head against the metal frame of the half-opened window and watches me talk to Talbot but doesn't look upset anymore. More like—sad.

"Will he get in trouble?" I ask, unsure if it's okay for Tom to return drunk.

"Nah. Don't worry," he says, waving away my concerns. "I'll get him back in. No one the wiser."

"I can put a good word in—with Lieutenant Colonel. If he needs," I offer. As strained as our evening has been, he wouldn't be late if not for my shoe-fixing attempt in the middle of the road.

"Please don't," Talbot says. "We're not out—officially—if you know what I mean."

I blink a few times, gradually processing the hidden message inside that statement.

"You snuck out?"

He shushes me, putting a finger to his mouth.

"Yes. Tom's restricted till next week. Everybody does it. There's a reason they don't fix that hole out in the west fence line."

"West? Through Nineveh?" The little town west of Camp Atterbury is known to be friendly to AWOL soldiers sneaking out for a night of fun.

"That location is 'need to know,'" he says, his slight slur making the declaration sound a touch ridiculous. "I know you don't give a whit about me, but if you want to keep him safe, you'll keep quiet about ever seeing us. You good at keeping a secret?"

He looms over me. My joints lock up in fear.

I nod.

"Yeah, bet you've got lots of secrets," Talbot says with a sneer, caressing my cheek with one finger.

"Would you knock it off? We've gotta go," Pearl shouts from the car, saving me.

"Keep your skirt on. I'm coming," he yells. With one finger to his lips, he stumbles back to the car. They drive away, and in the cricket-filled nightscape that's suddenly so peaceful and calm, I wonder how we didn't wake the neighbors. I take off my other shoe and run the rest of the way home through the damp grass.

The house is dark, which means that through some combination of pain medication, alcohol, and God's will, papà is asleep. Aria made it look like I was already home and tucked into bed. The poor girl—lying for her sister. I wonder if she ever talks about me in confession, about the lies I ask her to tell.

But if anyone can possibly understand the righteous nature of that deceit, it's Aria. And no matter what Father Theodore says, sometimes lying is righteous.

CHAPTER 19

Elise

Present Day
Elise's Hotel Room

"Wake up; wake up; wake up!" my mother chants as she lets herself into my suite, interrupting my morning Zoom meeting with Marla and a client.

"How'd you get in here?" I ask, muting my side of the call.

"I asked for a key at the front desk, told them we were sharing a room, and they were such angels."

"But we're *not* sharing a room." There's no way I could endure that.

"No, silly. But I wanted to wake up my girl with a surprise from her mamma." She holds a tray with two cups of coffee. She places them on the sitting area table and then rushes over to where I'm working, popping her head in-screen to give me a kiss.

In any other profession, this would be a mortifying moment of parental narcissism, but Hollywood is so enamored with Gracelyn Branson that she can get away with almost anything.

"Not sleeping, Mom. Working," I say, annoyed.

"Can they hear me?" my mom asks, waving at the patchwork of faces on my screen. "Unmute. I want to say hi."

"All right," I say, clicking the microphone icon.

"Oh, hey, cutie pie. You look delicious," my mom coos at a twenty-something member of the Hollywood "it" crowd. He was in a film with Mom last year, maybe the year before, played her grandson. Since then, he's leveled up to starring in a new HBO series.

"Did you know this is my baby girl?" she asks, squeezing my cheeks with her gloved hands. Of course, they all know, but I play along because everyone loves this story—Gracelyn Branson—mother extraordinaire.

"Yes. She's great—" he says as his manager finishes the sentence with a quick "Just like her mother."

"Oh, you're too sweet," my mom says. She lets go of my cheeks and starts shedding pieces of outerwear. "I'll let you get back to work. I'll be right over here, minding my own business."

"Goodbye, Gracie!" the young actor says with a hint of flirtation, which grosses me out.

I know nothing's going to get done with Mom in the room, so I close out my part of the presentation, pass the meeting over to Marla's capable hands, and turn to my mother. She looks stunning—as usual. Her lips, skin, and eyes have healed, and I have to admit, this round of touch-ups looks very natural.

"There's my big working girl. Look at you balancing everything. I bet when you start popping out babies, you'll be a badass mamma too. Let me take a look; anything cooking in there?" She runs her hand over my abdomen. I step away from her probing.

"No, Mom. Told you, not trying for a baby right now." She's always nagging me about babies, saying I should pass on the Snow/Branson matriarchal line, even though she already has four grandkids she hardly sees. Hunter is baby hungry, too, but I froze my eggs after Dean died, so my biological clock isn't forcing any rash decisions before I'm ready.

"This is the first and last time I'll ever say this, but—thank the Lord. We're already going to be hard-pressed to find you a gown with such short notice. But to find one that'll hide a baby bump, now that would be a feat. I'd have to bring in Hazel, and you know how hard she is to book." Hazel is Mom's ancient seamstress. She was Nonna's seamstress first and used to make all Mom's dresses when she was a girl. I don't know if it's even legal to force that old woman to work anymore and not get charged with elder abuse. But Mom worships the ground she walks on.

"I'll get one off the rack and pay for alterations like any regular person. I'm sure it'll be fine."

"Of course, it'll be fine," she says, using finger quotes around "fine." "But you have every right to be stunning, Lisey. Oh Lord, the Romona Keveza dress. That was breathtaking. *Breathtaking*," she emphasizes. "Totally out of style now but something like that—but not so outdated. That's what we need."

What *we* need. Yeah. That's my mom. Bringing up the wedding dress that I never wore because my fiancé up and died. What fresh hell have I signed up for?

The only positive so far is that no one is recording this conversation. I approach the stiffly upholstered love seat where my mother has landed and settle into the armchair beside her.

"Mac made us an appointment for a place in Indianapolis on Friday. It specializes in vintage pieces, so something—unique." Talking dresses should soften her up for my harder-hitting questions.

"You know 'vintage' is just another word for 'used,' baby," she says with a sour expression.

"It's what I want. Thought it'd go with the theme. And since we don't have Nonna's gown, this is a good secondary option."

"A good third option is Hazel. I'll have Patty reach out to her people. Give them a heads-up," she says, taking out her phone and texting her assistant, her long nails clacking against the screen. "I'm only say-ing—keep her in mind. I swear she has magical elves living in her sew-ing room." She laughs, and I get one of those glimpses into what other people see in my mom—a vivacious, charming woman.

"I'll keep her and her elves in mind," I promise.

"What are these?" she asks, spreading out the photographs stacked on the table next to the coffee cups. She picks up the two headshots of my grandmother and holds them up, squinting like she needs her glasses. "Oh my God! That's mamma!"

"Yeah, they're from the archives at the military base. I've never seen them before."

"This one"—she holds up the image with the fuzzy back-ground—"was her first headshot. Used it to audition for good ole Uncle Archie back before I was born. Where did you get it again?"

"One of the volunteers at the base. They have a little museum, and I guess these were saved in storage. Here, you'd know this—isn't this Nonna's handwriting?" I flip over a few of the construction pictures, and Mom makes a low *mmmm* sound.

"Undeniably hers."

My energy spikes.

"What about that guy? Do you recognize him?" I ask, handing her the picture of Antonio Trombello.

She reviews it quickly and then drops it. "Nope." She picks up the headshot again and stares at it. "I can't believe she ever looked this young. Such a beauty."

With the topic broached and her nostalgia wheels lubricated, I clear my throat and move to the edge of my seat, ready to jump in to all the other questions I've been waiting to ask until we could meet face-to-face.

"Did you get any of my messages last week?"

"Huh?" She doesn't look up.

"My messages, about Mac and Grandpa's grave? I left you a lot of messages. Patty and Connie must've told you. I asked Jimmy to call you and Chris. I had Farrah call you—a lot. Does this ring a bell?"

"Phone calls that ring a bell, very clever wording, dear." She dodges the question, pretending to be preoccupied with something on her phone and then in her purse.

"I'm not trying to be clever. I was hoping to talk to you about the situation now—before I lose you to Mac." She puts her phone down and focuses on me intently, her petal-soft hand stroking my cheek and then my hair. She smells of Crème de la Mer moisturizer, and I feel like a little girl under her touch. She holds my chin as she speaks.

"Sweetheart, you aren't losing me to Mac. You'll always be my little girl." It's the same speech she used to give every time she fell for a new man, and it's a piece of her worst acting. But she has to know that at thirty-seven years old, I'm not worried about losing my mommy to a new lover. She's intentionally manipulating the situation.

"Mom, Mac wants to dig up Grandpa's grave." She doesn't flinch, which means this isn't new information to her. He's already introduced this wild idea, and when my mom is entranced by a man, there's little that can be done to snap her out of it. But I have to try.

"I can't stop you legally, but professionally I have to tell you—it doesn't read well. I've told Mac and I'll tell you—I can't be a part of this project if you sign off on this." I try to keep a firm line, which isn't easy with my mom. I can hold out on a deal, or a tabloid, or a lawsuit, but Gracelyn Branson has powers over me akin to dark magic.

"You're making a big ole fuss over this, Lisey. Nobody's digging up your grandpa."

"Wait, what? That's great news."

"Yes. Now, will you stop freaking out and let Mac do his job?"

"I wasn't exactly 'freaking out.' And I still have questions . . ." Like why Grandpa isn't listed among the casualties for the Battle of the

Bulge, and the dates for the purchase of the headstone, as well as the wealthy Highwards of Philadelphia, and Father Antonio Trombello.

"We can have a nice chat later, but right now I'm bushed. I was up at three in the morning to get to the airport in time for my flight. I need a nap."

I sit stunned, staring at my mother typing on her phone again.

"Can you answer one thing, Mom? Just one. Is Mac gonna let it go? That whole storyline with the grave?"

"I already told you. No one's going to touch your grandpa's grave. I promise." She shrugs. "I'm sorry, honey. I thought I told Patty to text you about it last week. I was slammed. Press junket for *Finding Mrs. Franklin* was intense. You know how Toro and Brit Parsons hate one another. After they loved one another, I guess that is." What follows is a detailed retelling of the conflict between the lead and director on the set of the historical where my mom played the elderly version of Ben Franklin's wife. Mom acts like she's above such feuds because of her age and pedigree, but she actually revels in it all.

Her phone dings loudly, and she stops to check the notification. The font size on her screen is three times mine, so I can read it from where I'm sitting—a reminder to take her medication. She scrambles around in her bag, mumbling about how she'd been searched at security but was sure it was an attempt to snag a trophy or two for her rabid internet fans.

"It was only a little thing of mace on my key chain. Can you believe it? They made me take it off and throw it away even after I explained how important it is for a woman to defend herself these days. I swear I hate flying commercial. It's always a fiasco."

"So, not a rabid fan, then?" I ask with heavy sarcasm, still frustrated that I'll have to wait—again—for answers to my questions. We need to have this conversation about our family. Especially since anyone who is curious enough to turn on their TV will soon know everything. Is it wrong that I, as Vivian Snow and Tom Highward's granddaughter, would like to know first?

"What makes you say that? You don't think I have rabid fans, do you?" She takes half of the contents of her purse out, places the items on the cushion beside her, and then keeps digging, looking for her pillbox. "'Cause I do, Elise. I do. One man last month sent me a doll dressed like Suzie from that little stint I did on *The Cubical*, and it had real hair. Real *human* hair." She drags another load out of her handbag and shouts, "Ah-ha!" as she pulls out a complicated plastic container that looks way too big to be misplaced.

She gets up to search my minibar for "something to wash it down with" and asks me to reload the contents of her purse as she makes her way to the bathroom.

I assumed it would make a difference to talk with her in person without assistants or boyfriends around. But I always forget it's not any particular person keeping my mom from understanding me—it's just who she is. She's never understood me, and as my therapist said, the one I went to briefly after Dean died, I need to get used to the idea that she never will.

"Mourn it," my therapist used to say. But I already had so much to mourn at the time that I wasn't ready to mourn a mother who was still alive. So I didn't. And I'm not sure I'm ready even now. Though at this moment, as I'm refilling her purse with stacks of paper and empty notebooks and a confusing number of pens, I'm wondering why it seems so impossible. Other daughters have mothers who understand them. Nonna loved my mom, cared for her, sacrificed for her. So why didn't my mom learn how to be that kind of parent to her own children?

As I toss the last two items into her bag, I see an ancient-looking scrapbook and a flat rectangular box that looks like a COVID home test. I stop. The scrapbook looks familiar. I remember it sitting next to Nonna's bedside. When I stayed with her, we'd look through the pages at the postcard-sized drawings and watercolors of various exotic locales, some she'd visited and some she'd still dreamed of seeing with her own eyes.

I haven't seen this book in decades. I'm tempted to take a look inside, but then the other item pulls my attention. I place the scrapbook in my mom's bag and inspect the small box, checking to make sure she's still in the bathroom. It's not a COVID test after all. I hold up the box and read the packaging again and again, confused.

Why does my mom have a mail-in DNA paternity test in her bag? And why is the box empty?

I shove the test under the scrapbook and toss the bag with everything in it into the corner of the couch as my mom leaves the bathroom, holding the now-empty pill tray.

"Those antibiotic pills are so large they make me gag every time. Patty broke them up into smaller pieces, but they still stick to my throat, I swear. Don't get old, darling. It's not as glamorous as we make it look." She puts the tray back in her purse and then shoves the pictures into the envelope, drapes her coat over her arm, and puts her sunglasses on, even though we're inside.

"Mom, those pictures . . ."

"Oh, sorry, I thought they were for me."

"I was hoping to keep them until we had our talk."

"I totally understand." She reaches into her bag, takes out the envelope, and shakes it in front of me. "I'll send Mac's assistant down later, though. Get these scanned so we both have a copy. Sound good?"

I start to say no but find the word hard to say. Nothing works with my mom—nothing. She puts the envelope on the coffee table.

"Well, think on it. I'm heading up to my room. If you need me, I'm in suite 435," she says. That's Mac's room. I know it from the one-on-one interviews he films in the sitting area there. I shouldn't be surprised—of course she'll stay with him. But as she walks out of the room with as much flair as her entrance, I start to devise a crisis-management plan because it looks like I'm the only one watching out for this family, and I don't see that changing anytime soon.

CHAPTER 20

Vivian

Monday, June 7, 1943
Chapel in the Meadow

The lane is dimly lit by light streaming through the branches and thick leafy cover. If I didn't know we were still on camp property, I'd think we'd entered a fairy world. But the deep rumble of the military vehicle and the death clutch I have on the bar on the side of the jeep keeps me from straying too far from reality.

West, through Nineveh. Talbot's poetic confession came back to me the moment we headed out this morning for the chapel site. These woods border the small town of Nineveh and must be the cover used by soldiers brave enough, or foolish enough, to go AWOL for a night. It's also rumored that POWs use the forest as well. It's no wonder they make it in and out undetected—the land is rough and raw, untouched for the most part by humans. Besides the small POW cemetery, the only other vestiges of modern man are the tire tracks in the tall grass and the group gathered in the clearing ahead.

Finally, I'll stand on the actual spot where the chapel will be built. The river runs on one side of the path, with pussy willows hugging its edges like crinolines peeking from the bottom of a skirt. White-and-gray waterbirds dot the reeds, and a few ducks lounge in the water, unfazed by the influx of humanity. On the other side of the path, a broad meadow stretches along the barbed wire of the western side of the POW compound.

The foundation is scheduled to be fully dug and poured in two weeks. At that point, the exterior fence will be completed to make the structure officially part of the camp. If all goes as planned, the full project should reach completion before the weather turns cold. It'll be a small building, wholly made of cement and surplus building materials from the camp, but the planned artwork and masonry are breathtaking. Selfishly, I'm eager to get past the labor portion of the project so I can watch the artists as they work on the murals that'll line the walls of the chapel.

Private Craig angles the jeep up the slight slope to the cluster of prisoners and guards. The men use what look like old-fashioned scythes to clear the grass. A figure dressed in religious vestments stands in a northern corner of the clearing, sprinkling what I assume is holy water with a brass aspergillum.

Beside him, Trombello stands with his head bowed and hands clasped, likely the only one of the men to know by memory the Latin prayers of dedication. I don't recognize the other man, except I can tell from his dress that he's an archbishop. He's wearing a robe with red lining and a loose black cassock, red sash at his waist, and red zucchetto on the crown of his head.

Perhaps that's the reasoning behind the vestments, like the uniforms worn by the army men and by the POWs, the ceremonial clothing of the clergy lets others know to whom their loyalties belong.

Which is why things got so mixed up with Trombello. He's a sort of a plant, I think. A man of God living undercover as a man of war or perhaps the other way around. Which uniform did he choose, and which was forced upon him?

"Miss Santini, you're needed in the clearing." A guard helps me out of the jeep. My heels, borrowed from Mary, sink into the soft soil.

The prisoners have gathered around the archbishop. A knee-high wooden cross sticks out from the ground like a marker for a grave that hasn't been dug yet. Even with the June sun high in the sky, I shiver at the thought.

I haven't seen Trombello since dinner in the POW mess hall, and I've been preoccupied with confusion about Tom and excitement about Archie's business card I carry with me, but I still think of Trombello often. Mostly, I feel foolish for the strange reaction I had to the man who turned out to be a priest. Not that he'd given any indication he'd ever considered me anything other than an interpreter.

And though he's handsome, I'm not touched by his physical appearance. I'm not drawn to him like I'm drawn to Tom, who can make my insides boil in a delicious heat with one touch. I'm drawn to the *idea* of Antonio Trombello, that there are men in this world who are both strong and kind.

Perhaps it's the godly part of him I crave. Perhaps my silly, romantic mind had taken over, and instead of seeing Trombello's kindness and patience for what it was—a sign of his religion and life's work—I took it to mean something more.

But it means nothing.

It has to mean nothing.

"Buongiorno, signorina!" Trombello greets me with a wave that makes my heart flutter.

It has to mean nothing, I remind myself, clutching the leather satchel with the plans and paperwork across my body.

"Buongiorno, Padre," I respond, muted and without meeting his lively eyes. He speaks to me in Italian, so fast I almost can't keep up.

"Come and meet the Most Reverend Amleto Cicognani. He's finished his dedicatory prayer and would like to meet you."

"Meet me? Are you sure?" I smooth my skirt and tidy my hair, wondering how the archbishop knows I exist.

"Yes—all the men have had your name on their lips. *Parlano bene di lei.*"

"Singing my praises? Without an interpreter?"

"I did my best," he says in English before returning to Italian. "And it seems Lieutenant Colonel Gammell spoke of you as well."

I blush at the thought. As a secretary, I'm supposed to fade into the background, my work invisible, though necessary. But Trombello seems to be saying I'm important. Me. Vivian Santini. The praise doesn't match the level of my work on the project.

"I'm only doing my assignment."

"False modesty is a form of dishonesty," he says, wagging his finger. The mention of deceit stirs up my guilty conscience.

My heels catch on a clump of prairie grass, and I stumble.

"Attenta, signorina!" Trombello grasps my elbow, and I steady myself immediately.

"I'm sorry. My shoes aren't meant for trekking, I guess," I joke to calm my nerves and to distract myself from his hand on my arm.

"I suppose, no." He grips a little tighter but without any aggression, putting pressure on the bruise from when Tom yanked me into the car on Friday. I flinch.

"I hurt you?" he asks, stopping to inspect my arm. His eyes land on the bruise. I tried to cover it with makeup before work, but with the heat and the sweat from my skin and Trombello's hand, it's rubbed off.

"No, no. That's from another day. I . . . I . . ." I stammer through an explanation, every lie since my talk with Father Theodore sending up flares of guilt. What would it help to tell Trombello about my difficulties with Tom? This is what I don't understand—how do I tell the truth when it could hurt Tom's reputation or my own?

"I fell, and . . . and someone caught me. I'm lucky. It could've been worse." When I hear the false story, it sounds true, even to me.

But Trombello raises one eyebrow.

"You should see a doctor," he says, sounding overprotective.

"It's just a bruise. I'm all right."

He squints and takes a survey of the rest of my exposed skin, but not in a lecherous way. More like he's looking for any further damage.

"Promette?" *Promise?*

"Prometto."

He sighs deeply and mutters something I don't understand and then releases my arm.

"Follow me." He navigates a path through the crowd of men. Some I've seen before during the planning phase of the chapel; some I recognize from my dinner in the mess hall, but the rest are new faces. They say hello to Trombello, calling him *Padre*, and then offer shy greetings to me, and a cautious *bella* here and there, eliciting a harsh glare from my guide. I pick up the smell of unwashed men and hold my breath to hide my reaction. But overall, the prisoners are courteous, parting for me like the Red Sea in Exodus.

In front of Archbishop Cicognani, Trombello kneels.

"Vostra Eccellenza, I show to you—Miss Santini."

"Your Excellency," I say with a curtsy, taking his offered hand and kissing his ring, hoping I'm behaving in accordance with proper protocol.

"You're doing a good work here, Miss Santini."

"Thank you, Your Excellency." I fight off the urge to curtsy or bow every time I speak. He asks of my family and my parish; he speaks of Father Theodore as though he knows him well. I wonder if they reveal to one another what their parishioners confess. Is that covered by the seal of confession? I'd ask Trombello, but only a guilty person asks such questions.

"Miss Santini, I've heard you are a singer; is that right?" I want to deny it, but I can't fib to this man of God.

"I am, Your Excellency."

"Would you lead us in a closing hymn?"

"We have no hymnals," I protest.

"It doesn't matter much if they join you," the archbishop reassures me. "Your voice raised in praise is sufficient, my child."

He points to the open space in front of him, and I step forward, unable to refuse his holy request. The crowd goes still and silent, the birds chittering in the trees my only musical introduction.

I'm used to a big band playing me in and a microphone to project my voice. And usually, it's young American soldiers in the audience, not our sworn enemies. But at this moment, in this meadow that is now considered hallowed ground, and in front of the altar of our shared religion, I sing to them as brothers in faith and children of a shared God.

A clutch of birds takes flight on my first note. I haven't warmed up or practiced, so my voice catches in a few spots as I struggle to remember the verses of the Latin hymn I've sung in the Holy Trinity choir.

At first I sing alone, but soon Trombello joins in with a rich baritone, making me jump at first and then smile with gratitude. He knows the words better than I do, and with his bravery on display, the rest of the workers add their voices when we reach the chorus, timidly at first and then with increasing gusto, until the meadow reverberates with the song of praise as though we're singing in a grand cathedral.

We conclude our song, the echo of our raised voices still vibrating as Archbishop Cicognani says a few more words. He keeps it brief, those in the crowd growing restless knowing they have plenty of work ahead. Trombello walks with the archbishop as he departs with an armed pair of guards, leaving behind the cross where the altar will be and a symbolic stone placed where the foundation will be dug in the newly hallowed ground.

I retrieve my bag with the plans.

"You have a beautiful voice," Gondi says in Italian as he reviews the drawings. "We heard you are a *prima donna*, and it looks to be true."

I think of the business card in my waistband and shrug.

"Well, not exactly but maybe one day."

"One day, when?" he asks. "You won't find 'one day' here with ruffians like us," he says, gesturing to the men in blue prison uniforms, "or that American *cretino* at the mess hall. Your boyfriend?"

My spine stiffens at the mention of Tom.

"He's not my boyfriend."

"Not yet," Gondi says, pointing his finger up like he's made a discovery. "But let's say bread for bread and wine for wine. He's *un donnaiolo*."

A womanizer. I know the term is a dirty one. And though things with Tom are in a very rocky place, he's always seemed deeply interested in me, only me. And I guess Pearl . . . perhaps . . .

I scoff, the purity of the religious moment gone.

"You don't understand. It's very complex, me working here. He was only being—what's the word? Oh. Protective."

Cresci, sweaty and out of breath, joins the conversation. "Who? That American *stronzo*? Don't let him make you a fool."

"I don't plan on it," I mutter, tucking a curl behind my ear. I ready my pencil to take notes on the progress on the site using cement blocks and a piece of wood for a makeshift desk.

"It's him you need protection from, not us," Cresci continues. "We're your countrymen. Your blood comes from our home."

I slap my hand against the wooden surface but withhold my instinctive response. My father could be right—I shouldn't be here. Even the prisoners think I'm one of them. What happens if Lieutenant Colonel Gammell starts to question my allegiances?

"Don't you two have work to do?" Trombello asks, walking up the slight hill from the road, his sleeves rolled up and collar unbuttoned now that the archbishop's departed. A tuft of dark hair peeks out through the V at his collarbone.

"Yes, Father," Gondi says, eyes cast downward.

"Sorry, Father," Cresci says, grabbing the wheelbarrow next to the table. "Speak some sense to the girl," he adds quietly to Trombello, as though I won't hear it.

"Worry about your own grass, Vincenzo. Yes?" Cresci nods and heads off to literally tend to his own grass.

"They really respect you."

"They used to call me Father to make fun, but over time it changed, I think." He unrolls the chapel's plans on the table, his forearm brushing my hand as it crosses me. He stoops and places two large rocks on each end of the rectangle, and I notice the fresh dirt under his neatly trimmed nails. It reminds me of Aria and then of my mother.

When I was a child, my mother showed me how to dig a hole in the tilled garden soil deep enough to provide protection for the vulnerable seeds. I remember her delicate hands on mine, a thin film of soil the only thing between us. Those are the good memories, the ones I know Aria relives when she loses herself in the garden. I'm more interested in forgetting that version of my mother. Remembering her fondly brings me no comfort, not when I know she'll never be my loving teacher or protector again.

But when I see Trombello's hands, the dirt under his nails, it brings up repressed longing for a caring, consistent guide. And leaves me wondering what his hand would feel like over mine.

No. I shake the involuntary and completely inappropriate question away, forcing myself to return to the conversation at hand.

"What changed?" I ask. He doesn't seem to notice I'm blushing.

"I don't know. I'd like to say God softened their hearts after the battle at Sidi Barrani. The British army was *massiccio*. We knew nothing of war. General Bergonzoli said we'd understand how to fight when guns fired at us, but we didn't. Some of us ran toward the explosions; some ran away, and some stood still. On that first day, we saw so much death, so much."

He has a far-off look in his eyes as he stares at the pencil drawing of the chapel. I stand still, slowing my breathing to keep from distracting his recollection.

"I volunteered to be a soldier in '40. I thought myself a coward for staying behind to hide in a church when all the men I'd grown up with had been conscripted. When my friends and *commilitoni* crossed to the other world in my arms, I wondered if I'd made the right decision. But war needs God more than peace does. And I believe more service happens here than from the pulpit."

He looks out at the small group who volunteered their time to build this chapel. They've sacrificed paid work at local farms in order to create this sacred place and a piece of the home they miss so dearly.

"You chose to enlist?" I ask, finding the confession provocative and potentially frightening. "Are you loyal? To Mussolini?"

"I'm loyal to no man but God," he says as he looks to the sky. He lowers his voice and moves to my side, his arm hair tickling my skin. A line of perspiration races down the side of my neck. "The church has found Mussolini to be godless, and when I left, people were growing tired of fascism. Not all the soldiers here agree, but many do. From time to time, they have great arguments over politics as though they can change anything while inside these walls."

He tinkers with a camera, clicks the lens into place, and cocks a small lever.

"What of you?"

"Me?" I ask.

"Yes. Where do your loyalties lie?"

"My country," I reply automatically. "I'm loyal to my country."

"Just your country? Not your family, your *amore*, your church, or your God?"

"All of them, I guess."

"But which first, do you think? Who would you go to battle for if they did not all agree?"

Who would I go to battle for?

It's a challenging question. If all I hold dearest were in conflict—who or which would I choose? Would I abandon my father to please my country? Would I give up my religion to please a man I loved? Would I sacrifice my life before betraying my country? I'm too young to know these answers. Then again, I'm surrounded by younger men forced to make these choices every day.

He picks up the camera and takes a picture of the field and workers, and then another of the newly placed cross where the altar will soon stand.

"Not simple to say, eh?"

I shake my head, the uncomfortable weight of shame settling on my shoulders. My head bows.

"*Ehi*, pull up your eyes." He taps under my chin. "Don't be like a wilting flower. You'll know."

I'm about to open my mouth to say, "I'm not sure I will," when he lifts the camera again and takes a picture of me. I blink, surprised, and smile at his childlike antics. He takes another photograph.

"Trombello, *fermati*," I say, telling him to stop, laughing a little but also embarrassed my face will turn up in photographs of the building site.

"Excuse me. Miss Santini?" Private Craig interrupts our tête-à-tête and photography session. He's leaving, and I'm supposed to accompany him.

"You'll make sure these plans get back to me tonight?" I ask Trombello in English now that the soldier is listening. He's put down the camera and taken on a more officious and collected air.

"Yes, miss," the soldier replies as though I'd spoken to him, but Trombello nods, and I know he's understood my English instructions.

"Well then. Best of luck to you all," I say in English.

"Grazie. Ci vediamo presto," Trombello responds. *We will see each other soon.*

"Yes. Soon."

As I leave the meadow, I linger on Trombello's last words. I'll see him again soon, and that brings me peace. I'd like to say it's because of our shared religion or our shared heritage, but it's not. I just plain like him—the way his mind works and how words sound coming from his mouth. And I like who I want to be when he's beside me. I might not know all the answers to all his thought-provoking questions, but I do know this—I'm not ready to say *arrivederci* to him just yet.

CHAPTER 21

Elise

Present Day
Big Red's Place

"Two egg whites. From real eggs, not from a carton, please. And a side salad with as many tomatoes as you can give me. No dressing." The waitress takes my mom's menu. It shakes in her hand. She's serving *the* Gracelyn Branson. What an exciting day. Calloo! Callay!

I frown. Poor girl.

Nancy, the owner, has kindly kept my family connection under wraps. I've been using her diner as my office a few days a week for the past month.

My mom is in full makeup and wearing a designer blouse and a pair of high-waisted khaki-colored silk pants. Her hair is curled and sprayed. I try to see her through the eyes of her fans to understand how, even when she's borderline rude and as condescending as she was with that food order, little sixteen-year-old Kaylee doesn't mind.

"And you?" Kaylee asks me as an afterthought.

Kaylee must not remember that I already ordered and ate, so I follow up with a "no thank you" instead of correcting her. She doesn't move for a moment, smiling brashly while staring at my mom.

"Kaylee. Kitchen," Nancy shouts from her perch at the cash register. The trance is broken, at least for the time being, and Kaylee slips away to the back of the restaurant.

Mom and I don't acknowledge Kaylee's behavior because it's a part of pretty much any public outing with her. She arranges her discarded outer layers of clothing and settles into the vinyl seat.

"No work today?" Mom asks.

"Lots of work today," I say, gesturing to the evidence. Paperwork covers half the table, and my laptop sits open in front of me.

"Oh, sorry. Not that work." She flips her hand at the stacks of paper dismissively. "I mean, filming. Your day off?" The fact that my mom thinks of this documentary as my day job rather than as a favor I'm doing for her with great sacrifice to my real career is frustrating but not surprising.

"Not today. Remember? I drove in with the crew, but I'm not filming. Tomorrow, we shoot the Pre-Cana with Father Patrick, and then Friday—dress shopping in Indianapolis."

"Ah, yes. Father Patrick. 'The Hot Priest.' I've heard a lot about this fella." She giggles.

"Ew, Mom." My mother's gnat-like attention span with men has always bothered me, but this assessment grosses me out. "The Hot Priest" sounds like something you'd hear on a porn set.

"What? I think it can only help the film. How else do we fill a four-part series with your grandmother's early life? Most of the good stuff's been told before, so we have to, you know, lean into some of the smaller bits to bring flavor. Like when you simmer all the tasty pieces left over in the pot after cooking a roast to make the sauce." She dated a French chef for the first six months of the COVID pandemic, so now we get food analogies.

I take the opportunity to change the subject and ask her about the DNA test and all the other questions piling up.

"So . . . Mom." I lower my voice and close my computer. The diner is empty, so we have some privacy. "Remember how you said we could talk later—about Grandpa?"

Kaylee approaches with the worst timing ever. She delivers my mom's meal and asks if she needs anything else. Which, of course, Gracelyn Branson does. After two more trips to the kitchen for the right kind of sweetener and the answer to a question about the kind of salt used on the eggs, Kaylee disappears through the silver double doors after another reminder from Nancy.

"These are processed; I'm sure of it," my mom says before taking a bite. They look like any old egg whites to me, but I don't argue.

"As I was saying—can we talk now? About Grandpa?"

"Elise, I'm eating," she rebukes. As she takes another bite, she mumbles about how I've always been a touch nosy.

"I'm nosy?" I say steadily, used to hearing this narrative whenever I bring up something she doesn't want to talk about. "You're letting Mac make a movie about this shit."

She swallows and takes a sip of her iced tea before responding.

"Language!" she scolds as though I'm three and just said the *F* word in front of her industry friends.

She makes these discussions difficult on purpose—so I'll stop asking the hard questions. And, you know what? It works. It's easier to let Gracelyn Branson have what she wants. But this time, I'm not letting go.

"Mom. You can't keep putting all this off. You said Mac was giving up on the 'Grandpa' storyline, but I saw what was in your bag."

"Elise Toffee Branson." She uses my full name, trying to pull the Mom card on me. "How dare you go through my things? I wasn't supposed to show you that book till we were on camera."

"Show me on camera? What the hell does that mean?" I start to push for other answers but then pull back. She's trying to distract me. "No. Not the scrapbook. The other thing. The box . . ."

"Lisey!" She slams her fork onto the laminate tabletop. "Let it go for now, won't you?"

Normally that'd be it. I'd change the subject or excuse myself from the drama. Then I'd dodge her calls for a few days until we both cooled off. But that's not an option in this scenario. If I turn my back on my concerns, it could mean real damage to my grandmother's legacy or my mother's reputation. Damn it—it could even risk my own credibility.

"No, Mom. I'm not going to 'let it go.' And," I continue, "it's very controlling of Mac to tell you what we can talk about. I'm your daughter."

"A good director knows how to keep the emotions fresh for a scene. We'll have a false reaction if we talk about it now. I can't mess with the artistic integrity of the shoot," she explains haughtily.

"I don't expect a script. But I don't want to be surprised by something outrageous like that whole grave-digging thing . . . ," I explain calmly, knowing it's nearly impossible to change my mother's mind when she's trying to please a man.

"I told you—that grave thing is not happening." She's getting heated, and I know what that means. If I don't placate her, she'll storm out in a grand exit even with no cameras trained on her.

"This is real life, and that's what Mac specializes in—real life," she says, determined.

I roll my eyes. What I've seen Mac doing the last few weeks is nothing like "real life," but then again—what the hell does my mom even know about ordinary life anymore?

"I swear to God, Mom, if you blindside me, I don't care what my contract says, I'll be outta here so fast . . ."

That's all it takes to set it off—the theatrical exit. She throws her napkin on the table and stands to put on her coat.

"So help me if you embarrass me on this project . . ."

Our statements overlap, and Nancy is doing a good bit of acting herself, pretending not to listen. We're no longer discreet.

The bell on the door rings, and we both stop midstatement.

Standing in the doorway is Father Patrick because, of course it is. Damn it.

He waves and points to our booth so Nancy knows where he's headed. My mom looks over her shoulder and then at me.

"Is that him?" she mouths, eyebrows raised, argument forgotten momentarily. I don't have the emotional energy to respond. Instead, I greet the approaching clergyman.

"Father Patrick," I say, embarrassed at the scene he walked into but also grateful for the distraction. Mom strips off her coat, slides back into the booth, and puts her official persona on, smooth as her silk pants.

"Hey! Back in the office, I see," Father Patrick says, referencing the clutter on the table. He's seen me in here a few times already. His occasional visits aren't my reason for working at Big Red's Place, but I do like knowing I might happen to run into a friendly face here.

"Yeah, turns out you gotta work to make money. Go figure," I kid, and he laughs at my bad joke.

My mom clears her throat and rubs her lips together like she taught me to do when you don't have lipstick handy but need a fresh look. *I see what you're doing, Mom.*

"Oh, sorry. This is my mother—Gracelyn Branson, movie star extraordinaire. Mom, this is Father Patrick, priest extraordinaire. Father, Mom. Mom, Father."

"So honored to meet you." Father Patrick seems to find the word-play entertaining. He shakes my mom's outstretched hand, and she bats her eyes.

"Thank you. You're too kind."

"Not at all. I feel like I already know you a little. Elise is an extraor-dinary young woman."

"That she is," Mom says with a proud though forced glance in my direction. I return her insincere look with a closed-lip smile. She opens another packet of low-calorie sweetener and mixes it into her tea.

"Won't you join us for a spell? We'll be heading out as soon as Mac finishes his shot list for the day, which won't be long. I'd love to get to know you better." She sips her drink and wrinkles her nose like she's added too much lemon.

"Gosh, I normally would, but I'm actually grabbing dinner for Mrs. Lee. She's laid out with a broken arm. I thought some soup might help brighten her spirits."

"Got your order, Father," Kaylee says, standing behind the counter with a brown paper bag. I swear my mom tries to check out his ass as he retrieves the order.

"Isn't that the sweetest thing?" she says to both of us, but I'm the only one to see her wink and wiggle her eyebrows.

"Pre-Cana? Tomorrow?" he asks, riffling through bills in his wallet.

"Put that money away; we got it," Mom orders him even though she doesn't carry cash, never has. Usually, she has an assistant or someone nearby who keeps enough cash on hand for these moments. But Mom came without her assistants this time, so I guess that leaves the role of assistant to me.

"Add it to our bill," I reaffirm Mom's offer to Kaylee and then address Father Patrick's question. "Yeah, Pre-Cana tomorrow. Just you, me, and the entire film crew."

"And Hunter is Zooming in?" Mom asks. She's watching me, assessing me, seeing if she can stir up a little intrigue. I won't fall into her trap that easily.

"Yup, Hunter too," I say with a touch too much gusto.

Saying Hunter's name brings up inconsistent emotions. I can't wait to see his face, even through Zoom. We made up almost instantly after our disagreement, and we've spoken every day since. I want him close. Damn it—I need him close.

But I'm also nervous to have Hunter in the same room with Father Patrick, even virtually. It's nothing truly, this closeness we have. But will Hunter sense it? Will it make him jealous? Will it scare him away?

"That'll be nice. I know he misses you terribly," my mom says with extra emphasis.

"I miss him too." This is all a test—I can feel it. And it's even more uncomfortable being tested in front of Father Patrick.

I discreetly adjust the ring on my left hand.

"He's coming this weekend, right?" she asks, and then watches Father Patrick like she thinks he might be jealous.

"He is," I say simply, refusing to feed the beast.

"Won't that be nice? You'll have to make up for lost time. Take a trip to Louisville? I heard it's not that far away. Little pre-honeymoon honeymoon?"

"Maybe." Then, to spare us all, I gesture at Father Patrick. "Don't let us keep you. I'm sure Mrs. Lee likes her soup warm."

"Ha ha. Yes. Absolutely." He lifts the bag and backs away, a strange far-off expression on his face. "Thanks again for your charity. I'll make sure to pass on your well-wishes," he adds, sounding very priestly.

My mother says a majestic farewell and then looks at me with wide eyes once the door dings at his exit.

"That man is in love with you." She makes the statement like it's the most incredible news she's heard in her life.

"He's a priest, Mom. And I'm engaged!" I start packing up. There's no use trying to work here anymore, and hopefully the shoot will be over soon. I'm going to insist on driving myself from here on out.

"I know, which is what makes it even more fantastic. You two are so hot for each other, I need to take a cold shower to get my temperature down."

"Mother!" I'm not laughing. I'm furious. "Stop. Father Patrick is a good man. This kind of talk could ruin his reputation."

"And your engagement to Hunter, but look at whom you're jumping to defend first." My mom thinks she's incredibly insightful about relationships because she's had so many. No one has the energy to correct her.

"I'm going to pay and head to the car."

"To the car? Why?"

"Aren't we done at five?" I check my watch. It's five minutes to five.

"Oh no, dear. We're here till sundown. Reshoots. This job comes with long hours; you know how it is." She sounds like such a martyr.

Damn it.

"All right, then. I'm going for a walk." I put my bag over my shoulder, feeling an intense need to get out of my mom's orbit. I pass Nancy my credit card and hand her a one-hundred-dollar-bill tip with a giant, "Thank you." Mom joins me at the door, but Conrad intercepts her when we hit the sidewalk.

I call out as they walk away, "Please, *someone* remember to text me when you're finished."

I turn in the opposite direction of the shoot, taking deep, cleansing breaths in the cool evening air. The sun is low in the sky but hasn't set. Blossoming trees line the street. Main Cross Street has been shut down to traffic for filming, and I rush away before the next take. One more week of this chaos and then in three months—a quick wedding and reception—and boom, the film is a wrap. Hunter and I will be husband and wife, and I'll never have to worry about this Father Patrick situation again.

A pang in my chest hits as that understanding sets in. I'll never see him again. I know that's a good thing; I barely know the man, and he's a religious leader for goodness' sake. But it doesn't feel like a good thing, or the right thing.

I shake my head and pick up my pace. Mac shouts directions behind me as I approach Walnut Street. In front of me are Holy Trinity, the rows of ranch-style houses, the baseball field, and the cemetery. I turn to the right, putting Holy Trinity and Father Patrick behind me where they belong.

CHAPTER 22

Vivian

Thursday, June 10, 1943
Camp Atterbury

I lean against the bus stop sign, scraping at the dried mud on the bottoms of my shoes. It's the third time this week I've visited the construction site, and I'm not sure Mary will ever get these shoes back in wearable shape. Thankfully, our schedules haven't lined up for a few weeks, which means she doesn't know how badly I've ruined them. It also means I've been having to take the bus.

Though the crew only has permission to work part-time on the chapel, it's moving along quickly. They've dug the foundation, cleared the meadow, and built half the fence. Next, they'll pour the concrete foundation, but they have to wait until Lieutenant Colonel Gammell approves the concrete mix and a new load is delivered. Until then, the men collect cement bricks left over from the construction of the camp's sleeping quarters and will spend their three allotted days each week breaking the old concrete into a fine gravel to mix with the aggregate.

Before the war, I never would've thought twice about construction planning and supplies. But I now go to sleep thinking about where to acquire sand and the proper equipment for crushing blocks.

"I think it's time for new shoes." I look up to find Tom standing a few feet away. The two girls at the stop who've been chatting about ration recipes and soldiers they have crushes on go silent. They immediately focus on Tom. I'm sure they'll soon add him to their list of crushes. I'm less impressed. It's been almost a week, and the bruises he left on my elbow still haven't faded away.

"I think the time for new shoes was last Friday if I remember correctly." I dislodge another bit of debris from my heel, avoiding his eyes.

"I know," he says, regret in his voice. "I was hoping to get these sooner, but . . ."

He holds out an off-white box with red lettering on it reading *Styl-EEZ*. The blonde behind me, pretending not to listen, lets out a gulp. I stare at the offering, wishing I had X-ray vision.

"Here. Open it." He passes me the box. The contents rattle inside.

"Is this a joke? Will I lift the lid and find a garter snake in here?" I ask, eyebrow raised. "Because I'm not scared of snakes like other girls."

"It seems to me there are lots of things you're not scared of." Tom chuckles, appearing to find my caution entertaining. "It's not a snake. I promise. Just open it."

I lift the lid, and inside, under a piece of tissue paper, I find a pair of medium-heel shoes, black leather, a shaped bow at the toes and a silver buckle on each side. Unexpected tears fill my eyes, and I swallow a few times, trying to make them go away. I must look like a fool to cry over shoes.

"Judy told me your size. I hope they fit." Even with the pretty girls watching, Tom stays completely focused on me and my reaction.

"They're perfect." I finally get a few words out, but they hurt as I say them. "I can't take them, though. They . . . they're too much."

The blonde gulps again, and I want to shoot her a glare, but it'll have to wait.

"Too much? They're only a few bucks. Besides, it'd be such a hassle to send them back. My sister ordered them from Marshall Field's in Chicago; silly thing thought it was down the road. The post would be too slow, so she asked a driver to bring them down."

"You went through all that trouble?"

"It's only fair. I'm causing plenty of problems in your life; don't you think?" he asks, his charm turned to full blast.

"You certainly have a knack." I place the cover back on the shoebox and hold it out.

"Are they the wrong size?"

"I'll take them! I think they're my size," one of the girls chimes in.

"They're the right size. I just don't feel right accepting them. It's not proper," I say, hoping the girl will take a hint.

"It's not improper. Not when I'm the reason behind your tragic shoe loss." He gently pushes them back toward me.

"Tom," I say plaintively, finding it harder and harder to fight his charm. I'm sure he knows my resistance is fading. He runs a hand through his dusty blond hair and gives me a mischievous grin.

"There's a pretty simple way to make this even, you know."

"No. I don't know."

He steps close enough that I can smell his hair pomade and whispers, "Let me take you out to dinner Saturday."

The same furnace he ignited in me in the back seat of the Chrysler sparks again—his scent, his heat, his clear blue eyes, and the regulation haircut that still somehow looks like it belongs in a fashion magazine. To top it off, he's making the effort to set things right. His kindness adds fuel to the embers and sends up enough smoke to cloud what is proper and not proper.

"I can't," I finally force out.

"Damn it, Snow. Why the hell not?" His eyes narrow. "Do you have a fella already? Where's he stationed? Has he proposed? What, he couldn't get you a proper ring?"

His volume increases. I put the shoebox under my arm and place a hand on his chest to calm him.

"Shhhh. No. No one else. Just my job, like I said, at the USO. And . . ."

"And?" he asks, leaning into my touch, his heart racing under my palm.

"And," I whisper softly, "I don't want to contribute to your delinquency. If you get caught AWOL one more time, Talbot said you'd face some sort of discipline."

"Talbot, that dirty rascal," he says in a way that sounds friendly rather than angry. "Don't you worry yourself about that filthy gossip. I'm doin' fine, about to get promoted. Matter of fact, I'm off probation on Saturday, so it's all on the up and up. As long as I'm back for duty at twenty-two hundred hours. So, if you'd do me the honor—I mean, pay your debt—I'd love to take you out on a proper date."

I've never been on a proper date before, but Tom doesn't need to know that. He probably thinks I'm a woman of the world because of how I behave onstage. It's possible he thinks he can take advantage of me once we're alone—these shoes and his compliments payment for my services.

I'm about to reject him again when he takes my gloved hand and stares at it like it's made of gold.

"Please don't say no again. I can't take it. Pearl meant nothing to me if that's your worry. I was trying to get your attention because I think about you all the time. I can't stop. I've never had a woman plague me like you do. All I'm asking is for one shot. One."

One shot. I consider the risk—he could be a scoundrel, but that's a risk all girls face when dating. Or he could be head over heels for me in a way no man has ever been, the way papà used to be in love with mamma and would do foolish things to keep her happy and take care of her.

It's one date—what could it hurt, really?

"You'll have to meet my father," I say. Papà won't like it, but if I manage things carefully, he won't say no.

"I'd be honored."

"And no sneaking in or out. Just till ten. Like you promised."

"Scout's honor," he says with all the excitement of a Cub Scout. The bus rumbles up, the heavy exhaust announcing its arrival as audaciously as its squealing brakes.

"All right, then. Saturday evening at . . ."

"Eighteen hundred hours. Your address?"

I rip off a piece of the tissue paper from the shoebox, write my address down, and tuck it into his pocket. Without even a goodbye, I make it onto the bus as the doors are about to close and slip into the first empty spot. As the bus slowly accelerates, I let down the window and lean out and shout, "Thanks for the shoes."

He says something in reply, but I can't make it out.

I can't stop smiling as I sink into my seat. The two nosy girls who'd been eavesdropping at the bus stop take the empty bench across the aisle. Thankfully, I don't recognize them from the USO, so perhaps they're new to town like so many other girls these days.

"Hi, I'm Lilly," the blonde says, pointing to herself and then to her auburn-haired friend, "and this is Sue. We couldn't help but hear you talking to T. B. Highward. He's so dreamy. Are you his girl?"

"T. B. Highward?" I ask. "That's Tom Highward. And no—I'm not his—anything."

"He bought you shoes," Sue says, her voice squeaky like Minnie Mouse. No way she's older than seventeen.

"Yes. But he also ruined my shoes. So it was a fair trade."

"T. B. Highward *is* Tom Branson Highward. His dad owns half of Philly Steel. And T. B., sorry, Tom, is supposed to take over. When he gets back from the war and such," Lilly says as though she's reading from a history book.

Tom? The son of a wealthy steel magnate? No. Not possible.

"Dear," I say as condescendingly as possible, "rich men don't get drafted into the army. I'm not sure if you've noticed."

"They do enlist, though. To make their rich daddies angry," Sue chirps.

"I've never heard of joining the army as a great act of rebellion. Besides, how would you know this? You're close friends with the Highwards?"

"Nuh-uh," Lilly says, riffling through her purse and pulling out a hand-addressed envelope. "My mom cuts out Lolly and Hedda's columns every week and sends them to me. Never misses. He's T. B. Highward. I swear—he has to be."

She holds out the letter, but I wave it away. Tom isn't polished enough to be some rich man's son. That kind of money could've gotten him a cushy position in an office somewhere or even moved him through the ranks faster than he deserved.

Lilly shrugs and puts the envelope back in her bag. "I have a picture at home from the *Daily News*. His family threw this fancy party before he left, and there were photographers there, and a big article was written on it. It's a little hard to tell it's him in the picture, but I'd bet my grannie's dentures on it."

I cringe at the immature phrase and shake my head.

"No need for betting any such thing."

"So you believe us?" Sue asks, wide eyed and eager. This must seem like a real-life Cinderella moment from her sheltered, childlike perspective. The bus stops for the third time. It's my stop. I collect my things, including the fancy new shoes, and smile at the girls.

"In general, I believe nothing I hear and only half of what I see," I say, quoting some saying I've heard somewhere—maybe church or maybe a film I can't place. I feel quite dramatic as I turn on my muddy heels and leap down the stairs, leaving them with that enigmatic response.

They'll likely linger on it, and it'll become part of their T. B. Highward mythology. Tom, a rich fool who joined the army to prove something to his father? It sounds like the storyline for some comedy or an epic romance where the "playboy millionaire" learns life lessons while serving in the army. I guess it's possible. Nowadays everything seems possible—the good and the bad.

But there's one thing I know for sure: handsome rich men fall for small-town nobodies in movies, but in real life, they marry women with money and a pedigree that their families would approve of. T. B. Highward, whoever he may be, likely has a girl lined up at home for his heroic return from battle. And that girl could never be me.

My spirits darken as I wonder whether Tom could possibly be the same Highward written about in the newspapers. I turn down my street, wishing I had a way to hide the carton from Mrs. Brown, the busybody who lives on the corner. Unable to camouflage the bulky box, I walk as quickly as my tired feet allow.

I'll know soon enough who the real Tom Highward is, I guess. Saturday will solve the mystery. And though I know papà will be reluctant to let me go, I'm determined to be honest for once in my life.

Papà will meet Tom, and I'll be able to hold my head high the next time I go to confession. Perhaps God will see I'm trying. Life's more complicated than it's presented in church, and if anyone can understand that, it should be God since he made the world this way.

Balancing my belongings on my hip, I pull down the mailbox door and look for the damp washcloth Aria leaves me every night to clean the makeup off my face and dirt off my shoes before I see my father.

But today—it's empty.

My shoulders tense. Aria's never forgotten. Ever.

There's no sign of life up the gravel drive or behind the darkened front windows. The sun's setting, and the light on the front porch is off.

With trepidation, I make my way up the driveway, each crunching step bringing me closer to panic. I run up the stairs, the ringing in my ears reaching air-raid-siren levels. I won't know if it's a false alarm until I find my little sister.

I open the unlocked front door to the darkened living room and call out, "Aria?" and wait, hoping she'll rush in with an eager apology and a reassurance. But my greeting echoes in the seemingly lifeless house. I'm transported back to the day we couldn't find mamma, or the baby—the moment I learned life can irrevocably change forever. I close the door behind me, swallowed up in the darkness, and wonder if it's happening all over again.

CHAPTER 23

Elise

Present Day
Streets of Edinburgh

"Hey, you lost?" Father Patrick slows to drive next to me as I walk down West Perry Street. I've been walking around for half an hour and still haven't heard a word from my mom or Conrad or anyone else in the crew. I'm guessing (more like hoping) they're still filming and haven't forgotten me. The hotel is only three miles from downtown, and if I'd left right after my exit from the diner, I'd be in my swimsuit and hopping into the pool right about now.

"They're running over on the shoot, and I drove in with my mom today, so I'm killing time until whenever they finish. I'm thinking about walking back to the hotel." I squint down the road like I'm assessing the distance.

"I can give you a ride," he offers, leaning across the seat. "I dropped off Mrs. Lee's soup and have a few minutes."

"Yeah?" I ask, reaching out for the car-door handle, but then I stop short.

Is it a good idea to get in a car with Patrick given my discussion with my mom and the gossip that's festering about our friendship? Or a more difficult question—as an engaged woman, should I be alone in a car with a man I'm developing feelings for, even if he's a priest?

"You know what; on second thought, I'll walk it." I pat the car frame.

"To the hotel?"

"Yeah. I mapped it. It's not far."

He looks concerned. "It's a whole lot of cornfields and industrial complexes. Not exactly a walking path."

"I walk three miles in New York every day. Three miles in Edinburgh, Indiana, doesn't scare me."

"There are sidewalks in New York," he offers. "No one expects to come upon a woman in designer jeans and a blazer walking down Walnut. Some of these trucks are so big they might not notice if they crushed you."

I consider the options. I could let him drive me to the hotel and fight the guilt over how badly I want to say yes. I could let him bring me back to Main Cross Street, but then my mom would see me in his car. I could say no again—this time more forcefully. I think he'd listen if I really insisted.

But do I want him to listen? Not really.

"Fiiiine," I say, opening the car door and sliding into the passenger seat before I can mull over the decision any longer.

"I'm sorry?" he says, his apology sounding like a question. He moves a few file folders from the middle console to the back seat of the gray sedan. The upholstery is worn but clean, and the air in the car smells faintly of beef and barley soup.

"I meant—thank you," I say in a softer tone.

It's hard to be sincere with Patrick without feeling exposed, so I take out my phone and text Conrad and then my mom.

ELISE: I have a ride back to the room. No need to wait.

My phone rings within a second of the text going through. I answer, and my mom starts speaking without a hello.

"What do you mean you got a ride?" I can't tell if she's worried or mad.

"I got a ride back since things seem to be running late. Just giving you a heads-up."

"You staying by the mall?" Patrick asks in a whisper as he pauses at a four-way stop.

"Yeah, Haymark Garden Inn," I clarify.

"Perfect," he says, taking a left.

"Who is that?" Mom asks, and I cringe. Do I lie, or do I tell the truth?

"My Uber driver," I say with a guilty shrug toward Patrick.

"Mm-hmm. Sure it is," she says, her response loaded with suspicion and innuendo. Conrad says something in the background. She changes to a stage whisper. "Listen—take your time. We're stuck here for a while still. There's no shame in a harmless flirtation . . ."

I cut her off, not sure how much Patrick can hear.

"I better go, Mom."

"You're so your father's child," she says as though it's a massive insult, but I never take it that way.

"See you tonight," I say, preempting any further commentary with a decisive goodbye. "Love you."

"Love you, t—" she says, and hits the end button before finishing. I drop the phone into my bag and stow it in the back seat as we drive in silence for a moment.

"Mrs. Lee said thank you, by the way," Father Patrick fills in, not acknowledging the call, and I follow his lead, avoiding the topic of my meddling mother, assuming the dodge either means he heard nothing of the conversation, or he heard all of it.

"She should thank *you*. You're the one who did the footwork. Or is that your priestly humility?"

"It wouldn't be humility if I bragged about it," he says, making me laugh.

"Good point. I won't tempt you into pride."

"Yes. Get thee behind me!"

"I'm Satan now?" I ask after finishing the scripture reference in my head.

"No, no—not you! I was talking about pride. It's always been a challenge," he confesses like it's no big deal he's sharing his temptations and sins with me and not the other way around.

"You? Prideful?" I shake my head at the idea. "Spend one day doing my job and you'd see yourself more clearly. You just met my mom." Not talking about my mom lasted all of two minutes.

"Vanity and pride are not the same thing. Vanity is about what other people think of you; pride is about what you think of yourself," he says somberly, no longer playful.

"I bet you're too hard on yourself," I say, nibbling timidly on the edge of my manicured nail. I want to understand that secret something that changed "Patrick" into "Father Patrick."

"*Therefore I am content with weaknesses, insults, hardships, persecution, and calamities for the sake of Christ; for whenever I am weak then I am strong*. Second Corinthians, chapter twelve: verse ten," he quotes, which is a handy way to dodge a real conversation.

"I think I . . . *hate* that," I say as I digest the scripture, something about it hitting me the wrong way.

Father Patrick pulls into the hotel parking lot. I direct him to a spot closest to my room. He puts the car in park and turns to look at me.

"I don't know what to tell ya. It's from the Bible," he says, like that's the definitive word on the matter.

"I don't care if it's from the Bible or from Dr. Phil. I don't like it. I hate this idea religions glom onto that God gives out pain as some kind of prize to humans to teach us a lesson or make us grow. It's pretty messed up."

His forehead wrinkles at my vehement response.

"For me it's a relief—gives purpose to our earthly pains. How do I explain to a mom whose four-month-old was diagnosed with terminal leukemia that God is unwilling to heal her baby despite endless fasting and prayers? If I believe God loves us, then even the worst moments in our lives must be for some good." He speaks with an unintentional charisma, but it still doesn't sit right with me.

"You don't know how many times I heard that when Dean was sick. 'Everything happens for a reason.' But if I'm going to wrangle my brain into accepting the presence of God, I'd rather assume he doesn't get involved with human dramas. Because if he chooses to help Martha find her lost keys but not that baby with leukemia, then God's a jerk." I tap the dashboard passionately.

"God's reasons aren't necessarily our reasons." Father Patrick leans against the driver's-side door, his priest's collar more obvious at this angle. "If a toddler cries in his car seat, we don't let him out. It's about perspective."

"Perspective?" The term sounds so arrogant, like I'm narrow-minded or shortsighted and that's why I don't "get it." I unbuckle my seat belt and cross one leg under the other. "Do you know what it's like to lose someone?"

"I do," he says immediately, a touch defensive.

"Not like an aunt or your great-grandma but someone you really loved?"

I loved Nonna. It was painful when she died, and I knew I'd miss her, all the little things, the steadiness of her affection, the way she made pasta for my birthday and grew and dried her own garlic. But she was ninety-four.

With Dean, it wasn't only about losing what he'd been to me and his family and his fans; it was the vast and unwritten future snatched away from his deserving hands. That's the tragedy of losing someone young—all the "could've beens" buried along with your loved one in their satin-lined coffin.

"My fiancée. Magdalene." He says her name like it's holy, and I forget our debate. He picks at a loose stitch on the steering wheel, his eyes moist, voice thick. "I met her studying in the States, but we took that trip my senior year, the one I told you about—to France."

"I remember your saying something about the Louvre." Conrad interrupted his story—he was relieved; I was disappointed. I nibble on my nail again, eager to know more.

"It was right after that. I'd just met her parents. She was from a little town outside Toulouse. Beautiful."

"Magdalene or Toulouse?" I ask gently, seeing his emotions gathering like an infection under the skin by a healing wound.

"Both," he says with a wistful smile, looking up from the steering wheel. "Definitely both." He clears his throat, and his smile fades. He goes back to tugging at the little string sticking out from the faux leather upholstery.

"We had a few days until we were to fly home for graduation, and Magdalene suggested taking the train to Florence. But I wanted to drive. She didn't fight me on it. I remember she said, 'You have to go the slow way at least once in your life. Why not now?'" His voice breaks, but he keeps going; I hold still, not wanting to distract him from his reminiscence.

"We stopped after a few hours at Marseille for a late lunch, and then instead of heading east, we took a short trip into the mountains to the Cathedral Notre-Dame-des-Pommiers. It was a breathtaking drive, the commune nestled in this narrow gap between two long mountain ridges. I've no doubt heaven will look like the French countryside in spring."

He swallows loudly, and I can tell it's coming—the loss. I'm tempted to spare him the pain of telling it, from reliving whatever horrible moment hurt so badly he's been running from it ever since. But I also know that like with an infection, the only way to heal is to drain the wound.

"I didn't see it because of the hill. By the time I did, the truck was in our lane and only a few feet away. There was a tall wall of rock on Magdalene's side of the road, a low bank and a river on the opposite." He flinches as though he's reliving the impact in his memory.

"I chose the river, but it made little difference. There wasn't enough time. He hit us without braking. I had a few broken bones, but Magdalene . . ." He wipes at his eyes. I angle in, knowing what he's going to say and wanting to be there to catch all the fragments as they fall once he's said it. "When I tried to dodge the truck by driving toward the riverbank, I inadvertently put her directly in harm's way. They said she died on impact, but I swear I heard her last breath after the car came to a rest upside down in the shallows of the riverbed. Trapped in my seat, I held her hand until it grew cold and limp, praying God would change what I knew was unchangeable."

"And?" I ask, part of me hoping this is a story of a miracle. I'm leaning halfway across the seat, completely engaged.

"She died. Her parents buried her later that week, and I flew home alone."

"And became a priest?" I connect the dots, and he colors inside the lines.

"I had no interest in marrying anyone but Magdalene, and the only thing that brought me comfort was helping at my parish's shelter and community pantry. My parish priest, Father Francis, saw how the church had become a balm for my grief, and he suggested I consider the priesthood."

The thread he's been messing with snaps, and a bit of the stitching comes undone. He tosses the string and then rubs a spot on his knee.

"And you think God did that?" I ask. It's a real question, not accusatory or mocking.

"I do—or at least I want to."

"Because it gives meaning to something too terrible to understand?" I ask, knowing how tempting it is to cover a wound with placations. But those types of bandages never held up for me, always dissolving at the slightest provocation.

"No. More selfish. More—prideful," he says, taking us full circle to the start of the conversation. "It means I didn't kill my fiancée. It was God's will. And I can live with that."

I understand now that the screen between a priest and his parishioner during confession isn't only for the confessor. I hope he sees empathy, not judgment, when he looks at me. But he hasn't looked at me for a while, and if he keeps rubbing the spot on his knee, he'll damage it as badly as he did the steering wheel.

I cover his restless fingers, wrapping my own around them. He lifts his head and finally sees me. His priestly vestments now look like a hairshirt he's wearing to punish himself for the accidental death of his beloved fiancée.

I want to tell him that he's not responsible for Magdalene's death and that no loving God would kill a twenty-year-old woman to bring a man to his calling. But I don't because I know he's not ready to hear that. So I remind him of what I know is true.

"You're too hard on yourself," I say like I did earlier, but slowly this time and with added emphasis.

I squeeze his fingers, and he turns them up so they rest against mine. He's not watching my face anymore; he's watching our hands, my small, slender fingers running up his palm. He shakes his head without speaking and then grasps my wrist gradually like he's measuring it. It's a simple gesture, easily platonic. But as innocent as it seems, it doesn't feel like the touch of a friend. I run my middle finger over the smooth skin at the joint where I can feel his rapid pulse. He must feel my elevated pulse too.

"Agree to disagree," he says, withdrawing from our closeness and then readjusting in his seat so his hands rest on the wheel again. My fingers tingle, and it feels like we're running out of oxygen in the closed car. I think of a billion things I'd like to tell him but know I shouldn't—like how I worry I'll never love anyone like I loved Dean, or how sometimes I feel more connection with Patrick as my priest than I ever have with Hunter as my fiancé. So I say nothing other than a thank-you and a "see you again soon" as I slip out of the car, not waiting for a response.

I speed walk to the side door of the hotel and reach for my key card, eager to be alone in my room so I can think. But my pocket is empty. I pat my side for my computer bag and find it missing.

"You need this?" Patrick stands directly behind me, holding out my brown leather satchel.

"Oh gosh. Thank you," I say, reaching out to take it, our fingers brushing again. He doesn't let go of the bag immediately, keeping me close.

"I'm sorry I got a little intense back there. I don't tell that story often, and it's been a while," he says, staring down at me, seeming apprehensive.

"No—thank *you* for trusting me," I say sincerely. "I actually *completely* understand."

"I knew you would as soon you told me about Dean."

He shuffles closer, further closing the space between us. My mouth goes dry, and I wait for whatever he's going to say next, no idea what it might be. He takes a deep breath like he has a speech prepared but then lets it out, shaking his head again. He releases the bag and gives a simple wave before looking both ways and crossing the parking lot to his car.

I don't wait for him to leave. I rush inside and sprint up the stairs so fast it leaves me wheezing. Safe inside my hotel room, I toss my satchel onto the love seat and then fall onto the bed. My ears ring as I revisit the whole conversation.

I was wise to say no to his ride originally.

My phone buzzes. There's no way it's Patrick. Or is it?

Diving across the room, I retrieve the phone from my satchel and check my list of notifications. One is from my mom, inviting me to dinner with the crew in Greenwood. I have ten minutes to change. Three from work and one from Hunter and none from Patrick.

I read the one from Hunter, this time slower, and it drops a cold lump of dread into my midsection.

HUNTER: Hope you had a good day, baby. Can't wait to kiss my girl in four days!

I drop my phone on the newly made bed.

Shit.

Things are about to get really complicated.

CHAPTER 24

Vivian

Thursday, June 10, 1943
Santini Home

In the darkness, my question is answered immediately.

"Viviana! Vieni qui. Adesso." *Viviana! Come here. Now.*

Papà's inflection is harsh as he orders me to join him, and I flinch as though I've been hit.

Most evenings, I return home to a warmly lit house, the welcoming scent of dinner cooking, the sound of chatter, or sometimes music on the radio. But today the front room is empty, and I hear no sound other than the squeaking of papà's chair in the kitchen.

"Be right there, papà!" I call in Italian.

I shove the shoebox into the back of the closet and cover it with an umbrella and a stray scarf that I first run over my face and lips to remove any traces of makeup. With my hat hung and my purse in place, I check to make sure the business card is still hidden in my waistband. Then I smooth my hair and walk into the kitchen in my muddy shoes.

"No late shift tonight?" he asks with a sarcastic bite.

He knows. I don't know what exactly he's found out, but he's uncovered at least one of my lies.

"Not tonight, papà." I remove the green-and-white apron from its hook next to the icebox and tie it in a tidy bow around my waist. The chicken in the icebox should still be good, and we have tomatoes and basil from Aria's garden.

I take out the chicken. One breast remains, and if I hammer it thin and add lots of bread crumbs, it can serve all three of us. A loaf of bread from Marco, the chef at the POW mess hall, is in the breadbox, borderline stale, but it will make a nice bruschetta.

I know a confrontation is coming, but food calms papà. It's not just the food—it's seeing me working in the kitchen like mamma and his own mother, perhaps reminding him of another simpler time. Plus, I'd rather have my back to him when he's angry; then I don't have to see his anger, and he can't see my fear.

"Viviana, do you think me a fool?" he asks, sounding mournful rather than ferocious.

"No, papà," I say innocently, lining up the ingredients and washing my hands.

"You think I don't see you paid your mamma's bill? And the rent. And my doctor. And the grocer?" He hits the table, building up to a crescendo.

"I have a job now, papà. You know that."

"Being a secretary doesn't pay so well. I know this. I'm not the idiot my daughters take me for."

It's the job. He knows I don't work for Mr. Miller's company. Papà, notoriously suspicious of the phone, has been isolated for going on six months between his injury, surgery, and the lingering infection. But nothing stays a secret for long in a small town.

But does he know where the money is coming from? How could he? Unless . . .

"Where's Aria, papà?"

"She's watching Mrs. Brown's baby. The other one, the boy, broke his arm," he says like it's no consequence. I find the explanation comforting even if the news isn't exactly good.

"Timmy? Oh no."

"He'll be fine. Boys fall all the time at that age. Not so delicate as girls." He pauses, and I wonder if he's thinking of Tony and all the things he missed. "When Mrs. Brown came to fetch Aria, she and I spoke."

I use a small knife to cut the stem out of a tomato. The fresh and sweetly acidic aroma has a palliative effect that keeps my dread from rising to a point of crisis. I say nothing, knowing it's better to let my father continue without interrupting.

"She told me she saw you last Friday night arguing with a military man in front of her house. Thought about calling the police. She asked if I knew the man, and I had no answers for her."

My grip tightens around the knife. Tom. I knew someone would hear him, and of course it had to be Mrs. Brown—the street busybody. I grab another tomato and remove the stem, letting my father see me as calm and reserved and giving me some time to figure out what to say.

He continues talking, and I keep chopping.

"She said you sing and dance with men for money at the USO. Her father's mechanic plays a trumpet or some such thing and told her about you. At first, I thought she must be mistaken. But then I think of all the bills you pay. All your time away. And I wonder if it's true. So, I call Cummins engine company and ask for Mr. Irwin Miller. Ask if you are a good worker, and you know what he tells me?"

I dump the second tomato into the bowl and start peeling the paper-thin skin off three cloves of garlic, imagining my father shouting broken English into the receiver. My hands are shaking so badly now that I lose my grip.

"He says you don't work there. Haven't ever worked there." Another crack against the table and then a scrape of metal against linoleum tile.

"So, I ask again," he says, his voice strained, panting. "Do you think me a fool?" A clunk and a scrape followed by his thick, reddened hand on the counter beside me. "Because you make me look like one."

I put the knife down and step to the sink to get some space from my father. It's all happening too fast, and I haven't come up with a plan. I take out a large serrated knife and start slicing the bread.

"Like this bread," he says, yanking the loaf out of my grip and shaking it in front of my face as I clench all my muscles tightly and close my eyes to his aggression. "Where did you get it? Never before have I seen such bread in the house since your mamma grew sick. My daughters don't make such things. Last week—sweet rolls. Where do you get such things? Where do you go during your days?"

I don't answer, holding my breath when I smell the scent of alcohol as he speaks. My father isn't an angry drunk, but that's only because he's angry whether he's sober or sloshed. But when he indulges, he gets louder and forgets the pain in his leg, which makes him more mobile.

Usually, I'd calm him with platitudes or food or a funny story. But that won't work today. This is what I imagine Judgment Day must be like—being faced with all your sins and unable to deny them.

"Viviana—" he starts, eyes narrowed and his voice dripping anger. But it's a quiet anger this time. "Are you a *mantenuta*?"

I nearly laugh at his accusation despite my intense worries. *A kept woman?* He thinks I'm a mistress. Perhaps a prostitute who sleeps with men for money and favor. The Old World shows in him once again. He's unable to grasp that a woman can make a livable wage in a respectful manner, so he makes sense of it the only way he knows how.

"Oh, papà, no." Forced to face him now, I turn around, holding the knife across my chest like a sword. His face is red with rage and also from what looks to be a nearly empty bottle of Grappa Stravecchia I spot on the table. He must have been keeping it hidden somewhere in the house.

"Then what, Viviana?" He hits the bread on the counter with a heavy thunk. "What?" He hits it again. "What?" One final slam breaks the bread in half. My heart races. I know better than to cry. It'll just make him angrier.

"Sit, papà. I'll bring you wine and some bruschetta—"

"No playing your female games with me, *passerotta*," he says, calling me my pet name. He hasn't called me his sparrow since mamma left.

"You sit, and I will tell you everything," I say simply, and point to his chair while keeping the knife over my heart.

I don't know that I'd ever be brave enough to fight back if my father hit me. I've always convinced myself he'd never raise a hand to me or Aria, but when he gets this angry, I can't help but worry I'm wrong. Instinctively, I usually flinch or back away when he's lost to his rage. But I've been growing stronger as I've worked at Camp Atterbury and performing at the USO in front of so many strangers.

He must see something new in my demeanor because he returns to his seat and drops what's left of the loaf on the table in front of him. He's not resigned or friendly, but I can tell he's moving toward a gradual diminuendo. As he lowers himself into his seat, he stumbles a little. I reach out and steady him, and he lets me. I prop his bad leg back on the other chair and fluff the pillows underneath.

"No food. No wine. Only truth," he orders, gesturing to a chair on the other side of the table.

It's time to face judgment. I sit and straighten the off-white linen tablecloth before starting.

"I work at the army base," I say, deciding that if I must endure the pain of revelation, then it might as well be a full confession. "Camp Atterbury."

He shifts in his seat with a grumble.

"One of my friends told me about the position. I know how you feel about the internment camp, and I really didn't think I'd be placed there with my last name what it is, but . . ." I swallow, wishing I had a drink in front of me too. Papà's jaw tenses, and his lips turn white with the strain of holding his tongue. But I'll hear what he has to say eventually—there's no doubt about that.

"Do not tell me you work for the camps, Viviana. Do not tell me this."

I look at my hands. To lie about which side of the road I work on would be so easy. It would hurt no one. It would be a victimless crime. Father Theodore would understand. God would understand. I'm sure of it.

But I can't. Father Theodore says temptation is devious; it makes you think sin is not just permissible but that it's for the greater good. I won't fall into that trap.

"I'm a secretary in the main office of the prisoner of war internment camp, papà. It's a very good job, and they pay double what my salary would be anywhere else."

"You work in the same place that makes people hate us? This camp where they bring the worst of our kind who steal jobs for little pay? Do you want to be locked away like they did with the Japanese? Do you want this, Viviana?"

He speaks with his hands like he's directing his own symphony. I understand his position, and it's not completely unfounded. When the military base became a POW camp, people in Edinburgh and the surrounding towns were filled with fear and resistance. Even before that, it wasn't easy to be an American with an accent and a foreign last name. And though they haven't come for us yet, my father's fear is real and fed by life experience.

"You know I don't, papà. And I've been afraid, too, but don't you think if I'm working for the army, it might help keep us safe?"

"My daughter is spending time with prisoners. With Blackshirts? You sound as though you respect these men—these fascists."

"No, I don't respect fascism, papà. But there are rules that all the countries in the war follow, and Lieutenant Colonel Gammell says we must follow them exactly, or our men will be treated poorly in POW camps overseas. I do as I'm told. I follow orders." The complexities of the Geneva Conventions are not something I'm prepared to explain, not that I fully understand them myself.

"And you lie to me about it? You make Aria lie? It's no good, Viviana. No good at all."

He fills his glass and rips off a hunk of the bread, seeming to consider what I've said. He's softening ever so slightly. I continue as he chews.

"I know, papà." Tears of shame spill down my cheeks. "It was wrong. In confession last week, Father Theodore told me I must be honest with you even though . . . I've been afraid."

"Of what, *passerotta*? Of what?" he asks, with something akin to tenderness in the gruff question.

He clearly doesn't know how frightening he is to his children. Even if I told him, I don't think he could possibly understand.

"I was afraid you'd make me quit, and I want to work and help you take care of mamma and Aria. And I'm doing well in my position. I've already had a promotion."

"A promotion?" He chuckles cynically as he swallows a mouthful of grappa. "What? You type faster, now? What kind of promotion do they give women typists?" he asks skeptically, his old-fashioned ideals continuing to cloud his understanding of the present-day workforce that employs more women than ever.

"I'm an interpreter," I explain, filled with an unexpected pride. "And they have me assisting on the building of a chapel on the base for the Catholic prisoners. I work with some artisans, builders, a priest even. Oh," I add, seeing the doubt in his expression, "I . . . I met Archbishop Cicognani last week. He had me sing at the dedication of the site."

"A chapel?" he asks.

"Yes, papà. A chapel."

He shifts in his chair, intrigued at least for the moment, but then he turns dark again.

"And what do you call singing and dancing with men for money?" he asks, the accusation clear. It could seem like a blow, but I know better. He's accepted my first confession, along with the lies that accompanied them. He knows we can't live without my paycheck, and anything that has to do with the church, papà sees as blessed.

I can keep my job—for now at least. Relief brings me an extra surge of courage.

"It's the USO, papà. United Service Organizations. The government runs it. There are tons of rules and chaperones, and I get paid to sing, not to dance. The dancing I do as a volunteer. They call it a patriotic duty. Mrs. Portia from church, she's in charge. And Mrs. Tawny is a senior hostess. You can call her if you like—she'll tell you it's all on the up and up."

He raises one eyebrow, still suspicious.

"If that's true, then who was the man you were with late at night? The one in the uniform? Mrs. Brown said you were fighting."

I think back to that horrible night, and I can only imagine what it looked like from fifty yards away and through the lens of the town gossip. I've gotten this far on honesty, but I can't tell him everything, not about that night and not about Tom. But I will give him as much of the truth as I can.

"I was going to talk to you about that tonight. It wasn't a fight. Tom—"

"Tom? That's his name?"

"Yes, Tom Highward—he's a technician fifth grade at Camp Atterbury."

"You were alone with this man?"

"No, no, papà. I'd missed my bus and was walking home alone and . . ."

"Viviana!" he says, tapping his forehead, which I know means he thinks I'm brainless.

"Tom—and his friends—picked me up and drove me the rest of the way home."

"These friends. Men as well?"

"No!" I rush to correct the narrative, knowing how dangerous it sounds. "No. My friend from the USO, Pearl. Her brother drives her and a few other girls into Edinburgh every week. They were giving Tom a ride back to the base. I swear."

"This Tom—is he trying to court you? I told you—no army men. Not to be trusted. Doesn't even come meet your father and shake his hand. That's how it's done. I went to your grandfather and asked if I could take his lovely daughter to the church supper. He said yes. We went. Two months later, she was my wife."

"It was late, papà. And . . . and we aren't courting . . . or whatever you used to call it back then."

"He doesn't want to court you? You are beautiful and sing like a bird. He could be so lucky to spend time with you." His temper is rising again, but this time I find some humor in his words, and I'm touched by the rare compliment. He lifts his finger to the sky. "Ah. It's because you're Italian!"

"No, papà," I blurt. "He *wants* to take me out and to meet you. Tomorrow, in fact. I was about to tell you."

Papà tears off another piece of bread and then uses it to gesture as he talks.

"This man—is he Catholic?"

"I don't know, papà," I say, collecting the bread and the grappa bottle, attempting to act as though his passions, as he calls them, have passed. Which may or may not be the case—I'll know for certain in the next few minutes.

"He has a good family? A good home?" He continues to ask questions I don't know the answers to.

"I don't know, papà. It's our first date."

"You know nothing of this man. Stranger. Foolish girl." He shakes his head, but I'm not discouraged. I know papà wishes he could give his daughter to a man from Italia, but it's far safer to let me be seen with a GI. This works in my favor. "And this man—where will he take you? You go nowhere till this man shows his face to me."

"He is coming to meet you, papà. He wants to. You can ask him all the questions you like then." The last thing I want is for my father to question my date, but then again—it's Tom. Not only can he take a little ribbing—he kind of deserves it.

When papà reaches for his empty glass, I pour him a mixture of lemon and strawberry that Aria's made out of flavor packets and fruit from the garden.

"Have this, papà. It's good for you."

"What is this mess? Look at this," he complains without tasting it. But I'm so relieved, I don't care about his grievances now. I know we'll speak of all this again. It'll come up when he's frustrated or angry or worried about the future. But for now, my father has decided, unilaterally, that we no longer need to discuss the lies I've told. And I know why.

It's not because he approves of even half the things I'm doing outside our house—but he understands something I hadn't realized until now. If he pursues the conflict, it will ultimately uncover layers of his insecurity. It'll reveal the real reason I work outside the home—because he cannot provide for his family. And it will be a reminder of how his wife, the love of his life, has lost her mind, placing a heavy burden on us all.

We, his daughters, are his only shield from reality and from a society that doesn't care if he lives or dies. Fear fuels my father's anger and encourages my lies. We are not too different in that way, my father and I—he attacks perceived threats, while I dodge them with a smile, a story, and a laugh.

CHAPTER 25

Elise

Present Day
Holy Trinity Catholic Church

"My parents were divorced when I was three. My dad's been remarried three times, my mom four," Hunter says through the computer screen. The first two Pre-Cana sessions I did alone, but Father Patrick reminded me at our last session that he's required to speak with both the bride and groom for at least half the lessons. Hunter agreed to the Zoom meeting today, and the in-person meeting this weekend brings us up to the requirement. It's the last step before we're officially cleared for our wedding.

Hunter arrived early today. When I logged into Zoom, with my laptop positioned between us on Father Patrick's desk, he was sitting there waiting in his favorite Tom Ford suit, navy blue, with a slate-gray tie and engraved golden tie clip. He's hot, like David Beckham hot, smart, successful—now and then I wonder if he's an actor being paid to pretend to love me. Which would make sense with all the cameras and lighting equipment around.

He greeted me with a "Hello, hot stuff," and I blushed.

Patrick didn't flinch, which means he either has a great poker face or I was reading into things last night. When he walked into the office this evening, his hair parted neatly on one side and a sweater over his collared shirt, I felt it all again. I can hardly breathe when he's nearby, which makes "playing it cool" even more difficult.

"Thank you both for sharing about your family of origin. It's important to look at how your families process conflict and communication in order to build a new and evolved healthy marital relationship," Father Patrick reads from the binder in front of him and then flips to the next tab and clears his throat. "*Section four. Marital Intimacy and Sexual Purity.* I'll start our next topic by reading a scripture from First Thessalonians, chapter four: verses three to eight. *For this is the will of God, your sanctification: that you abstain from immorality; that each one of you know how to control his own body in holiness and honor, not in the passion of lust like heathen who do not know God . . . For God has not called us for uncleanness, but in holiness.* Any comments on this passage?"

The computer mic picks up Hunter's chuckle, and I'm sure my eyes are wide. I knew a little about the Pre-Cana from my time as an all-in Catholic, but I guess I didn't consider that Patrick would lead a discussion with me and Hunter about sex and purity. Especially not on camera. I address Mac directly rather than express my not-so-holy thoughts about the Bible verses we just heard.

"I'm not comfortable with this."

"Sorry, dear. What don't you feel comfortable with specifically?" he asks in his charming British accent, looking at me over his monitor.

"Talking about my sex life in front of a viewing audience," I clarify, bristling at his pushback. Mac doesn't respect my boundaries—must be why he gets along so well with my mother.

"I don't mind," Hunter chimes in through the screen, straightening his suit coat. "What's wrong, babe? Worried we'll make 'em jealous?" He's joking, and normally I'd laugh, but this isn't some cute banter between the two of us about our sexy love life. Father Patrick is the last man I want thinking about me having sex with my fiancé.

"It's a cheap gimmick—you know—'sex sells,' etc., etc. It's gross," I explain, twisting my face up like the idea of it makes me ill.

Father Patrick closes the book with his finger keeping his place. "It *is* a part of the curriculum, but if Elise is uncomfortable, then she shouldn't be forced into an embarrassing public conversation."

Mac rolls his eyes and sighs. "Fine. We'll take a break. You get through all the naughty bits, and we'll be back in ten, okay?"

"That works," I say, still dreading the conversation with Patrick and Hunter but hating it a touch less, knowing it won't be on camera. The room empties faster than if I'd yelled fire, and Patrick reopens the binder and clears his throat.

"Should I read the scripture again?"

"No," I blurt. "I think we got the picture."

"All right, then—what have you observed from the verses?" he asks, looking between Hunter and me. The Patrick I knew from last night is nowhere to be found. This formal young priest is a stranger in comparison.

"Uh, pretty much that we're terrible, terrible sinners," Hunter says, his eyes on me in that hungry way they get when we've been apart for too long. And I can't stop the little involuntary smirk I get when we talk about our sex life. Which is playful, innovative, intense, and dare I say—aerobic. I shake my head, trying to discourage flirty innuendos, but I'm sure my facial expression is sending mixed signals.

"What? Don't tell me you're all holy now. The only time you've mentioned God before is when you're screaming."

"Hunter!" I scold, trying not to laugh. "Stop. This is serious."

"I'm just saying—we don't need a sex ed lecture. We know how the parts work. We're grown-ups. You know?"

"I do, I do," Patrick says, biting his lip and bobbing his head up and down. "You know what? Since there's a time constraint, I'll just read what it says here." Father Patrick shifts in his chair and reads from the binder. "Do you live together?"

"No," Hunter and I say at the same time.

"All right. That's good." Father Patrick makes a note on a form next to the binder, then goes back to the printed instructions. "It's suggested that you refrain from living together until you've made your marriage covenant."

"That one's easy," Hunter says. "Don't even live in the same state right now. Is there a box to check for that?"

"Uh, no," Father Patrick answers, scanning the page with his pointer finger, serious. He summarizes the next point without looking at either Hunter or me. "It also is suggested you refrain from physical intimacy from now till the wedding."

"Once again, not in the same state," Hunter says, and then mouths "for now."

Father Patrick accepts his answer and doesn't ask me anything directly. His cheeks are flushed, and though Hunter likely thinks he's a sexually repressed religious ideologue, I can tell this isn't easy or comfortable for him.

"I know we're short on time, so I'll read the closing of this section. It's a good summary, and I'll copy the pages for you to look through on your own." He turns three pages and then points to a paragraph at the bottom of the last one.

My head pounds as he reads. *The Catholic Church teaches every act of sexual intercourse is planned by God to express love, commitment, and openness to life. It is a gift of total intimacy.*" He glances up at me and then back at the page, the brief eye contact sending a shock through my nervous system. I watch his mouth make the shape of each word as he closes his reading with, "*This, we believe, is only available in marriage.*"

Total intimacy.

The phrase sticks with me, and I consider my relationship with Hunter. We have physical intimacy, and we have some emotional intimacy, for sure. But *total* intimacy? The phrase loops through my mind, creating a hypnotic buzz that overrides anything Patrick is saying.

"And just to be clear—we do have that 'openness to life' part. We definitely want kids. Right, Lisey?"

I blink. I want kids. I've wanted them since before I said yes to Dean six years ago. It's why I pay the bill at the cryo center every month to keep my eggs safe so my biological clock wouldn't impact my decision to be a parent. But am I ready for them *now*? With Hunter?

"Yeah," I respond, catching up with the pace of the conversation. "Eventually."

"Don't say that in front of the priest, babe. You know how they feel about birth control," Hunter jokes. Father Patrick's face is flat without any traces of his usually active sense of humor.

"Children are a gift from the Lord," he mumbles, and writes something in his binder. "You can let Mac know we're ready to move on," Patrick adds, turning to the next section, and I slink down in my seat, sending out a quick text to Mac, trying not to think about babies or intimacy any longer.

Hunter looks at his watch and changes the subject before Father Patrick can give any further family planning advice.

"Oh, really quick before they get back in here. Not to rush you at all, but I have a call with Australia at seven, so I'll have to ditch out in a few. I know—bad timing, but it popped up today, and I can't miss."

Seven o'clock? I check the time on my phone. That's ten minutes from now.

Thirty minutes. That's how long he spared for this meeting. I've seen him make four-hour international conference calls during a merger. He's ditched out of all our previous Pre-Cana sessions and joked his way through this one. This whole stupid documentary was more his idea than mine, but somehow, it's ended up on my plate entirely, as though I don't have my own life and my *own* business to run.

"We'll fit in what we can," Father Patrick says as Mac and the crew file in, and I'm glad he replies because I know my irritation will be noticeable if I respond.

"Ready?" Mac asks, and with the clack of a clapper, we're rolling again, this time talking about safer topics like household budgeting and balancing family time with work. The subject matter is boring, and I can't imagine Mac finding much to work with, but I love seeing Patrick doing what he's most passionate about—helping others. He makes me feel safe to share my thoughts and emotions. He protected me when I didn't want to have an audience witness my most private secrets.

Total intimacy.

No. It's not something I have with Hunter. And despite what the church says, I don't think I'll suddenly find it when I'm married to him. But Patrick . . .

"Love you, babe. Call you later," Hunter says as he logs off.

"Love you too," I say back, following the age-old script for couples saying goodbye.

"Let's call that a day," Mac declares, and the small crew works to strike the equipment. Father Patrick stows the Pre-Cana binder in a drawer and snakes his way through the organized pandemonium. I slip my computer into my bag and follow him. He's leaning over to rearrange the hymnals in the rack on the back of the front pew.

"Hey, sorry about that," I say, using my thumb to point to the office door.

"What for?" he asks, sounding uninterested.

"That meeting. How awkward I made it. Hunter leaving early. All of it."

"Seemed pretty normal to me," he says, moving down the row to the next rack.

"That was normal?"

"It's always difficult to bring up sensitive topics. And grooms can be harder to engage in this kind of thing."

He clearly doesn't want to talk about the counseling session, the unease remaining from last night still lingering. I feel it, too, but if one of us doesn't step up and force an interaction, the tension will only get worse. I sit in the front pew and lean over the back of it on folded arms.

"I totally forgot to tell you about a new development with the 'my mom' stuff." I refrain from referencing the conversation in the car, hoping we can get back to normal. "I confronted her when she got into town, and you wouldn't believe what I found in her purse . . ."

I take a breath to tell him about the picture album and the DNA test, but he drops a hymnal into the rack on the opposite end of the pew and then moves to the next aisle, two rows away now.

"No thank you," he says, overlapping my explanation.

"What?"

"I'm not available to counsel with you right now," he says, not breaking his serious priest persona.

"What, do I have to sign up for office hours or something?" I look around for any cameras or hidden mics but see nothing obvious. "You know you're not on camera, right?"

He moves closer to my end of the pew; though he's still two rows away, he's close enough I can see his face more clearly. His lips are taut and white, his brows pinched together like he's concentrating. I move directly in front of him, the back of the pew the only thing between us. He steps back and sighs and then moves to the next row.

"What the hell is up with you?" I ask, his cool responses beginning to hurt my feelings.

"Nothing." The books make a rhythmic thump, thump, thump as he works. "I have work to do, that's all." He steps down the pew, and I don't follow him because I can't pretend to not comprehend. He needs space—from me. The balloon of warmth that fills me whenever we talk deflates. I respect him too much to try to change his mind.

"I understand," I respond, gathering my things. "Have a good evening, Father," I say, tripping on the braided edge of the runner protecting the wood-paneled main aisle.

"God be with you," he says, moving to the next row, the thump, thump, thump echoing off the vaulted ceilings. On the verge of tears, I rush down the front steps to where I parked my Ford Explorer, the twilight dimmed further by a cool mist that kisses my cheeks like it knows they'll soon be wet with my tears.

It's grief I feel—not the paralyzing heartbreak that comes with the death of a loved one but a uniquely tragic sorrow, the loss of something still alive and yet wholly unavailable.

Total Intimacy.

That phrase runs through my mind again as I rush into my car and slam the door, breaking down as soon as I'm alone and the mist has stopped its gentle caresses. Sure, I'll never have total intimacy with Hunter, but it's possible that's why I said yes to him three months ago. Because intimacy equals vulnerability, and vulnerability leaves me wide open for loss. That's where I messed up with Father Patrick—I believed it was safe to let him in, to be vulnerable, intimate. But I was wrong. And as a result, I risked my heart, and I'm sure he feels he's risked his soul.

I put the car into drive and pull away from the church on the hill, watching as it fades in the rearview mirror, the sound of tires over damp asphalt muting my troubled breathing. As much as it hurts to give up our friendship, he's right. We must walk away now—before we get in too deep and lose more than we ever bargained for.

CHAPTER 26

Vivian

Saturday, June 12, 1943
Santini Home

"Wear the red," Aria says, admiring the contraband lip color lined up on our shared dresser. Tom is due any moment.

"You should try it, Ari," I say, uncapping the tube and holding her delicate chin in place.

"No, no. Papà will be mad." She wiggles away from my attempted makeover, the fear in her eyes familiar and frustrating.

"We'll take it off right away. He'll never know."

"He'll know," she says, sitting on the bed, her legs crossed like a pretzel and wearing mamma's old brown gardening trousers.

"He won't," I say as I pin back a rogue curl that keeps falling onto my forehead.

"You don't know that, and I'm stuck here with him, so . . ." She shrugs and disappears inside papà's tattered old flannel. "I don't want to rock the boat."

"I'll be home at ten at the latest; I swear. Tom has to be back on base by then anyway. It's not forever."

"Not yet."

"Not yet?" I spin around and look at my baby sister sitting on our neatly made double bed, the faded brass frame mamma and papà brought from Italy when they immigrated. It's the bed we were both born in.

We used to sleep on a hard mattress papà found in an old, abandoned house on Vista Drive, but around my ninth birthday, mamma got it in her mind her girls should have a pretty bed with a white cast-iron frame and a soft-as-clouds feather mattress. So papà saved and saved till he could afford a mail-order one from the Sears catalog.

"Yeah, not yet but soon. I mean, you're gonna leave one day."

She picks at the scratch on the bar across the foot of the bed, part of the bronze finish dulled from the rub of bedding and my mother's restless feet in the night. I plop down next to Aria and pull her to my side.

"I'm only going out for a few hours. I promise. Nothing will change." I pet her hair and kiss the crown of her head, glad I'm not wearing any lip color yet.

"Things always change," she says into my shoulder like she's breaking bad news.

"Of course, but it's not always bad." I hold her out in front of me, her dark lashes framing eyes that look just like mamma's. "Think about the seasons. Your garden brings many harvests for our family. Sweet strawberries in the spring. Watermelon, tomatoes, and beans in the summer. Pumpkins, corn, and sunflowers in the fall."

"It's not the same," she says, touching her upside-down reflection in the bed frame.

Bronze, not white like the cute little frame papà ordered. When it was finally delivered, it was exactly what mamma wanted, ornate white iron posts and a soft-as-feathers mattress. But it was half the size she'd expected. To save money, papà had ordered the twin instead of the double, and he didn't seem to understand her gasp of surprise.

"Our little birds have a little nest," papà said as Aria and I squeezed our small bodies into the twin-sized bed. Mamma bounced Tony as he nursed. She smiled and said nothing about her secret disappointment, but I picked up on it. I'd seen that look on my mamma's face before, but my father never seemed to notice.

Aria and I only spent a week in the pretty white bed before mamma was put away. Papà traded beds with us, saying his was too big without mamma there.

"There're some changes we can't stop, Ari. You'll blossom soon enough, whether you like it or not." I push her hair back, wild and unbrushed from her afternoon outdoors. I see the walls of the prison our parents have created for Aria more clearly than I see the walls of my own, I'm sure, but I wish she'd pound on those barriers, test them occasionally.

"You be a flower, and I'll be a carrot. How about that?" Ari asks, giggling.

"With this hair, you sometimes look like the top of a carrot. Heavens!" I grab my horsehair brush and pull it through her tangled strands, finding two sticks, a blade of grass, and one unidentified bug that makes us both squeal.

By the time the doorbell buzzes, Aria is smiling again. She puts her hand on my cheek.

"Back at ten?" she asks like I'm her mother leaving for a glamorous night out.

"Back at ten." I kiss her cheek before putting on a quick coat of red lipstick, knowing papà won't say anything to cause a scene in front of Tom. I blot the color with a tissue, pin on my hat, then buckle the shoes Tom gave me, check my teeth for any stray smudges of lip color, and then pose for my sister.

"He's gonna fall in love with you," she says loud enough that Tom could possibly have heard.

"Aria!" I gasp, and toss a tissue across the room.

"What? Who *doesn't* fall in love with you?" She laughs and rolls off the side of the bed onto her feet. "Now, get out there before papà takes out his pistol."

"Oh, heavens. Don't even joke."

I blow Aria another kiss and rush out to the front room where papà stands, leaning on his cane, and Tom sits on the floral love seat. I know papà must be in immense pain standing upright, but I also know he's showing his strong presence to the young soldier, letting him know that Anthony Santini is not to be messed with.

"I've been with the Eighty-Third Infantry since August last year." Tom points to the black inverted triangle on his shoulder and then to the other patch with stripes and an embroidered *T*, signifying "technician fifth grade."

"È a Camp Atterbury da agosto, papà," I translate, surprising both men with my interruption. "Tecnico di quinto livello."

My father has no way of knowing what any of this means.

"What does this even mean? Technician? I don't care," he says in Italian, and makes a face like he's tasted something sour, which Tom misses as he rises and greets me with a small wave. He holds a bouquet of flowers and smells of a rich aftershave. After a quick search of his eyes and the color of his cheeks, I'm relieved to see he's sober.

Papà continues his line of questioning with me. "What matters more is what does he do when he doesn't have a rifle in his hands?"

"Tom, this is my father, Anthony Santini. Papà, Corporal Tom Highward," I say in English without acknowledging my father's question. I'm sure papà performed his own introduction while I wasn't in the room, but I can't rely on his version of hospitality in this situation.

"So nice to meet you officially, Mr. Santini." Tom extends his hand, which papà looks at with disdain for a moment before asking in broken English, "Where you from?"

"Papà, sii gentile." *Papà, be nice.*

"No, Viv, it's okay." Tom drops his hand and chuckles like he's entertained. I don't interrupt again, also curious after my conversation with Lilly and Sue the other day.

"From? Pittsburg, Pennsylvania."

My eyebrows rise; one detail matches the outrageous story Lilly told.

"East Coast?" Papà asks, keeping up well enough with the conversation.

"Yes, sir. East Coast."

"You job? Not this." He gestures to Tom's uniform, and I wonder if he understands.

"He wants to know what job you had before the army," I say in a low whisper, similar to how I translate in meetings with Gammell.

"Sa cosa sto dicendo. Lascia che quest'uomo parli," papà orders. *He knows what I'm saying. Let the man speak.*

"Scusa, papà," I say, my cheeks hot.

"I think I get the drift," Tom reassures me, and then hands me the bouquet of roses with baby's breath wedged between the large fragrant blossoms. "By the way, hi."

"Hi," I say, taking the flowers with a restrained smile. Papà stamps his cane to get Tom's attention.

"My apologies, sir. Yes. I have a job back home, but I'm also going to school. Law school." He speaks slowly, which makes it easier to continue listening as I take the flowers into the kitchen to put them in a vase.

"Law school? For policeman?" Papà asks, and I understand the confusion. I return to the front room and position myself between the two men in case I'm needed.

"Lawyer? Attorney?" Tom explains.

"Ah—*avvocato*?" Papà asks to confirm.

"Yes, papà. *Avvocato*."

"Ah-ha," he says, proud of himself for figuring it out on his own. "This is good job, no? Your father—is he also a—" He gestures at me to help.

"Lawyer?"

"Si. Lawyer."

Tom, hands behind his back now, shakes his head. "No, he's more of a . . . businessman."

"Business is good. And you—*Italiano*?" he asks like it's the last item to check off his wish list. I can see his sense of humor shining through, but I'm not sure Tom picks up on it.

"Italiano?"

Papà gives me the look, and I fill in again. "He wants to know if you're Italian."

"Ha. Sorry, no." He addresses papà. "My father's from Ohio? Does that help?"

"Eh?" Papà says, clearly having no idea what nationality this "Ohio" would fall under.

"It's fine. He was joking. He knows you're not Italian," I clarify to Tom, even though I know it was only partially in jest, and then turn to my father.

"Papà, Tom e io dobbiamo andare presto," I say, letting him know we need to leave soon. I've done my due diligence as a good daughter. Tom's been far more impressive than I'd expected, and it's better to cut our losses now and leave before something starts to unravel.

"Okay okay okay," he says in English but so rapidly it sounds like he made up a new word. "Home by ten," he says to Tom, pointing at him with his crooked left index finger.

"Yes, sir," he says like a good soldier. He turns to grab his hat off the love seat, and papà whispers to me in Italian.

"What is on your mouth? You look like a street walker."

In the haze of the interrogation and distracted by Tom, I forgot about the lipstick.

"Sorry, papà . . . I . . ."

"Excuse me, sir," Tom interjects, and papà turns away from the blazing red paint on my lips. "I almost forgot. My uncle sent this last month from Cuba. I thought you might like them."

Tom gives him a paper-covered box that papà hands over to me, leaning into his cane, which tells me he's tiring quickly. That's likely why he's not pushing back harder on my lipstick or interrogating Tom about his intentions. I open the hinged cover, revealing stacked rows of rolled cigars; the earthy smell fills my nose. It hits papà a moment later, and he grunts.

"Per me?" *For me?*

"Yes, papà," I say in English before transitioning into Italian. "I'll put them in the kitchen, but only one tonight. All right?"

"Yes, Viviana. Yes," he says irritably, but there's a youthful gleam in his eye I haven't seen in a while. "Thank you," he says to Tom with a grateful tip of his head. Then to me in Italian, "Be good. Be careful. Be back before ten."

"Arrivederci, papà," I say with a kiss to his forehead, and then call to my sister who timidly pops her head out from the hallway like she was there listening all along. She gives a shy wave to Tom, and he rewards her with one of his most memorable smiles.

"Help him to his chair, please, Ari."

She nods, biting her lip lightly.

"And there's a box of cigars on the table. He'll try to finagle you, but only one. Okay?"

"Okay," she says, bouncing on her bare feet before grabbing papà's arm and escorting him into the back of the house. I turn to Tom, who's now only inches from my side. He takes my elbow and guides me out the door.

"You're really sweet with him," Tom says once we're in the car he borrowed for our date.

"My father?" I laugh, wondering what he'd think if he could understand everything said tonight.

"Your sister, too, I guess. You're like the little mother of the house. It's sweet."

"You said that before. 'Sweet.'" I twist my mouth like I've tasted something sour.

"Does that bother you?" His eyebrow is raised in mock scandal. "I thought a girl like you would like to be called sweet."

"I'm not sure. There's such a thing as being too sweet, I guess."

"Hmm, I suppose." I'm leaning forward, considering the statement, when he reaches across my body, his arm grazing my breasts as he opens his glove compartment. He takes out a silver flask and unscrews the top with one hand. Taking a long swig, he offers it to me.

"No thank you." I push it away.

"That's what I thought. Sweet," he says, closing the cap and reaching for the glove compartment again.

Sweet. The way he says it hangs in the air like the heavy stench of a skunk's spray. Tom Highward—brave, successful, handsome, possibly rich, and most surprising of all—papà likes him. And he thinks I'm some brainless little doll who plays the roles expected of her. As if I don't have my own mind or make my own choices.

I snatch the flask from his hand and unlatch the cap.

Tom looks at me, stunned but entranced, like he's daring me to do something that'll surprise him.

I take a long drink, swallowing the burning liquid in one, two, three gulps. It's whiskey, and it's strong. I wipe the smudge of red lipstick off the rim and toss the damn-near empty flask into the glove compartment. I take out my compact and touch up my lipstick as a subtle buzz floods my body.

"That was—" Tom starts to say but stops like he can't find the right word.

"Sweet?" I finish, clicking my compact closed.

"No. Definitely not sweet," he says, chuckling. He revs the engine, sending a whirlwind in through the half-rolled windows. "Unexpected," he says, finishing his previous sentence, his lip curling up in a way that could only be rivaled by Rhett Butler himself. "That, my dear, was deliciously unexpected."

We shoot down Route 31, going faster than I've ever gone. I close my eyes and pretend I'm flying.

~

"I've been selected for Ranger training," Tom says, his head tilted against the headrest in the back seat of the Cadillac.

We have one hour left until Tom turns into a pumpkin, so after a decadent dinner and several cocktails at the Palms Café in Columbus, I said yes when Tom suggested we spend the last of his freedom parked by the river.

My head is heavy and spinning, and I think I'm drunk. It feels great sitting here beside Tom, listening to him talk about his dreams for the future. He hasn't said it straight out, and I'll never ask him, but he does indeed seem to have an unlimited supply of money.

His cavalier attitude toward finances is almost more intoxicating than the whiskey he keeps encouraging me to drink or the sweet words he whispers in my ear or the current that goes through my body every time we touch. What would it be like—a life without worrying where our next house payment would come from or how to pay mamma's hospital bill? What would I worry about if the burden of debt were taken off my mind?

"Ranger training?" I gasp, impressed and partially heartbroken. I remember overhearing Lieutenant Colonel Gammell say the training doesn't take place at Camp Atterbury. "But isn't that in Tennessee?" I shouldn't reveal this bit of information, but I relish the opportunity to seem important to Tom.

"Where'd you hear that? Lieutenant Colonel?"

"Uh . . . I think so?" My head spins as I try to remember the moment clearly. "But I could be wrong. He doesn't talk much about 'the other side of the road.'" That's what he calls the military base side of Camp Atterbury—*the other side of the road*. Which is the perfect way to describe it—like a reflection in a mirror, the same but opposite. Especially when it comes to who lives on each side.

"They haven't told us where we're going yet, but Tennessee is as good a place as any. Only thing I know for sure is—I'm on the list." He takes another gulp, and I wonder how he can seem so levelheaded after finishing half of the bottle.

"Golly," I say, my lower lip trembling. I could cry, though I'm not sure if it's the liquor or the idea of losing Tom just as we've finally connected. My tongue loosened by too much to drink, I told him everything about my life at dinner—my dreams of Hollywood, the pressures I face at home; I even told him about mamma and the day Tony died. I've never told anyone but Father Theodore the truth about that day or why my mamma doesn't live with us. But I trust Tom—and now he's leaving me.

"Oh, doll, no. Don't do that. You'll break my heart." He cups my face and runs his thumb over my bottom lip, around the edge at first and then presses it into the smooth, moist flesh where it meets my top lip. He stares at my mouth like a hypnotized creature. My breathing becomes rapid, and the rear window gathers a film of condensation like it's granting us an unspoken wish for privacy.

"You're so perfect," he says, using his thumb to trace along my cheekbone and down my neck to my collarbone above the neckline of my dress. His caress sends shivers through my whole body and spreads a warmth through my midsection and a strange and delicious tingle between my thighs.

"Mmm," I mutter reflexively, which is embarrassing but out of my control.

"You like that?" he asks, retracing the trail from my jaw to my collarbone, dipping lower this time, closer to the outline of my brassiere. And then again, this time his fingertips linger only centimeters from the swell of my breasts. I hold back another gasp, licking my lips and squirming in my seat. It feels good, so good, and shockingly—I want more.

But I can't want more. Even in my intoxicated state, I know this is a sin. Besides, Tom is leaving; he just said so.

His fingers reach my breasts and graze my nipples through the fabric of my dress as he leans in to place a hot, gentle kiss on my neck. The thrill his caress sends through my body brings me back to sanity. I put both my hands on his shoulders and push him away.

"Tom, no." I'm breathing so fast that I sound like I've been dancing the jitterbug at full speed. He pulls back but keeps his hand resting on my right breast like it's meant to be there.

"No?" he asks, eyebrows raised in confusion. "Why? You clearly like it."

I do like it. I'm ashamed of how much I enjoy the way he's exploring my body inch by inch, and I don't want him to stop. But I'm no idiot. Good girls, drunk or not, don't fool around in the back seat of a car on a first date. I might not be "sweet," but I'm also not loose.

"I can't, Tom. I'm sorry." I remove his hands from my body, hoping I'll think more clearly once the magic of his touch has worn off. He hits the seat between us and groans, which makes me jump and makes my heart race in a new way.

"You're killing me, baby." Without making contact, he runs his hand over my face, neck, abdomen, and legs, never touching my skin but close enough that his body heat leaves a trail of goose bumps behind. "How's a guy supposed to be around a girl like you and not fall madly in love? That's like sitting a starving man in front of a feast and telling him not to eat."

"Love?" I sit up, pressing my back against the side door, as far away from temptation as possible in the back seat of a Cadillac.

"Damn it, Viv. Yes." His eyes are glossy with drink. Or could it be with emotion? "Why do you think I go so crazy sometimes?"

I shrug, thinking back on how intensely he's pursued me, how upset he gets when I give any other man attention.

"Do you love me back?"

Love? I think about the word again. *Is this what love feels like?* I wonder. It's what it looks like in the movies. Desire, jealousy, passion, love. I've always considered my parents' story to be the epitome of true love—my father supporting and loving my mother through all her mental anguish and their terrible mutual losses. But what if that's not real love? What if that's only endurance?

Who am I kidding? None of this matters anyway.

"I can't love you, Tom," I say, knowing it's the only safe choice.

"That's a lie." He slides across the seat and presses his thigh against mine. "I can tell you love me. You're fighting it, but you do."

"Do you blame me?" I ask, looking up into his face, tears gathering in my eyes. It's easier to speak to him now, with the effect of the drinks at dinner and the flask and whatever's in that bottle. "You're leaving. You'll love some other girl in the next town, but I'll be stuck loving you forever if I let myself."

"I knew it. I knew you love me," he says triumphantly.

"That's not what I said. I said . . ."

"I don't care what you said. I care what I heard, and I heard that you love me." He takes my left hand and kisses the finger where I'll one day, if I'm lucky, wear a wedding ring. "And you'll keep loving me even when I'm in other towns or other countries, or even if I'm gone from this world. That means so much to a soldier, a beautiful, talented girl like you loving a guy all the way to the eternities."

"I can't, Tom. I can't love you. You'll break my heart—I know you will." Now I hear it, too, all mixed in with my denial. I do love him, even if I wish I didn't. And my heart will break when he leaves.

"What if I don't break your heart? What if I don't run off and find some other girl because you're my girl and why would I need anyone else?"

"You want me to wait for you?" Plenty of girls wait for their soldier to come home and start a life together. But it's a gamble that keeps most girls from saying yes without an engagement ring or a wedding.

"If you stay here waiting for me, I'll come home to find you married to some famous actor you met in Hollywood; I know I will." He chuckles at the fantastic prospect, but I can hear real anxiety behind it. "The only way I want you to wait for me is as my wife."

"Your wife?" I echo, the revelation making my head spin.

"Yes, doll. My wife. You wanna marry me?" he asks officially, holding up my left hand and tracing the empty spot he'd been kissing.

As soon as he says the words, I'm sober. Tom Highward wants to marry me. Me. A little Italian girl from rural Indiana whose mamma lost her mind and whose baby brother drowned, who could easily end up an old maid taking care of her daddy till her belly is round and hair gray, and who might lose her mind one day just like her mamma. Me. A small-time performer with nothing more than a stage name, a couple of hand-me-down dresses, and a useless business card from a talent scout.

I know I should ask him questions, find out if he's as rich as he's rumored to be, if his family will accept me, if he's chosen me in an act of rebellion. But I don't ask him a thing. Even if Tom is only half of what he appears to be—at least he loves me. And when we're married, I can move out, make choices outside of my father's control, have a partner to help shoulder my burdens.

I nod and smile sweetly and say, "Yes, I'll marry you."

Tom pulls me in for a kiss, my first ever. His embrace is softer than in my dreams. And when his tongue brushes past my lips and into my mouth, I greet it willingly, taking him in, grasping at his neck and shoulders, and twisting my hands up into his hair. And as his kisses go from my mouth to my neck to my breasts, I lean back and allow him to know parts of me I've saved just for him. Because I do love him. And I want him to know me—all of me. I am his, now, and he is mine. Forever.

CHAPTER 27

Elise

Present Day
Elise's Hotel Room

My phone buzzes on the bedside table. Then again. And again. I peek out from under the heavily starched hotel comforter and look at the glowing numbers on the clock.

5:30 p.m.

I headed upstairs for a nap after our morning trip to the vintage wedding boutique so I'd be awake enough to pick up Hunter from the private airport in Greenwood at eleven tonight. It's an hour-and-a-half drive each way, and I know he could hire a car, but Hunter is my partner, my future husband; I want to be there waiting for him when he gets off that plane.

The trip to the boutique was exhausting.

I know my mom would say I'm being paranoid, but I swear the crew made every effort to keep us apart when we weren't on camera. We drove in separate cars, both ways, and Mac placed a chair directly next to him where my mom sat for the majority of the shoot.

The women running the boutique were starstruck by my mother but extremely helpful. They pulled gown after gown out of storage and used fitting clips to show the potential in each one.

I had shown Cammi and Wanda a photo of my grandmother's dress, but my mother dismissed each gown they brought out. "You cannot wear long sleeves in June, Elise," she said repeatedly.

"We can make any alterations in-house. Including removing sleeves or adding embellishments," Cammi explained.

"No, thank you. We have our own seamstress," my mom, who can be as cold as she can be charming, snipped back.

"Vintage-inspired works too. Long transparent lace for the sleeves would give you the silhouette you're looking for, but with a tight, trendy bodice. Train or no train? Satin was very much the fabric of the day, but lace works too. Or we can go with something more modern," offered Wanda, the older of the two women, a pincushion on her wrist and pencil tucked into the expanse of her graying hair.

All the dresses were beautiful and had intricate details, buttons, embroidery, beading. But when I looked at my reflection wearing white, off-white, or even ivory, the bride staring back didn't look like me.

"Veil or no veil?" Cammi asked, holding a floor-length veil the same ivory as the dress.

"Veil. Must have a veil," my mom said from her seat on one of the green velvet couches in the fitting room. "But a simple one like the Pronovias veil that went with the Dean dress."

My mother is not an evil woman; she's not cruel, and usually I believe she's not calculating. But saying Dean's name in the fitting room of the bridal boutique was a step too far, and despite her intentions, I lost the slowly slipping grip I've kept on my grief during this whole process.

Warm, heavy tears dripped off my chin and onto the lace collar of the gown.

"The bride gets the final say in these things," Cammi said to my mother, which I found brave as Gracelyn Branson's superstar status usually mutes even the strongest personalities.

"I think the bride could use some privacy," Wanda said solemnly, seeing my tears, like a nurse asking visitors to leave a patient's room when visiting hours end.

It took some doing, but Wanda and Cammi cleared the room and helped me take off the dress, passing me tissue after tissue as I continued to cry the tears I'd bottled up for months, maybe years.

"I really do love Hunter," I said to Cammi as I sat on the elevated platform where I'd been showing off my dresses.

"I'm sure you do. This is very normal, I promise," she said, hanging the gown.

"Nothing about this is normal," I said, gesturing to the tripods and can lights.

"I guess that's not normal, but your tears are." She handed me another tissue. "Weddings are stressful, and throw in an opinionated parent or two, and something little girls dream of their whole lives becomes a big ole nightmare."

"I guess," I said, but what I thought was, *But it didn't feel like this with Dean.* My mom was still my mom back then, so what's the difference?

"The advice I give to every girl going through 'mamma drama' is— this is your wedding and your marriage. This is your story—you have to live with what you write. So don't let nobody take your pen away."

It was a deep moment from Cammi, who I doubt was more than a year or two out of high school, but it's what I needed to hear. I wiped my tears away and had Wanda call Lisa back in to redo my full face of makeup. Within an hour, I'd chosen a dress, and we took the ninety-minute drive back to Edinburgh in silence.

Buzz. Buzz. Buzz.

My phone explodes again on the bedside table.

"Ugh." I blindly grab for it, keeping my eyes closed for a minute longer.

I squint at the screen. It's full of notifications. Texts, social media tags, emails. I scroll through, searching for one that clearly explains whatever media disaster we've somehow stumbled into. Did one of my clients tweet a sexist comment? Forget to wear panties to a club? Have a total meltdown? Die?

Oh God, I hope not.

Whatever it is, I'm sure it's something we've seen before at Toffee Co. Usually I'm insulated from it, the news filtering through one of my associates or assistants. But clearly, I've been gone too long, and someone has dropped the ball. Which I can only partially blame on my team because I'm spending most of my days in a one-gas-station town, planning a wedding, worrying about dates on headstones, and accidentally stalking the local priest. Who am I?

I tap on a random notification. As the social media app opens, my phone rings. It's Marla, my VP. Damn. This must be big.

"Hey, Mar, what's up?" I ask, trying not to sound groggy, which is pretty much impossible.

"Are you okay?" she asks, her voice sounding as tired as mine.

"Uh, yeah. Long day but I'm fine. Why? What's going on?"

Dead air.

"You haven't heard?"

"Uh, no. I've been . . ." I try to think of a better excuse than napping. "On set. What should I have heard?" I put the phone on speaker, curiosity growing, going back to my list of notifications as Marla hems and haws. I've never heard Marla like this. She's a no-nonsense businesswoman who tells it like it is. Whatever the disaster, it must be huge, and it must affect our company directly.

"Marla, give it to me straight. What's the lowdown?"

"I don't know what happened. I thought Terry at ZTM was our inside guy."

"Marla. Stop. I can't be any help if I don't know what happened. You know what—hold on. I'll brief myself."

I tap on the blue-and-white Twitter logo with a shocking number of notifications in a red circle in the corner. The app pops open, and so does a grainy picture of two figures sitting in a car in an intimate conversation. Another photo of the figures standing outside a hotel, looking as though they're holding hands. I zoom in on it to get a better look.

It's me and Patrick.

My stomach drops, and I click on the link.

The headline pops up: ELISE BRANSON CAUGHT WITH PRIEST LOVER! I read the first few lines.

> Our sources say Elise Branson, former fiancée of deceased star Dean Graham, and currently engaged to business icon Hunter Garrot, showed she has more in common with her famous grandmother Vivian Snow than her smile when she was discovered outside a hotel in a compromising position with a local religious leader, Father Patrick Kelly. Mac Dorman's newest documentary on the early life of icon Vivian Snow reveals a similar love triangle in the actress's early life. Like grandmother like granddaughter, it seems . . .

"Shit," I say into the phone. "Shit. Shit. Shit. Shit."

Marla lets me have my moment of panic. It's a normal response; I've seen it countless times with my clients.

All the things that I roll my eyes at when other people say them pop into my mind. I want to tell off every single one of my contacts at ZTM. I want to sue everyone who picked up the story after the picture was leaked. I want to write a comment on every post to rebut the claims. I want to send out my own statement ASAP, correcting every assumption made in this stupid article.

But I know that's not how things work.

"Well, what do you think?" Marla asks eventually.

"I think we need to find out who the source is," I say, scanning through the rest of the article that's filled with claims not only about my "relationship" with Patrick but also my grandmother's relationship with an Italian prisoner in the POW camp in 1943.

The prisoner's name is familiar—Antonio Trombello.

Oh my God—the guy from the pictures and the one who bought Grandpa's burial plot. It's extremely specific information that could only come from someone working on this film.

"I agree. I'll reach out to Terry, but you know he's pretty tight-lipped about these things."

"I know, which usually is good for us . . . ," I say, recognizing the irony.

"Messaging strategy?" she asks, going through the crisis checklist.

"No statement. Not yet. So far, it looks like it's just trash mags that have anything. Retweets by a few Snow/Branson fans. I'd like to know the media impressions if Farrah could run that. And have Helen add some alerts for my name, Hunter's name, Father Patrick Kelly—you know what—just everyone named in that article. I don't want to be surprised again."

"Agreed," Marla says, typing as I speak. "Your mom? Hunter? Should I call them, or do you want to?"

Hunter. My fiancé whom I'm supposedly cheating on with a priest. Oh my God. Hunter, who this very minute is probably getting ready for his flight, who is supposed to spend the next four days here. Hunter, who has enough staff to keep on top of every single media hit mentioning his name.

"I'll call them. Please tell everyone to insulate Hunter and my mom from this as much as possible, okay?"

"Will do." Marla pauses, and it sounds like she's waiting for a statement or some words of wisdom from me.

"Just so you know, it's not true," I say, wanting to maintain my dignity with my staff. I may have feelings for Father Patrick, and I may have let things go a little too far, but he's not my lover in any way, shape, or form.

"Okay," she says with doubt in her voice.

I get it—it's not our job to determine if our client is telling the truth. It's our job to create a positive image and then help protect that image in moments of crisis. But I wish I knew she believed me. I need someone to believe me.

"Reach out when you know more. I'll go talk to my mom and have someone get in touch with Father Patrick to give him a heads-up and fill him in on some best practices."

"Perfect plan. I'll brief the team while you call Hunter." When I hear her say his name, intense anxiety crushes my lungs. I feel like I can't take in even the smallest amount of oxygen. "Good luck," she adds, the phrase turning up at the end like it might be a question.

I hang up without a goodbye, still struggling to breathe. What can I possibly say to him?

Hey, Hunter. I know the papers say I'm screwing the local priest, but don't worry—that picture isn't what it looks like.

What if he doesn't believe me?

Well, whether he'll believe me or not, I have to call him. I rush to the bathroom, nauseated. I fill a plastic cup with water from the tap and chug it, fill it again and chug until I can take a breath. Then I pace around the room, each buzz from my device amping up my anxiety until I can't take it anymore. I dive onto the bed, pick up the phone, and call Hunter's number.

Oh God, I might vomit.

I roll onto my back, my waterlogged stomach bloated and near bursting.

The call goes straight to voice mail. I hang up and call again with the same result. One more time. Nothing. I switch to text.

ELISE: Can't wait to see you soon! Call me as soon as you get this. Crazy tabloid shit going on today. I'll tell you everything when you call.

Send.
The blue message turns green; then a red warning appears next to it.

This message is undeliverable.

I send another test text, just to make sure. Same result.

He's either turned off his phone, which is likely if his is blowing up as much as mine, or . . . he's blocked me. No. That's too childish. Hunter isn't the kind of man to hear a rumor about his girlfriend and block her without a discussion. That's teenage melodrama stuff. Not millionaire businessman stuff.

I go into the settings and put my phone on Do Not Disturb to silence all the notifications, and I approve only two contacts to break through the barrier—Marla and Hunter.

I can't do anything more without talking to Hunter, so I shove the phone in my pocket, put my bra back on, and wrestle my feet into my gym shoes. No one's in the hallway when I rush out of my room with only my wallet in my hand and my phone in my back pocket. I run to the stairwell, avoiding the elevator and anyone whom I might bump into there. I'm out of breath when I finally reach room 435. I knock three times on my mom and Mac's door.

Now for step two of my crisis management plan—talking to Mom and Mac. Even though Mac's documentary is mentioned in the gossip columns, it's my mom I'm the most worried about. She's so wrapped up in her relationship with Mac that I wonder when she's finally going to realize what all this is leading up to—a question of who her real father is and whether she's been lied to by her mother, the iconic Vivian Snow.

Though there's a chance she already knows—the DNA test in her bag could be a sign that I'm the only one on the outside of this secret. No matter what the truth is and how embarrassing this hit piece is, at least I know my mom and Mac can't ignore me or my questions anymore. I'm about to get answers, and that takes the edge off my nerves enough to keep me from vomiting.

I knock again.

This time I hear voices on the other side of the door and a scratching at the doorknob. I tidy the strands of hair sticking out from my ponytail and tickling my face. I go to readjust my tangled bra straps when the door swings open. I look up, expecting to see my mom or Mac or even Conrad. But instead, standing in front of me in a pair of Armani slacks and a white button-up shirt, his tie loosened, is the last person I expected to see—my fiancé.

CHAPTER 28

Vivian

Monday, June 14, 1943
Camp Atterbury

It's been two long days and nights since Tom's drunken confession of love and subsequent proposal. By the time I got home, papà himself was drunk, and the house was filled with cigar smoke. He must've known I'd scold him for it because as soon as I crossed the threshold, he excused himself and went to bed. I washed my face and brushed my teeth until my gums bled, floating in a post-romance haze. When I crawled into bed beside Aria, I kept my face turned away so she wouldn't detect the alcohol on my breath.

The next two days went by in a blur of embarrassment and hope. I was unsure if I was in fact an engaged woman or if Tom had changed his mind after sobering up. Getting on the bus this morning felt like joining a funeral procession in which I didn't know if the person in the casket was dead or alive.

But as soon as we turn onto Hospital Road, I can make him out, standing on the corner waiting for me. One of the girls across the aisle gives me a meaningful look. Apparently, Lilly and Sue have spread conjecture about me and Tom to every female at Camp Atterbury.

I'm too nervous to be overly annoyed. As I tromp down the bus steps, Tom offers his hand, helping me to the ground.

"I want you to wear this," he says, taking me aside and pulling out a ring he's made from what looks like tin. Metal of any kind is hard to find nowadays, so I suppose I'm lucky to have a ring at all.

"I ordered a big diamond from Tiffany's. It won't get here for a few weeks, but I wanted to see a ring on your finger right away."

"Tiffany's?" I've never dreamed of having anything from such a fancy store. Girls at college would cut out Tiffany & Co. ads from magazines and pass them around at lunchtime, seeming to me more persnickety about the ring than the man they'd spend their lives with.

"I hope you like it. I had my sister pick it out. She knows better than I do about that sort of thing."

"That's right; you mentioned her as your accomplice with the shoes." I don't know a whole lot about my future husband.

"Yeah, Moira. She's a doll but a little spoiled; you know how it is." I don't "know how it is," but I act like I do. "You'll meet her in a few months, after Ranger training. Think what my family will do when I show up with you on my arm."

"You're not gonna tell them till then?" We're nearing the gate where we part ways. I have so many questions, and it seems like there's never enough time to ask them.

"They'd do something stupid like try to change my mind or send Franklin, my older brother, down here to stop things before our wedding." My eyes widen. "Oh, don't worry your little head. It'll be all spiffy, once we're official for a while. That's why we gotta get this wedding done lickety-split, before my transfer. And Moira knows. She's a gem, though. She won't spill the beans. You didn't tell your pa, did ya? It might be better to wait till after we're married—when I'm far enough away he can't shoot me."

He laughs, and I fake a chuckle. I haven't told papà yet mostly because I was worried I'd imagined the whole thing, but I hadn't planned to keep it from him for long. Though I can see some benefit to eloping. No fights with papà. No issues with Tom's family. And no need to wear my ring during auditions. But since Tom is a GI, I guess we wouldn't be able to keep it a secret for long here at Camp Atterbury.

Eloping. My Lord, I'm about to elope.

"Can I tell my sister?"

"I don't see why not. She seems like she'd be a far worse shot than your dad." He winks, and all the jiggly warm feelings I had in the back seat of the car return, and I'm dizzy again, drunk on his charm.

He leans in to kiss me when a truck going through the gates catches my eye. It's the one that transports the workers to the chapel construction site. My team stands in line thirty feet past the fence. They watch me. Only Trombello tries to be discreet, pretending to look at something on the ground. The other men point toward me. Even with his thick glasses, Gravano can see us and waves until Trombello pulls his arm down.

Tom notices the change in my focus, and his demeanor goes from light and hopeful to stormy.

"They act like they know you," he says, moving his body between me and the line of men. "It's disgusting."

"We work together," I say, trying to explain.

"Work together? Together? Can you hear yourself?" he asks, tapping my temple. "What am I supposed to tell my company? That while we're out fighting, my wife's back home giving these dagos a hard-on, swaying her hips, and laughing at their stupid jokes?"

"Tom," I say, reprimanding his crass language. But his intensity only rises.

"I heard these yucks are having a dance next week at some church. Dancing with local girls. Can you believe that?"

I startle at the mention of the POW dance. I'm helping to plan it. Archbishop Cicognani and Father Theodore proposed the event and offered up the school gymnasium behind the church. Gammell says it's a reward for the men working on special projects.

"It's not against the rules," I say defensively, stepping back.

"It should be. How would you like it if I was captured and went out dancing with foreign women while you were here alone? Nazi women?"

I consider the possibility, and it doesn't bother me as much as the idea of Tom dancing with Pearl again.

"I think I'd be glad they let you dance." I throw up my hands, a touch of my father's fiery nature flaring up. "That's the whole point of this camp—to treat the prisoners how we'd like our men to be treated."

He stamps his foot and snorts like a bull preparing to charge; then unexpectedly he grabs my upper arms, pinning them tightly to my sides.

"I don't like it. This job, this whole mess with coddling these fascists. My wife won't be a part of it, Viv. After we're married, you gotta quit. I can't stand it. I just can't." He shakes me hard enough to make one of my bobby pins fall onto the ground between my shoes—the new shoes that he gave me.

The whole line of prisoners is watching now.

"I can't quit." I wriggle against his viselike grip. "Papà needs me . . ."

"I can take care of you and your family. I'll send you all my pay. I don't need it. And I have . . . other ways." It's clear he doesn't want me to know about his wealthy family, which is fine. I guess if I were well off like him, I'd want a woman to love me for me. But still—I'm not taking his money. I want to work.

I shake my head. "That won't work. We aren't telling papà we're married, not till after your training. That's what you said. He'd know something's wrong. He's not stupid."

"I wouldn't exactly call him smart," he mumbles loud enough for me to hear.

"Beg your pardon?" I ask, offended and unwilling to ignore this particular insult. He scowls at me and then lets me go. I shake out my hands, which have been growing numb.

"Nothing," he says calmly, straightening my sleeves so they cover more of my reddened upper arms. "You can keep this job until I'm officially a Ranger. Okay?"

I nod my head as he retrieves the bobby pin, putting it in the palm of my hand. This Dr. Jekyll and Mr. Hyde–like shift makes me flinch away from his kind touch. Then he unceremoniously shoves the tin band onto my finger.

"Now, put this on so those dogs know who you belong to."

I don't resist. I can barely register the band of cool metal there, my fingers still in the process of regaining feeling.

"There we go," he says, putting his hands on my hips and yanking me toward him into a kiss. I attempt to dodge his lips by turning my head to the side, but he won't let me. This time his touch doesn't elicit steam and excitement. I'm cold inside, frozen solid. I don't know how he can't feel it, the icy block I've become.

He steps away with one more peck on my cheek and promises to find another time to see me today so we can make more solid plans. I agree and smile the perfect, frozen smile of the ice creature I've become.

I rush through the gate, late for the first time in my tenure at Atterbury. And as I hurry up the stairs into the office, the truck pulls away. It's loaded with men in blue denim huddled together. One upturned face watches my ascent. Trombello. He acknowledges me with a nod, and I nod back; then I turn away and enter the office, shame my only companion as I cross the threshold.

CHAPTER 29

Elise

Present Day
Room 435

He knows. I can see it in his body language as soon as he lays eyes on me, like he's fighting against his natural instincts to reach out and take me in his arms. His eyes are red, and he has a five o'clock shadow, which I rarely see since he shaves twice during the day to keep his jaw smooth.

"Hey! I thought you didn't get in till later." *Act normal,* I tell myself. Which shouldn't be hard since I haven't done anything wrong. I *am* normal.

"I got in an hour ago."

"An hour ago?" The timing doesn't make sense. If he didn't know about the article, he would've told me he was coming in early. If he did know about it, how did he find out before me or any of my staff?

"Let's get out of the hall." He holds the door open and presses his body against the wall so I can get past him. He smells of Creed, and I want to hug him but can tell he wouldn't welcome it.

My mom's sitting on the couch in the living room area, and Mac stands behind one of the armchairs. Neither of them greets me at first. Then my mom extends her hand, inviting me to sit beside her.

"Oh, baby. Come here."

I collapse next to my mother, grateful to have a sympathetic figure nearby. She engulfs me in a warm embrace, petting my hair like when I was a little girl. I refuse to cry. Perhaps I'm out of tears from my cry earlier today at the boutique, but I also worry that tears might read as guilt, and I'm not guilty, I remind myself again.

"Paparazzi are the lowest form of humans; am I right?" She kisses my temple and then holds my face in her hands.

"This is such a mess," I say to my mom but also to Hunter, who's taken the chair to the left of me, close enough to make eye contact but not close enough to reach out if he even wanted to.

"We know. We know. This is all too common during films. Isolation from loved ones. Close friendships form. It's nothing to be ashamed about."

"Wait, what?" I stiffen and pull out of her embrace, turning to Hunter. "No. There's no truth to any of this story. I hardly know Father Patrick. He's a priest, for God's sake."

Hunter's brow is furrowed, and his lips are set in a straight line. He's hurt—massively hurt. I don't know how to convince him I'm telling the truth.

"Sure, baby. Sure. That's the right way to handle it with the press. We know."

"No, that's the truth." I feel like I'm being gaslit. Having feelings for someone, feelings, by the way, that we both walked away from instead of embracing, isn't the same as cheating. "I want to know who leaked this, because there's some information in that article that's far too specific to come from a paparazzo with a camera and a misleading angle."

"Leaked?" Mac asks, finally speaking up. He pushes off the back of the chair he's been leaning on and crosses his arms. "We've all signed NDAs. No possible way there's a leak from my crew."

"It has to be," I insist. "Antonio Trombello—that name. It's in the article. How'd they get that information?"

"Research?" he says, "Same kind we're doing. It's all public record."

I bounce back and forth between looking at my mother's and Mac's expressions. My mother's face is dewy and made up, but every visible crease drags downward in a sad, droopy kind of way. And Mac seems nowhere close to concerned or worried about the article.

"I'm sorry—what's going on here? Doesn't anyone care about this pile of bullshit? We might not be able to do anything to stop the story, but can't we all agree to be on the same side?"

Mac nods at my mom, and my mom gives him a knowing look. She lets go of my arm and reaches around behind her for something. Staring off into space, Hunter sits stoically, his toe tapping against the wooden leg of the coffee table.

"There are a few things you should know, Lisey. Here." She places the familiar album on my lap and unties the green bow on the side. "I know you recognize this."

"Nonna's scrapbook," I say in agreement, still confused.

She opens the album to the middle where a paper bookmark sticks out. The yellowing pages hold the same drawings I remember from when I was a little girl: one, a hand-drawn Italian villa with climbing vines dripping off the awning of the house; another, a waterfall in the middle of a jungle in watercolor. There's another drawing of an old woman sitting with a basket of kittens in her lap, cobblestones beneath her feet. I was right—it's the same book my grandmother shared with me when I was younger. We'd play pretend with each picture, making up stories about where it was and who lived there.

"I'm sorry. I don't know what this has to do with anything."

"It'll all make sense soon, baby," my mother says, sliding her finger under the cardstock of the image of a statue in a park.

"What are you doing? We aren't supposed to take them out. Nonna said they're fragile." My instinct is to stop her from ruining something my grandmother cherished, but the card is out. There's writing on the back and a canceled stamp up in the corner.

"They're postcards?" I ask, confused why my globe-trotting grandma collected postcards from someone else's travels. It seems more likely that she'd go to the locale herself.

"Read it," my mom says, handing the card to me. It's in a tidy hand, black ink, likely penned by a man. It's in Italian.

"I can't." My mother used to claim Italian as a second language, but it turned out she only knew a few phrases.

"Not the whole thing. Just the name—at the bottom." She points to the compact script that's small but easy to read.

"Antonio Trombello?" I ask, not believing what I'm seeing. "Like the man in the photograph? The priest from the POW camp?"

"Yes, darling. As far as we can tell." The postcard is dated 1954. But I remember her adding illustrated cards to the album even when I was a little girl.

"And so—what does this mean? In your opinion." I flip through the pages, stunned at the number of postcards contained within. "What does it mean to us and Nonna?"

"He was a prisoner at the internment camp while your grandmother was there. They remained close until his passing in 1999," she says, locating the picture I'd given her earlier that week. "I think this man is your grandfather."

CHAPTER 30

Vivian

Thursday, June 17, 1943
Holy Trinity Catholic Church

The church is empty except for Aria, Carly, Mary, and Tom's witness and best man, Talbot. It isn't a wedding like the one I'd hoped for since I was a little girl with a big white dress and my mamma crying tears of joy as papà handed me off to my fiancé's loving embrace. Papà doesn't even know he's giving his daughter away, and the only one crying is little Aria who's sure I'm abandoning her forever. But Tom ships out next week, and he made it clear—he doesn't want to leave unmarried. Marriage is the only way.

When I went to Father Theodore for confession and told him of what transpired between me and Tom in the back seat of his borrowed car, he agreed that a marriage needed to happen, that it was the only path to my redemption. He arranged for the ceremony to take place before Tom's departure and agreed to keep the elopement confidential until my soldier returns.

I'm wearing Mary's blue dangling sapphire earrings and Carly's wedding gown, a lovely ivory color with long embroidered tulle sleeves and a train. It's loose around my waist and tight around my bust, but with a few inconspicuous stitches and a veil that hides any evidence, I fit the role of bride well enough. I still can't believe I'll be Mrs. Tom Highward by the end of the night.

I'm honestly surprised Carly showed up with the dress, after she threw a small fit when I told her I was engaged to Tom.

"I never took you as one of those girls who's pinned her future on 'getting a man,'" she said, her hands on her hips, the only person I'd confided in about my audition next month.

"It's not like that," I insisted, wanting her approval. "I love Tom. He loves me. And it's not like I'm giving up on performing. Tom said he doesn't care if I keep singing with the band and go to the MCA audition."

"He doesn't care. How generous of him," she said, her tone heavy with contempt, none of her dreamy memories of her long-deceased husband softening her reaction. "From what I've seen of that boy, he's just another man who'll tell you what you can and can't do in your life."

I wish Carly could remember what it was like to be in my shoes. She's been a widow for six years, making choices as a single woman but with the rights of a married one. She could live the rest of her life without the threat of sacrificing all her other dreams and ambitions on the matrimonial altar. I guess when she saw I wasn't going to be deterred by strong words of warning, she chose to be by my side anyway. I'm glad—I don't know what I'd do if I lost Carly's support.

Mary, on the other hand, squealed like a little girl, in love with the idea of our whirlwind romance and marriage. I'm not fool enough to believe in Mary's imagined version of marriage. Sure, there will be sacrifices. But the more I envision my life as a married woman, the more I understand that marriage for a girl like me isn't only about romance. It's stability. It's freedom. And it opens doors that a single girl living at home would never have, especially in the culture I've been raised in.

Besides, Tom supports my dreams. He said, "You just watch—I'll come back from Europe, and my girl will be a movie star!"

His girl—that's what he calls me now. It thrills me every time. I know he's mercurial. But he apologized for his outburst in front of the compound and explained that he loves me so much that it causes this sort of explosive episode.

Of course, I forgave him. But it's impossible to explain his apology to my Italian crewmen. When I showed up at the work site last Monday, they greeted me with a cold silence that was out of character.

"So much progress!" I said animatedly, overcorrecting in response to their chilly reception. The foundation is still bare, but the grounds are groomed. A gravel drive trails down from the hill where the chapel will stand, the road a little over a hundred yards away. The trees have been cleared, the grass cut, and the iron fence put in place. All that's left is the actual construction. Which is why I knew the piece of paper I found on my desk that morning was of utmost importance. The long-awaited concrete had arrived.

"I have good news!" I said to Trombello loud enough for the nearby committee members to hear. Trombello didn't look up from the plans, and Puccini continued distributing tools and shoveling gravel.

"Hey, did you hear me? I have good news."

"We already saw," Cresci said, handing Trombello a shovel and then walking away with a disappointed scowl.

"What the heck is wrong with everyone today?" I asked.

Trombello shook his head while staring at the pages in front of him longer than could possibly be necessary. Sighing heavily, he finally raised his eyes to me, with a look of care and a touch of frustration.

"We saw you with that man again. The one from the mess hall."

"I saw you watching," I said, choosing not to play dumb.

"He's no good for you, *mia figlia*."

My daughter, he said, as though he were *my* priest. Even though my arms still ache where Tom gripped me, I feel defensive. What right do these prisoners have to judge me and my life? I've always been friendly toward them, and though they're my country's declared enemies, I've never treated them as such.

"You don't know him," I said, picking up the paper with the good news, hoping to change the subject, but Trombello continued.

"I know this, and that's enough." He very lightly traced a finger over the red lines peeking out under my sleeve. I flinched away and yanked the fabric down, not liking his insinuations or how his touch gave me goose bumps.

"We got the concrete." I tossed the paper in his direction. He read the page and put it aside with a rock on top to keep it from blowing away. No reaction. "We can pour the foundation now."

"Yes," he said with little emotion, lining up his writing utensils.

"And the dance? Saturday night? Will you all be there?"

"I don't know."

His noncommittal attitude felt like a rejection. I'd been through a rough moment with Tom in front of my place of employment, and now Trombello treated me indifferently—the one truly kind man I've met in a long time.

"What should we call you?" Trombello asked as I started to step away, ready to go back to the safety of my desk.

"Huh?"

He pointed to my tin ring. I was about to explain the whole thing, how Tom loved me and I loved him and how he was transferring for Ranger training. How we were going to get married even though his family wouldn't like it, and he promised to take care of me and my family, and he supported my dreams. But Tom was right—no one would understand. It's a secret—our secret. For now, at least.

"Snow," I said, using my stage name, grief coming over me. I'd thought Trombello might be the one person I could be myself with. The one man who might see and accept me for who I really am—Vivian Santini. But I guess not. So, I'll be Vivian Snow for Trombello and all the men at the USO and Archie Lombardo and even for my father, whether he knows it or not.

And even though by the end of this ceremony I'll be Mrs. Tom Highward, I'm still Vivian Snow to my future husband. I wonder if I'll ever be the real Vivian again.

"It's time, Viv," Aria says, stopping in the doorway and holding a bouquet of flowers from her garden. Her hair is neatly braided for once, and she's dressed in her best dress, blue as the sky the day Tony drowned. Her mouth drops open. "You look like a movie star."

"Don't make me cry," I say, looking up to keep tears from ruining my makeup.

"I'm already crying," Ari says, rushing into my arms and resting her head against my chest.

"I wish mamma were here," Ari says when she pulls away, drying her face.

"Me too, love. Me too."

"You're not gonna leave me too, are you, Viv?" I shake my head and tuck a strand of hair behind her ear.

"Never, darling. I promise." And I won't. Even if I go on tour or to Philadelphia with Tom or to Hollywood, I'll always be back. I'll leave Tom before I leave her.

The organ starts to play in the church. I can't wait any longer.

"Get in there! Hurry. Hurry!" I urge her out with a little wave. She mouths, "Love you," and I do the same. She rushes away, and I take a moment to sneak one last look in the mirror, checking my lipstick and veil. But even with the organ music vamping in the background and the little tap on the door, Carly coming to get me this time, I stare at my reflection.

I do look like a different version of myself. She's calm and collected and pretty enough, I guess. I'll get used to this girl. I think I'll have to.

"Goodbye, Vivian Santini," I say to the reflection in the mirror, and then walk out the door to my future.

CHAPTER 31

Elise

Present Day
Room 435

"You knew Grandpa wasn't your father?" I ask my mom, my head swirling with all the new information.

"No, no. I was always told Tom Highward was my father. Always. He and your grandmother were legally married in 1943. But it turns out he didn't die in the war. That was a lie Archie came up with to get around the morality clause when mamma signed her contract with MGM. I never considered, never once till now, that he wasn't my daddy after all."

"And you don't think Mac knew this when he started his project?" I ask, pointing a finger in her boyfriend's direction. "This was all a setup; can't you see that?"

Mac holds up his hands like I'm pointing a gun at him.

"I did know some of it," he says. "I knew Tom Highward didn't die in battle. I knew he wasn't buried in Rest Haven, and I even knew his family was wealthy and had shunned your mother and Vivian after he abandoned them. But only recently did I learn about the priest—the one in the albums, I mean," he clarifies, and I cringe at even the slightest reference to Father Patrick.

"And that's why you had that DNA test," I say to my mom. Mac's storyline is coming together. He started out to tell the story of Vivian Snow's granddaughter getting married in the same small town where Vivian had her own wedding eighty years ago. But somewhere along the line, as he learned more salacious details about a potential love affair and the possible illegitimate offspring of a Hollywood sweetheart, he couldn't resist.

My mother nods dramatically, tears glittering on her lower eyelids. "I'll have the results in a few weeks. I'd like to have you there when I open them."

"Of course." I take my mom's hand. I can't imagine how difficult it must be at seventy-nine years old to possibly have the whole framing device for your life change. My father took a paternity test as soon as they were widely available. At the time, I was offended. But years later when I was starting to understand my mother, I was grateful for the undeniable knowledge that he is my dad. And that can't be taken away from me in some shocking revelation of infidelity or deceit.

"I guess what I need to know from you and Hunter," Mac addresses both of us, patting the air like he's trying to keep us calm, "is if you'd like to go through with the wedding at Holy Trinity. Now, I understand that we have a few kinks to iron out with these new revelations. How would you feel about changing the venue? Perhaps somewhere in Italy. We could track down Antonio Trombello's family line, find a lovely church in the local town or village. Make it an international affair?"

I shake my head, anger turning into outrage. I've gotten so lost in the story of my grandmother and grandfather, whoever he may be, I've become distracted from the real reason I'm in their room. And why Hunter is here at all.

"No, no. I don't want to even think about that." I wave violently, my volume turned up to an eight or a nine. "Mom, I'm sorry about your dad. I'm sorry Nonna kept things from you, well, from all of us. I'm still trying to imagine a scenario where she'd do something like this. And Mac—I'm glad you're there for my mom or whatever you're doing for her. But I cannot focus on your stupid documentary right now. I have a life. And now, because of my soap-opera-worthy family, it's in shambles. So if you'll excuse me and Hunter, I think we need a minute."

"Of course. I wasn't trying to pressure you into an answer immediately. I wanted to put it out there for consideration," Mac says. Then, taking my mother by the elbow, he tenderly helps her up from her seat. "Come, dear. Let's leave the children to chat, shall we?"

"Absolutely," she says, kissing my cheek one more time. "You'll always be my baby no matter what the test says," she says, as though I'm the one waiting on DNA results for my parentage.

"I know, Mom," I say, humoring her out of compassion. I give them a moment to clear the room before scooching over to the edge of my seat so I'm close enough to Hunter to touch his knee. I spread my hand out on his leg and squeeze, my grandmother's engagement ring catching the light. He doesn't withdraw from my touch, but he doesn't return it either.

"Hey," I say as my opener. He's staring at my hand on his thigh, or maybe the engagement ring he gave me three months ago with my mother's help.

"Hey," he responds finally.

"I'm so glad you're here," I say, whispering, knowing Mac and my mom can likely hear through the wall.

"Yeah?" he asks, touching the diamond with his pointer finger.

"Why wouldn't I be? I told you—it's all gossip. I'm here because of *you*. I've been dying to see *you*. I was planning *our* wedding. You can ask Father Patrick. There's nothing between us. I promise. Nothing."

He nods, and I hush the nagging guilt I feel from saying "nothing" so emphatically. But I don't think I can find a way to explain that despite starting to have feelings for Patrick, I didn't indulge those feelings. Hunter would never believe me.

"So, you still want to get married?" he asks, a sweet, soft vulnerability in the way he looks up at me.

"Of course I want to marry you, babe. I love you. But not here." I gamble and try a laugh, hoping Hunter doesn't think I'm taking things too lightly. But he joins me, chuckling.

"No, not here. I've only been in this town one hour, and I'm ready to get the hell outta here. So, Italy?"

"With Mac? No damn way. I'm so done with this thing. They have enough material without us now. I just want to focus on us," I say, taking his hand and pulling him in for a soft kiss. I've missed him, missed those lips, missed his smell and his easy smile. I breathe him in, and my nerves start to calm.

He pulls away and touches my cheek and my damp lips and then grasps my chin between his finger and thumb, cocking his head. I expect something sweet, healing, or an apology for not believing me.

Instead, he asks, "Are you sure? After all the work you've done on the documentary. I mean—it's Italy."

His comment feels like a shift from a major key to a minor key, making my chest tighten.

I lean back so I can see his expression more clearly.

"Can I ask you a question?"

"You're asking a question about asking a question?" he jokes. I usually like his humor, but right now it hits me wrong, like he's trying too hard to be charming or he's trying to distract me from something. I continue without laughing.

"Why are you here early?" It struck me as odd when I first walked into the hotel room, but I was so wrapped up in the moment, I nearly forgot to ask.

"I got done with work early. Thought I'd surprise you but heard the news on the way and didn't know what to do, so I came up here to talk to your mom."

I nod at the very reasonable explanation. I want to believe it. I want to ignore the alarm bells ringing louder than ever before. They rang back when he had my mom sneak him my grandmother's ring for his proposal. They rang when he talked to my mom about the documentary before he'd discussed it with me. They rang when he pushed me to have our wedding in Edinburgh, and they rang when he didn't mind the idea of being followed around by cameras or the idea of my family's dirty laundry hung out for the whole world to see. They rang again when he didn't answer my calls and again when he didn't comfort me when he opened that hotel room door.

"Why are you so dedicated to this film, Hunter?"

"I . . . I don't know. It makes me feel like part of the family, I guess." He shrugs and then, standing up, releases my hand. "We can talk wedding stuff later. I'm starving. Let's grab dinner and then make up for lost time?" he offers, trying to change the subject. When he retrieves his suit jacket from where it's draped over the desk, something heavy hits the floor.

"What was that?" I ask, on my feet and by his side in a flash.

"I . . . I don't know," he says, kicking something under the desk to my right. I fall to my knees and reach under the lower edge of the frame and pull out a compact camera. I've seen it on pretty much every interview we've shot so far. It's Mac's camera—and it's recording.

"What the hell is this?" I ask, holding up the device. I'd turn it off, but I don't know how.

"I have no idea. I was just putting on my jacket." He holds up his hands like he's showing me he's not a criminal. I don't believe him. "Mom! Mac! Come out here," I shout as loud as I can, holding the camera while scanning the rest of the room for equipment.

My mom bursts out from the bedroom like she was listening through the wall, which she likely was. Or through headphones or a screen, because just as she notices I'm holding a camera in her direction, I find another one, this one a bigger model, also running. A mic sticks out from behind the picture above where I was sitting with my mom, and I spot another one clipped to the lamp shade. How'd I miss any of this?

"You were filming me?" I ask my mom and Hunter at the same time. A dozen other moments I'd assumed were private flash through my mind. Were those recorded too? I don't address Mac because the idea of him invading my privacy isn't shocking, but the other two—I thought they loved me.

"I'm sorry. It wasn't my idea. They already had it set up when I got here." Hunter's being honest, finally. But it's too late for me to be moved by honesty. I'm wounded, maybe mortally so. What else has he hidden from me?

"What the hell? Why are you so invested in this?" As soon as I say the word, I know. *Invested.* Is Hunter the anonymous investor who's been funding this whole project?

"I thought you'd like it. I thought it'd be fun or something. I didn't know it'd end up like this."

"Are you, like, Mac's partner?"

He stares at me in silence and then mutters, "You weren't supposed to find out . . ."

"What the hell . . ."

"It's not his fault, baby," my mom jumps in. "Don't be mad at Hunter and Mac. They meant well . . ."

"Oh my God, Mom," I gasp, feeling like a lamb cornered in a den of lions. "Don't you see—your boyfriend leaked the story and called the paparazzi. He's willfully ruining my reputation for what? A little free publicity?"

"I did no such thing," Mac says defensively, his accent giving him an air of dignity I don't think he deserves. "I knew more than I let on, and Hunter has been instrumental in getting this project off the ground, but I've done nothing I'm ashamed of. It can take some finagling to get a project like this out of development and into production. But I never leaked a story or pictures to anyone. I do have *some* journalistic integrity."

"That's doubtful," I say, glaring.

"No, dear, it's true," my mom says, coming to her man's defense, as always. She never sides with her children, her family, not even herself—*always her man.*

"Mom, stop standing up for this guy. He's clearly lying."

"He's not lying, hun. I was the one who called ZTM and gave them the pictures. I'm the source."

I drop the camera. My mother. Not Hunter or Mac but my very own mother. I can't be in this room, this building, anymore. My surroundings spin, and I pivot on one foot, glad that I'm wearing gym shoes.

I run.

I run into the hall and down the stairs. I run through the side door and past the antiques mall and Cracker Barrel and follow the wide asphalt road that goes past industrial parks and smells of freshly tilled earth now that it's planting season.

I should've known better. I've lived and worked long enough in entertainment to know that everything around me is a mirage. They'll be close behind me, I'm sure, trying to reason with me or change my mind or pay me off. But for now, I'll run to the only place I've known without a doubt is real—the church on the hill and the man inside it.

CHAPTER 32

Vivian

Saturday, June 19, 1943
Edinburgh Middle School Gymnasium

I exit the stage with a bow, and the men whistle and cheer in their native tongue. I've never performed in front of a crowd where English wasn't the primary language, and during the performance, I found myself talking to the gathered prisoners in Italian.

The dance was officially organized by the Italian American Organization (IAO), Father Theodore, and the parishioners at Holy Trinity, but Lieutenant Colonel Gammell asked me to act as a liaison between the groups and the camp. The leaders from each of the divisions were awarded passes along with a few hand-picked men seen as deserving of a special reward. Those in the chapel construction crew were a part of that limited list.

The dance is held in the middle school gym at the rear of the long rectangular building behind Holy Trinity, with Father Theodore presiding as the host and chaperone. The women attending are of a slightly different sort than those at the USO dances. These girls have been bussed in from other Catholic parishes in the area by the IAO. Their skirts are longer and hair darker, and many have accents that blend in with the men they dance with.

And the band isn't my usual ensemble—this one is made up of POWs playing old, beat-up instruments that barely hold a tune. But we know enough of the same songs, and our performance is made more vibrant by the rarity of it.

At the bottom of the rickety stage stairs stands the whole committee, Trombello included. Gravano and Cresci clap and grin like I'm their daughter or niece finishing a school recital. Other than Trombello, the men softened toward me over the week, especially with the dance looming ahead. My priestly friend is still kind enough, but it seems to take great effort.

"You are a *bella prima donna*!" Gravano declares, helping me down the last step.

"Why did you keep this secret?" Cresci demands.

"It wasn't a secret! I sang at the dedication of the altar."

"Eh, different."

"No, it's not," I laugh as the band starts up again. Gravano asks for a dance. I've already danced with all the men from our little crew at least once—every man but Trombello, who stands on the side of the room, declining every dance request from every girl who has the guts to ask.

But I'm tired. I've been married two days, and I spent the first night at the fancy Hotel Severin in Indianapolis with my new husband, talking, drinking, dreaming, and making love. I told papà I was visiting mamma at Mount Mercy Sanitarium, and he didn't bat an eye. I almost feel more guilty about that lie than eloping.

On Friday morning, my husband and I woke after only an hour of slumber. Hung over and exhausted, we drove the hour back to Camp Atterbury. He dropped me off at my gate and then drove off in his borrowed car to make the most of the rest of his twenty-four-hour leave. I haven't seen him since. He left a message with Aria that he'd gotten back onto base on time and he'd call again soon. As of dinnertime tonight, the only evidence I have that I'm married is the signed marriage license I passed off to Carly's care after the wedding and the ring tucked into the waistband of my skirt alongside Archie Lombardo's business card.

"I need to sit this one out, but I promise you my next dance."

"Yes, *bella*. Yes."

"And me!" adds Ferragni, his pale eyes glowing in the dim lights.

"And me!" Gondi echoes the same request.

They see something new in me, something different. Trombello steps forward and takes my hand, gesturing for his fellow prisoners to leave.

"Shoo, shoo. Let the girl rest."

"Yes, Padre," they say in near unison, like altar boys reprimanded by their Sunday school teacher.

"Come. Come with me," he says, tugging gently and guiding me to the refreshment table. He passes me a cup of punch and leads me to a seat in a dim corner of the gymnasium.

"Thank you. You saved me."

"You deserve a break," he says, taking the chair next to me.

"I don't know about that." I stare at my punch, Trombello's awkward kindness making me shy.

"You do. You've made many things possible for us, and we are indebted to you."

"You're acting like we're done working together. You're all stuck with me for a while longer," I say, taking a drink of the overly sugary red liquid that's stained the inside of the cup. Tom wants me to quit my job once he's a Ranger, but he'll be away at training for months, and I hope I'll have found a way to change his mind by then. The only way I'll consider quitting is if I get an agent.

"But I thought with the wedding . . ."

"Tom supports my career," I say defensively. "I'm auditioning for the USO Camp Shows next week. He said if I make it, he'll help me get headshots . . ."

"Yes, yes," he says as he eyes my bruises. He obviously doesn't believe me, and I can't blame him. He's only seen the Mr. Hyde side of Tom.

"I know he seems bad, but . . ." I try to think of a way to convince Trombello my husband isn't a controlling jerk, when a loud clank echoes through the hall, interrupting the big-band music. The lights in the gym flick on, and the dancing comes to a stop along with the music. Uniformed men enter the room.

"All right. Night's over. Time to go," a man shouts into the crowd. "Women on the back wall. Men in line. Let's go."

This was not how it was supposed to end. We reserved the building until ten thirty, and it's only ten. The girls twitter and squeal as the uniformed men urge them to one side of the room. And the POWs stand in place, clearly not understanding the orders.

I rush up to the stage, pushing past panicked girls and confused prisoners, and take the mic to translate. I steady my voice, trying to make the announcement sound routine, although I'm sure the prisoners sense the tension in the air. Finally understanding the orders, the men groan with disappointment and follow the directions without hesitation.

As I stand onstage and scan the crowd, a familiar face approaches. Tom. It's not surprising I didn't recognize him at first. This man isn't my handsome, Dr. Jekyll Tom but the dark and dangerous version, a version of my husband that scares me.

He shoves several of the prisoners aside, trying to get to the stage.

"What the hell are you doing here?" he demands. I move closer to the edge of the elevated platform and cover the mic to keep our conversation private.

"It's a paying gig," I say, trying to make it sound reasonable.

"Get off that stage."

"In a minute," I say, holding up the microphone and repeating the directions again in English and then Italian. As I finish, I feel his hand around my ankle. He's leaning across the stage, and before I realize what he's about to do, he tugs at my leg. I wobble, losing my balance. I reach back to break my fall but tumble onto my bottom, dropping the microphone and jamming my wrist in the process. An ear-piercing squeal goes through the sound system. Two of the POW band members rush to my side, thinking I slipped.

"Stai bene?" *Are you all right?* one asks.

"Sei ferita?" *Are you hurt?* the other inquires as they crowd around me. I hold my wrist and nod my head.

"Sto bene," I say, insisting I'm fine. Tom is storming up the stage stairs, and I don't want them to get hurt, so I urge them away once they've helped me to my feet.

"We're leaving," Tom says, grabbing the same arm I hurt in my fall. I wince.

"I can't leave. I have work to do." The room is a disaster, and after the abrupt and premature ending to the dance, the trembling girls lined up along the back wall need to be reassured before they're sent home. Then another realization rushes in. "Besides, aren't you on duty?"

Tom growls, and his brow furrows as he pulls me off the stage and down the stairs. He drags me toward the side exit through the locker rooms.

"That's none of your goddamn business. Just because they let you run things over there at the summer camp doesn't mean you get to question my assignments."

I open my mouth to voice my suspicions that this has nothing to do with "orders" and has more to do with bitter feelings that've been brewing for some time, but this isn't the time or place for a domestic dispute.

"I'm sorry," I say softly, hoping to calm him.

We push into the boys' locker room, and a heavy scent of sweat and mold assaults my senses. Tom pulls at me, and a stab of pain in my left arm shoots all the way up to my shoulder.

"Baby, you're hurting me," I whimper.

"I'm hurting you?" he asks, stopping for a moment, his question imbued with sarcasm. I can see pain mixed with the anger in his eyes. "I told you what I thought about this mockery, and you came anyway. Don't you think that hurt *me*?"

My fear is rising.

I've seen papà get angry, but never uncontrollably. And I know how to calm papà—an apology, a nice meal, a refill on his drink. But Tom—I know so little of my husband. I don't know the rule book for his anger yet, how to manage it or avoid it. I wonder if all men are like this, bombs waiting to go off if handled improperly. I ignore my own pain and instead work to defuse the situation.

"I didn't think about . . . It was an assignment . . . from work. Lieutenant Colonel Gammell . . ."

"I don't care what Gammell told you—I'm your husband. You listen to me now," he orders, and then holds up my already swelling left hand. "Where's your ring? Clearly you don't need the one I ordered after all. Do you want to look like you don't have a husband? You know what they call women who get paid to entertain men, don't you?"

"Tom, you know it's not like that. Papà doesn't know yet, so I took off my ring . . ."

"You have an excuse for everything, don't you?" He sighs like I'm the biggest idiot he's ever run across. His eyes are sunken as though he's been drinking, and he looks like he's about to cry. "I thought I was in love with you, Vivian, but you're a little whore, aren't you?"

The word "whore" hurts more than anything he has done to me physically.

"Excuse me, *signorina*. Are you all right?" A heavily accented voice bounces off the walls of the locker room, and I recognize it immediately. Trombello.

"What the hell? This guy?" Tom says under his breath, and then speaks directly to Trombello, who stands by the swinging locker-room door. "She's fine. You'd better get outta here, or you'll be in for a lot of trouble, Padre."

"Miss Snow. They call your name. Come to see." He's working hard to find the right words in English. I know what he's trying to say, but Tom is irritated and confused.

"Can't you see my *wife* and I are having a conversation? Get the hell out, or I'll make you get out."

"I not leave *fino a che* Miss Snow leave too." Trombello's fists are clenched at his sides, and the veins in his neck bulge. He's always seemed a peaceful man, but now I see Antonio Trombello isn't inherently passive or wary of conflict. He's a man with strong ideals who chooses to contain his antagonistic instincts. But the aggression remains beneath the restraint, and it seems Trombello knows exactly how to release it when he needs to.

Tom lets go of my arm and steps toward Trombello. Reaching into his pocket, he withdraws a small rectangular object that flips open into a blade.

"I told you to mind your own business and get out of here, you greasy fascist dago." I flinch at the nasty slur as though he said it about me as well as Trombello.

"*Signorina.* You go now?" Trombello asks without acknowledging Tom or his weapon.

"Hey, don't you talk to my wife, you hear me?" Tom says, holding the knife up threateningly.

"I'm all right, Padre. You can go." I urge him to leave with a trembling voice, hoping to save him from injury and save my husband from doing something I know he'll regret when the heat of passion has worn off.

"Non è sicuro." *It's not safe,* he warns in Italian this time. "Per favore vieni con me." *Please come with me.*

"Hey, hey! No. None of that." Tom slashes at the air between them. "I get it. You have a little crush. You're a priest, but I'm sure your little dick still works." He gestures with the blade. "But she's my wife, okay? Get the hell out of here, or I swear to God I'll cut your throat."

"Tom . . . ," I start to reason, but he stops me, yelling loud enough that his reverberating voice feels like it will burst my eardrums.

"Shut *up*, Vivian. Shut the fuck up!" He waves the knife at me now, hurrying over to where I'm standing, holding my damaged wrist. I stiffen as he presses the knife against my throat.

"I'm sorry, Tom. I'm sorry," I repeat over and over, but it doesn't work. It doesn't turn off his rage. The knife starts to dig into the delicate skin on the side of my neck when a loud thump and an audible "oof" send Tom reeling away.

Trombello stands behind him with a bat in his hands. He drops the makeshift weapon and takes my hand.

"Correre!" *Run!*

Tom writhes on the floor, the wind knocked out of him but seemingly fine otherwise. I take Trombello's hand and rush for the door to the gym, but we don't get far. Tom catches his breath and regains his footing. Using one of the wooden benches as a booster, he leaps across the tiled floor and tackles Trombello, who falls to the ground still holding my hand. I trip, and our hands break apart. Tom lands a blow on the side of Trombello's head, and I scream, thinking he's still holding the knife. But his hands appear empty.

Tom pins Trombello to the ground with both knees on his chest. The priest twists from side to side, trying to free himself but unable to budge an inch.

"Tom, stop! Stop!" I scream, tugging at the back of his uniform, but it's like he can't hear or feel anything other than his rage. He takes Trombello's head in his hands and slams it on the hard floor, and my stomach turns. With or without a knife, he's going to kill him.

I spot the bat on the floor a few feet away next to the open switchblade. I slide across the tile and confiscate the knife to keep Tom from grabbing it again. I can't figure out how to close the blade, so I hold it in my injured hand and then pick up the bat.

I'm not strong and the bat is heavy, but if I don't act now, Trombello won't stand a chance. I swing as hard as I can with my one good arm, and the solid wood bat lands with a heavy thunk against the back of Tom's head and shoulders. It's not hard enough to cause damage, but he definitely feels it.

"What the . . . ?" He glares at me over his shoulder, touching the place where the wood met his skull. "Are you kidding me? Did you just hit me with that?"

Tom drops Trombello like a cat dropping a dead mouse. The priest's chest rises and falls regularly enough that I know he's still alive, but there's blood on tile, and that can't be good. I hold the bat up in front of me like a shield.

"That was stupid, Vivian. Really, really stupid." He takes the bat from me with one yank and tosses it against the lockers with a crash. Trombello moans in the background. I switch the knife into my right hand and hold it defensively.

"Leave us alone."

"Us? You and that dirty fascist are an 'us' now? I should've known when I met your father that you were nothing more than immigrant trash." I want to bite back at his insults, but I'm too scared to speak; my hand is trembling, and if I had anything of substance in my stomach, I'd likely vomit. He lunges for the knife, and I slash at his hand, making contact.

"Ow! Oh shit, Vivian. Damn it. What the hell?" he yells. I'm instantly immersed in guilt. Did I overreact? Did I hurt him seriously? Am I in the wrong here?

"I'm sorry, Tom. I'm sorry," I say, crying now. But I keep holding the knife up. I'm shaking so hard that I'm not sure how I'm keeping a grip on the handle.

"You're not sorry. You're a crazy woman just like your mother, aren't you? Damn it." He cradles his hand and then pulls a handkerchief out of his inner uniform pocket.

"I . . . I'm not crazy," I say, sniffing, watching him bandage the wound.

At least I think I'm not crazy. Is this what crazy feels like? Is this how my mom felt when she lost her mind? I'm sure my eyes are glowing wildly like hers used to—like a trapped animal. He might be right. Maybe I'm losing my mind. My head swims with the possibility. I want to wipe the tears from my eyes, but my left hand is throbbing and the other still clutches the knife. I can't put it down. Whether I'm crazy or sane, the one thing I'm definitely not is safe.

I back away. He pursues me with slow, methodical steps until I back into a row of lockers, the brackets poking into my back through my dress. I consider thrusting the knife at him, sinking it into his chest, but I've never intentionally hurt someone before. This man is my husband—I don't want to hurt him. I love him.

As soon as he senses my resignation, he moves in swiftly and pins the knife to my side and wraps his uninjured hand around my neck, squeezing.

"They'll put you in the loony bin after this."

I try to shake my head, but he clamps down harder, my breath wheezing loudly through the shrinking airway.

"Or I could squeeze a little tighter, crush your windpipe, finish off your priest over there, and blame the whole thing on your illicit love affair." He crushes my neck against the metal cabinets, bringing up his bandaged hand to increase the pressure. The edges of my vision turn gray and then black. I'm going to die.

With the darkness closing in, my other senses pick up. I hear the scratching of tables being folded and put away under the stage in the gymnasium. I taste the blood in my mouth as my airway closes off. I smell the scent of Tom's fancy cologne mixed with the whiskey on his breath. And I feel the handle of the knife still in my hand.

I grasp it as tight as I can and drag one last miniscule breath past his crushing pressure, and then, with all my might, I shove the blade outward and upward, not stopping when I meet resistance.

All at once his hands drop, and I collapse to the floor, my hair catching in the metal latches on the row of light blue lockers. When I come to, my breathing is ragged, and the lights are dim. The copper taste of blood sours on my tongue. But my hand is empty. That I can tell.

A calm touch gets my attention. Trombello checks my breathing, my eyes, my pulse. I breathe in and out deliberately, and soon the scene comes into focus. Slumped on the floor in front of me is my husband, the dirty knife in his hand and a pool of blood around the seat of his pants as though he's messed himself.

"Tom," I say, my voice deep and raspy like an old man's.

"He's gone, little one," Trombello says in our shared language.

"What?" I ask, but I know he's right. The only person I've ever seen dead up close is Tony, but whether it be a baby or a grown man, I recognize death immediately. Tom is dead.

"You need to leave. Now." He helps me up. With the volume of blood on the floor, I'm shocked none is on my dress. The room starts to spin as soon as I get to my feet.

"I can't. Tom." I gesture to my lifeless husband. "And you."

"Go, *mia figlia*. Go." He walks me to the door that leads to the middle school's hallway. Gravano takes me by the waist and half carries me through the corridor. Gradually, I realize I've been unconscious longer than it seems. Trombello and the crew have a plan, and they're sparing me the details.

By the time Gravano gets me to the end of the hall, I can walk steadily. He shepherds me out the door where a car idles next to the curb with Father Theodore in the driver's seat.

"It's not safe to walk alone," my priest says as I climb into the back seat. When I try to speak, he puts his finger over his lips. "We'll speak soon. But not now. Not now."

I want to tell him everything, ask if I'm mad like my mother, if I'm all the things Tom said I am. But I can tell he doesn't want to know what happened inside that locker room, and I understand why. The only way he can help me is if he doesn't know the truth. I can tell him in the confessional later when he can't be seen as complicit. Only then can I tell him everything—and ask him everything—including if I'm a murderer and if I can ever be forgiven for my sin.

CHAPTER 33

Elise

Present Day
Holy Trinity Catholic Church

By the time I arrive at Holy Trinity, the sun has set, and I'm walking instead of maintaining the sprint-like pace I'd started with when I bolted out of the Haymark Garden Inn. I turned off my phone completely so I wouldn't be tempted to check any messages or pick up the calls that started within minutes of my grand exit. I hope my mother took notes because that exit was epic—and well deserved.

It's Friday-night confessional hours, so I know the church will be occupied, though I have no idea if I'll see Father Patrick or Father Ignatius inside. I also don't know if they're aware of the developing scandal, which means I might have to tell them. I suppose I'd rather be the one to talk them through it than have them hear it from a member of the community or, God forbid, a member of Mac's staff.

I pick up my speed and run up the front steps two at a time until I reach the top, out of breath. I know I must look a mess. My gym shoes and yoga pants are not exactly church attire. I put my hand on the curved metal handle and work to slow my breathing and the slam of my heartbeat against my rib cage.

Inside, all the lights are on. A mother and her child sit in one of the pews, and a gray-haired man kneels by another. The atmosphere of the room is contemplative and peaceful—exactly what I need. I sit in the back row, hoping to identify which priest is in the confessional before facing either of them one-on-one. I don't want to step into that box, that space I know my grandmother and Father Patrick view as holy, and distract Patrick from his religious life more than I already have. But then again, I have to talk with him, and it might not hurt to have a wall between us.

A middle-aged woman I recognize as the assistant librarian exits the confessional. It's a wooden structure with a latticed door in the center where the priest sits and an open but shielded area with a step where the penitent kneels. The little girl takes her turn, bouncing into the confessional with a lightness that comes with youth. I long for the innocent confessions of eight-year-old me.

I mimic the reflective pose of the man in the front row, kneeling, folded hands, eyes closed, only without the constant movement of my lips in prayer. Though if there's ever a time to pray, this is it. I don't know the entire anatomy of my mom and Hunter's betrayal, but I'm slowly piecing it together. My relationship with Hunter was real; I know that. He loved me, and I loved him. But did he propose after only six months because of Mac? Does it go back that far? And Hunter is not a naive fool—he saw the potential rewards in a quick engagement. I'm sure of it.

In the PR arena, relationships and engagements and weddings are tried-and-true methods to improve or change an image. And plenty of agents and publicists participate in this kind of manipulation. More often than not, the two personalities might not even know each other beforehand. There are contracts, signatures, details as specific as where and when the individuals can be photographed together.

I decided early on with Toffee Co. that we wouldn't dip our toes into those waters. If a client is looking for that kind of a quick boost, I have plenty of references willing to help them. But my relationship with Hunter didn't feel orchestrated—no contract to sign, no stipulations, no nondisclosure agreements. Just proclamations of love and plans for our future. Perhaps the other way is better—a business agreement instead of a fairy tale. That way, everyone knows what to expect.

I peek up over my clasped hands, the sound of two men engaged in a whispered conversation pulling me out of my introspection. My throat tightens, and a low note hums in my ears, making it difficult to hear what they're saying to one another.

Patrick sits beside the contemplative man in the front row, a white garment over his black vestments and a purple stole around his neck, deep in conversation. I get off my knees and sit on the wooden pew so I can see them better. The man wears a burgundy sweater with a hole at the elbow, his thinning hair askew on the top of his head. It's obvious the man is in crisis and Patrick—Father Patrick—is counseling him. Father Patrick takes the man's hand and bows his head in prayer, and they sit like that, communing with God together.

I grow emotional as I watch them, one man helping another man find access to his God. I know I don't believe the same way they do, Father Patrick and his parishioner. I don't know if I believe in a deity much less one specific church. But I do believe in what Patrick is doing. If there is a God and if there is a Jesus and if any religious thought is real—then this kind of brotherly love and charity are what I believe in. Even if it's not real, if we're alone on this planet and when Dean died, he was gone forever and all he got were those few brief years on this earth—this is still good.

Patrick may have entered the religious life to find purpose in Magdalene's death, but I think he stayed in it because he found a purpose greater than his own personal redemption.

"Miss Branson, may I help you?" Father Ignatius stands beside me between the pew and the stained-glass window that looks like a patchwork of dark purples and blues and reds now that the sun has set.

"Oh!" I start, not expecting to see anyone standing there, much less the elderly priest.

He puts a finger over his lips, shushing me. I check to see if I've caught Patrick's attention unintentionally.

"This is a time for meditation and prayer. We'd appreciate your reverence," he scolds, and I feel like a child in Sunday school not knowing the right answers. I haven't seen the senior clergyman since my first day in Edinburgh nearly a month ago, and I wouldn't mind living the rest of my life without interacting directly with his sparkling personality. If Patrick is an example of the good of religion, Father Ignatius is the embodiment of why people my age are leaving traditional belief systems in record numbers.

"I'm sorry," I mutter. "I was waiting to talk with Father Patrick."

"Father Patrick is otherwise engaged tonight. If you have specific needs to discuss, I'm available, but unfortunately, he's not."

I thought I'd have the courage to tell Father Ignatius about the article, but I don't. It's none of his business, anyway. I'm sure Father Patrick will be in enough hot water as it is; he doesn't need more judgment.

"I can wait," I say, ready to return to my kneeling position, hoping Ignatius will walk away and give me privacy. But he calls my bluff and remains in the same spot, unmoved. Stagnant and complacent.

"I'm sorry, Miss Branson. He cannot meet with you tonight. If it's something of import, we can speak in my office . . ."

"I really need to speak with Father Patrick specifically. There's been a"—I search for the right words to convey gravity without giving away all the details—"development with the documentary, and we'll be leaving immediately. He's been a significant part of the film. It's important we speak."

He holds his ground, hands clasped on the curve of his belly. "You're in luck. We are well aware of your so-called 'development,' so you're free to go."

"You know?" I'm clearly too late. They know.

"Yes, Miss Branson. We know. Now, I think you've done enough. If you'd please leave."

I look over to Patrick. He's still talking to the man, but I'm sure he must notice the conversation between me and Father Ignatius. He's not blind, and he's not hard of hearing, so that means he's made the choice to leave my pesky interruption to his colleague. Father Ignatius is right—I've done enough.

"I'll go. But if you need any help here"—I gesture at the structure, but I mean the church in general, as though the ancient religion needs anything from little ole me—"I can reach out to my team. We're developing a strategic response, and I promise to protect him." I gesture at Patrick protectively. "He did nothing wrong. If you need me to testify or however things go with priests—I will."

"That will not be necessary," he says.

"All right." I check around my seat for my belongings, but I brought nothing other than the clothes on my back and my turned-off phone, so my hands are as empty as my heart. I take in the church one last time. Until two hours ago, I thought I'd be getting married here. God, till two hours ago, I still thought I'd be getting married, period. But everything's changed.

My mother betrayed me; my fiancé manipulated me; and I've irrevocably damaged my career. I've been humiliated in the press. And on top of that, my grandmother is not who she led me to believe—a salacious affair, a love child, a rogue husband, and too many lies to count.

There's only one person I want to talk to about all of it, and I'm being cast out from his presence. Is this why people crave a god so much—so when all else is lost, at least they still have one being that won't reject them?

Perhaps. But that's not where I can find my comfort, not today at least. Father Ignatius shuffles in place like he's dying to usher this sinner out of his holy home. I have no desire to be escorted out, so I leave, watching my feet with each step, head bowed low. Father Ignatius follows behind me to the end of the pew and then keeps watch as I travel the last few feet alone.

Once outside, I glance around, sure I will see a familiar car or Hunter with a bouquet of flowers, looking for me, but as far as I can tell in the pale moonlight and the muted shine of the streetlamps, no one's come to find me. I walk to the landing above the bottom steps and sit, turning on my phone. It erupts with buzzes, and color badges fill my screen. My mom called seventeen times and left six voice mails. Hunter sent one text saying that I seemed upset, and he'd let me have my space. He's getting his own room, and he suggests we talk in the morning. How cute—he thinks I'll still be here in the morning.

There are missed calls from contacts at various publications and more than one from Toffee Co. agents. My voice mail must be full at this point. The shock has worn off, and now I'm left with numbness. Usually, I'm a forward thinker, ten moves ahead of the game, but right now, I'm going one teeny tiny wobbly step at a time.

I open my Uber app and order a car. It'll be here in thirty minutes, faster than I anticipated. Then I open my travel app to find the next ticket out of here and hit the purchase button. I won't spend one more night in Edinburgh, Indiana.

"Excuse me." The man who was counseling with Father Patrick steps by me as he leaves the church.

Well, confession must be over. The rectory is in a house on the other side of the church through a rear exit, so at least I don't have to worry about either clergyman happening upon me while I wait for my ride. But just in case, I fold myself in tighter and lean against the metal railing, hoping I'll blend into the background.

Then I close my phone, wrap my arms around my upper body, and watch my breath mist up into the air, beneath the yellow glow of the streetlights. From here on the hill, I can see the town laid out in lines of illuminated streets, dots of light where uncovered windows project ambient warmth into the inky blue-black of the night. The evening air is cold and the sky cloudless. I shiver, the sweat on my neck and back having soaked into my long-sleeved shirt.

I feel cast out, and I think about the Bible story of the woman "taken in adultery" who was to be stoned by a group of men filled with righteous indignation. Jesus stepped in; I remember that part. He stepped in and said something about not casting stones if you live in glass houses, or something like that. Even though I can't remember the exact story, I do remember how I felt hearing it years ago. First, I thought, *Where's the guy she was cheating with? How come he's not being stoned?* And then I thought, *Why did all the people rushing toward the trembling woman care so damn much about what she did that they were ready to kill her?*

No one's about to stone me. But I still feel as if I were that woman cowering on the ground, preparing to be pelted by strangers, while the people I love most have abandoned me.

I hear the loud slapping footfalls of a runner heading in my direction— someone out for a late jog, I guess. I put my chin on my knees and hold my breath so the frozen water vapor of my exhalations in the air doesn't give me away.

"Elise, there you are!" Father Patrick comes to a halt at the bottom of the steps, out of breath, hands on his hips. He's removed his stole and white vestment. His collar is open without the white insert. I've never seen him like this —so . . . normal. "I thought I missed you."

I blink and shake my head, trying to make sense of what I'm seeing. It took a lot of restraint to leave him alone and not make a scene with Father Ignatius, but now he's here, outside, underdressed, and looking for me. I'm overcome with gratitude. Even if he's here to tell me he never wants to see me again and that I ruined his life—it's better than the stonewalling.

"I'm waiting for my Uber. Father Ignatius passed on your message."

"My message?" he asks, the haze from his heavy breathing obscuring his face.

"That you didn't want to talk to me." It hurts to say it. Tears spill down my cheeks, and I curse my inability to stop them. "Which is completely your prerogative. I'm sorry you got caught in the middle of all this."

"You're sorry?" he asks, moving into a puddle of light that illuminates his light blue eyes, making them glow. "No, *I'm* sorry. This is all my fault."

"No, it's my fault and my family's fault. God, it's even Hunter's fault." I run through the list, laughing ironically. "The only person I don't blame is you."

"I can't let you do that. The pictures and accusations, sure, we can blame that on human frailties like greed or pride. But my sin remains the same. I . . ." He stumbles over his words, staring at his hands pressed together in front of him. "I knew after our first meeting that I needed to be careful. It didn't take long to develop *very* strong feelings for you. I allowed myself to have them, and I nurtured them inappropriately."

He's avoided direct eye contact until now. When he meets my gaze, it's there again, the electricity that nearly struck me down when he touched my hand across his desk after our first interview. Damn that current. Damn how right it feels. Damn how badly I want to be held in his arms and protect one another from all the stones hurled our way.

He looks away first, following the line of the church steeple, his eyes turned toward the heavens.

"Father Ignatius will be completing your Pre-Cana and performing the ceremony. I'll be transferring in the morning."

"Transfer? They're sending you away?" Talk about being cast out—I'm sure my consequences look like nothing compared to his.

"No, I want to go. I can't be here while . . ." His eyes grow glossy as he stares toward the cross on the top of the steeple. "I can't be here while you are."

I look over my shoulder at the symbol he's focusing on and then back at him, spinning my engagement ring around my finger over and over again.

"I'm leaving tonight for New York. Hunter and I—I don't think we're gonna make it."

"Oh no. I'm so sorry," he says, sounding concerned. He looks up at me, his face filled with compassion and regret.

"Hey, don't be. It has very little to do with you. Really."

Well, it has something to do with him or at least the way I feel about him and the contrast it's provided to my relationship with Hunter, opening my eyes to its flaws.

"That's sad to hear. You know I wish you the best, either way." He gives a little bow and a smile I know he doesn't mean. One minute he's leaving town because I'm too tempting or whatever, and then the next he's wishing me well in my possible future marriage. I can't keep up with it all.

"I don't blame you for your feelings," I explain, frustrated with him in a way that's hard to pinpoint. "I have them, too, and you're right—it all feels . . . irresistible when we're together," I disclose, so exasperated that I don't recognize the importance of us both acknowledging our feelings for each other. "So, I agree—that means we have to stay far apart, but you don't have to be so goddamn magnanimous about it all."

A car with a *U* illuminated in the window pulls up to the curb. Thank God, my ride is here. I left all my belongings including my rental car key at the hotel. I'll have Conrad pack it up and mail it. For now, I have my wallet and my phone, and that's all I need. No way I'm going back to that place and risking being surreptitiously filmed again.

I stand, wobbling as blood returns to my legs and feet.

"I gotta go. I wish you well too, Patrick." I make it to the second-to-bottom stair just above where he's planted. He doesn't step aside, and he doesn't look away. In this position, we're close to equal height, and he has to look me in the eye.

"Hold on. Please. Let me explain." His cheeks are a bright pink from the cold and his eyes red rimmed like he's spent the day crying. I should leave; it's safer for us both.

But I don't.

"Go ahead."

"All right," he says, and then continues, labored, like he's fighting off a muzzle. "I wanted to tell you to leave Hunter," he says, uttering Hunter's name like it's a dirty word, his breath touching my cheek with each word, "and I want to go back in time to a place where I had a right to offer you all the things you deserve." He scrutinizes me between each statement, his assessment feeling like a caress. "Do you really think I don't dream of waking up next to you? It haunts me, that thought." He tucks a strand of hair behind my ear, and I melt at his tender touch. "My vows have never felt heavy. But now they're like chains that keep me underwater when all I want to do is breathe you in—your mind and soul and, God curse me, your hair, your lips, your embrace . . ."

I bite my lower lip when he mentions them and then tilt toward him, our bodies practically touching.

"I'm sorry I haunt you," I kid, touching his cheek. A rumbling sound comes from deep in his throat, and I hate how it builds my longing for all the things he listed.

"I wish things were different," I say, fighting the urge to give in to temptation and press my mouth against his, let his arms take me in, his fingers grasp at my back, pulling me into his chest so tightly I can't breathe.

"Me too," he says, watching my lips, fighting the same demons that I am.

"But they're not," I say, stating what we already know and removing my hand.

"No, they're not," he agrees, shuffling far enough away that a cool wind chills the pool of heat that had gathered between us.

"Goodbye, Father Patrick," I say, putting out my hand formally. He takes it.

"Goodbye, Miss Branson," he returns. We shake and then we reluctantly let go. I run to the waiting car like I'm being chased by the devil himself.

Turning my eyes downward, I stare at the glittering three-carat diamond ring my grandfather supposedly gave to my grandmother. I once asked her how he'd afforded such a fancy ring when he was reportedly such a humble man. She said it was a family heirloom, which meant it didn't really belong to her, but it belonged to the next generation and the generation after that. I take it off and slip it onto the ring finger of my right hand.

Why did I only feel worthy enough to wear this ring when a man gave it to me? I wonder.

As the car carries me away, I turn around in my seat for one more look at Father Patrick, at Edinburgh, and at Holy Trinity. Patrick stands in front of the church where I left him, but his eyes are no longer cast up toward the steeple, the cross, or heaven itself. Instead, he, in his black shirt and slacks, head bowed low and buried in his hands, is gradually swallowed up by the darkness.

It's better this way. For both of us.

CHAPTER 34

Vivian

Sunday, October 17, 1943
Camp Atterbury

"Vivian! Is that you?" Judy jumps to her feet behind the glass partition and leans against the desk to get a better look, and I know why. I've been away for four months, and I'm returning a different woman from when I first walked into this office six months ago.

My two-piece crimson Adele Simpson dress and blue felt hat with a wide brim are newer additions to my wardrobe, along with the matching wool polo coat draped over my shoulders. Archie says it's important to always look the part of a star even if you aren't in front of the camera because you never know who's looking. USO Camp Shows provides all our stage costumes, but for meet and greets and dances, we're expected to supply our own wardrobe. Most girls use their whole paycheck to fund the glamorous look Archie encourages. But I've been sending my paycheck home.

Judy bursts into the lobby as I'm stuffing my gloves into my envelope purse. As she wraps me in an intense embrace, I take a brief glance at the hallway that first led me to my new life. I had no idea where things would lead back then—but I'm sure the six-months-ago me would be proud of my dress choice at least, even if she might not be as impressed with some of my other decisions.

"When I heard you and Tom ran off and got married and then you were chosen for the Camp Shows, I about lost my mind with envy. Now you're back and all elegant and polished. And look at that ring!" She picks up my left hand. I'm not wearing the tin one Tom gave me here on base. I save that one for when I'm on the road or when I'm home with papà, playing the role of a good wife. He knows of my elopement. I told him as soon as the officers started coming around looking for Tom. Our marriage was legal and binding, so of course they'd question me first.

Tom's been AWOL for four months, and there's still an investigation as far as I know. I've had several conversations with the military police. They finally seem to believe I'm not helping him hide out somewhere to avoid being deployed.

His family's paid to keep it out of the papers and ignored any evidence of his marriage to me, an unknown country bumpkin. They blame me, I'm sure, for his disappearance, which is only fair. Going AWOL two days after a secret wedding looks a lot like buyer's remorse. So far, I've stayed away from the Highwards, and they've stayed away from me, and that's been working fine. I don't think I could face them, anyway. Not with how things ended between me and Tom. What I did.

Thankfully, I was able to convince papà that Tom is missing in action. With his limited English, I don't have to worry too much about him hearing otherwise. It's the story I tell everyone. And since I'm a married woman, even old-fashioned papà couldn't keep me from auditioning with Archie Lombardo or saying yes when I was offered the touring position.

Judy clutches my hand to examine the ring. "Yeah, it was delivered right before I left for Chicago. It's a bit much for a USO girl."

"No. It's beautiful."

The stone sparkles in its white gold setting—three carats. I have no need for a three-carat diamond. The moment Ari and I opened that box, I was filled with guilt. If things hadn't taken a turn, if Tom were around and we were happy, I'd make him take it back, get something a little simpler, and use the rest of the money for more important things like family and our future.

At first, I planned to sell it. I hoped that if I got rid of the ring, I'd get rid of the guilt. But that was right around the time the military police started showing up searching for Tom. So I needed the ring—to avoid suspicion. But I didn't need the stone.

What Judy doesn't know, and what no one will ever know, is that the stone in the ring is as fake as my status as an army wife. I sold the real diamond weeks ago. I paid off mamma's debt at Mount Mercy and papà's medical expenses, and I set up an account to pay for Aria's college in case something happens and I get sent away. Everyone is taken care of.

Well, almost everyone.

"All right. It's decided. I forgive you." She stares at the ring and then at me like I'm the luckiest girl around. "How long are you here?"

"Just for the chapel dedication. I have to be back on the tour tomorrow." I have twenty-four hours to make the trip from Chicago to Edinburgh and back. I'm already blurry eyed from the late-night drive and nauseated from my empty stomach, but as soon as I got Trombello's latest postcard with his sketch of the finished chapel, I knew I needed to be here. "But I'll return for a few months soon."

"Oh yeah? You gonna take your old desk back?" she asks, looking at the tidy desk in the corner and the sweet little blonde girl sitting there tapping away.

"Ha. No—this is not a hostile takeover. I'll be busy with . . . other things." I keep my response vague and check my watch. "I should sign in and get over to the meadow. You coming?"

Judy passes me the sign-in log and shakes her head.

"Nah. Prisoners only, besides you and some guards and the priest doing the service."

Priest.

The term brings up so many emotions. It used to be a word of safety and comfort, but it's very different now for many reasons. I haven't seen Father Theodore since the night he drove me home, bruised and bloodied, my voice scruffy from Tom's hands around my throat. He debated taking me to the hospital, but I begged him not to. My family couldn't afford one more medical expense, and the doctors would have had questions I couldn't answer.

I never went to him and confessed what happened that night with Tom. And to this day I don't know what happened after Gravano escorted me out of that middle school locker room. All I know is Tom never came back. And Trombello and the rest of the crew never mentioned the incident. I ran away to audition for Archie in Chicago as soon as my throat had healed enough for me to sing again.

"Well then. We'll have to catch up when I sign out. I want to hear all about your guy and what's been going on here since I left." I give her arm a little squeeze as I head toward the door, both dreading and desiring my next challenge.

"Sure. Sounds great. And how about a cup of coffee, you know, when you come back round Christmas?" Judy asks, hand on her hip, pencil buried in the curls of her bob haircut. "Mary should be back by then. We can all complain about our husbands and exchange casserole recipes like all the good married girls do."

Mary found her own soldier and married him only a month after she watched me walk down the aisle. She's visiting his family in North Carolina for a few weeks, but we write often, and she promises to be home for Christmas. I hope her dreams of marital bliss have come to a happier ever after than mine.

"It's a date," I chirp cheerfully, pretending I'm the same as Judy and Mary, worrying about my housekeeping and meal planning.

As I take the transport to the chapel site, I do all I can to maintain a cheerful expression. I keep up the façade, not to hide my feelings about seeing Judy or the familiar scenery, or the regrets that pop up at the most unexpected moments, but to hide how I feel about coming home again in December and the reason why.

Archie's going to call it medical leave, say I have pneumonia. But pneumonia rarely leads to a baby, so that'll only work for so long. There's no scandal in a married woman having a child, but it does change how a casting director sees an actress, and so Archie suggests keeping it as quiet as possible. A child is far easier to explain than a husband who never comes home from a war he's not fighting in, but I guess I have some time to figure out those details.

When the truck takes a left instead of a right at the front gate, my attention shifts. We're heading through the heart of the camp, passing the barracks and the mess hall, to the westernmost border of the camp. The ride is bumpy, and I have to grab my hat a few times to keep from losing it. And the rough drive does little for my already tender stomach.

Thankfully, the ride is over shortly. As we approach the old rear gate, I see the barbed-wire barrier has been extended to enclose the rear meadow. A tall, octagonal wooden guard tower overlooks the fields. All the trees and wild brush have been removed and the ground turned to a rough, packed clay on one side and a tidy sports field on the other. The transformation is dizzying, and I'm not sure how the chapel can keep the moniker of Chapel in the Meadow when the meadow looks more like a dirty tundra.

Mass has already begun. A large crowd of POWs dressed in dark slacks, the blue collars of their PW uniforms sticking up neatly from the tops of their thick, black woolen sweaters, surround the finished chapel in a hushed reverence, virtually encompassing it with their number. The compact, one-room structure is only big enough for the officiant, his deacon, and altar servers. The inside of the three-walled chapel is covered with colorful paintings of saints on the plaster and cherubs behind the altar.

The colors are vibrant, though I know the lack of supplies meant that the men created the art out of found items and reused plaster. The crimson-colored steps lead up to the altar, painted in a pattern like tiles in an ancient cathedral.

Despite the surroundings—the fences, guns, towers, and uniforms—our little chapel is perfect. As I watch the men take Communion, I notice something I hadn't before. The *PW* on the men's sleeve is gone. It reminds me of another reason I couldn't miss the opportunity to visit today. Soon the Italian men and the melody of their voices will be replaced by German prisoners who may not have much use for the Catholic chapel.

Since Italy surrendered last month and declared war on Germany just four days ago, these men in blue and black are no longer our enemies—they're our allies.

A cutting wind whips through the field, sending debris against my legs and a shiver through my bones. I slip my arms into my coat. I'm sure it'd be warmer nearer the crowd, but I'm not prepared to take Communion—not yet.

As the congregation moves into an orderly line to receive the Eucharist, I spy Trombello heading my way. He looks much like he did before, a strong jaw and kind eyes. But there's something else in my priestly friend now, something I'd expect from a man coming home after war. It's a strength I respect but also a coolness that I fear comes from sacrificing who he thought he was in order to protect those he cared about. It's even more painful to see, knowing I'm the cause of it.

He catches my eye and I nod at him.

When Mass has ended, I move with the congregation away from the chapel and spot Trombello standing a short distance away, watching me approach.

"Signora Highward, è così bello vederla." *Mrs. Highward, so good to see you,* he says, using my married name to greet me.

319

"Buongiorno, Padre," I say, letting him take my gloved hands. We've stayed in touch the past few months with postcards and drawings. But only so much can be said on a three-by-five piece of paper that'll be screened by the authorities before reaching its intended recipient. Trombello covers only the basics, and even those are limited, though meaningful.

"Lei è luce per i miei occhi." *You are a light for my eyes*, he says, the Italian version of "you're a sight for sore eyes." And I feel the same about seeing my friend again—any shift in his countenance hasn't changed a thing about how he makes me feel. In these moments, I'm jealous of sharing his charity with others and that the church has him in a way I never can.

"It is beautiful," I say in Italian, gesturing to the chapel. Trombello beams with pride and then turns somber.

"We'll be leaving soon," he says.

"Back to Italy?" I ask, uneasy, wondering how the POWs will make it through the havoc of war-torn Europe or Africa to get back to their terrified families and villages.

He shakes his head.

"No, here. In America. There are jobs for men who sign papers of allegiance."

"You're staying?" A flash of hope flares up.

"Only till the war is over," he says.

"Oh," I say, allowing my disappointment to show. "I'd hoped . . ."

"I know," he says, letting his fingers brush against the back of my hand as they hang parallel at our sides. "But you are strong on your own. With your work and your marriage certificate and your mamma and papà cared for. God will watch over you now."

"I doubt God has any kind feelings for me, Father."

"You are wrong. He is all love," he says, sounding like the priest I often forget he is.

"But my sins . . . Tom . . ." I've had no one to talk to about that night—about what happened to Tom. What the knife felt like in my hand as it pierced his flesh. How there are times I'm suffocated by guilt and other moments I'm sure I did what had to be done.

"Do you blame a soldier for killing his enemy on the battlefield?" Trombello asks before the tears gathering in my eyes make their way to my cheeks.

"No. Of course not, but . . ."

"No 'but.' You were a soldier, *figlia mia.* A brave soldier. God knows of it, and so do I."

A soldier. It feels sacrilegious to think of myself as a soldier with the horrors of war facing our brave young men every day. But when Trombello says it, I understand his meaning.

"I'm pregnant," I blurt without preamble. Trombello stiffens and then responds mechanically.

"Congratulazioni per la bellissima notizia." *Congratulations on the great news.*

I didn't tell him in order to seek his felicitations. As this life has grown inside of me, I've wondered if it is God's way of telling me that actions have consequences. If caring for this child is my penance, for myself, for my family. To make up for what I've done to the child's father, to make up for the life my brother didn't get to have.

"What do I tell my child?" I have so many questions I need answered. I want the guidance I can get from only one source. "How do I tell him his father is gone? That I am the thief who stole his father away. How do I repent?"

Trombello gazes at the chapel. It's a long, unbroken stare.

"Tell him his father died at war." I nod. Trombello's body sways as his knees lock, and the breeze tosses my hair into my face. I don't panic at his withdrawn demeanor and far-off look. I know it's not an easy question, and I don't expect a simple reply. At long last, he says, "One day, when your child learns of God, tell him this in addition and nothing else—his father is buried on consecrated ground, with last rites, and God will open the gates of paradise to him if he is found worthy."

I imagine my child sitting on my knee, wanting to know stories of his papà. I'll tell him of a man who didn't exist, not really, not in any way I'd want my little one to know of. My child will worship a fable. I touch the scar at my neck where Tom cut me with the knife that killed him moments later. I grew up knowing who and what my mother was. Her darkest moments were also mine. If I can protect my child from such a harsh understanding, I will.

And I'll be the mother mine was unable to be because of the way her mind worked, and the way life failed her. I'll care for my child and carry the heavy burdens of life so he doesn't have to, no matter what sacrifices are required.

Finding the first modicum of peace I've felt since that fateful night, I follow Trombello's gaze, grateful. He lingers on the cross at the apex of the chapel's vaulted entrance like he's witnessing the holy sacrifice of Christ himself. An unsettled nausea gathers in my belly that goes beyond morning sickness. This is a holy place now. But it's been con-secrated ground since Archbishop Cicognani dedicated the altar last June. Consecrated ground. The phrase chills me. The foundation to the chapel was poured immediately following the night of the dance.

Consecrated ground.

I shake off the potential realization. I don't want to know.

If Tom rests under that chapel, and Trombello spared his soul in those final moments of his life by administering last rites, that's some-thing Trombello can carry. For now, I'm carrying enough, including Tom's innocent child.

"I wish things were different," I say quietly as Cresci and Gravano wave and make their way to us across the field.

"As do I, *figlia mia*. As do I."

I've seen an ally turn from a stranger into a dance partner, into a lover, into a husband, and finally into an enemy. And I've seen my enemy turn from an adversary into a colleague, then a friend, a rescuer, and finally my only true ally.

I've been many things in my life as well, and soon enough I'll become a mother. I don't know if I believe Tom will be waiting inside the gates of heaven when I make it there one day. I don't know if I'll be allowed inside either. But I do know that my child doesn't deserve to inherit the sins of his or her father or mother. And I will do my best to protect her and provide for her. Whatever it takes.

CHAPTER 35

Elise

Two Years Later
RROCK Headquarters—Refugee Resettlement Organization and
Community Kitchen

The boardroom table seats twelve, but right now it's just me, my chief operations officer, senior vice president, and general counsel sitting across from a bright-eyed Harvard grad in a tailored skirt and jacket. Her résumé is impressive—master's degree in public health and social work and an undergrad degree in linguistics. I can already tell her vibe will fit in perfectly with our team.

"I interned at the UNICEF headquarters. It's a great organization, but I wanted to go somewhere more grassroots. My roommate told me about an opportunity with the Peace Corps in Togo working in public health, so I applied."

"Africa?" I ask, impressed. This young woman has her head on straight. She's the kind of employee I've been looking for since opening RROCK a little over a year ago.

"Yes. Africa. Togo is a beautiful country, and I spent two years there. But when I left, I felt like there was more I could do to help, and that's when I heard about RROCK. You're new—totally ground floor in the nonprofit world. But that's what I'm into—building something new. Like, literally and figuratively. In Togo, we had to rebuild our house and help our neighbors and friends do the same when a brush fire came through and turned the town into dust. That's just one town. I'm totally passionate . . ."

I take notes as she shares her experience. Ciara and Oscar ask her some additional questions. In all actuality, this applicant has more real-world experience than I do even as president of the Refugee Resettlement Organization and Community Kitchen. But I rely on individuals far more educated and experienced than myself. I provide expertise from running Toffee Co. and a good amount of funding from my sale of the company and the residuals from the documentary.

"Thank you for your time, Monique. We'll be reaching out before the end of the week with our final decision," Ciara says, bringing the interview to a close. We take turns shaking hands and exchanging nice-ties as we walk her to the door.

"Oh, Ms. Branson, I hope you don't mind my saying so, but I'm a huge fan," Monique says as she's about to leave. Her professional mask slips and reveals a much younger side that the old PR Elise would label "in touch with the eighteen-to-twenty-four demographic." A little young to be a fan of my grandmother, or even my father or mother, so I assume she must be referring to one of my siblings.

"Thanks, Monique. I'll pass it on," I say, without asking for specification. Now that I'm out of the entertainment industry and fewer people know of my background, these kinds of comments bother me less. I never actually "pass it on" like I promise, but I don't think that matters as much as receiving the compliment graciously, a familial proxy.

"Pass it on?" she asks, her manicured eyebrow raised.

"To my family. I'll pass it on."

"Oh no. I'm talking about you. I'm a fan of yours. I've seen *Bombshell* like ten times. It's why I applied at RROCK. I didn't know anything about Vivian Snow or even those POW camps. Then the part about the refugees and the big revelation at the end . . ."

"Well, thank you. I appreciate it," I say, hoping to bring the conversation to a natural end, surprised and a little destabilized by having the documentary brought up in my professional arena.

I've never seen the final cut of the four-part film. I asked Marla, my former VP, to watch it for me, and she gave me a CliffsNotes version, but I can't go back to that six-week period of my life that gutted me so entirely that I had to start over from scratch.

But I know enough from Marla's twenty-page summary to understand the narrative. The story wasn't about my wedding because it never happened. Mac cut the majority of the wedding prep and Pre-Cana with Hunter but kept the scenes with me and Patrick and used the friendship as a framing device for the first few episodes. He then used the paparazzi pictures and ensuing breakup as an effective cliff-hanger at the end of the third episode leading up to the results of the DNA test. That was the last scene I appeared in, a month after leaving Edinburgh. I was eager to know the results, and the only way I'd find out ahead of the rest of the viewing public was if I let Mac film the big reveal.

Perched on the edge of her velvet settee, I sat there in my mother's penthouse, considering who my grandfather might be. I'd pondered Antonio Trombello often and wondered if my grandmother had somehow fallen for the same kind of forbidden fruit that I'd been tempted with.

With the cameras rolling, my mother did her best "loving mother" impression, even though we hadn't spoken in four weeks. Chris and Lawrence were there too. Chris had refused to be in the same room with my mom for years but was suddenly desperate to be by her side. Jim was still on location, so he couldn't attend the big moment, but he also didn't need the publicity as much as my other brothers. One boy on each side, holding their mother's shoulders for support. And me by myself, spinning the ring on my right hand, counting the seconds till we finally knew the truth.

Using a fancy golden letter opener, my mother opened the sealed envelope in one swoosh. The DNA had been provided from the Highward family, which was just about all my long-lost New York cousin who had no idea of our familial connection until our visit was able to supply. All the samples were processed in a prestigious facility, and it was finally the moment of truth. She took her own sweet time sliding out the paper and unfolding it dramatically.

"He's my dad," she said, teary-eyed. But it wasn't clear whom she was speaking about, so Mac made her try again.

"Tom Highward is my dad." We all reacted again with hugs and relief, yes even me. As far as we know, this great scandal was nothing more than my sweet grandmother covering for her deadbeat, AWOL husband. The Highwards seemed to know even less than we do about Tom, contributing only a few pictures from his childhood and stories told by his sister, Moira Highward, before she passed. Some "bombshell" that turned out to be.

On our way out of the boardroom, Monique gasps and points to my right hand like she's a kid at Disneyland who has spotted Mickey Mouse.

"Is that the ring? The one your grandma passed down?"

The three-carat stone sparkles up at me. Even with its pristine luster, it's easy to forget about since I rarely take it off.

"It is," I say, covering the antique piece of jewelry with my bare left hand.

"I love that you wear it even after . . . everything. Boss move," Monique says.

"Thanks," I say, feeling nothing like a "boss"—not in the way Monique means it at least. People read far too deeply into the ring. Some people say I wear it for revenge; others say I wear it because I can't let go—that I'm not over Hunter or even Dean. Of course, it has to be all about a guy.

What the internet gossips fail to understand is that I left Hunter after the shady stuff with the documentary, not the other way around. The more popular narrative is that Hunter dumped my ass after the story broke about the priest scandal, but there's little need for a public correction. Mac could've cleared it up easily if he'd included the entirety of the hidden camera confrontation, but instead, it ended up on the proverbial cutting-room floor.

The story went away quickly, flaring up only briefly when *Bombshell* went through its publicity cycle and again when awards season hit. But none of it hurt Hunter's image; in fact, it seems to have been a net positive. He married a wealthy entrepreneur/reality show star within a year of our breakup. From what I hear, they have a baby on the way.

I knew I was over him when I could see a picture of the pair in my newsfeed and not unfollow that particular media outlet. I don't believe Hunter did what he did because he wasn't in love with me. I think it was more likely because his view of love was so altered by his upbringing that he didn't know how to have a real relationship outside of the media spotlight. And it turned out that I wasn't interested in that kind of relationship.

My marriage to Dean may have worked—we were young enough and naive enough to give ourselves over to love wholeheartedly. But who knows? Maybe that was a broken heart waiting to happen too. In a way, I'm glad I'll never know.

"I'm not even kissing up to try and get a job. It's the truth—you guys deserved those Emmys." Monique continues with her compliments, and though I know she means well, it's getting a bit awkward. "And Mac Dorman's acceptance speech? I see clips on TikTok all the time."

"Well, thanks, Monique," I say, smiling at her reference to all the things I've actively avoided. "You should hear from us soon. Oscar will show you out," I add quickly, ready to escape.

Mom and Mac had broken up by awards season, and she attended with my thirteen-year-old niece, Nora, keeping the fame cycle running for another generation. Nonna passed a lot down to us—*Variety* says it's her smile, but that's one minor part of our inheritance. She worked tirelessly for her place on the screen, and it pulled her and her family out of poverty. I do wonder whether it's fair to benefit from her fame rather than pave our own paths. It's a hollow existence wondering every time I find success if I'd have reached it without my family's name following my own.

I politely disengage from the conversation, and Monique eventually departs. RROCK is my domain now, and I want to be immersed in it. As Oscar and Ciara walk Monique out and greet our next candidate, I return to my spot and think of Nora at the Emmys all dolled up in a gown and fake lashes. I'll see if Jim will let her spend part of her summer with me working in the community kitchen, maybe taking a trip to my dad's ranch. I'm not pretending to know what's right for my brother's kid, but I know what helped my soul, and very little of it had to do with red carpets or flashing lights. If I'd remembered that a little sooner, I would've walked away from *Bombshell* before all the damage happened. No boom mic; can lights; camera lenses; Edinburgh, Indiana; or Father Patrick.

My phone buzzes just in time to keep me from going down the well-trodden path of regret labeled "Patrick Kelly."

OSCAR: Got our next one. Be right in.

It's no use reliving that storyline anymore. Walking away from Patrick was different from walking away from the film or Hunter or even my mom. Patrick was innocent. He was my friend. He was real. And unlike Hunter—I still miss him.

I take out the next résumé without looking at it and place it on the table as the boardroom door opens. I hope our next applicant doesn't know me, or if she does, she isn't gutsy enough to bring it up. Though it's pretty likely any candidate will do a healthy amount of research before their interview, so maybe it's a red flag if they haven't seen the documentary. I chuckle at the irony as everyone returns to their seats.

Oscar clears his throat and starts the meeting.

"Good afternoon. We're so glad you made it out today. I know Hanna and Luis met with you earlier this week and you and Ciara had a long call yesterday and you finished up a tour of the kitchen and our other facilities. Now, we wanted to bring you in today to meet both myself and our president, Ms. Elise Branson, for a few questions and to see if you had any for us. So—welcome." Oscar rattles off his spiel as I finish fidgeting with my notepad, forcing myself to come back to the present moment.

"Thank you. I'm honored to be here." A masculine-sounding voice with a temperate quality to it replies, making me check the résumé. And there, on a stiff, white piece of paper is the name I've been running away from for close to two years.

"Patrick?" I say, just as surprised as the first time he played a switching game on me as I pontificated about stained-glass windows in Holy Trinity. Sure enough, when I look up, there he is—dark hair, kind eyes, playful but steady smile.

"Well, yeah. Or 'Mr. Kelly' if you're looking for something more formal."

Oscar laughs, and Ciara presses her trimmed nails against her lips like she's covering up a grin. Patrick is dressed in plain clothes: a neat dark blue pair of jeans and a Ralph Lauren jacket that was popular four or five years ago. His short boots are a rich brown leather. Most interesting of all is the dress shirt he has on. It's not the white oxford shirt itself that catches my eye. No. It's the lack of a clerical collar.

"M . . . Mr. . . . ," I stutter, caught on the casual title but trying to look professional. "Mr. Kelly." I read over his résumé and find it matches what I know of Father Patrick, which apparently also applies to Mr. Kelly.

"Ms. Branson," he responds, calling me by my formal name in a good-humored way.

"You two know each other, then?" Oscar asks.

"Uh, yeah. In a way, I guess. We knew each other from . . ." I don't know how to describe how we know one another. From planning my wedding? From the movie we did together? From church? From the tabloids? From conspiracy videos on TikTok?

"Operation Allies Welcome. Working with Afghan refugees at Camp . . ."

"Atterbury. Yes. Mr. Kelly was a big part of that project." I'm speaking to my team now in order to avoid eye contact with Patrick. "Actually, seeing the lack of resettlement resources for that particular base was one of the inspirations for RROCK."

"Well, isn't that full circle?" Oscar asks, holding his pen in the hand clasped under his chin. "Your résumé struck me as particularly *unique*." He lingers on the last word, and I'm sure it's because he's savvy enough to know not to bring up an applicant's religious beliefs in a job interview. "What brings you to our organization?"

Patrick sits up in his chair and straightens his jacket like he's preparing for a one-on-one with Mac Dorman rather than a job interview.

"A lot like Ms. Branson, I've recently made a huge shift in my career," he says, speaking directly at me, uninhibited. "And I've always been passionate about helping others."

"Wait," I blurt, wedging myself into the conversation, dizzied by the unexpected cameo. "Your career changed?"

I haven't seen Father Patrick since the night we parted in front of the church. I considered reaching out more than once, but after that last conversation with Father Ignatius and several conversations with church officials investigating the photograph situation, I thought it'd be best for Patrick if he never saw my face again. Why would he even want to talk to me, much less work at my company?

"Uh, yeah. It's a long story, but—to answer simply—yes. Yes, it changed." He rubs his chin and uncrosses his legs and then lays an envelope on the table. "I was freed from the clerical state at the end of last year and have been laicized. It's all in here if you need the documentation."

"Well, your religious orders are really none of our business," Ciara reminds Patrick and the rest of the room, pushing her long, curly hair off her shoulders like the tension is making her warm. It may be none of Ciara's business or Oscar's or RROCK's business for that matter, but it damn well seems like one of the main reasons he's come here is to give me that piece of information.

"You know what—could Patrick and I have a second? I think we need to catch up before we continue. You all right with that?" I ask my team, knowing full well they have no other option but to say yes.

Both executives clear the room without protest. Once we're alone, I settle into a chair closer to his but not so close as to seem aggressive or presumptive.

"You know you could've just called me, right?" I ask, taking him in from this closer proximity. He's different. Not quite so buttoned up, literally and figuratively. His hair is neatly combed but touching his ears and collar. And from here, I can see a light stubble on his chin that's ruggedly handsome to say the least.

But he's also completely unchanged, and so is my reaction to him—his mannerisms, humor, the way he makes me feel like he knows all the worst parts of me and doesn't give a shit about any of them. Our eyes connect in that way that makes my insides melt and my ears ring.

"I wanted to. But I didn't know what you'd think of me now." He gestures to his new look or perhaps his new self.

"A wardrobe change or a title change isn't important to me. I thought you'd have known that."

"I know, but . . . ," he says, unable to finish the sentence coherently. I tilt my head, confused.

"If you knew, then, why'd you stay away so long?" I thought he was focused on his spiritual life. I thought I was helping him avoid temptation or whatever people like Father Ignatius might call the glowing embers of what we had together.

He sighs, readjusts in his seat, and then leans in toward my chair.

"When you left the church that night, I went after you. You don't know that, but I did. When I got to the hotel, though, Hunter was in your room and told me you were gone. He said he knew the pictures were embellished and tried to act like you'd reconciled. I only halfway bought it, but it did take some wind out of my sails. I went back to the rectory, and I'm not kidding when I say I was about to buy a ticket to New York."

"You were?" It sounds ridiculously close to the end of a cheesy romcom, but even so, I find it touching.

"I did," he says, reticent, a touch of pink coloring his cheeks. "Then Father Ignatius came to speak with me, convinced me to not throw away everything I'd been working toward. He said, 'If it's God's will today, then it will still be his will tomorrow' and asked me to not make a rash decision. So, I didn't transfer. And every day I'd pray, and every day Father Ignatius would ask if I'd decided to stay, and I'd say I didn't know. And then one day he said, 'If you're still asking God the same question after all this time, you know your answer.' And I knew he was right. I hadn't gone one day without thinking of you. Not one. And that's a lot to say to someone without, you know, freaking them out," he acknowledges sheepishly.

"You left the priesthood because of me?" I stare at him, taking in his confession, not sure what it all means but also feeling like I'd just figured out the final puzzle on *Wheel of Fortune* with only a few vowels and consonants in the right place.

He looks uncomfortable with my chosen wording.

"I stayed away because I *didn't* want to leave 'because of you.' I wanted to make sure I was leaving because it was right for *me*. And that's why I'm here looking for a job instead of calling you with"—he gyrates his hands in the air, symbolically—"other intentions."

Two years is a long time. I've been through a major breakup, a total career change, family drama, and multiple public relations nightmares. I'm not the same person I was two years ago, and neither is he. And I think that's a good thing.

"I can't hire you," I say matter-of-factly, which I can tell surprises him after he revealed his emotional vulnerability.

"All right, I understand," he says after a brief pause, folding up his notepad and placing the envelope in the crease.

"Hey, no, wait. I'm not asking you to leave." I touch his sleeve, wishing I had the courage to take his hand, but I can't, not yet. "I'm saying I can't be involved in hiring you because I'm"—I search for the right word—"biased."

"Good biased or bad biased?" he asks, placing the notepad back on the table.

"It's not bad. It just means I have a vested interest in your doing well, so it's not fair to everyone else." I bite my lip and say the thought that's flashed into my mind. "But you're too skilled to lose that easily, and we don't have an art program here . . ." I let the suggestion trail off, allowing him to fill in the gaps of my impromptu proposal.

"That sounds amazing," he responds, taking out his résumé again.

"It might take some time to get funding. I'll have to pass it by the board and the rest of the executives. And we'll need to come up with a strong proposal."

"I have time, and I have mad PowerPoint skills," Patrick says, his face lighting up. I laugh.

"I'm not even going to ask how you honed those skills in your last job," I say as I text Oscar and Ciara to come back into the room. They'll be the first ones we'll need to pitch the idea to.

"Let's just say my liturgy was audio and visual," he clarifies.

I've missed this. Him. All of it.

"Sounds like all we need to do now is shake on it," I say, standing up and offering my right hand, the one with Nonna's ring. It looks small and white in the space between us. He gets up from his seat and we shake, my fingertips dragging across his palm. And though it's been two years since I first felt it, his touch has not lost its charge. The sensation is so intense, I instinctively draw away, and so does Patrick.

The boardroom door swings open, and Ciara and Oscar take their assigned seats. Patrick clenches and unclenches his fist like he's checking for damage.

Unless my board sees something I don't, I'm positive there's a place here for Patrick Kelly. And I think it's clear neither of us is ready to dive into this connection without looking. I know one thing for certain—Patrick Kelly, this man with the electric touch, is back in my life, this time without the barrier of religious office and clerical collar. And I am without the specter of fame and the expectations that accompany it. It's possible we'll get used to the electricity between us or that it'll go away entirely, but there's also the chance that we'll discover a new power source that'll change lives, including our own.

ACKNOWLEDGMENTS

Thank you to the people of Edinburgh and the Edinburgh-Indiana Memories Facebook group. Your pride in your town and its rich history is beautiful, and I loved every minute of my visit. I hope you enjoy a fictionalized story based on the true history of your community and Camp Atterbury.

Thank you to Camp Atterbury and the Camp Atterbury Museum for preserving and sharing the dynamic history of this facility. As I researched the camp's background as a military training facility, WWII POW camp, and the very real Chapel in the Meadow—I also learned of Atterbury's ongoing legacy of military and humanitarian service. I was impressed and inspired. Thank you to all who have walked those grounds and given their service. I write stories based on fact and colored with fiction, but the truth is many lives have been dedicated to or lost in the service of their country, and I bow my head in gratitude to each and every sacrifice.

To Dave Hunter of GreenRoom Video—thank you for letting me tag along and learn the art and science of documentary filmmaking. You were generous with your time and expertise. I appreciate your support and enthusiasm and feel lucky to have such a willing resource and friend. PS—Sorry I dramatically choked on my water in the background of a take and ruined it. Just know that I think about that exact moment at least once a week with great embarrassment and shame so . . . that's fun.

Thank you to my beta readers—in particular Agnes Orth and Beverly Barbaro. Thank you for your insightful thoughts and well-researched notes. You have great eyes and brilliant minds, and this story is better because of you.

Thank you to my adopted family at Improv Playhouse. My life is richer and definitely far more hilarious with all of you in it. You keep me sane by letting me be slightly insane onstage with all of you.

Thank you to my developmental editor, Jodi Warshaw. You opened my mind and helped me continue to learn to trust my creative process. Thank you for your guidance and trust. You were a joy to work with. I love how your brain works. I hope I get to see it in action up close again soon.

Thank you to the team at Lake Union Publishing, including Kyra Wojdyla and the production team. You make this process a joy, and I appreciate all your hard work and effort.

Thank you as well to the Lake Union author community—you are such a wonderful and supportive group of pseudosiblings. I cheer for you each individually, even if you don't hear it from behind your computer screen, and I appreciate every minute you invest in me as well.

And my editor, Melissa Valentine, I truly believe we were meant to work together. Thank you for taking on this story and believing in it wholeheartedly. I've enjoyed our journey together, and I know we have more greatness ahead of us.

Marlene Stringer, my amazing agent and guide—thank you for literally everything. You've been by my side since the beginning. I know for a fact that I am where I am today because of your belief in me. Thank you, Marlene. Thank you, always.

To my family—I adore you. You continue to come through for me and my little crew, and I love you for it. Thank you for accepting us for who we are. We love you.

To my sister Elizabeth—I'd never be able to do this without you. Thank you for being so many things in my life—my best friend, my confidant, my maid of honor *and* officiant, my beta reader, and my cheerleader. I love you more than I can explain and love watching you continue to succeed in life, love, and motherhood. Let's keep taking those less traveled roads, okay? Deal.

To my Bleeker kids—my brave, strong, beautiful humans—I'm humbled every day to be your mother. Motherhood is my greatest joy and teaches me more than any other class, book, or life experience. I promise to keep learning and cheering and supporting for the rest of my livelong days. Thank you for your endless patience and love. You are the reason I do this.

And to my two newest kids, Anthony and Michael Barbaro—thank you for accepting me and showing me so much love and warmth. You are bright, funny, and intelligent men. I'm grateful your parents have shared you with me. I look forward to including you both in all this book stuff . . . endlessly . . . for the rest of your lives. Be warned—it's gonna get annoying. Sorry.

My very own Italian lover (and loving husband), Sam. They say write what you know, but I wrote about love for a long time without ever having fully experienced it. For some time in my life, I wondered if I'd ever know what it was like to be loved without reservation and to give that love in return. Now, I get to have both experiences because of you. Thank you, my love, for being my person. Thank you for loving me and the unique family we've created together. Marrying another creative person and finding ways to support our individual pursuits brings such richness to my life and creative experience. Thank you for listening to me read out phrases over and over again, assisting and correcting me on my Italian translations, and making me the best egg sandwiches a girl could ask for. We make a great team, and I look forward to celebrating all our successes and comforting each other through all our inevitable sorrows as we go through life together.

And to my readers new and old alike—thank you for giving me a shot. Thank you for getting lost in the worlds I hold inside my head. I love, love, love sharing them with you. I hope you keep coming back because without you, I'd just be a lady making up people on my computer. These stories are for you. Thank you for reading them.

ABOUT THE AUTHOR

Photo credit Organic Headshots

Emily Bleeker is the bestselling author of seven novels. Combined, her books have reached more than two million readers. She is a two-time Whitney Award finalist as well as an Amazon Charts and *Wall Street Journal* bestseller. Emily lives in the northern suburbs of Chicago with her husband, their kids, and her kitten-muse Hazel. Along with writing and being a mom, she performs with a local improv troupe, sings karaoke like no one is watching, and embraces her newfound addiction to running. Connect with her or request a Zoom visit with your book club at www.emilybleeker.com.